Janet Heijens

A Wrongful Conviction Mystery

Janet Heijens

SNOOK WALLOW

A Wrongful Conviction Mystery

www. canterburyhousepublishing. com
Sarasota, Florida

Canterbury House Publishing
www. canterburyhousepublishing. com

Book Design by Tracy Arendt

Library of Congress Cataloging-in-Publication Data

Names: Heijens, Janet, author.
Title: Snook Wallow / Janet Heijens.
Description: First edition. | Sarasota, Florida : Canterbury House Publishing, [2017] | Series: Wrongful conviction mystery ; 1
Identifiers: LCCN 2016056231 (print) | LCCN 2017003120 (ebook) | ISBN 9780997011951 (softcover : acid-free paper) | ISBN 9780997011968 (ebook) |
ISBN 9780997011968
Subjects: LCSH: Cold cases (Criminal investigation)--Fiction. | Murder--Investigation--Fiction. | Human trafficking--Fiction. | GSAFD: Mystery fiction. | Legal stories.
Classification: LCC PS3608.E3655 S66 2017 (print) | LCC PS3608.E3655 (ebook)

| DDC 813/.6--dc23
LC record available at https://lccn.loc.gov/2016056231

First Edition: April 2017

Author's Note:
This is a work of fiction. Names characters, places and incidents are either the product of the author's imagination or are used fictitiously, and any resemblance to actual persons living or dead, business establishments, events, or locales is entirely coincidental.

for Elinor

PROLOGUE

As the band played a Buffett song under a palm-thatched hut, Logan concentrated on the girl. Thong straps, pale pink against brown skin, arched over broad hips before disappearing under denim shorts leaving little to the imagination. Her halter-top, damp with sweat, clung to her body. When she leaned over and shouted her order to the bartender, Logan noticed the tattoo on her shoulder blade, a pair of folded wings. The girl turned, rested her elbows against the bar, and wiggled her hips to the beat of the music. Logan's gaze lingered on the rise of her breasts before dropping to the silver ring in her navel.

The bartender interrupted Logan's fantasy by slamming two wet bottles of beer on the bar. The girl twisted around, pressed money into the man's palm and waved away the change. Picking up the drinks she mouthed *thanks* with a smile worth ten times the tip.

Logan caught his friend, Boyd Skinner staring as the girl disappeared in the crowd.

"Hands off," Logan said. "She's mine." He glanced back, but she was gone.

"Never gonna happen." Boyd grinned. "Take a lesson from Ty here. He knows his limits. I'm not saying you should settle for the hookers in the fish camp, but—"

"Speak for yourself." Tyler Fox flipped Boyd the finger. He turned to Logan and slapped his back. "Don't pay no attention to Boyd. I say go get her."

"I just might do that." Logan lifted his empty bottle and peered through the brown glass. Feeling a little dizzy he glanced in the direction where the girl had wandered off.

The sandy clearing serving as Snook Wallow's dance floor was packed with sweaty bodies pressed tight against each other. The dancers joined in the chorus, drowning out the band. Logan figured the girl was down there somewhere.

"Can't believe the boss had us doing roof work in this heat." Boyd continued to scan the crowd.

"You spent the whole day sitting in the shade, guzzling Gatorade," Ty shouted over the noise.

Logan smiled, a wave of drunken affection for his friends washing over him. He looked across the clearing toward the flat-roofed building that housed the rest rooms and tapped Ty on the shoulder. "Gotta take a leak."

"Right, a leak." Ty gave him a knowing nod. "You ready for another round?"

Logan reached into his pocket and pulled out a few crumpled dollar bills. He tried to figure out where all his money went. The first three beers went down cold and fast, his body absorbing the fluid in minutes. Egged on by his friends, he chased the next one—maybe two—with vodka shooters.

"I'm almost tapped out." Logan stood, holding the bar for support.

"I'll get this one." Boyd drained the last few drops from his own bottle and waved the bartender over.

"Get me an order of hot wings while you're at it." Logan passed him the six singles. "I'll be right back. Maybe."

Logan missed the first step, grabbing the railing just in time to keep from falling off the deck. As he pushed through the crowd he kept his eyes open, looking for the girl. The pressure on his bladder grew worse with every step. When he arrived at the bathrooms and saw there was a line, Logan stumbled a few yards down the old mule path that ran along the river. As soon as he stepped beyond the cone of light cast down from the lamppost, the night closed in. He turned off the path using one hand to ward off the low hanging branches. With the other he lowered his zipper. The ground sloped downward and he slipped on the mud, skidding down the bank. Once he found his footing, he did what he had to do and with a sigh of relief, turned to make his way back to his friends. Hit with a wave of dizziness, he reached out to steady himself against a mossy oak. He pressed his face against the cool, damp bark and closed his eyes. The faint strands of "Margaritaville" drifted through the trees.

The smell of rotting leaves filled Logan's nose as he slowly came to. He remembered leaving the deck, the long line at the toilets, stepping off the path and then . . . nothing. Logan raised his hand to check the illuminated dial of his watch. Rolling onto his back, he looked up to the sky wondering how he lost more than two hours. There was a half-moon up there somewhere but all he could see was the occasional flicker of distant lightning behind dark clouds. With a moan, he closed his eyes and drew a deep breath. The only sound to reach him was the singing of frogs. By now Ty and Boyd were probably long gone. It was time for him to find his way to the parking lot, mount his Harley and get out of there.

Back on the mule path something caught his eye. He blinked to make sure he did not imagine it. There it was again, a light coming from one of the derelict buildings down the path. The cabins were the oldest structures on the property, built when Snook Wallow was nothing more than a fish camp. The only people to use them now were the prostitutes Boyd was so fond of, or the occasional junkie looking to score from one of the pimps that stayed in the shadows. As Logan watched, the light winked and died, leaving him to wonder who was down there. Knowing only that he wanted to avoid whoever it was, he turned and started back to the main building.

With his first step he tripped and fell, landing in something wet. "What the . . ." He pushed himself to his knees and wiped his hands on his jeans.

The clouds chose that moment to part, the white glow of the moon lighting the ground around him. He looked down and drew in a sharp breath.

"Hey, what are you doing here?"

His eyes fixed on the tattoo. The girl from the bar lay on her stomach, her head turned toward him, her hair a curtain of black silk covering her face. Except for the sandals on her feet she was naked, the sheen of her skin beautiful in the moonlight. Placing a hand over her tattoo, Logan shook her.

"Wake up." He glanced around. A minute ago, he had hoped to avoid whoever was back there. Now he wished someone would show up and give him a hand. "Come on," he begged, shaking her harder.

Fighting a rising panic, he tried to turn her over. She was heavier than he expected but somehow, he managed to roll her onto her back. Her head lolled to one side, her arm flopped against her limp body. His gaze rested on the ring in her belly. A few inches higher he saw the knife.

Logan knew that she was dead but his instincts told him to get that thing out of her. He gripped the handle and pulled. The knife came free with a slurping noise.

Standing on trembling legs he called out. "Is anybody out there?"

He listened for a reply, the sound of footsteps on the path, anything. The knife fell with a soft thud on the bed of damp leaves. Then the silence was complete. Even the frogs had stopped singing.

ONE

Logan Murphy was as good as dead. Over the phone, I heard frustration creep into Ben Shepherd's voice as he explained Murphy had reached the end of his appeals. I couldn't help thinking Ben was off tilting at windmills once again.

"There's a lethal injection with Logan's name on it. If you don't help me, the State is going to kill an innocent man."

"You just told me the guy was a convicted murderer," I replied. "I don't believe in the death penalty any more than you do but your client raped a girl, stabbed her to death and left her body to rot in the woods. The police were convinced they had the right guy. The jury found him guilty. What makes you so sure he's innocent?"

"He's not my client. Not yet, anyway. But at the time of the murder he was barely eighteen years old."

I pictured the pout on Ben's face when he said it. "You know as well as I do. Age is not a defense."

Ben was a criminal lawyer. He also happened to be my sister Nancy's pride and joy. One year ago, he graduated first in his class from an obscenely expensive law school in Manhattan. Despite several job offers from high-profile law firms, Ben turned his back on the chance to earn big money and offered his talents to a non-profit organization for a salary that barely covered his rent. And I'm talking about Gainesville, Florida rent, not New York City rent. His employer, the Defender Project was dedicated to freeing men and women convicted of crimes they did not commit. My sister went ballistic, ranting about his student loans but I admired my nephew for sticking to his principles.

"Listen to me, Aunt Cate." A patronizing tone crept into Ben's voice. "Logan has been on death row for ten years. He was just a normal kid, letting off steam with his friends at a local bar when he happened to find the girl's body. There were no witnesses, no DNA evidence and the victim was never identified. So tell me, if Logan killed the girl, why would he call the police instead of walking away without a trace?"

Before I had a chance to respond, Ben answered his own question.

"Because he didn't kill her, that's why. Logan was a straight-A student. He never had so much as a speeding ticket. I looked him square in the eye and he swore he didn't kill that girl. I'm telling you, Logan Murphy is innocent."

"You think he's innocent just because he reported the murder? That doesn't make a whole lot of sense."

"Nothing about murder makes sense. That's not my point. My point is I believe him. I'm looking at a complete failure of justice here. One by one Logan's appeals have been rejected and my firm won't take the case. I have to do something to help him."

I smiled, thinking of Ben's tendency to rail against injustice. While in law school Ben rejected a well-paid internship with a corporate law firm, opting instead to work for free, for Pro-Choice America. Despite what his mother thought of his career choices, I believed his job with the Defender Project was a good fit, a chance for Ben to do some good in this world. As the greenest lawyer in the firm, his job was to evaluate petitions from Florida prisoners with the aim of identifying cases that met the Project's criteria. Ben wasn't able to convince his boss to accept Logan Murphy as a client but I knew he wouldn't walk away from something he believed in just because his boss told him to drop it.

"There are hundreds of convicts on Florida's death row." I paused for a moment to emphasize my point. "Each and every one of them probably swears he's innocent."

Ben sighed and I wondered if I went too far. I thought of all the cases that cross his desk and wondered how he decided which deserved a last shot at justice.

"Most are guilty," he admitted. "But sometimes the system gets it wrong. That's what keeps me here. I'm simply asking you to meet with Logan. Before I take this any further, I want to get your opinion."

"What do you mean by taking this further?"

"After you hear Logan's side of the story, if you don't believe him then I'll drop the whole thing. But if he convinces you he's innocent, then I want you to help me with this."

"I've never practiced criminal law, Ben. I spent my career preparing wills and negotiating divorce settlements. What makes you think I can help?"

"You're the smartest lawyer I know."

His flattery won me over. Still, driving three hours to face a convicted killer on death row was not my idea of fun.

"I'd like to know more before I agree to meet this guy. Email me his court summary and I'll take a look."

"I'll send it right now."

I was a soft touch when it came to Ben. To be honest, I was pleased he valued my opinion so highly. But I didn't want to give an appearance of giving in too easily.

"You know, this is coming at a bad time. I'm trying to get settled into my new house. It took me all day yesterday to get my computer hooked up to the Internet, and this entire place is littered with unpacked boxes. I can't even find my—"

My computer pinged, alerting me to the arrival of a new email.

"I think that summary just came in." I clicked my mouse and opened the message.

"It's titled Murphy v. State. Let me know if you have any trouble accessing the file."

"I know how to open an attachment. I may be old, but I'm not an idiot."

"You're not that old." Ben paused, letting the silence stretch between us. "And no one could ever accuse you of being an idiot."

"What's the procedure for visiting someone on death row?"

"I'll make all the arrangements. In the meantime, I can send you a link to the prison's website so you can read the visitor guidelines."

I scanned the first page of the court summary, wondering what I was getting into. The cover page was marked one of sixty-three. The boxes in my garage would have to wait.

TWO

The following morning Ben selected one of his seven white shirts from the wardrobe in his studio apartment, grabbed a blue tie to go with his gray suit, and tapped a reminder into his phone to stop by the cleaner's after work to pick up his other two suits. With his messenger bag strapped across his back, he left the apartment and walked to the corner bakery to grab his usual, coffee and donuts. The girl behind the counter flirted with him, holding the bag a few seconds longer than necessary, their hands touching until he smiled and gently pulled the bag from her grip. A few minutes later he arrived at the office.

Though Ben's law firm was based in Manhattan, they operated satellite offices in states where capital punishment was still the law of the land. They offered their services for free, surviving largely on grant money and donations. Most of their legal assistance came from law school volunteers but the organization had a core of paid staff in every location where they had a physical presence. Ben was one of five employees who worked out of the Gainesville, Florida office.

He took one of the two coffees from the bag and set it on the desk of the firm's paralegal before settling into his own office. Pulling the strap of his messenger bag over his head, he sat down and turned on his computer. After taking a bite of his first jelly donut, he reached for the large stack of papers on his desk and pulled a new legal pad out of the top drawer. He had already committed to memory everything he needed to know about his new client, Ricky Castro. But to prepare a case summary for his boss, Ben set to work distilling the lengthy document to a few bullet points. It always helped to hit Greg with the key legal issues of the case before going into detail.

When he was satisfied with his summary, he turned to his computer and noticed he had an email from his aunt, Cate Stokes. Scanning the message, he saw she'd already read Logan's court summary. Before he reached the end, Ben heard someone clearing their throat. He looked up to see Stephanie, the firm's paralegal, leaning against the door and staring at him with her green eyes.

"Hey, Shepherd, what time did you get in this morning? My coffee is cold."

Stephanie wore one of her black power suits—tight skirt, jacket cinched at the back and fastened in front with a single button. The bright pink blouse clashed with her orange hair that she pulled back in a ponytail. Stephanie raised her paper cup. A crooked smile played on her lips.

"Nuke it. While you're at it, zap mine too, will you?"

"What are you working on?" Stephanie took a few steps into Ben's office and reached for his untouched coffee. "You didn't even hear me come in."

"An extracurricular project."

"Like you don't have enough to do." She glanced down, her eyes rising from the computer to meet his. "You're still working on Murphy? I thought Greg told you to turn him down."

"Yeah, but—."

"Just write the rejection letter and move on. Where are you with Castro?"

Ben gathered his notes and slipped everything into a folder. "Actually, I've just finished prepping for my presentation. Did you get a chance to pull those records I asked you for?"

"You'll have them before lunch. What are Castro's chances?"

"Ricky is a great candidate. The police screwed up the chain of evidence and the prosecution's key witness was a jailhouse snitch. On top of that, if we get lucky, we'll be able to clear him with DNA testing. But we need to put effort, not to mention money, into building a case. Of course we'll have to hire an investigator. Bottom line, his chances are as good as or better than most. I think Greg will green-light this one."

Greg Farley, the lead attorney for the Gainesville office had a reputation for working miracles. As a junior lawyer in the firm, Ben was amazed by Greg's near psychic intuition when it came to picking cases they could win. With limited resources, the Defender Project could not afford to waste time on lost causes. It was Ben's job to sift through all the candidates and come up with cases that were worthy of their efforts. Greg rejected his recommendation to take on Logan Murphy, but Ben hoped he could convince his boss to go with Ricky Castro.

Stephanie disappeared with the cold coffee and soon Ben heard the fan of the microwave start. With a tap on the screen, he called Cate. As the phone rang at the other end, he began to wonder if it was too early in the day to make the call. A sleepy voice answered.

"This better be important. The best thing, I mean the *very* best thing about being retired is that I don't have to get up at the crack of dawn. What time is it, anyway?"

Ben ignored her question. "I got the email you sent last night. Give me a minute while I pull up Logan's court summary." His eyes scanned the document. The name and file number headed the report followed by the date and disposition of the case. *October 31, 2005, decided*. Below was the list of counsel for both the plaintiff and defendant and on the next line Ben found the name of the judge.

"Alan G. Higel," he read out loud. "You were right."

"Look at the name of the prosecutor."

The microwave pinged. Ben's eyes moved up the page until he found the name of the lawyer who represented the state. He shook his head, still amazed that he did not catch it earlier.

"This may be a coincidence." Ben clicked the mouse and closed the file. "Higel is a pretty common name down in Venice."

He heard Stephanie's high heels click on the tiled floor as she returned with the coffee.

"I don't believe in coincidences," Cate said. "What are the chances that the judge and prosecuting attorney had the same last name? Dollars to donuts they are related. Unless they disclosed the nature of their relationship before the trial began—"

"Right, I'll look into that. Listen, I can't talk right now, but I'm going to Raiford in a few days to meet a new client. Can you meet me there?"

"I haven't agreed to meet Mr. Murphy yet."

"But you will, right?"

"Don't I need an appointment?"

"Well . . . I sort of booked one for you already."

"Why am I not surprised? Okay, but if I don't buy his story, you're going to drop this case and I'm going straight back to unpacking boxes. That was our deal, right?"

"It won't come to that."

Ben ended the call and slipped his phone into his pocket as Stephanie handed him his cup. He nodded his thanks and took a sip. She arched her eyebrows, giving him a pointed stare.

"You're on thin ice here," Stephanie warned."What if Greg finds out you're still working on Murphy?"

"I'm done with Logan. I just referred his case to another lawyer."

"You expect me to buy that? I know you, Shepherd. Once you get hooked, you can't let go."

He shook his head in denial. "I'm telling you, I've got someone else looking into Logan's claim. Listen, I need those Castro records sooner rather than later. Greg wants me to brief him by the end of the day."

"I said you'd have them before lunch." With a look that told him she didn't believe a word he told her about Murphy, she moved to her desk, turned on her computer and got to work.

THREE

Before I pulled up stakes in New Hampshire, nobody told me Florida summers were prone to unrelenting rain, turning the world into a sweltering steam bath. Though I wasn't exactly looking forward to visiting Logan Murphy in the State Prison, getting out of the house would be a welcome break. Assuming of course the prison was air-conditioned.

I carried my breakfast—black coffee and a box of Marlboro Lights—to the lanai and glanced out to the area I had cleared for a vegetable garden. A sheet of gray water blanketed the soil. Earlier that week I picked up a dozen tender tomato plants that I intended to put in the ground as soon as the rain let up. From my initial poking around, I seriously doubted if the sandy soil could ever produce the same tomatoes I used to grow in my garden back home. I took a drag of the cigarette and exhaled.

My husband and I started smoking in college when it was sexy and cool. Like fools we kept right on smoking even after the Surgeon General told us it was just plain stupid. After thirty years of marriage, Arnie was diagnosed with lung cancer. His death should have been enough to shock me into quitting but living alone in the house we shared for half my life was tough and the cigarettes got me through long days without him.

Then two years after Arnie died I suffered an angina attack. The doctor called it a warning shot across the bow and read me the riot act. He not so gently reminded me that I wasn't getting any younger and needed to start taking my health seriously. I took that to mean parting company with my beloved Lights, getting more exercise and avoiding stress. The next day I quit my job and put my house on the market. The house sold quickly and the minute the papers were signed I moved into a little bungalow near the Gulf of Mexico in Venice, Florida. My plan was simple. Walk the beach, practice yoga and relax in the sun. In my spare time I planned to write my own great American novel. Hopefully that and puttering in my garden would be enough to keep me—not to mention my weak heart—happy.

Ben's call changed all that. Not that I minded. Ben was like the son I never had and to be honest, I appreciated the distraction. Angina attack or not, I wondered if I was ready for retirement. One morning, I went down to the public beach and joined a few dozen senior citizens for my first yoga lesson. Turns out I'm not cut out for yoga. I was sore for days. And as for basking in the sun, well I've read all that stuff about skin cancer.

If getting rid of the stress was easy, quitting smoking proved to be more challenging. Returning inside, I poured a fresh cup of coffee and tapped a second cancer stick out of the box. Time to have another good look at Logan Murphy's court summary.

During the past few days I spent hours studying all the information Ben sent me. Before driving up to see Murphy, I wanted to be sure I had the facts of his case clear in my mind. I flipped past the pages that covered the case history and the cast of characters. When I reached the description of the crime I stopped. Every time I read this, my belief in Murphy's guilt grew stronger. A girl estimated to be in her early teens was raped and stabbed to death. Her naked body was left on a path in the woods where she was killed. The prosecutor presented a compelling case, the hard evidence sealing Murphy's fate. His fingerprints were all over the murder weapon, his shoe prints imprinted in the mud where the victim was found, and his clothes smeared with her blood. Ben's faith in Murphy was puzzling. I flipped back and scanned the section covering the various appeals and saw that at every pass the original trial conviction was upheld. I never had much exposure to criminal law during my years working in a family law firm, so the legal mumbo jumbo was beyond my understanding. I planned to ask Ben to explain the grey areas when I saw him. I tried to keep an open mind but on the surface the effort seemed pointless.

Reading the summary sparked another craving for nicotine. I cast a look of longing at my Lights, resisted the urge and grabbed my car keys. I had a long ride ahead of me.

The drive from Venice to the Florida State prison took me three hours. I lost NPR somewhere around Ocala, and had to choose between country music and silence. I chose silence. When I arrived in Raiford, I started looking for Millie's Pancake House where Ben suggested we meet. The idea was to catch up over lunch prior to entering the prison grounds. I would have preferred a cup of coffee from Starbucks, but after passing a burned-out fruit stand, a Dollar store and a boarded-up Smokin' Pig restaurant, I got the picture. Millie's Pancake House was the best—make that the only—choice. I spotted Ben in a booth at the far end of the restaurant. The only other customers were a pair of state troopers, armed to the gills with pistols, batons and stun guns. They both looked up as I approached. I suppose, finding nothing interesting about me, they turned back to their lunch, pancakes drenched with syrup and melted whipped cream.

"You found me." Ben smiled as I slid into the bench across from him. He waved to the waitress who looked up from her crossword puzzle. With a sigh, she picked up a pot of coffee from the burner and filled my cup with high-test before I could tell her I wanted decaf. She produced an order pad from her apron which stretched tight over her bulging midriff and stained with what appeared to be strawberry jam. She stared at me expectantly.

"What do you recommend?" I asked.

"Pancakes are the safe choice."

I ordered a garden salad, and when the waitress turned her back, I cleaned the table with a disinfecting wipe from my purse. Looking up I caught Ben watching me. It had been a few months since we'd seen each other, and though he smiled, there was a dark, serious look in his eyes that I never noticed before. Seemed his new job was knocking his reckless youth out of him.

"You look good. How do you like Gainesville?"

"I'm still adjusting, I guess. Everything moves slower here than back home."

"The whole world moves slower than Manhattan." I glanced down at my untouched coffee. How could one cup kill me? I took a sip and felt the caffeine surge through my veins.

Ben chuckled and took a swig from his own cup. "You look great. Mom thinks you've lost your mind, retiring in Florida. She predicts you're going to get lonely and run back to New Hampshire within a year. I told her moving to Venice was the best decision you ever made."

I accepted his comment about my sister with a grimace. Nancy didn't fully grasp what I wanted in life. I was through with my old life. Gone were the makeup and high heels, the heavy jewelry and perfume. I pinned my hair, streaked with silver, into a twist on the back of my head. Today, following the prison guidelines that Ben sent me, I wore a loose cotton blouse, dress slacks and loafers. Nothing too sexy or distracting. As if I could manage sexy at my age.

"You tell your mother that this is my life and if I want to move to Timbuktu I will." I reached across the table to pat his hand. "But the truth is, I'm glad you're not too far away."

"Are you ready to meet Logan?"

"I'll admit I'm a little nervous about this whole thing. I've never been in a prison before. Which reminds me, when I looked at the website, I noticed there's a three-week lead-time for a visitor's pass. Are you sure they'll let me in?"

"I sent in your application last month. As long as you remembered to bring your photo ID you'll be fine."

"Last month? You only called me a few days ago."

A glimmer of mischief in his eyes told me all I needed to know. "A precautionary measure. I could tell by the way my boss acted that he intended to turn Logan down so I had to come up with Plan B. Then out of the blue you decided to retire down here and I thought—."

My surprise gave way to laughter. The waitress returned with our lunch and looked at me.

"Most folks come visitin' the prison aren't in such a good mood as y'all," she said.

"How do you know where we're going?" I asked.

"Only people come in here are lawyers or relatives of the inmates. I figure he's the lawyer." She gave a nod in Ben's direction. "And you're somebody's grandmother. Hope y'all have a good visit."

I caught Ben's eye when she walked away and smothered my laughter with a napkin. Grandmother, indeed.

As Ben drove under the arch that marked the entrance to the Florida State Prison, I saw before me a double ring of soaring chain-link fence topped with coils of razor wire that surrounded the grounds. Between the two fences, a pack of Dobermans patrolled the perimeter. Inside those prison walls, a cell the size of my bedroom closet was the home of Logan Murphy.

The smell of industrial disinfectant hit me the minute we passed through security. Ben and I parted ways soon after the first gate clanged shut behind us. He headed toward the attorney's conference room to meet his client, a man by the name of Ricky Castro, while I was escorted to the visitor's area to meet Logan Murphy. The correctional officer who led the way was stony faced, speaking to me in monosyllabic instructions. "Left . . . hold . . . stop." We walked through a series of more iron gates that the officer opened by punching a keypad with his stubby finger. I jumped each time the gates clanged behind us, my nerves stretched tight by the time we finally reached a narrow room lined with three-sided booths. Each was fitted with implanted devices that enabled communication between visitors and inmates. The guard gestured for me to raise my arms so he could frisk me. I had already passed through a metal detector at the front door and surrendered my pocketbook, watch and cell phone when I signed in. Not to mention there was no way for a visitor to pass anything to an inmate. Death row visits were strictly non-contact.

Before we left the restaurant, Ben reminded me that I was simply there to listen. To be convinced of Murphy's innocence. Though he did his best to prepare me, I had no real idea what to expect.

"Ask him to tell you about his appellate lawyer's strategy. The motion for post-conviction relief."

"What was the basis of the motion?" I asked.

"It was actually a pretty good idea," Ben replied. "His lawyer thought of a way to get the review board to commute Logan's sentence to life without parole. When I heard Logan wouldn't go for it, I knew there was something to this case. Just ask him about it."

I was sharply aware of the guard's presence as I sat facing the Plexiglas, waiting for Murphy to appear. I wondered if I would recognize the inmate from the mug shot of the boy who was arrested for murder ten years ago. When he finally appeared, I wasn't prepared for the bespectacled, clean-shaven man dressed in an orange T-shirt and blue pants who sat down and smiled at me. I figured he was about Ben's age, not yet thirty. Though his hands were cuffed, he appeared to be relaxed, his manacled legs stretched out as if he sat across from me in his own living room. There were no scars on his face, no tattoos that I could see, no sinister glimmer in his eyes. I had to remind myself that he was, after all, a convicted murderer, no matter how docile he seemed.

"Thank you for seeing me, ma'am. Ben told me you weren't sure about coming. And I understand that, I do. I just want to let you know I appreciate you being here."

He spoke with a Florida accent in quiet, measured words. Logan Murphy was so unlike the man I expected. A thousand questions rose to mind. I wanted to know what his life was like, how he spent his days, if he constantly thought about the fate that awaited him.

"Do you get many visitors?" I asked.

"No, ma'am. But my grandmother, she comes to see me every month. I'm lucky that way. Most guys here don't have anyone."

"What about your friends?"

"My buddies from Venice?" The young man shook his head. "I haven't heard from them since the trial. My real friends are all here now. The guys on The Row."

His comment jarred me to silence. I understood that with few exceptions the inmates were confined 24/7 to their cells, small rectangular spaces furnished with one cot, a toilet and a sink. How could friendships be forged in such a place?

As though Murphy read my mind, he explained. "I have neighbors on either side of my cell. We can't see each other, but we talk. And we're allowed out in the exercise pen six hours a week so yeah, I have friends here. Every now and then they decide to move us around or change our exercise schedule so we lose contact." He shrugged. "It's one of the ways the warden tries to remind us that we have no control over our own lives."

"What do you talk about?"

"The news, politics, books we're reading, our favorite television shows."

"You have a television?"

"They give us a small black and white set, no cable. Personally, I only watch PBS. Best programming if you ask me. The rest is junk."

I felt like I was chatting with a new friend, getting to know about his life that, despite the circumstances, approached normal. No, not normal, I reminded myself as I glanced at his cuffed hands, the leg irons. There was nothing normal about this place.

"Ben told me to ask you about your lawyer's idea for post-conviction relief."

Murphy nodded in understanding. "That was my first lawyer. Since then my case has moved to the State Supreme Court so I have a new team working for me now. Anyway, his idea was . . ." Murphy paused, looked down at his hands and sighed. "Back in 2005, the U.S. Supreme Court decided it was illegal to give the death penalty to a minor. So if the Medical Examiner thought that girl died before midnight, I wouldn't be here talking to you."

"She died on your birthday?" I remembered hearing Ben say Murphy had just turned eighteen when Jane Doe was murdered, but it was only now that I realized the implications.

"Real bad luck, right?" An ugly laugh burst forth, the first sign of Murphy's suppressed frustration. "Anyway, my lawyer hired a forensics expert who disputed the M.E.'s autopsy report. He said the victim died sometime within a range that included a few hours before I turned eighteen. My attorney used that to try and convince the board to commute my sentence to life."

"Sounds like a good idea."

"Yes ma'am. And right around the time of my review the Florida House passed a bill to allow juveniles a sentence review after serving twenty-five years. So if things went well with the board, I would be moved off the Row and out of here in fifteen years."

"What was the problem?"

"They wanted me to confess to the crime." Logan looked at me without blinking. "And I refused to lie. I did not kill that girl."

The assertion stated so quietly and calmly, sent a shiver down my arms. Now I understood why Ben wanted me to take this case. He wasn't basing his opinion on a belief that the law was improperly executed. Or because he had doubts about the legal procedures that led to this young man's conviction. Ben simply knew, deep down in his heart, that Logan Murphy was innocent.

And much to my surprise, I did too.

My armed escort, the surly correctional officer, guided me back to the front entrance where Ben stood waiting. I recovered my belongings and hurried out the door. Overhead, black clouds threatened an afternoon thunderstorm. I slipped into the passenger seat of Ben's old BMW and stared straight ahead, trying to shake off the aura of the prison.

"The first time is always the toughest. Are you okay?"

"Fine. Let's find a place where we can get a cup of coffee and talk. Preferably not Millie's."

We found a McDonald's five miles down the road, but by the time Ben pulled into the parking lot the rain was pouring down. I ducked under the overhang and reached into my bag for a cigarette. Ben scowled as I lit up.

"Just give me a minute." I turned away to exhale the smoke from my lungs. I felt better already.

"I'll meet you inside. Black regular, right?"

"Decaf. Doctor's orders."

I followed him with my eyes as he stepped up to the counter. He carried our coffees to an empty table, pulled out his phone and started checking his messages. Looking at Ben, I felt a surge of admiration for the work he did. Knowing innocent people were locked inside that prison, Ben fought their battles and could still maintain a positive outlook on life. Standing there, watching him rapidly tap messages with both thumbs, I made my decision. A ragged bolt of lightning hit something near, the thunder shaking me from my thoughts. Stubbing out my half-smoked cigarette, I joined Ben inside.

"How did your meeting go?" I asked.

Ben placed his phone on the table and pried the plastic cover from his coffee. Blowing across the surface, his eyes scanned the restaurant. Aside from the workers behind the counter, we were the only ones there.

"Do you really want to know?" Ben raised an eyebrow.

I nodded.

"My client, Ricky Castro worked in the tomato fields of Immokalee. He met his girlfriend, Marcela de la Vega at a bar he frequented after work. They fell in love and pretty soon they made plans to leave town and start a new life together. In the end, things didn't work out so well. The girl ended up dead, and Ricky is on death row for her murder. The case is messy, but the one thing I'm sure of is that Ricky didn't kill her."

"Can you help him?"

"I think so. My boss must think so too because he approved the case. Now tell me what you think about Logan."

"I never thought I would say this, but you're probably right about him."

Ben replied with a smile.

"Don't gloat."

"I'm glad to hear you agree with me, that's all. I guess I'll have to work on this behind my boss' back until I can find something to change his mind."

"You can't risk your job to help that boy, no matter how much you believe in his innocence. Let me help. Point me in the right direction and I'll do the research for you."

"You sure you want to get involved?"

"Where do I start?"

"Try to get in touch with the people who could tell you more about what happened the night of the murder. You might start with Ty's grandmother, Annie. She lives near you in Venice."

"Give me her number and I'll call her tomorrow."

Ben pulled his phone back out. After he made a few taps it made a whooshing noise. "I just sent you her contact information. After you meet her, I suggest you track down Logan's friends who were with him that night. See if they remember anything new. In the meantime,

I'll email you the trial transcript and everything else I have regarding the case. Once my boss pulled the plug I had to stop digging, so we'll have to figure out how to get the rest of what you will need later."

"Let's take this one step at a time."

"Okay," Ben agreed. "If you need to get in touch with me, you can always reach me on my cellphone. Make sure you never discuss the case in a public place. We're good here because we're alone, but . . . well, you never know who might be listening."

"I understand. What are Logan's chances?"

"I'll be honest with you, they're not good. Legally, I don't see any hope for a wrongful conviction. In the past ten years Logan has been working his way through the appeals process and his lawyers have been turned down every time. All we can hope for is for you to find something new, a fresh angle, something everyone else missed that we can use to build a case. Are you sure you're up for this?"

I only wished I felt the confidence my smile conveyed.

FOUR

With the rain showing no sign of stopping, I decided to drive the short distance to Annie's house. I grabbed the keys to my Prius and five minutes later, parked behind the rusted VW Beetle standing in her carport. Annie's flat-roofed house was made of painted cinderblocks, one of many in the neighborhood built around fifty years earlier. Tucking my chin against my chest, I ran across her lawn, my sandals slipping on the spongy St. Augustine grass. Several sets of chimes on the front porch blew wildly in the wind. Annie caught me staring at them when she opened the door.

"Good morning." Her smile revealed a chipped tooth. I couldn't help but notice her hair was a mess of tangles and that she was still dressed in her nightgown.

"Oh, I'm sorry. I thought you expected me."

Annie waved me into the house. "I just put the kettle on for tea. Down the hall to your right. Fix yourself a cup and I'll be with you in a minute or two."

I set my dripping umbrella on the cracked ceramic tiles and followed the sound of the whistling kettle. The kitchen looked like it had not been updated since the house was built. A plastic grate in the drop ceiling concealed twin fluorescent tubes that flickered against the gloomy morning. The refrigerator hummed loudly. I removed the kettle from the burner and read the label on the tin of green tea. *Pure Organic*, whatever that meant. One whiff and an earthy smell filled my nose. I set the tin back on the counter.

Hearing Annie's bare feet slap against the tiles, I looked up to see her wearing a cotton kaftan. A string of beads hung around her neck, her frizzy, gray hair pushed back from her forehead with a headband. She looked like a seventy-year-old version of Janis Joplin as she crossed the kitchen and pulled two cups down from the cabinet.

"Milk and honey?" Annie asked.

I held up my hand. "I've already had my coffee this morning, thanks. I explained on the phone that I'm here to discuss Logan's umm . . . his situation."

"Coffee?" Annie scowled. "Don't you know how bad that is for you? This will help you get rid of the toxins in your body." She filled both cups with hot water, spooned a few twigs and leaves into each and set them on the table. She then grabbed an unlabeled jar of what appeared to be honey and set that on the table too.

Edging the cup to one side, I thanked her.

"I'm sure my grandson doesn't get anything like this tea up in Raiford. Every time I go to see him I try to smuggle some in, but the Nazis that run that place confiscate it before I can get past security. Logan tells me the food they serve is crap. Nothing fresh, all loaded with preservatives. I shudder to think what being in that place is doing to his body."

"He looked well when I saw him." In my opinion Annie worried about the wrong thing. Certainly the last ten years on death row had done more damage to the state of her grandson's mind than to his body. If he was released, his main challenge would be finding his way in a world that had passed him by.

"Does he know you're here?" Annie asked.

"He sends his love. I understand you raised him."

"That's right." Annie nodded. "Logan was only two when my son and his wife died in the accident. He doesn't remember them at all. But I tell him that all he has to do is take a glance in the mirror to see his father looking back at him. That's Dylan, his father, in that photo there." She stood and pulled down a framed print from a shelf and handed it to me. I studied the picture of Logan's father in a leather jacket straddling a motorcycle. His hair was dark, a shock of bangs falling over his eyes. For whatever reason, he didn't smile for the camera. What struck me the most was how young he looked, I judged him to be in his mid-twenties, a few years younger than Logan was now. Annie was right. The resemblance was uncanny.

I passed the photo back and she took a minute to gaze on her son's image. Her eyes welled up with tears and she turned her attention to the steaming cup of tea before her.

"I understand this is hard for you," I said. "But I need to ask you about the night of the murder."

Annie nodded. Stirring honey into her tea, she kept her eyes fixed on the cup. "Those pigs got it fixed in their minds right off that Logan killed that girl."

"Why don't you start by telling me how the evening began?"

"Logan and his friends went to Snook Wallow every Friday night to have a few drinks, pick up girls . . . you know how teenaged boys are." Annie's gaze shifted and she stared out the window. The rain pelted against the pane, blurring the pepper trees that grew in the back yard.

"They worked together, right?" I already knew this from speaking with Logan, but hoped Annie could give me a better understanding of the relationship between the three friends.

"They were close, those kids. Logan and Ty especially. Inseparable. The two of them planned to leave for the University of Florida at the end of the summer. Now Boyd, he wasn't exactly college material, but obviously that hasn't hurt him any."

"What do you mean?"

"After high school Boyd got a job working for his father in real estate. He's done pretty well for himself. Ty too, in his own way. Who knows what Logan might have done with his life if it wasn't for . . ."

Annie choked back a sob. I pulled a clean tissue from my purse and passed it to her, waiting while she blew her nose.

"Do you keep in touch with them?" I asked.

"Ty comes over every year on my birthday with a bunch of red tulips and a box of chocolates. He's got a wife, Bibi and two kids. Real nice family. Boyd now . . . I haven't seen him in years. You can see his for-sale signs stuck in front of high-end houses all around town. From the look of things, his business is doing well. Ty tells me Boyd never married, but I get the impression they don't see each other much."

Interesting, but not surprising. From what Logan told me it sounded like Ty and Boyd were heading their separate ways even before the event that split the trio apart. I made a mental note to contact them both.

"You said they went to Snook Wallow together. What time did Logan leave the house?"

"Around eight or so. I heard Boyd pull into the driveway."

"How did you know it was Boyd and not Ty?"

"Boyd's Harley idled in a funny way. Sputtered like it was going to stall out, then roared back to life when he gave it gas. Anyway, Logan ran out, jumped on his own bike and off they went to pick up Ty."

"And what time did he return?"

"Two fifteen. Of that I'm certain. I always slept with one eye open when Logan was out. Anyway, I checked the clock when I heard his bike and thought at the time that it was later than usual for him to come home."

"What happened then?"

"At first I stayed in bed, pretending to be asleep so Logan wouldn't think I was keeping track of him or anything like that. When he knocked on my bedroom door, I turned on the light. He stood there, covered in blood . . ."

Annie buried her face in her hands. Her shoulders shook and a moan escaped her throat. I reached across the table and placed a hand on her arm, feeling the bones under her parchment-thin skin.

"I understand why people think Logan killed that girl." Annie looked up with red-rimmed eyes. With the back of her hand she wiped the tip of her nose. "But I know my boy, and I'm telling you, he would never hurt a fly. Those cops made a terrible mistake."

While I felt enormous sympathy for the woman, nothing she told me would help prove her grandson's innocence.

"Tell me what happened next," I gave a gentle nod, prompting her to continue.

"I called 911 and the cops showed up within ten minutes or so. Before they arrived, I told Logan to wash up. Then I took his clothes, stuffed them in a garbage bag and threw everything in the trash outside." Annie looked at the palms of her hands and wagged her head.

"Why? Did he say anything to suggest—"

"No, of course not. Everyone assumed I was trying to get rid of evidence or some such nonsense. It never occurred to me that the cops would think Logan had anything to do with that girl getting killed. The sight of all that blood made me sick, and his clothes . . . I just wanted to get them out of my house."

"You must realize how that looked."

Annie threw me an annoyed look. "Of course. I know that *now*. But do you think I would put Logan's clothes out with my own trash if I was trying to hide them from the cops? I'm not stupid. I just wasn't thinking clearly, that's all."

"Okay, what can you tell me about Logan's knife?"

"What about it?"

"Well, you must know that the killer used a fishing knife to kill that girl. The police claim you bought one just like it the year before the murder."

"We never tried to hide that fact. When the detective asked me if Logan had a fishing knife, I told her that I gave him one for his seventeenth birthday. All his friends had them and that was the only thing he asked for, talked about it for weeks. Logan kept his in his tackle box."

"But it wasn't there when the police detective asked to see it."

"Logan explained to the cop that it went overboard the last time they went out fishing in Boyd's boat. He didn't tell me at the time because he knew how much that thing cost and he was ashamed to admit it was gone."

"Tell me, is it possible that Logan recognized the girl? Maybe he saw her before and—?"

"He told me that was the first time he laid eyes on her. My grandson doesn't lie."

I reached out to touch Annie again. "Teenagers don't always tell their parents—in this case a grandparent—everything."

Annie jerked her arm away from me and lifted her chin in defiance. "I told you, Logan is not a liar."

I felt it was time to wrap up our interview but I needed one more thing before I left. "Do you have the telephone numbers of Logan's friends?"

Annie rose from her chair and pulled an address book from a kitchen drawer. "I don't have Boyd's home number," Annie said as she scrawled something on a scrap of paper. "But you should be able to reach him at his office. This is Ty's cell phone number."

In reading the trial transcript, I noted that for the most part Ty responded to every question from the prosecution with, "I don't remember, exactly." The only exception was when he said he and Boyd went home before the band stopped playing, sometime around eleven thirty. The lawyer's frustration came through loud and clear, and after several attempts to get answers from Ty, he asked the judge to consider him a hostile witness. On the other hand, Boyd offered a complete account of the evening, including Logan's fascination with the girl they all saw at the bar. The murder victim who the County labeled "Jane Doe 04-05".

Pocketing the paper, I offered Annie my hand. Instead of shaking it, she pulled me close and gave me a hug.

"Please help my boy," she whispered in my ear. "You're his last hope."

I could still smell her herbal shampoo when I stepped outside and glanced up to the sky. The rain showed no sign of stopping.

The Skinner Premier Real Estate Agency logo was printed on for-sale signs planted on the lawns of multi-million dollar properties overlooking the water. Estates that were so exclusive potential buyers had to submit to a credit check just to view them. Boyd Skinner had done well for himself, especially for a kid who, as Annie put it, wasn't exactly college material.

"I'm sorry, Mr. Skinner isn't available at the moment," the receptionist said. "May I take a message?"

I gave her my name and number, and when the woman asked what the call was in reference to, I replied, "Tell Mr. Skinner I'd like to speak with him about Logan Murphy."

If the receptionist recognized the name as belonging to a convicted murderer on death row, she didn't let it show in her voice. She assured me that Boyd would call back at his earliest convenience. I thanked her and hung up.

When I dialed the number for Ty, the call went through to voice mail. His message said he was on vacation, and would return all calls the following week when he returned. I left a message, and slammed down the phone, my impatience getting the better of me. My visit to Raiford and the interview with Annie raised more questions than answers. Why did Logan leave the scene of the crime? Could I believe Annie's explanation for throwing away her grandson's bloody clothes? Nothing I'd read or heard suggested Logan was innocent, and yet . . . I looked around my house at all the corrugated cartons. Failing to generate the will or energy to start unpacking right then, I sat down at my desk in the kitchen, drumming my fingernails on the stone countertop as I waited for my old computer to boot up.

I decided to start looking for news stories or any other information about Logan Murphy that might be available online. After all, the murder of an unidentified girl on the banks of the Myakka River must have been big news in this small town. When at last the icons stopped popping up, I positioned the mouse over the Internet icon and clicked. Fingers poised above the keyboard, I took a deep breath and typed, "Logan Michael Murphy, Venice, FL." The results astonished me. A long list glowed on the screen. Clicking the first link, I tried to send the page to the printer.

Then I remembered. I hadn't yet figured out how to connect my new printer to the wireless service. In my old house I simply plugged the printer into the side of the computer. But this was one of those new, wireless gadgets, and I had no idea how to get it working. While the rain streamed off the flat roof of my lanai, I pounded the counter with my fist. Realizing that wasn't going to solve anything, I got up to fix myself lunch and sat back down in front of the computer. I took a bite of my sandwich and chewed slowly, deciding to read everything online. When I found something I wanted to keep, I'd make a note and print it out later. Long after I finished lunch, I was still reading. The press did a pretty good job of convicting Logan before the jury had their say. The evidence was indeed compelling, but something nagged at my brain. Who was Jane Doe 04-05? What was her story? I knew I needed answers to those questions to help Logan.

I craved a cigarette. Flipping back the lid, I counted the filters and blinked. The day was half gone but only one cigarette was missing from the box.

FIVE

I cruised north on I-75 for forty-five minutes, the odometer on my car holding steady at seventy-eight miles an hour. Two miles south of the Bradenton exit traffic ground to a halt. I could see red taillights stretching to the horizon. The windshield wipers pounded a steady thump, thump, thump while I listened to Terry Gross interview Tom Hanks on the radio. If I had any spare time, I'd like to see Hank's latest movie, but with all the unpacking still ahead of me I had no time to spare.

For the next thirty minutes I inched along until I finally left the interstate. Coming off the ramp I hit the gas, skimming through a series of yellow lights until I flew past the Manatee County Courthouse. Realizing I missed the turn, I slammed on the brakes and made an illegal U-turn onto 12th Street. Going slowly now, hindered by speed bumps on every block, I passed a string of shabby buildings with barred windows and signs advertising *Se habla español.* A few blocks in, the neighborhood changed. Pawnshops yielded to trendy cafes. Tables with closed umbrellas belted like trench coats against the rain spilled out on the sidewalk. At the end of the street I pulled into the Twin Dolphins Marina where multi-million dollar boats strained against their lines, resisting the wind. I left the car and opened my umbrella, making a mad dash to the restaurant, two minutes late for my lunch date with Ben.

I looked around. Ben hadn't arrived yet. I selected a table on the covered patio and waited for a waitress to notice me. Since I was the only one sitting outside, it took her a while. When she finally appeared, I tried hard not to bite her head off and ordered a decaf. As the rain poured down, the air became almost too thick to breathe. I crossed my legs and lit up. By the time I saw Ben approaching, I was on my second Marlboro Light.

"I thought you were trying to quit," he said with a disapproving frown.

"I am." I stubbed out the half-smoked cigarette.

Ben peeled off his suit jacket and hung it on the back of a chair before sitting across from me.

"You still dress like you're in the city," I teased. "I understand you were going for a certain look when we went to the prison, but you're the only one wearing a tie here."

Ben shrugged. "Uniform of the trade. I'm meeting with my investigator after lunch to discuss the Castro case." Ben caught the waitress's eye and waved her over.

The waitress, who had been eyeing Ben ever since he came in, sashayed to our table. Ben ordered another coffee for me and a beer for himself.

"Sorry I'm late. Traffic was terrible. I hoped to have time to catch up over lunch, but since we're getting a late start . . ." Ben reached into his pocket and pulled out a flash drive. Sliding it across the table he said, "Logan Murphy's trial transcript. Also, I looked into that issue you raised about the judge. Higel is serving his twenty-first year on the bench. No reversals, two mistrials. Both of those were due to jurist issues so no reflection on the good judge. He has a reputation for running a tight court, a no-nonsense guy. The kind of judge both sides appreciate."

"What about the prosecutor?" I asked.

Ben nodded. "George Higel. A distant cousin. At a preliminary hearing the judge made a full disclosure of the relationship and the defense didn't object."

The waitress returned with our drinks and a pair of menus. Ben thanked her, flashing that boyish smile I knew so well. She batted her eyes and I swear, winked at him before telling us that the specials were listed on the back of the menu. He turned his attention back to me when she left us alone.

"That thing about the Higels was a good catch on your part. But at the end of the day, it appears that everything was done by the book."

"I read through the brief you sent. The one you submitted to your boss when you pitched Logan's case. There's quite a bit about this I never encountered before. I spent my career preparing wills and divorce settlements. Can you explain how the appeal process works?"

"As soon as someone is sent to death row the process automatically kicks in with court appointed lawyers. These legal teams are highly specialized. They look for all the stuff that might get their client a wrongful conviction hearing—false testimony, inadequate representation, suppressed or mishandled evidence, you get the idea—and the case keeps working its way through the system until either the conviction is overturned or the lawyers find enough cause to advance it to the State Supreme Court. That's Logan's next step. His team is waiting to hear if the Supremes will hear his case."

"Does he have a chance?" I asked.

Ben set his glass on the table and shrugged. "There's always a chance, but there's something you have to bear in mind. The moment Logan was convicted, the burden of proof shifted. It's now up to him to prove that either the case was mishandled or that he is innocent."

I leaned back in my seat and nodded. "I've been thinking. The only way we'll get to the truth is to find out who the victim was."

"Do you have any ideas?"

"Not yet. The police investigation focused on Logan from the start, and everything else seemed to fall by the wayside, including any real effort to find out who that girl was."

"Have you had a chance to speak with Logan's friends?"

"I've got an appointment with Tyler Fox this afternoon. Boyd Skinner still hasn't returned my calls."

The waitress reappeared to take our order. Ben waved her away saying he needed more time to look at the menu.

"If we don't order soon you're going to be late for your meeting."

"Lalo won't even notice," Ben laughed.

"Who is Lalo?"

"Eduardo Sanchez, the investigator I hired to work on Ricky Castro's case. He prefers to be called Lalo." Ben tilted his head and glanced at me over his menu. "You should meet him."

"I don't have time. I've got to meet Ty."

"Lalo could help you find out who Jane Doe was."

"Doesn't he only work for your clients?"

"I'm not suggesting anything official. He may be willing to put in a little time, pro bono. He's got all the tools of the trade, access to information that you may find difficult to get your hands on. It's worth asking him. The worst he can do is say no."

Ben put the menu down on the table and waved the waitress back. He gave her a smile and said, "My aunt here just reminded me that we're in a hurry. We'll both have the special. And could you please bring the check with our food?"

"Sure thing." She winked at him again and wiggled her behind as she headed for the kitchen.

Outside the rain had faded to a steady drizzle, the wind reduced to a soft breeze. I followed Ben out of the restaurant and down a few steps to the docks. When he offered his hand, I refused. That small stand for women's equality turned south when I slipped on a wet board and fell, landing rather ungracefully on my rear end. To his credit, Ben didn't laugh. We walked down the pier, passing several yachts—each more stunning than the next—until we reached the end where an old wooden boat lay in its slip. The vessel appeared deserted, rocking gently with the movement of the water. Ben called out, and a massive Rottweiler appeared through a set of open doors, stumpy tail wagging in greeting.

"I thought we were going to meet your investigator," I said.

"We are. This is his home."

"He lives on this boat?"

Ben nodded. Climbing onto the deck he motioned for me to follow. I shook my head, preferring to remain on solid ground. Not that a few planks suspended over murky water met any definition of the word "solid" but anything was better than stepping onto a floating death trap.

"What's the matter?" Ben asked.

I peered at the boat. The teak floor was dark and slick, the wooden rails that embraced the back deck splintered and weatherworn. Mildew-stained plastic screens covered the windows, blocking the view inside. The boat was big, maybe forty feet long or more, but the size didn't do anything to allay my fears. On the contrary, I could easily imagine the whole thing sinking under its own weight.

The Rottweiler turned and trotted back into the cabin. From where I stood on the dock I could see beyond the seawall all the way out to the Manatee River. Though the water in the protected marina rolled uneasily, it was nothing compared to the angry river beyond. I watched as a few pelicans sailed over the whitecaps. That signaled the worst of the storm was over, but just looking at the swells made my stomach turn somersaults.

One corner of Ben's mouth turned up in amusement. "I didn't know you were afraid of boats."

"Did I say I'm afraid? I just don't trust them, that's all."

"Don't worry, we're not going anywhere." Ben offered his hand, and this time I grabbed and held on tight. Despite his assistance, I tripped over the railing, thanking my lucky stars that I landed upright. With both hands, I clutched a grab bar and glanced through the open doors into the cabin. An upholstered chair was screwed to the floor in front of a panel with various gauges and switches. A computer screen glowed green. The radio squawked and I jumped, my heartbeat breaking a hundred. When the dog clambered down a set of steps leading deeper into the ship, I realized that this upper cabin was just the cockpit. The bulk of the vessel lay below.

"Is anybody home?" Ben called.

A bear of a man peered up at us from the foot of the stairs. His hulk seemed far too large for the boat, his head nearly brushing the ceiling. When he saw me, his dark, almond shaped eyes opened wide and he removed his fishing hat to reveal a mass of coarse, blue-black hair.

"Welcome aboard, *amigo*," the man said.

"Good to see you again, Lalo."

After Ben scrambled down the stairs, I held onto the handrails for dear life and slowly made my way behind him. Lalo took my hand into his giant paw when Ben introduced us. Curiosity was written on his face, his thick eyebrows arched in question.

"This is my umm . . . this is Cate Stokes. She's volunteered to help me with a case. I thought you might want to hear about it."

"In other words, you're looking for pro bono work from me too." Lalo smiled at me. "At least you're a better looking lawyer than Ben. Have you done work for the Project before?"

"Me? No, I'm not familiar with criminal law."

"Then what kind of law are you familiar with?"

"My field is . . . that is I used to work in a family law practice but I recently retired," I struggled to maintain my composure under his dark stare. Something about the man put me on edge.

"A retired family lawyer, well that explains everything." His mocking smile rubbed me the wrong way.

"It seems to me the main qualification necessary for this job is a belief in the innocence of the client." I sat up straight and gave him one of my best, withering stares. "I could ask if you meet that same criteria with every case you take."

"You have me there. Take a seat while I get you both something to drink."

"I'm not staying. I need to get back to Venice for a meeting."

"But you just got here. Please, I insist." He gestured toward the U-shaped bench wrapped around a pedestal table secured to the floor.

I sat. The dog hopped onto the bench next to me, met my gaze with her dark, gold-rimmed eyes and leaned closer to take a sniff. Her breath smelled like pond water. I leaned back, and Lalo smiled wide, revealing a gap in his front teeth.

"What would you like? Beer? Soda? Tequila?"

"Water, please." I nodded.

Ben settled on the bench across from me. "The case Cate is working on is strictly unofficial. The odds of success are outside the range of Greg's comfort zone."

"So Greg didn't green-light a project that you believe in and you're going rogue." Lalo raised his eyebrows. "That could be fun. Hit me with the highlights."

"Ten years ago the client, Logan Murphy, was convicted of killing a Jane Doe. She was never identified."

"Interesting." He set the drinks on the table, waved the dog off the bench and slid in next to me. I scooted over to give him more room. My stomach turned in protest as the boat gently rocked.

"Someone must have known her." Lalo looked directly at me. "Her mother, a sister, a lover? Sooner or later someone always turns up to ID the body."

"Usually," Ben agreed. "But not this time."

"And you think your guy is innocent." His eyes locked with mine. "Missus . . . Miss Stokes?"

"Mrs. And yes, I do."

He glanced down at my wedding ring and shrugged. "What makes you so certain?"

With every passing moment, I disliked this man more and more. I picked up my glass and sipped water in an attempt to settle my stomach. Reaching a decision, I set the glass down with a solid thump.

"This is a waste of time." I turned to Ben. "Thanks for lunch. I need to go or I'll be late for my appointment."

"Hang on." Lalo placed his hand on my arm. "Let's assume you're right. Do you have any theories about who killed the girl?"

"Cate says the answer to that question lies in finding out who Jane Doe was."

"She's probably right."

Lalo sat inches away, intently staring at me. I leaned back, claustrophobia compounding the distress of my already troubled stomach. "Tell me what you know about this Jane Doe."

"She was young, beautiful . . . ," I began.

"Do you have a photo?"

I already made up my mind to leave, but I couldn't resist the chance to show the man that I wasn't just an idiot Ben dragged out of retirement to help with the case. I dug into my purse and pulled out a folded sheet of paper that I pressed against the table. It took me a full day speaking to a heavily accented person on the cable provider's help desk to get the new printer working. Once I got it going, I was able to print out everything I had earmarked for my file.

"The press ran this sketch of the victim for days. The local newspaper even offered a reward for anyone who could provide information leading to Jane Doe's identity. But as Ben told you, no one came forward."

Lalo took another pull on his bottle, his eyes fixed on the image that looked up from the paper.

"A Latina," he said quietly.

I glanced down and wondered why, after looking at Jane Doe for hours, I never saw the obvious. The girl could indeed have been Hispanic.

"I've got to go. I'm going to meet a friend of Logan's who was with him on the night of the murder."

"That won't get you anywhere." Lalo voice was a low baritone. "If the friend knew anything, the cops would have looked into it long before now."

His arrogance lit my anger. "Coming here wasn't my idea," I snapped.

"I'll do it." Lalo raised his bottle and clinked it against Ben's. "I'll help you with this one."

Ben nodded. "Thanks, Lalo. If the two of you dig up new evidence, something that convinces Greg to approve the case, we'll make this official. At that point we'll try to find money in the budget to at least cover your expenses."

"I don't need his help!" My voice rang shrill in the cramped space.

"Oh yes, you do. There's a reason why no one came forward to speak for this girl, and I can help you find out why." Lalo spread his hands out, palms upward. "No offense, Ms. Stokes, but I've got a little more experience with these things than you do."

I hated to admit it, but he was right. Ben looked at me, willing me to agree. I nodded.

"I'll put feelers out in the Hispanic community to see if anyone knows anything about our Jane Doe. In the meantime, let me know what you learn from the friend who was with your client that night."

"Thanks, Lalo, the two of you will make a great team."

All the way home, I replayed the events of the afternoon in my head. I wasn't happy. By asking for Lalo's help, Ben showed a lack of confidence in my ability to get the job done. And Lalo's interest in the case felt strange. I couldn't quite put my finger on it, but the moment he saw the victim's picture, it seemed to me he made up his mind to help. For some reason, Lalo wanted to be involved. I considered calling Ben to say I quit. Lalo could work this case on his own.

I stewed in my thoughts until I arrived in Venice. The windshield wipers, set on auto, stopped. The hazy afternoon sun hung low in the west, not a cloud in the sky. I turned down Annie's street and saw her sitting out on her front lawn, eyes closed, face turned toward the sun. She looked up as I passed and waved. No matter how slim my chances of success were, I realized I couldn't let her down. Like it or not, I promised to help her grandson. Even if that meant working with Lalo Sanchez.

SIX

After watching Cate drive away, Ben's thoughts turned to the Castro case. The Defender Project used Lalo when they needed an investigator who was fluent in Spanish and had connections to the Latino community. Other than knowing he was a guy who could get the job done, Ben did not know much else about him. He was pleased to have secured Lalo's help for Cate, but was anxious to get down to the business at hand. Yet when Ben returned to the cabin, he found his investigator was not in any hurry to change the subject.

"Where did you find her?" he asked.

"Who?"

"Cate. I get the feeling you've known her for a long time."

Ben sighed, realizing Lalo would find out sooner or later anyway. "She's my aunt."

Lalo laughed. "I figured something like that."

"She's convinced Logan got a raw deal and she wants to make it right. And believe me, when Aunt Cate sets her mind on something, she doesn't let go 'til she gets what she wants."

"Must be hard for your uncle, living with someone like that."

"Uncle Arnie died a few years ago."

"I see."

"Can we talk about Ricky Castro?"

"Sure. Tell me what we're working with here."

"What do you know about Immokalee?" Ben asked.

Lalo turned his head slightly, his gaze fixed on something outside the small, round window in the cabin. He did not blink, his breathing slowed, his hand closed tight around his empty bottle of beer. Ben wondered if he should repeat the question. Lalo appeared to be in another place, another time. Finally, with a deep breath, his investigator spoke.

"ImMOKalee. Rhymes with broccoli."

"So you know the place," Ben said.

"Why do you ask?"

"My client, Ricky Castro grew up there."

"What else do you know about Castro?"

"He was born on this side of the border to illegal immigrants. Father originally came from Puebla, Mexico and ended up in Immokalee where he died at the age of thirty-nine to liver cancer. Ricky's mother fended for herself, Ricky, and her only surviving daughter until she got sick too."

"Her only surviving daughter?"

"Yes, apparently Mrs. Castro gave birth to two stillborn girls after Ricky and his sister were born. Her last baby suffered from a birth defect and died when she was two. Ricky was only thirteen when his mother passed away from lung cancer. That's when he quit school and went to work in the tomato fields to support himself and his sister."

"Unfortunately, I've heard that kind of story before." Lalo continued to stare out the porthole. He mumbled a curse under his breath. "The lawsuits stopped the growers from spraying insecticides on the crops with the workers in the fields, but the cancer rate down there is still off the chart. So tell me, who did Castro kill?"

"The whole idea here is that he didn't kill anybody."

"Sorry. Who did he *allegedly* kill?"

"His girlfriend, Marcela de la Vega."

"And did she work in the fields?"

"No. She was a prostitute."

Lalo jerked his head around, his fascination with the outside view broken. He ran his hand down his face, and shook his head slowly from side to side.

"*Chin*," he swore. "How did she die?" His voice was subdued, but there was a growl in his throat that sent a shiver down Ben's spine. Something about the case obviously struck a nerve.

"She was strangled." Ben tried to decipher the look on Lalo's face. "The autopsy report suggested she was raped before she was killed. Possibly by more than one man."

Lalo stood and crossed the cabin to pull another beer out of the refrigerator. He offered one to Ben, but the young lawyer shook his head saying he had a long drive back to Gainesville. Lalo returned to his seat, patted the empty space on the bench next to him and the dog jumped up, resting her head on his lap. Lalo stroked her absentmindedly, the beer clutched in his hand, his attention returning to the view outside.

"I know something about Immokalee, but I have to warn you, it's what I don't know that will give us trouble."

About fifteen minutes into his drive home, Ben's phone rang. Glancing at the screen he saw it was Stephanie, calling from the office. He chose to ignore her, deciding to return the call after he had time to process his discussion with Lalo and think things through.

The investigator was not interested in reviewing Castro's trial summary or any other information that Ben offered to share. He insisted on forming his own opinion, and wanted to get started by pulling Castro's arrest report at the Collier County Clerk's office. Lalo assured Ben that he had access to everything related to the police investigation. That puzzled Ben. Arrest reports were a matter of public record but detectives guarded case files like their own personal property. He decided not to press the issue, offering a helpful suggestion instead.

"I usually begin with the trial summary and work backwards."

"Yeah, well I like to do things my own way," Lalo said. "I'll let you know when I want to see the court records."

"I'm not trying to tell you how to do your job. I only thought . . . never mind. You're running the investigation. When do you want to interview Ricky?"

"I'll apply for a visitor's pass this afternoon. As soon as I'm cleared I'll go."

"Let me know when and I'll join you. In fact, you don't have to bother with that visitor's pass. I'll register you with the prison as my investigator and you can get in with me anytime."

"But I want to see Logan Murphy too," Lalo said. "And you're not *his* lawyer so I'll go ahead and get that visitor's pass anyway."

"Tell me honestly. Do you think you can help Logan?"

"Maybe." Lalo nodded slowly, his eyes moving back and forth while he tossed an idea around in his head. "I have a theory why the authorities never found out who the victim was."

"Why?"

"If she was an illegal, then there wouldn't be too many people in her circle of friends willing to come forward and report her missing. But it's too soon to say for certain. I'll let you know when I find out more about our Jane Doe."

As he drove home, Ben's thoughts revolved around Logan Murphy. Running the investigation against Greg's explicit order wasn't exactly a great career move. But Ben was convinced Murphy was innocent, and unless Cate or Lalo could produce evidence to challenge the conviction, the case would never be taken up by the Project. He took this job to help people just like Logan and in his mind, going against his boss was worth the risk.

As the numbers on the mile markers increased, Ben picked up his phone and called the office. Stephanie answered on the first ring.

"'Bout time you checked in, Shepherd. I tried to reach you an hour ago. How did it go with Lalo?"

"He wants to do things his own way."

"Let him. Believe me, you might not want to be witness to some of his methods. Lalo Sanchez doesn't necessarily work within the confines of the law, but he always gets results. Any chance he'll be coming into the office?"

"Not for a while. Why?"

"Did you not look at him?" Her voice went up a notch. "Sexy doesn't even begin to describe that man."

Ben laughed. From his perspective, Lalo was a slightly overweight, unkempt Mexican-American, pushing sixty, maybe sixty-five.

"Really? I wouldn't have figured him for your type. So other than sitting around, fantasizing about our investigator, did you get anything done today?"

"Yeah, I found all the information you wanted on Immokalee."

"ImMOKalee, rhymes with broccoli." Ben, smiled to himself.

"No kidding, I've always wondered about that. Anyway, that place is not exactly a vacation spot. Are you ready?"

"Shoot."

"Forty-four percent of the residents live below the poverty line, seventy-five percent of the population Hispanic, median household income under twenty thousand a year, blah, blah, blah. Do you want to hear this crap?"

"You're not telling me anything I couldn't have guessed. What about the crime rate?"

"Bad. *Real* bad. For a town that size, violent crime in Immokalee is one of the worst in the nation. If you're planning to drive through there I recommend you lock your car doors when you stop for red lights."

"Okay, I get the picture. There's something else I need you to check."

"Does this fall anywhere in the realm of paralegal work, by any chance? I've got three other attorneys here that I'm supposed to be working for. And the other guys expect me to do actual legal research while you come up with wild-ass goose chases that make no sense. I sometimes wonder why I do this stuff for you."

"We both know why. It's because I'm irresistible." Ben chuckled. "And much sexier than Lalo."

"In your dreams," she said with a snort. "So what do you want?"

"I want to know what you can find out about the tomato fields down there. Who owns them, how do they operate, any lawsuits pending, that sort of stuff."

"Are you kidding me? What's that got to do with anything?"

"Background."

"Yeah, right. Greg's got me on something else right now but I should be able to start on your tomato fields first thing in the morning. See you at eight?"

"I'll bring the coffee," Ben replied. "And Stephanie?"

"Yeah?"

"You're the best."

"Shoot, Shepherd. Tell me something I don't already know."

SEVEN

I raced back to Venice for my appointment with Tyler Fox. Cruising Seaboard Industrial Park, I read the numbers on the buildings, glancing every now and then at the paper clutched in my hand to make sure I had the address right. Rolling down the window, I called to a man loading a spool of cable onto a utility truck and asked for directions. He wiped his brow and pointed to the building across the street before going back to his task without a word. I pulled into the weed-infested parking lot that backed onto a canal and checked for a number. Nothing. Walking around the side of the cement block building I saw the sign: T.F. CONSTRUCTION COMPANY. A quick check of my watch confirmed I was right on time.

When no one responded to the bell, I looked over my shoulder. Three other cars were parked in the crushed gravel lot, so I pounded the door with the heel of my hand. The door opened almost immediately to reveal a girl who looked to be about eighteen. She wore pink glitter eye shadow, red lipstick, three-inch heels and cologne that smelled like cotton candy. The tattoo on her wrist read, "Randy."

"The doorbell don't work," the young lady said, popping her gum. "I keep tellin' Ty to get it fixed, but he don't ever listen to me. 'Course we don't get many visitors, only salesmen, sometimes a subcontractor, and they all know about the bell so Ty says he don't see the point. And the thing is, anyone comes lookin' for work, we're not hirin' so he says it don't matter. Still, broke is broke, right? So I keep telling him, he oughta get it fixed." She snapped the gum in her mouth without missing a beat. "I'm guessin' you're the one he's expectin'. Come on in and I'll call him."

I stepped into the reception area, a closet-like space that contained a dented metal desk and a pair of folding chairs. The girl squeezed behind the desk, picked up a microphone, keyed a button and shouted, "Ty, your visitor is here." She looked up, blew an alarmingly large pink bubble, sucked it back into her mouth. "He's loadin' the truck out back for tomorrow's job. Make yourself comfortable, he won't be long."

I settled on one of the chairs and looked around. The top of her desk contained a computer plastered with sticky notes, an old fashioned adding machine, a mess of papers and a handful of weird animals made of seashells. Pinned to the wall was a calendar promoting a national paint company and taped next to that was a photo of a shaggy-looking mutt.

"Is that your dog?" I asked.

"Yeah, Ringo. He's like, old. I've had him since I was a kid."

By any definition, the girl was still a kid, but I nodded like I was impressed. "How do you like working for Mr. Fox? What is he like?"

"Ty? Oh, he's great, really, really great, never yells at me or nothin' even when I make mistakes, which I don't. At least not too often. Well, there was that time when the friggin' computer kept locking up on me and he thought I was doing somethin' wrong, but that was like months ago. So yeah, he's great. Still, I don't wanna work here forever, just until somethin' better comes along, I got my application in at Home Depot. My boyfriend, he works there and he says they got great benefits. Ty don't give me health insurance or nothin'."

The smile on my face masked the utter despair I felt at the failure of the education system to teach this girl how to speak. I suspected she was inches away from getting pregnant with the boyfriend—presumably Randy—and thus the allure of a job that offered health insurance. Tyler Fox entered from the back of the shop just in time to save me from wasting my breath on sound advice about birth control that the girl would probably ignore.

Ty's polo shirt stretched tight over his chest, damp with sweat. I had to crane my neck to meet his brown eyes as we shook hands. I knew he was in the same high school class as Logan Murphy so I figured he was twenty-eight, give or take a year. When he smiled, I found myself smiling back.

"Thanks for taking the time to see me," I began. "I know you're busy."

"No problem," he replied. His eyes shifted to the girl who still stood there, staring at us. "Stacy, did you offer Mrs. Stokes something to drink?"

"Oh snap, I totally forgot," Stacy looked at me. "That's somethin' he's always tellin' me, don't forget to offer visitors somethin' to drink, but man, every time . . . we don't got ice but I keep the bottles in the fridge so it should be cold enough, I guess."

I accepted the plastic bottle and asked, "Do you have a glass I could use?"

"A glass? Like to drink out of? I think there's one in the bathroom."

"Never mind, I'm not thirsty." I handed the water back to her.

I followed Ty back to his office, a small room with the same type of gray metal desk wedged into a corner. Same calendar pinned to the wall. Same clutter on the desk. No shell animals. I took a seat at the only visitor's chair in the room.

"What can I do for you, Mrs. Stokes?" Ty asked. "You told me on the phone that you work for Logan's law firm?"

"Not exactly. And please, call me Cate."

"Not exactly?" Ty's genial expression clouded over. "I don't have time for games. Are you here to help Logan or not?"

"I'm doing pro bono work for the Defender Project. Logan has requested our assistance but we can't commit resources to the case until we have more information. That's why I'm here, to ask if you can tell me anything that might help your friend."

The scowl remained on Ty's face. I watched patiently while he mulled things over in his head. Slowly the crease between his eyebrows disappeared and he eased back in his chair.

"We were good friends back then. But I haven't seen Logan since the trial. My saying so doesn't change anything, but I know Logan didn't kill that girl. Sure, I'd like to help him if I could, but I honestly don't see how."

"Let's start with Snook Wallow. Do you remember seeing the girl that night?"

"We all saw her, Logan, Boyd and me. Logan saw her first and said something about her being hot."

"Was she?"

"What?"

"Hot. Did you think she was hot?"

"Yeah, I guess."

"Did Logan speak with her?"

"No, not even close. She bought two beers and left." Ty shrugged. "That was it."

"Two beers? Did you notice if she was with anyone?"

He paused, looking up at a corner of the ceiling as he thought that one over.

"Didn't notice anybody in particular. But a girl looks like that, she's not alone, you know what I mean?"

"What happened then?"

"Logan left to take a leak and never came back. After a while I went looking for him but he was gone. Boyd and I didn't have any luck picking up girls that night so we decided to leave early."

"Was Logan drinking heavily?"

"We all were. That's pretty much what we did back then."

"Why did you leave Logan behind?"

"That was the deal. We always went together, but if we got lucky and hooked up with someone, there was no waiting around. I figured Logan caught up with the girl and I wasn't going to interfere with whatever he had going."

"But neither you nor Boyd found a . . . a date that night?"

Ty shifted in his seat. "Like I told you, we left early. Before the band quit playing."

"The police assumed Logan left the bar to follow the victim. It sounds to me like you made the same assumption."

A guarded look crossed Ty's face. He leaned forward, both arms resting on the desk. "Look, what I just said about Logan catching up with the girl . . . that was a guess. He never actually said anything like that. I thought you wanted to help him."

"I'm simply trying to find out what happened."

"Logan claims he went to take a leak and when he got down to the river he passed out. Knowing the shape he was in at the time, I'd say that's exactly what happened. Like I keep sayin', I don't believe Logan killed that girl."

"I don't either. But the problem is we need proof. Is there anything else you can tell me?"

"If I knew something, I would have told the cops when they talked to me ten years ago." He sat straight, pushed his chair back from the desk. "Are we through here? I've got work to do."

"I understand. Will you call me if anything else comes to mind? Sometimes a small detail, something that didn't seem important at the time can open a new avenue of investigation."

"Yeah, sure, I'll do that. Listen, don't get me wrong, I hope you can do something for Logan. He doesn't deserve what happened to him."

I nodded agreement. "I promise to do my best."

Lately, it seemed like that was all I could offer. Empty promises.

I called Ben later that evening to update him on my meeting with Tyler Fox. I hit all the highlights while Ben listened without interruption. When I finished, he remained quiet. I asked him what he thought.

"What is your gut feeling about the guy?" he asked.

"I liked him. He's a hard working family man. His employee says he's a decent boss. And there's no question about his loyalty to Logan."

"What makes you say that?"

"He made it clear that he didn't think Logan murdered that girl."

"You did well. If Jane Doe bought two beers, that means she was with someone that night. And that's something that never came up during the trial. Ten years is a long time, but keep at it. Sooner or later you'll find someone else who remembers something we haven't heard before."

"I was thinking, when I get a chance, I'll go out to Snook Wallow and see if I can track down the bartender. We have one thing going for us; this was a big event in a small town. Anyone who was at Snook Wallow that night would remember Jane Doe's murder."

"How soon can you get out there?"

"Not for a few days. I've got to get my things unpacked. Living here amid all this chaos is making me crazy."

"Fair enough. All in all, this turned out to be a productive day, huh?"

"How did your meeting with Lalo go after I left?" I asked.

"Great. What do you think of him?"

"He seemed nice," I lied.

"You hated him," Ben said with a laugh.

"Okay, so there's something about him that rubs me the wrong way. But that doesn't mean I can't work with him if I have to."

"That's good. Of course his first priority will be the Castro case, but if you need anything, just call him."

Calling Lalo Sanchez was not on my list of things to do.

"I'm sure he can contribute." I measured my words carefully. "He is going to speak to people within the local Hispanic community to see if they know anything about our victim. That would be a great help, but I don't know if I'll need him for anything else. I've got things pretty much under control."

"Have you figured out how to get a copy of the homicide detective's case files?"

In typical fashion, Ben hit me with a problem I hadn't yet solved. While every report, every note the homicide detective made was considered an official document, I had absolutely no idea how to go about getting my hands on them.

"Any suggestions?" I asked.

"Lalo has contacts within the Sarasota County Sheriff's department. He knows how to cut through the red tape down there, and believe me, there's plenty of that to go around. Call him and see what he can do. And while you're at it, it wouldn't kill you to be nice to the guy. I think he likes you."

"If he can get me a copy of the detective's records, I'll let him take me to the prom."

I heard Ben chuckle at the other end of the line. "Why don't you bring him with you to Snook Wallow? I hear they serve deep fried alligator bites."

"Ugh, no thanks."

"No, I'm serious. Not about the alligator bites, but it's a good idea to have Lalo with you when you speak with the bartender."

"Okay, I'll give him a call. But I swear, if he brings that smelly dog . . ."

The sound of Ben's laughter drowned out the rest of my words.

EIGHT

Twenty-nine cartons labeled KITCHEN and no clue as to which contained my dishes. For days I'd been eating off paper plates and drinking out of plastic cups. I refused to spend one more day camping out in my own house. I dragged one box to the center of the room, thinking it was heavy enough to hold stoneware. After slicing through the tape I pried open the flaps. Inside I discovered a collection of old wedding gifts—a tarnished silver casserole dish, two cut crystal vases and a pair of candlesticks—which I never used. A quick scan of the cabinets reminded me I had to store everything in half the space of my old kitchen. Setting the gifts on the counter, I attacked the next box and discovered two fondue pots, six canapé plates, a pressure cooker, two coffee makers—one hadn't worked in years—and a set of twelve wine glasses. No dishes. I realized the problem. Even though I shed my old house, I simply never considered getting rid of things I didn't need. The cabinets were already half full, and I had yet to unpack anything useful. Left with no choice, I pulled everything back out and started culling. Before long the boxes were refilled. With a black marker I scratched out KITCHEN and wrote GOODWILL underneath. I felt liberated, but still hadn't found my dishes.

By noon the kitchen floor was covered with crumpled packing paper that swirled like tumbleweeds when I moved around. Just as I felt a rush of victory at finding my silverware, the doorbell rang. The sun streamed in, backlighting Annie Murphy with a yellow glow.

"What a nice surprise." I blew my bangs out of my eyes. "Come in."

"I brought you a little house warming present." She extended her hand and dangled a bit of glass at the end of a thread.

"How lovely." Even as I accepted the gift, I wondered what I was supposed to do with it.

"It's an earth guardian crystal. They emit a comforting aura. Just the thing to help you adjust to your new home."

I took a second look at the irregular crystal, and noticed the shape vaguely resembled an angel. Of course I didn't take all that nonsense about auras seriously, but I didn't want to offend her. Even as I attached the thing to the curtain rod over the sink, I had thoughts of throwing the little angel in the Goodwill box after Annie left. As I stood back, the crystal caught a ray of light, turning from clear to pale pink.

"There, it's working already," Annie gave a warm smile.

Strange though it seemed, I did feel better, if only a little bit.

"Can I offer you something to drink?" I asked. "Iced tea?"

"That would be great, thanks."

I placed a pitcher of tea and two wine goblets on a tray and carried everything to the lanai where things were a bit more settled. At least we could sit down without having to move boxes or other random items that hadn't yet found a home.

"Nice glasses," she said with a smile as she accepted the tea.

"Still unpacking," I replied. "Haven't found my tumblers yet."

"How's your investigation going?"

"I'm just getting started." I took a sip of my tea. "I went to see Tyler Fox a few days ago. He is nice but I don't think he can be much help. He doesn't know what happened to that girl any more than Logan does."

"Any luck catching up with Boyd?"

"Not yet. I left lots of messages, but he doesn't return my calls."

"I'm not surprised. I haven't seen Boyd since the trial, as I told you."

In the awkward silence that followed, Annie's glance fell on the tray of tomato plants sitting on a shelf. They looked the worse for wear, limp and yellowing.

"I've been waiting for the ground to dry so I can plant them," I explained.

"You can put them in now. We're built on sand here, so the soil drains quickly. Just be sure to add compost or the plants will starve to death."

"I bought a bottle of fertilizer."

Annie wrinkled her nose and shook her head. "Throw that stuff out. The plants will grow all right, but the tomatoes will absorb all those toxic chemicals and you don't even want to think about eating them. There's a guy in Nokomis who sells great organic compost. I'll look up his address and give you a call when I get home."

I thanked her for the advice, and she took her leave. As I finished emptying another box, my doorbell rang again. Thinking it might be Annie returning with the name of the compost guy, I opened the door to see Lalo standing there. He wore a Yankees baseball cap, a dark brown polo shirt that matched the color of his eyes and khaki trousers. He scanned me up and down, an amused look on his face. I brushed my bangs off my forehead with the back of my hand. With Annie, I didn't think twice about how I looked. Under Lalo's scrutiny, I was painfully aware of my old work shirt and torn jeans.

"Are you going dressed like that?" he asked.

"Going where?"

"Snook Wallow. We have a date for lunch."

"Date? Nobody said anything about a date. I asked you to meet me there tomorrow so we could speak with the bartender."

"Oh, well I'm here now so let's go."

"Did it ever occur to you that I might have other plans?"

"Do you?"

"No, but . . . oh, never mind. Come in but don't mind the mess. I need a minute to change."

When I saw my reflection in the bathroom mirror, I was appalled. Not only was my hair plastered to my scalp with sweat, I had a charcoal black smudge of something on my cheek. I desperately needed a shower, something presentable to wear and more than a light touch of makeup. Thirty-five minutes later I emerged to find Lalo sitting in my living room glancing through the latest copy of *Florida Gardening*.

"You like flowers?"

"Flowers, vegetables, I love to grow things," I replied.

"Not me. Had too much of that stuff when I was young."

In my opinion, anyone who didn't like flowers had something wrong with them. Deciding to drop the subject, I went into the kitchen and gathered my purse. Looking around in surprise, I noticed the crumpled balls of packing paper were gone and the empty boxes were folded and stacked neatly in a corner. I turned to see Lalo holding the door open, waiting.

"You cleaned up the mess?"

"Nothing better to do while you made yourself beautiful." He shrugged. "Let's go. Maya is hungry."

I glanced past him to see the Rottweiler waiting on my front porch. She panted like a locomotive, her tongue dripping drool. Lalo opened the truck door and the dog pushed past me, scrambling onto the back seat. As we pulled away from the curb, Maya placed her front legs on the armrest between us and stared at the road ahead. Her breath was terrible, the smell of her fur nauseating. I adjusted the vents to blow cold, filtered air in my face, but the odor was inescapable. When at last the truck bumped down a dirt road that ended in Snook Wallow's empty parking lot, I threw open the door and drew in deep breaths of fresh air. When I stepped out, the dog jumped onto my seat and followed.

The place reminded me of my childhood summer camp. The rough boards of the main structure suggested the building was cobbled together long before the existence of any building code but I saw evidence of recent improvements. The buildings were painted a bright green and the aluminum screens on the wrap-around porch looked brand new. A towering oak grew in the middle of a clearing, a fake Interstate sign nailed to the trunk that read, "Exit 207 Circus Brewing."

"It's deserted."

"They're probably out back." Lalo placed his hand in the small of my back, guiding the way.

We climbed the steps to the porch and walked around to the back of the building. The unleashed dog trailed behind. All eight tables stood empty. I peered over the railing into the Myakka River below.

"This time of year the place only gets busy on weekends. Come January when the snow birds return you have to fight for a table. Do you know where the body was found?"

The place was so quiet and tranquil that I almost forgot why we were there. I pointed to a small structure about two hundred feet away. "Somewhere on the path between those restrooms and the fish camp."

Lalo followed my gaze. "We'll take a walk down there later. Let's eat first, I'm starving."

An overweight waitress appeared and set down a bowl of water for Maya. She ran down a list of specials—including alligator bites—but before I could say anything, Lalo ordered two grilled grouper sandwiches, a hot dog and three orders of fries.

"Do I get the fish sandwich or the hot dog?" I asked after the waitress disappeared.

"The fish sandwich. They're pretty good here."

"But what if I don't want the fish sandwich?"

"Do you want the hot dog? Because Maya likes grouper so you could switch with her."

"No, I don't want the hot dog!"

"If you want the fish sandwich, then what's the problem?"

"The problem is, you didn't *know* I wanted the fish sandwich."

"I told you, they're good."

"You're missing the point." I took a deep breath and counted to ten. "I prefer to order for myself."

"Why?" He peered at me as if seeing me for the first time. "You're not one of those liberated women, are you?"

"Well, I always believed that—"

"I'll call the waitress back so you can tell her yourself that you want the fish sandwich."

"No, that won't be necessary. It's just that—"

He tipped his head and a crease formed between his thick eyebrows. "That's the problem with women. If I live to be a hundred, I'll never understand you."

"Let's change the subject, okay?" This conversation wasn't doing anything to enhance our working arrangement. "I take it you've been here before?"

"A few times. I come for the grouper." His face broke into a wide smile revealing the gap between his front teeth. I couldn't help but smile back.

A soft *whoosh* broke into our discussion, and I turned to see the whiskered nose of a manatee break the surface of the river.

"Look," I shouted, rising to my feet and peering over the railing. The sea cow sank slowly, disappearing under the brackish water.

"Next time you see a manatee, you might want to tone it down a little."

I felt foolish for scaring the creature, but Lalo didn't seem to hold my outburst against me. While we waited for our food, he gave me a brief history. Years ago bootleggers ran the place. In time four cabins were built along a tributary of the river and the fish camp grew from there. The murder certainly didn't help the restaurant's business, and in recent years the owners declared bankruptcy. The new operators did a good job of turning things around. In addition to the improvements to the main building, Lalo told me that the fish camp was converted into vacation cabins for tourists.

"With the change in management, I doubt that anyone who worked here ten years ago is still around." Ben shook his head.

The waitress must have overheard him as she set our plates on the table. "Charlie's the only one. He's been here forever."

"Charlie?" I asked.

"One of the bartenders. Only works weekends. Comes in at four and stays 'til closing."

"Are the cabins rented this week?" Lalo asked.

"Three of them are, why?" She winked at Lalo. "Are you two looking for a little get-away?"

"No, of course not," I replied annoyed. "We're here to—"

"Yeah, maybe," Lalo interrupted. "Can we have a look?"

"Sure, honey. I'll bring you the key. They're fixed up real nice, you'll like it."

With the arrival of the food, Maya sat up. Lalo grabbed a bottle of barbecue sauce, smothered the hotdog and fries and set the dog's lunch on the ground. She cleaned the plate, pickle and all in three greedy bites, took a long drink of water and sniffed the ground to see what she missed. Finding nothing, she gave Lalo a soulful look. He laughed, shook his head, pointed to the ground and said something to her in Spanish. She promptly curled up in the shade cast by our umbrella. I could sense her eyes following my every move as I finished my sandwich.

"Tell me what you know about this murder," Lalo said, breaking the silence.

I gave him the basic facts of what I learned about Jane Doe from the court summary. He listened carefully, his intense stare never leaving my face. When I started to tell him about Logan's refusal to confess to the sentencing review board, Lalo cut me off.

"I'm not interested in the legal issues. If Ben says this man is innocent, that's good enough for me. Our job is to find out who Jane Doe was, which maybe will lead us to finding out who killed her."

"Any idea how we can do that?"

"We start here, where the girl was killed."

The dog rose to her feet when we pushed back our chairs. As we made our way down the path toward the fish camp, she trailed behind. When we passed the building containing the restrooms, it struck me as being woefully inadequate for the number of people who filled the place on the weekends. I tried to imagine Logan on the night of the murder, staggering down the same path we now followed along the river. He said there was a long line of people waiting to use the toilets, and I believed him. As we moved along, a canopy of trees closed above us. The ground under my feet grew soft and a thick bed of oak leaves cushioned our steps. At a sharp turn in the path, I stumbled over a hidden root. Lalo caught me, saving me from a fall. He held me a moment longer than necessary, standing close enough so that I could smell his aftershave.

"Look there, straight ahead," he said.

I pulled away and peered through the trees. In the distance, I saw a small cabin painted the same bright green as the main building.

"Logan saw a light from one of the cabins," I thought out loud. "The body must have been on this side of the bend. He wouldn't have been able to see anything from back there."

Lalo nodded at the slow-moving river to our right. While the bank next to the restrooms sloped gradually, there was a steep drop where we stood. A chill ran down my arms. This was where Jane Doe's blood soaked the ground. Maya started sniffing around, plowing her nose through the leaves. A gecko darted across the path and disappeared into the underbrush.

"Let's have a look at that cabin."

The wooden steps creaked under Lalo's weight as he climbed onto the porch. Two brightly painted rocking chairs faced the water. I assumed the dog would follow us in, muddy paws and all, but Lalo gave her another signal and she dropped down on her belly. The two brown spots above her eyes seesawed. She didn't look happy, but the stump of her tail beat a steady rhythm and she stayed put when we entered.

A slowly rotating ceiling fan cooled the one-room cabin. A small kitchen was tucked into one corner, a bed and dresser in another. The majority of the space was set up as a living room. The furnishings looked like they came from one of those stores that sell cheap sets for a whole room, but the place appeared to be clean and comfortable. Lalo stood in the center of the room, staring at the bed. He seemed lost in thought. I wondered what went through his head.

"What are you thinking?" I asked. My question seemed to shake him out of his trance. He looked at me, and without a word he turned and walked out, leaving me standing alone. I found him outside, sitting in one of the rockers. He stared into space, absent-mindedly scratching Maya behind the ears.

"The cops assumed she was killed on the path. There was a lot of blood there, so that's a pretty good assumption. But if I was going to rape a girl, it wouldn't be out in the open where someone could come along."

I nodded agreement, wondering where he was leading me with this line of thought.

"So here's what I'm thinking," he continued. "The killer had her somewhere down here, maybe in one of these cabins where no one could hear her scream. After the guy raped her, the girl tried to run. When he caught up with her on the path, he stabbed her to death."

"That's a big assumption."

"Yeah, maybe. But it makes sense. Did they ever find her clothes?"

"I didn't see any mention of them in the trial transcript. I imagine the police looked everywhere, certainly in and around the cabins. How can I get my hands on the homicide detective's case file to check the details?"

"What is his name?"

"Her. Detective Geraldine Garibaldi.

"Geri?"

"You know her?"

"You could say that." A half-smile replaced the somber expression that clouded his face since entering the cabin.

"Will she cooperate with us?"

"That depends."

"On what?"

"On whether or not she's still mad at me."

I took the bait. "Why would she be?"

"Detective Garibaldi is my ex-wife."

NINE

Ben could not decide. Either Greg was a great mentor or his boss was setting him up for failure. When Greg assigned him to the Castro case, Ben felt euphoric. But once the initial excitement faded, he realized Greg expected him to work on the case while maintaining his other responsibilities. For the past two weeks, he was first to arrive in the morning and the last to leave at the end of the day. Still, he was drowning under the rising tide of work. Most nights he went home, grabbed a sandwich and dropped into bed only to catch a few hours of sleep before returning to the office by sunrise.

On Friday afternoon, buried under a mountain of paperwork and facing another late night, he heard the clatter out in the bullpen as the team of law school interns packed up for the day. With a sigh, he gathered the papers strewn across his desk, stuffed everything into a folder and threw it on top of a stack of similar files piled on a shelf behind him. The whole day slipped by without one minute spent on the Castro case. Hours of work still stretched before him.

From the start, Greg reminded Ben that his job was to find a legal solution to Castro's release. In discussing the case strategy, Greg pointed out certain weaknesses in the prosecution's case. Ricky's guilt or innocence was immaterial as far as the boss was concerned.

Ben looked up when Stephanie poked her head into his office.

"Another late night? If you're trying to score points with Greg, you're wasting your time. He left an hour ago."

"I think I'm onto something here," Ben replied. "But I'm not sure how to get my hands around it."

"Need a sounding board? She set her designer bag on the floor, sat down in Ben's visitor's chair, slipped out of her shoes, and reached down to knead her left foot. "It's not like I have anything better to do tonight."

Her offer surprised Ben. Stephanie looked tired, ready to call it a day. He studied her for a moment, making sure she was serious. He had been pursuing an idea for days, only to hit a dead end at every attempt. Stephanie was right, a second opinion would be helpful.

"What happened to your hot date?" he asked.

"I ditched him. Things were getting a little weird."

Not for the first time, Ben wondered about Stephanie's love life. With her gorgeous looks, sharp wit and killer body she had no problem attracting men. But for some reason, she had a habit of breaking up after a few months and moving on to someone new. The news that she was once again single did not come as a surprise.

"So let me tell you what I've got. I'm pretty sure the prosecution used a snitch to offer false testimony against Ricky. At the trial, a guy named Diego Salazar claimed he heard Ricky confess to the murder."

"When did this alleged confession occur?" Stephanie shifted in the chair and started working on the other foot.

"A few hours after the cops discovered Ricky standing over Marcela's dead body. Salazar—a drug dealer—was thrown in a cell with Ricky while he waited for a court-appointed attorney to show up."

"Okay, let me get this straight. Castro is sitting in jail, in shock from discovering Marcela's body, and as if things couldn't get worse for the guy, the cops accuse him of murder. Then out of the blue a drug dealer appears in the cell with him and Castro tells this Salazar–-a complete stranger—that he killed his girlfriend? I don't buy that."

"It won't sound so crazy when I tell you Ricky knew Salazar. The guy was Marcela's dealer."

"You think the cops planted Salazar there on purpose and offered to drop the drug charges if he could help them seal the deal with Castro?"

"I sincerely hope so. That could be Ricky's golden ticket off death row."

"Okay. So it seems to me that it's time for you and Salazar to have a chat."

"That's proving to be a little difficult. Salazar is dead."

Stephanie stopped massaging her feet and gave Ben her full attention. He met her gaze and nodded.

"Shot in the head two months after the trial ended,"

Stephanie rose from her chair, reached for the phone on Ben's desk and punched in a number.

"Who are you calling?" Ben asked.

"Tony's Pizza. Sounds like this is going to take a while."

Hours later, only a few scraps of mozzarella and congealed grease remained in the pizza box. At Ben's suggestion, they mapped the events leading up to Marcella de la Vega's murder by drawing a time line on his white board and populating it with colored sticky notes. The time line started at 11:00 am in Ricky's apartment where he last saw Marcela alive. At the other end a note indicated the time their client found Marcela's body in an alley behind a bar called El Rincon.

Ben sat down and rolled his chair back to get a wider perspective of their work. He stretched, flexing his neck muscles.

"We know exactly where Castro was all that time, but almost nothing about what Marcela was doing." Stephanie placed a hand on her hip and shook her head.

"Then let's focus on what we do know."

Ben scanned the board, nodding as he mentally checked off everything his client told him about that day. Ricky and Marcela had been fighting. The night before she agreed to run away with him and leave Immokalee for good. But in the cold light of day, she tried to back out of her promise. She said she needed more time to pay off her debt to the people who brought her into the country. Ricky was furious. He said her only way out was to run. She insisted they would track her down and bring her back. In a fit of panic, Marcela grabbed Ricky's car keys and drove away.

"Ricky waited for a few hours, but when Marcela didn't return he took the bus to her boarding house," Ben said. "He found his car parked out front but the only person in the house was Norma Martin, the landlady who runs the place."

"And she insisted she hadn't seen Marcela. . . . Did Castro believe her?"

Ben shrugged. "Let's just say there isn't any love lost between Ricky and Norma."

"Meaning?"

"Norma keeps the girls who live in her house on a short leash. It's her job to collect what small amount of money the girls earn and turn it all—almost all—over to the people who smuggle them into the country."

"So if Marcela planned to run away with Ricky and Norma found out, she'd be . . ."

"I think the word you're looking for is 'screwed.'" Ben leaned back in his chair, his eyes turned toward the ceiling. "Not only would Norma lose her percentage of the business, she'd have to answer to her boss, whoever that is. And if Marcela broke free, other girls might get it into their heads to run. Norma had a lot to lose if Ricky took Marcela away."

"Did the police question her at the time of the murder?"

"There's no mention of her in the trial transcript, so even if they did she wasn't called as a witness to testify. I guess I won't know more until I get a look at Tom Moreno's files. He was the homicide detective on the case."

Ben cracked his knuckles, breaking the silence that settled over them. Stephanie winced, throwing him an annoyed look.

"Creeps me out when you do that. What's bothering you?"

"I need to go down to Immokalee so I can speak with Moreno."

"Not your job. Totally outside your wheelhouse. Ask Lalo to meet with the guy. As an ex-cop, he'll connect with him on a level you never could. Not to mention that Greg won't exactly be thrilled if you skip out of the office for a day when you're so far behind with your other work."

Ben groaned. Just thinking about all the other cases he had to review depressed him. But after a minute he made up his mind. The Castro case had to take priority over everything else on his desk. If Greg gave him a hard time about leaving the office for a day, well he would offer to work through the weekend and make up the lost hours.

"I have to go. Moreno was the lead detective on the case, and there's always more to learn about an investigation than what you can find in the reports. But if it will make you happy, I'll ask Lalo to join me."

Stephanie cocked her head to one side. "I can't wait to hear how that goes." She picked up her shoes from the floor and slipped them on her feet. "So, are we finished here?"

"For now. Maybe we'll get lucky and Moreno will tell us he arranged a deal between Salazar and the DA."

"No chance, Shepherd." She opened the door. "If there was a deal, Moreno won't admit it." She paused, casting a glance over her shoulder. "But I have to say, you have balls to even think about asking him."

Stephanie was gone. The overhead light blinked and hummed as Ben stared at the white board. For all her wise cracks and tough exterior, he had a feeling Stephanie liked him. Why else would she stay late to help him with his case? With a sigh, he slung his messenger bag over his shoulder and gave the board one more sweeping glance. Shaking his head, he turned off the lights and locked the door behind him.

TEN

"*Cafecito, amigo*?" Lalo sat in a canvas chair on the back deck of his boat, his coffee cup raised in greeting.

"No thanks," Ben replied. "I've had three cups already. We should get going. According to my phone, it'll take us two hours to reach Immokalee."

"Less than that if I drive." Lalo tipped the remains of his coffee overboard and pushed himself out of the chair with a grunt. When he stepped off the boat, Maya rose to her feet and jumped onto the dock.

"You're bringing the dog?"

"We'll be gone too long to leave her alone."

The truck came to life with a roar, shaking violently until Lalo settled the engine by punching the gas pedal. Shifting into reverse, he shot out of his parking spot, changed gears, and tore into the oncoming traffic without casting a glance in either direction. An angry horn blasted behind them. Ben tugged the strap of his seatbelt, pulling it tight across his hips. Maya stretched out on the back seat and closed her eyes.

"I did a background check on Norma Martin," Lalo said after he merged onto the interstate. The speedometer edged up, leveling out at eighty-five. "Thirty-one years old, owns her own house, no mortgage. Runs a consulting business." As Lalo said the words, *consulting business*, he took his hands off the wheel and wrote quotation marks in the air with his fingers. When the truck started to drift, he grabbed the wheel and continued without missing a beat. "Excellent credit score. I checked the social networking sites, but couldn't find anyone using that name. The house is wired for high speed Internet and basic cable. No landline. She does have a wireless family plan that includes ten cell phones. Unfortunately, I can only provide you with the main number."

"You found all that out in one day?" Ben asked.

"No big deal," Lalo replied. He turned to face Ben, a wide grin on his face. "And frankly, I don't think any of that stuff will be particularly useful. But I did find something interesting."

Once again, the truck drifted dangerously, and the tires rumbled over the rough shoulder. Lalo gave the wheel a quick adjustment that brought the truck back to the middle of their lane.

"Okay," Ben shifted in his seat, righting himself. "What else have you got?"

"Norma Martin didn't exist until ten years ago. She seems to have appeared out of thin air. Her social security number? Who knows, maybe legit, maybe not. You'd be surprised to learn how easy it is to get one. I need to stop for gas."

Lalo nearly missed the exit ramp, swerving right without cutting his speed, hitting the brakes only when they reached a red light at the first intersection. The dog rolled off her seat with a thump. Ben turned around to see her struggling to her feet. She climbed back onto the seat as if nothing had happened.

The light changed, the truck lurched ahead and Lalo pulled into a gas station. He slammed the door behind him.

Ben sat thinking about Norma Martin while the dog pressed her nose against the window and watched Lalo fill the tank. After they resumed their trip on the interstate, Maya settled down and once again closed her eyes.

"Do you want to hear about your snitch?" Lalo asked.

"Sure."

"There's not much that you don't already know. Salazar was probably illegal. No record of a birth certificate, no driver's license, no credit history, *nada*. Five years ago, the cops picked him up on a drug charge. Illegal possession of prescription painkillers with intent to distribute. Salazar was Mirandized, and the cop who tagged him filed a buy-and-bust report. All standard. A few hours later the cop decided to let him go. After that, Salazar's record remained clean until the night of Castro's arrest when it was déjà vu all over again for Salazar. Catch and release. The guy was Teflon coated."

"Why didn't the police press charges? Or better yet, if he was illegal why not deport Salazar when they had him?"

"If you want answers to those questions you need to ask the arresting officer. But here's where the story gets interesting. Two years ago—two months after Salazar testified at Castro's trial—a homeless guy looking for lunch found his body in a dumpster. Single gunshot to the head."

"That much I already knew. Did the police run the bullet through ballistics?"

"No match."

"Real life is nothing like you see in the movies or on TV, right?" Ben sighed.

"Not even close. The case is officially still open, but I promise you, nobody cares. The murder weapon is probably at the bottom of Lake Okeechobee, together with a million other guns that will never be found."

As Ben counted down the mile markers, he remained deep in thought. Solving Salazar's murder wasn't his issue, but the timing of the man's death was suspicious. Sixty days after Salazar offered damaging testimony at Ricky Castro's trial he turned up dead, his murder unsolved.

Ben hoped Detective Moreno could help shed light on the mystery. Lalo said that when he called Moreno to set up their meeting, the man sounded friendly enough, offering to help with Castro's case in any way he could. Ben glanced at the dashboard and noticed the truck's speedometer held at a steady eighty-five. At their current speed, they would arrive in Immokalee in another sixty minutes or so. With the sun streaming through his window, Ben drifted off until Lalo's voice broke into his light sleep.

"Do you like to fish?" he asked.

"Fish?" Ben snapped awake. "No, I never tried it."

"Me, I love to fish. You can't believe how stupid fish are. Always going for the bait, no matter how many times they are caught. So I catch the same fish over and over, throwing them back if they're too small. Catch and release until they are big enough to keep."

"Interesting." Ben thought the whole exercise sounded pointless.

"I think Moreno might be a fisherman too."

"Why?"

"Because he also catches and releases, waiting until his fish is big enough to keep. Only in this case, I'm not talking about fish. I'm talking about a drug dealer. Can you guess the name of the cop who arrested Salazar five years ago?"

"Thomas Moreno?" Ben asked.

He didn't need to see Lalo nod to know he guessed right.

They took the main road into town, passing through the most impoverished area Ben had ever seen. Low-slung cement block buildings, broken windows, rusted road signs, weed-infested parking lots. As an impoverished law student commuting to Manhattan from his fleabag apartment across the river in Jersey, Ben witnessed first hand how low an industrial area could sink when the local economy wilted and died. But this was different. Immokalee looked like it had *never* known prosperity. This agricultural area struggled every minute of its existence. Chaparrito's, the restaurant where Detective Moreno suggested they meet for lunch, was located in a flat-roofed strip mall. Painted signs nailed above each unit identified the various businesses—a thrift shop, a tattoo parlor, a bar. Lalo pulled his truck into one of the two parking spaces allocated to the restaurant. When they entered, Ben saw there were no other customers.

The waitress, a pretty round-faced Mexican with large, dark eyes greeted them in Spanish. She pointed to Maya, gesturing toward the door. Lalo ignored her and led Ben to a booth in the corner. Maya trotted behind as the waitress shook her head and disappeared behind swinging doors that led to the kitchen. Ben scanned the greasy, laminated menu, printed in Spanish like everything else in the town.

Minutes later Tom Moreno came through the door as the waitress reappeared from the back of the restaurant.

"*Buenos días, Tomas.*" She smiled at the detective like he was an old friend.

"*Hola, Valentina.*"

Moreno looked around and spotted Ben and Lalo sitting at the table in the corner. He pointed to them, rattled something to the waitress in Spanish and headed their way.

When they stood to say hello, Ben saw Moreno's head barely reached the level of Lalo's shoulder. He looked like a boxer gone to seed, his upper body solid, his tan pants belted below a beer belly. His face was scarred by acne and the puffy skin below his eyes suggested too little sleep or too much alcohol.

While they exchanged business cards, the cook emerged from the kitchen, his white chef's hat contrasting sharply with his black hair and dark skin. He removed the stained apron from around his waist and threw it on the back of a chair before pulling Moreno into a bear hug. Ben noticed the man was even shorter than the detective, but something in his appearance suggested the cook was the more powerful of the two.

"*Hola, Tomas. ¿Qué tal?*" the cook said.

"*Bien, gracias a Dios,*" Moreno replied. "I'd like you to meet these new friends of mine. They're representing that kid who killed Marcela de la Vega a few years back. You remember, right? The girl was killed in the alley behind the bar a few doors down."

"*Claro que sí,* I remember," the cook nodded gravely. "The killer was Marcela's boyfriend, *verdad*?"

"Did you know Marcela?" Lalo asked.

"I saw her around sometimes." He pointed at Maya who lay under the table. "Is this your dog?"

"It's too hot to leave her outside," Lalo said.

"No problem." There was a flash of gold tooth when the cook smiled. "Everyone is welcome here, even the dog."

After a few rapid words of Spanish to Moreno, the cook picked up his apron and returned to the kitchen. Soon the waitress returned, burdened with plates piled high with food. Easing into the conversation, Moreno explained that the cook actually owned the restaurant. He originally came from the State of Michoacán, south of the border. The food before them was a specialty there. While he shoveled rice and chorizo stew into his mouth, Moreno asked Lalo about his family. The two men commiserated over their multiple divorces, estranged children and the burden of alimony. When they discovered their fathers both came from Mexico City, they started to compare notes about their favorite restaurants in that crowded city. Ben shifted in his seat, anxious to get down to business. As soon as the waitress cleared the dishes from the table, he spoke up.

"Can we ask you a few questions about the murder?"

"Sure kid," Moreno replied. "That's why you're here, right? But first, I want to show you something."

Moreno guided Ben and Lalo through the back door and into an alley that ran behind the strip mall. They passed several rusted cars before they reached the end. Behind the last unit, a stack of empty cartons lay in a heap next to an overflowing dumpster. The smell of stale beer and vomit rose above the reek of rotten garbage. Dozens of flies circled the dumpster. Ben recognized the name on the door from the trial transcript.

"This is where Ricky found Marcela's body."

"Exactly. When I arrived on the scene, Castro sat on the ground, holding the victim in his arms." Moreno pointed to a place next to the dumpster. "No question that she was already dead. The look of her skin, the blue lips. I told Castro to move aside, but he wouldn't let her go. One of the uniformed officers had to pull him away so his partner could check for a pulse. The body was still warm."

"What was she doing here?" Ben asked, thinking out loud.

"She worked at El Rincón," Moreno answered, nodding at the name on the door. He wrinkled his nose and brushed away a fly that landed in his hair. "Stinks out here. Let's go inside where we can talk."

When they entered, the bartender looked up in surprise. He broke into a grin when he saw Moreno. The detective offered his hand and the bartender took hold and pumped twice before giving him an affectionate slap on the arm. Moreno ordered three beers, then led Lalo and Ben to a table in the back.

"I know you work for Castro, so you probably don't want to hear this, but your client murdered that girl. My case was solid. The jury returned a unanimous verdict."

"We still have to ask," Lalo said.

"You have your job, I have mine." Moreno shrugged. "You came all this way so I'll tell you what I know. Castro admitted he and the girlfriend had a big fight earlier in the day. He wanted to take her away from here, get her off the drugs. She told him to go to hell, he got angry and . . ." Moreno shrugged again. "Unfortunately I've seen this kind of thing before," he said. "An act of rage."

Ben shook his head. "That's not how I heard it. Ricky claims that when he got here Marcela was already dead."

"No, no, my friend. He definitely killed her. That poor girl, may she rest in peace . . ." Moreno made the sign of the cross. "She loved her drugs way more than the boyfriend. Right after she left Castro's apartment she drove home and called Salazar. She then came here to turn tricks so she'd have enough to pay for the drugs. The autopsy showed signs of rough sex, lots of tears and bruising. Blood down . . . you know." Moreno pointed between his legs. "She had one hundred and fifty dollars stuffed in her bag. To have that much money, she had sex with more than one man. When Castro came looking, he found her out back, lost his temper and . . ." Moreno raised both hands, grabbed an imaginary throat and squeezed.

"Why did he look for her here?" Ben asked.

"He must have known she worked this bar. Let me tell you, when I saw him holding onto that girl's dead body, I almost felt sorry for him. He cried like a baby." Moreno shook his head from side to side. "But let's face it, he got what he had coming to him."

"There was a stain on the hem of the victim's skirt. Why didn't you test it for DNA?"

"Look around, kid. Do you think I can waste money on that kind of thing when I've got a rock-solid case without it?"

"But that evidence has to be kept until—"

"Until the execution? You're the lawyer, you tell me." Moreno shifted in his seat, and threw a quick glance at the bartender who caught his eye. He nodded slightly and turned back to Ben. "I need to get back to work. Is there anything else you wanted to ask?"

"Just one thing. On the day of the murder, Marcela's dealer, Diego Salazar was picked up on a drug charge and put in a cell next to Ricky. I understand you knew Salazar from a prior arrest?"

Moreno looked calmly at Ben. After a slight pause, he answered. "I wouldn't say I knew Salazar, but yes, I picked him up once before."

"Was he a snitch?"

"Not in the sense you're suggesting. Salazar was a small-time dealer. When I picked him up I reminded him that this was his second offense and he wasn't going to get a free ride like I gave him the first time." Moreno paused again, studying Ben. "And as you just admitted, the victim was one of his customers. News spreads fast on the street and Salazar, he wasn't stupid. So he says to me, if you put me in the cell next to Castro, maybe I'll hear something that will help your case."

"Did you promise to release him if he gave you something you could use against Ricky?"

Moreno's face clouded over, a smoldering anger creeping into his eyes. His hands curled into fists as he seethed, "You have some *cojones,* kid. I'm doing you a favor here. What you're suggesting is illegal and you know it."

Ben held Moreno's cold stare. Before he could say anything more, Lalo stepped in.

"What do you know about Norma Martin, the lady who runs the boarding house where Marcela lived?"

"I guess you could call Norma's place a boarding house." Moreno leaned back in his seat, flexing his fingers. With the change in subject, the charged air around him seemed to ease. "We know about her business of course, but we have bigger problems in this community than a harmless lady looking after a few prostitutes." Moreno gave Ben a pointed look. "Or small-time *drogueros*. Unless someone gets hurt, we live and let live around here."

"But someone did get hurt. Marcela de la Vega is dead," Ben said.

"I solved that murder to everyone's satisfaction," Moreno replied. "Everyone, except the killer's lawyer who doesn't want to accept the facts." He looked at his watch, picked up his beer and drained the last drop. Slamming the glass down on the table he said, "I have work to do so if you don't mind . . ."

"Can we have that copy of your case file?" Lalo asked.

"I almost forgot. It's in my car."

They followed Moreno to the front of the building where he extracted a blue binder from his black Dodge Challenger and handed it to Lalo.

"Just one more thing before you go." Lalo reached for his wallet and pulled out a newspaper clipping. "Do you recognize this girl?"

Ben recognized the clipping as the article Cate discovered while researching Logan Murphy's case.

Moreno stared at the sketch, squinting at the image, he shook his head. "No, I don't think so. Who is she?"

"The victim in an unrelated case I'm working." Lalo stuffed the paper back into his wallet.

"Sorry, I can't help you there," Moreno offered his hand to end the meeting.

They shook hands and Ben watched Moreno stand next to his car until they drove out of sight. Back on the road, Lalo started humming. Ben recognized the Mexican folk tune he heard in the restaurant.

"What do you think?" Ben asked.

"About Moreno?"

Ben nodded.

"I think you pissed him off."

"I don't believe what he said about Salazar," Ben replied. "That guy was his snitch. Moreno traded favors for false testimony. I'm sure of it."

A faint smile crept across Lalo's face. "I suspect you're right, but Moreno didn't admit anything, so what did you gain?"

"Nothing, I guess. Except maybe the satisfaction of knowing I got under his skin."

"It's never a good idea to attack a Mexican head-on."

"Well, now's your chance to show me how it's done. How far to Norma's house?"

"Ten minutes."

Ben leaned back and closed his eyes, listening to Lalo hum his tune.

ELEVEN

With one hand grasping the open door and the other braced against the jamb, Norma Martin fiercely guarded the entrance to her house. *Firecracker* was a word that came to Ben's mind. He judged her to be somewhere in her early thirties, a smoldering beauty with unblemished olive skin, thick black hair and a heart-shaped face. Norma was petite, no more than five feet tall, but judging from the set of her jaw, there was no denying the woman was a force to be reckoned with.

As Lalo attempted to reason with her, Norma glared at him. Ben's high school Spanish served him well enough to follow the one-sided conversation. Lalo turned on the charm as he explained they were investigating Marcela's murder. Aside from casting a few nervous glances at the dog, Norma remained unresponsive. Her silence made it clear she was not about to help them. Considering they represented the man convicted of killing one of her girls, Ben was not surprised.

After several futile attempts, Lalo appeared to give up. He reached into his back pocket and pulled out his wallet. For a moment, Ben thought he intended to offer Norma a bribe as a last-ditch effort to get her cooperation. But instead of money, the investigator pulled out one of his business cards and offered it to her, "Give me a call if you want to talk."

Norma stared unblinking at the card. She shook her head, refusing to take it.

Lalo bowed slightly, thanking Norma for her time. He fumbled with his wallet, cursing when the card slipped out of his hand and drifted to the ground. As he bent down to retrieve it, Maya rose to her feet, pushed past Norma and trotted into the house.

Her face livid, Norma erupted in a torrent of Spanish. Lalo responded with a shrug and a sheepish grin. He tried to calm the excited woman while returning the wallet to his pocket. When he politely requested permission to enter the house to retrieve his dog, Norma renewed her verbal assault but grudgingly stepped aside and let him pass.

As Lalo disappeared into the house, Ben said, "I'm sorry if we've upset you."

Norma ignored him, casting a nervous look over her shoulder.

"I don't know what got into the dog. She's usually well behaved," Ben tried again.

"Why he ask me about Marcela?" Norma demanded.

"He's investigating her murder."

Norma cocked her head, studying Ben. "Marcela killer in jail."

"I believe Ricky Castro is innocent. The justice system failed him."

His comment seemed to hit a nerve. Norma laughed, a raw, bitter laugh. "Justice," she spat with venom. "*Una broma, no*? A joke, your American justice."

Ben was about to ask her what she meant when Lalo reemerged from the house. Maya followed close behind, pink tongue lolling out of her mouth. Lalo muttered a few final words of contrition to Norma and shoved his business card into her hand. Grabbing Ben by the arm, he propelled him down the front walk.

Glancing down at the dog, Ben could swear Maya smiled.

Lalo threw the truck in gear, made a U-turn and headed back toward the center of town.

"What happened back there?" Ben asked.

"Thanks to Maya, I got a good look inside."

"And?"

"We're going to meet one of Norma's girls at the bus stop in an hour."

Lalo explained that when he went inside, he found Maya scratching on a closed door at the end of a hallway. Inside Lalo discovered a teenager curled up on one of four single beds in the room. The girl's name was Luci.

"When we rang the bell, Norma sent Luci to her room and told her to be quiet until we left. Needless to say, Luci was surprised to see me."

"So Norma expected us?"

"Moreno probably called and warned her that we were on the way. Anyway, you should have seen the face of that girl when I opened the door. Not just surprised. Terrified is more like it."

"Then why is she going to meet us at the bus stop?"

"I offered to pay her."

"For what?" Ben's mind jumped to the obvious. "You do know Norma's girls are prostitutes, right?"

Lalo turned toward Ben, the corners of his mouth turned up. "For information. How much cash do you have?"

Ben pulled out his wallet and counted the bills. "Forty-three dollars."

"We need to find an ATM."

"How much is this going to cost me?"

"More than forty-three dollars."

"She's only going to tell you what you want to hear. Someone like her will do anything for money. You can't believe a word she says."

Lalo jerked his head around and glared at him. He gave the steering wheel a sudden pull. The truck veered off the main street onto a county road. They headed north, skirting the town until they reached the outskirts. Tomato fields stretched ahead as far as Ben could see. Wearing straw hats and long-sleeved shirts, a gang of brown skinned workers methodically thrust thumb-length starter plants into plowed rows covered in ribbons of black plastic. A steady stream of workers with stacks of empty trays approached the trucks at the edge of the fields, departing under the burden of full ones.

Ben gazed across the fields, fascinated by the activity spread out across the landscape. "Stephanie told me about these tomato fields. I don't know how those guys can stand working in this heat."

"They're grateful to have a job," Lalo said. "But yes, it's a hard life. This is the best time of year since the rains have stopped and the summer heat is easing. In a few weeks they'll start tying the plants to stakes in the ground. It's backbreaking labor. Ten, even twelve-hour days. They work until the boss tells them they can stop. The heavy work begins a few months from now. The harvest. But what choice do they have? There is a Mexican expression, *hay que trabajar*. You have to work."

"How do you know so much about growing tomatoes?"

Lalo nodded, keeping his eyes on the workers. "I grew up in a migrant labor camp near here. My father worked these fields. Our air conditioner didn't work, the burners on the stove leaked gas and the septic system was so overloaded it ran over into the back yard. Cockroaches the size of bats lived under the sink." He twisted the key in the ignition, staring straight ahead while he continued. "Life here is a constant struggle. Parents die young and their sons leave school to work in the fields. Their daughters do what they can to survive."

"You're telling me I have no right to judge Luci just because she's a prostitute," Ben said. "I didn't mean to—"

Lalo turned to look at him. "I thought you should see this, that's all. Let's hear what Luci has to say."

Lalo waved five twenties in front of Luci, pulling it back as she tried to snatch the money from his hand. Sitting on the back seat, the girl stroked Maya's head, her eyes darting back and forth between Lalo and Ben. Waif-thin, her dark eyes rimmed with black eyeliner giving her an Asian look. With a nervous jerk, she tucked a strand of hair behind her ears. Dressed in a tight T-shirt, an even tighter mini-skirt, three-inch heels and large hoop earrings, she looked ready for a long night's work.

Lalo began by asking the easy questions. Questions regarding the relationship between Norma and the girls who lived in her house. Luci's answers came slowly at first. She told Lalo to drive around while they spoke. She slouched down on the seat mumbling something about not wanting anyone to see her talking to them.

"How does the money work?" Lalo asked.

In a mixture of Spanish and broken English Luci explained that she turned all her earnings over to Norma who deducted room and board. The balance went to pay down her debt to the smuggling cartel that got her across the border. Every night Norma sent the girls to various bars—El Rincón was one—and the bartenders kept track of how many tricks they turned so they couldn't skim the cash. Norma gave the girls money when they needed something. Clothes, booze, drugs. Every penny was added to their debt.

"How long have you worked for her?" Lalo asked.

"*Tres años más o menos.* Three years, more or less."

"And how much do you still owe?"

"Too much," Luci replied. "More than when I come to this country."

Ben judged her to be about fifteen or sixteen. She would probably never be free. Not until she lost her usefulness to Norma. It was anyone's guess how the girl would survive then. He had never given much thought to what Marcela's life might have been like. This new insight made her death even more tragic.

Lalo lowered his voice to a whisper. "Tell me what happened to Marcela."

Luci flashed him a sly look, held out her hand. "*Dame el dinero.*"

"You know how this works, Luci. I give you the money when I get something in return."

Slowly she withdrew her hand and resumed patting the dog, eyes downcast. "I see her right before . . . you know, right before."

"At the bar?"

Luci shook her head. "At the house."

"How did she seem to you?" Lalo spoke in slow, calming tones. Ben sat straight in his seat, listening to every word.

"She is in a hurry. She tell me Ricky will take her away from here, but she need money. I try to stop her."

"Tried to stop her from leaving?"

"No, I try to stop her from going in bedroom of Norma. I warn her, but she is taking too much time and . . ." Luci drew in a deep breath and squeezed her eyes shut.

"And what?"

When Luci looked up, she had tears in her eyes. "Marcela try to steal from Norma. I never think that . . ." She drew in a deep breath. "*Tengo la culpa*. My fault, yes. But you must see. I have no choice. So I call Norma."

Maya nudged Luci's arm and the girl buried her face in the dog's fur, her shoulders shaking. Ben stared at the tattoo on the base of Luci's neck. A barcode marking her as somebody's property.

"Luci." Ben reached back and touched her gently. Luci knocked his arm away. She sat up, wiped the tears from her cheeks. One blink and the distraught girl transformed back to a street-smart prostitute.

"You make Norma pay for what happen to Marcela," she hissed.

"Are you saying *she* killed Marcela?" Ben asked.

"No, not Norma. She make call and he take Marcela away. If she know I speak to you, she will call again and he take me too."

"Who did she call? Who came to take Marcela?" Lalo asked.

Fear crept into the girl's eyes. She rubbed the crook of her arm and glanced out the window. "No more. I give you what you want. Now my money. *Rápido*. If I am late to work she will know."

Lalo pulled into a side street and brought the truck to a halt. He turned around in his seat to face her. Ben clearly saw something in his investigator's expression that he never expected to see. Compassion.

"Luci, listen to me. You are in danger. Come with me now. I'll find you a better place to live, a good job. It's not safe for you here."

A hard tone crept into her voice when Luci answered. "I cannot. I have a brother here. If I run, they hurt him."

Lalo nodded acceptance. He reached into his wallet and pulled out the folded sketch of Jane Doe. Adding another bill to the money he already held in his hand, he passed everything to Luci.

"Do me one more favor before you go. Take a look at this girl and tell me if you recognize her."

Luci gave the drawing a cursory look and shook her head. "No, I do not know." She shoved the money into her canvas shoulder bag and passed the paper back to Lalo.

"Keep it. I wrote my number on the back. Call me if you change your mind. I promise I'll come back to take you away from here." Lalo patted her hand.

She nodded her thanks, stepped out of the truck and walked away without a backward glance. Hips swaying, heels clopping on the cracked sidewalk she joined two more girls just like her and leaned against the building on the corner. A buyer's market.

TWELVE

Thanks to Annie and her organic compost my tomato plants thrived. A generous dose combined with two weeks of unrelenting sunshine transformed the wilting plants into healthy specimens that promised to bear plenty of fruit. I was working in my back yard, tying the plants to their stakes when my phone rang. The person on the line identified herself as Detective Garibaldi, the homicide detective who headed up the investigation into Jane Doe's murder. The tone of her voice was brusque, businesslike. She advised me that the office closed in one hour, giving me little time to drive to Sarasota if I wanted to see her before the end of the day.

The Sheriff's offices were located on Ringling Boulevard, a main stretch of road in downtown Sarasota where the County Courthouse dominated the skyline. The street was named after John Ringling, one of the famous circus brothers who settled in the area and wielded his sizable fortune as a developer of the town. The building, with its impressive columns and courtyards, was built when Ringling's influence was at its strongest—right before the market crash of '29. I parked my car out front, taking a brief moment to pause and appreciate the beauty of the structure.

Once inside I placed my purse on the conveyor belt and passed through the metal detector without setting off any alarms. After retrieving my things, I asked for directions to the county investigative bureau. The gloved guard pointed to a bank of elevators. After several wrong turns, I found the right place. Detective Garibaldi sat at her desk in a large room shared with three other detectives. She studied me for an awkward moment before gesturing for me to sit down.

"You're not what I expected."

"Excuse me?"

"You certainly fit the bill physically, it's just that Lalo prefers . . . how can I put this politely? Younger women. Last I heard he was shacked up in that floating firetrap of his with a *chiquita* young enough to be his daughter. So naturally, when he called to say he had a friend who wanted to talk about the Jane Doe murder, I expected something different."

"Friend?" I looked at the detective in disbelief. If I wasn't what she expected, then I guess I felt the same way about her. Though I knew she was once married to Lalo, I couldn't picture them as a couple. I estimated the woman tapping the desk with the eraser end of her pencil, to be in her early fifties, ten years younger than me and a good fifteen years younger than Lalo. She wore a black jacket over a low-cut T-shirt. A gold cross hung on a chain around her neck, dangling between her breasts. Her lipstick was candy apple red, the same color as the shirt. Her hair, streaked blond by the sun, was cut short on one side, long on the other. The photo on her badge flattered her. In person, her blunt personality tarnished that beauty.

"I'm sorry but you got the wrong idea. Lalo and I aren't friends . . . that is, I hardly know him. As a favor he offered to set up a meeting with you so I could—"

"Yeah, yeah," Garibaldi snorted. "I see the ring on your finger. It's none of my business anyway. Normally I wouldn't give Lalo the time of day but he got my attention when he told me what you were working on."

"Why?"

"Of all the murders I've dealt with—and let me tell you, I've come across more than my share—this is the one that keeps me awake at night."

"Why?" I felt like an idiot, repeating the same question over and over. At least I found comfort in the fact that she didn't seem to notice.

"You probably know enough about the case to answer that yourself. I'm curious, why are you doing this? Have you found a legal loophole that will help your client?"

"No. I simply believe Logan Murphy is innocent."

I gave Garibaldi a hard stare, holding her in my gaze until she broke away and looked down at her hand, still tapping away. Sticking the pencil behind her ear, she pushed back her chair and stood. Hoisting a cardboard file box from her desk, she motioned for me to follow.

She led me down the hall to a conference room with the thermostat set so low, goose pimples erupted on my arms. I sat across a square table from the detective and faced a mirror that covered the entire wall. She produced a pair of black-rimmed glasses from her jacket pocket and put them on.

"I've seen all the cop shows on television, Detective. Is someone watching us on the other side of that mirror?" I asked.

"Call me Geri, and I assure you, we're alone. I have my own reasons for keeping this conversation private." Tapping the lid of the box with an acrylic nail she said, "Everything related to my investigation is in here."

"Oh, then thank you." I was surprised at how readily she handed over her files. Outside of the room I could hear the sounds of people pushing their chairs back and packing up for the day. I stood and reached across the table, ready to take the box and go.

"Not so fast." Garibaldi slammed her hand down on the lid. "This box isn't going anywhere. Sit down and listen to what I have to say."

I dropped back into my chair, wondering what kind of game she was playing. Still, I knew my only viable option was to play along until I could figure her out.

"I totally nailed this case. When the press got hold of the story we were front-page news for weeks. Because of all the publicity, the county prosecutor, George Higel assigned an up-and-coming attorney, Dick Hale to the case. Hale put it all on the line by asking for the death penalty. You could argue that he overreached with a case involving a teenaged boy who stabbed an unknown girl to death, but knowing this would be a high-profile trial, Hale figured he could make a name for himself. And he was right. The press stayed with us every step of the way. When the verdict came in, everyone called Hale a friggin' hero. And to top it all off, when it came to sentencing, the jury voted seven to five for the death penalty. I'd bet Hale had an orgasm when he heard that."

I looked at her, incredulous. "Seven to five? I thought the verdict had to be unanimous in a death penalty case."

The detective squinted at me. "What kind of law do you practice, Mrs. Stokes?"

"I recently moved here from New Hampshire."

"Well, welcome to Florida." Geri stared at me from behind her dark-framed glasses. "You only need a majority in this state."

"An innocent man is behind bars." I was at a loss to know what was going on behind those ice blue eyes. After what seemed like a long time, she spoke.

"You may be right. I'll admit that when the dust settled, a few things about this case started to bother me. But after a win you move on, right? I had plenty of other work to keep me busy so I left well enough alone."

"What bothered you?"

Geri shook her head. "Here's the thing. It would be professional suicide to start making noise about a case that made Dick Hale a superstar around here. He's now ASA Hale, an Assistant State Attorney and if you believe the rumors, he's in line to take over when George Higel retires next year. So even if some things about this case don't add up,

I'm not going to risk my career by re-opening the investigation without cause. You get that, right?"

She was telling me she cared more about her job security than admitting she may have made a mistake. I could barely hold my temper in check. Before I blurted something I would later regret, I picked up my purse and pushed back my chair.

"Where are you going? We're not finished here."

"I have a job to do," I replied, lowering my voice. "A job that doesn't keep me awake at night."

"Sit down. I'm not through with you yet." She tucked a lock of her hair behind her ear and peered at me over the rim of her glasses.

I held her stare as I placed my purse back on the floor and crossed my legs.

With a satisfied nod, Geri continued, "When Lalo called to tell me the Defender Project is thinking about taking Murphy on as a client, I thought kismet, right? Fate. The gods gave me a chance to set something right."

"What do you mean?"

Geri pulled her pencil from behind her ear and resumed tapping the table with the eraser. "I honestly don't know." She looked me in the eye. "Listen, in any other case I would interview the victim's friends, family, anyone who could help me determine motive. Near as I can tell, your client didn't know who that girl was any more than you or I do. Are you following?"

I nodded my head, encouraging her to continue.

"Murphy had no motive to kill that girl, and that above everything else, bothers me. If you find out who she was, you'll have a fighting chance of finding the son-of-a-bitch that killed her. Assuming it wasn't your client, that is."

"What did you do to try and identify her?"

"I pulled out all the stops. Dental records, fingerprints, DNA, Missing Persons Register, all by the book. No results. I even ran her tattoo through the FBI database. Zilch. We opened a tip line and the local paper ran a picture of her, even offered a reward to anyone who could give us a handle on who she was. We got a ton of calls but nothing leading to her ID. The girl was a ghost."

"Lalo is passing that picture around the Latino community to see if anyone recognizes her," I offered.

"Don't get your hopes up. Ten years is a long time. Listen, I can't let these files leave the building. And for obvious reasons I can't risk having

Dick Hale drop by and catch you working on this stuff in my office. So here's what I'm offering. After you leave I'll take everything up to PD12 where you can work on this without any chance of Hale finding you. He never goes near the place."

"PD12?" I asked.

"PD12, the public defender's office for district 12. Ask for Dix Powers. She's the A.D."

"A.D.?"

I guess that was one too many idiotic questions because Geri snorted a laugh before giving me an answer. "Administrative Director of the Public Defender's office. Dix runs a program where volunteers help organize case files for court-appointed defense lawyers. Anyone sees you there they'll assume you're part of the program. I cleared everything with Dix this morning so when you come back on Monday, she'll be ready for you. Her office is on the fifth floor."

It took me a few seconds, but I caught on quickly. I even considered looking into this volunteer program. It sounded like it might be something interesting for me to do after I finished with this case. And after I finished unpacking my house, of course. I stood and extended my hand. Detective Garibaldi took it in her firm grip.

"Thank you, Geri. I appreciate what you're doing here."

"Listen," she waved off my gratitude with a shake of her head. "My hands are tied with regard to re-opening the Murphy case, but if you ever want to talk, or if there's something else I can do, give me a call, okay?"

I returned to my car empty-handed but looking forward to Monday when I could start plowing through Geri's files. Her comments confirmed my belief that any hope of vindicating Logan Murphy rested on putting a name to the victim. But if a seasoned homicide detective was powerless to identify the girl, I wondered what chance I had.

The interior of my Prius was roasting. Turning the air-conditioner to maximum, I waited for the car to cool down, taking the time to reflect on what I had just heard. Geri admitted there were some things about her case that didn't add up. I wondered what I would find in her case files. If Logan was innocent—I now believed that more than ever—there had to be something in those boxes that would set him free.

THIRTEEN

I pulled up behind the drawbridge gate and waited for a sailboat to pass. Glancing down at the houses lining the Intracoastal Waterway, I noticed the expansive back yards braced behind sea walls with small yachts tied to private docks. For a few minutes I was so taken by the decadence of those homes that I didn't notice the sign planted on one of the lawns. I blinked, struck by an idea. Picking up my phone, I dialed. Ben answered on the first ring.

"Write this down." As the sailboat glided by, I gave him the number on the sign. Boyd Skinner's number.

"What is this about?" Ben asked.

"Skinner has been avoiding me. I figured the only way to pin him down is to have him show me one of his listings. I'd call his office myself, but the receptionist will recognize my voice so I'm thinking if you make an appointment for me . . ."

"You're starting to think like a real investigator," Ben chuckled. "When do you want to see this house?"

"As soon as possible. When you get through, give me a fake name. Smith or something."

"No problem. As a matter of fact, I was just about to call you to see if we could get together tomorrow morning. If you make the coffee, I'll bring breakfast."

"Are you driving all the way down from Gainesville just to see me?"

"Not quite. Lalo and I got back from Immokalee later than expected yesterday so I spent the night on his boat."

"Breakfast sounds perfect. I can't wait to fill you in on my meeting with Detective Garibaldi."

"Would nine o'clock be okay?" he asked. "I wouldn't want to get you up too early, now that you're retired."

"Don't be a wise guy. I'll see you then."

Bells clanged as the drawbridge finished its slow descent. The gate blocking the road lifted, traffic lights turned green. As I crossed onto the island, the bridge tender waved at me from high up in his tower. Though I only lived on the island for a few short months, it already felt like home.

Ben held out a pink and orange bag from the donut shop on Tamiami Trail. Taking it from him I took a peek inside. Two apple-cinnamon muffins and a sesame seed bagel. No question who was going to eat what.

"Let me warm the muffins in the microwave," I offered. "Make yourself at home while I get your coffee."

"This place is great." Ben looked around. "I didn't realize you lived so close to the beach."

"Just down the block." I handed him a steaming mug.

The microwave pinged. Setting the muffins on a plate, I grabbed my bagel from the toaster and sat down across from Ben. The rich coffee aroma rising from my own mug only partially masked the sweet, artificial smell of the muffins.

"Your mother thinks I made a mistake, retiring down here. But I intend to stay busy, do a bit of gardening, and walk on the beach. And ideas are bouncing in my head—there's a story that I want to write. But since this thing with Logan cropped up, I haven't had time for anything else. In the last few weeks I haven't caught a single sunset on the beach."

Ben laughed and gave me a knowing look. "I'm sure Logan and his grandmother appreciate what you're doing. Have you discovered anything I can use to get my boss interested in the case?"

"Nothing yet. But I can tell you one thing. I'm coming up with more questions than answers."

"Such as?"

"Detective Garibaldi has second thoughts about her investigation. I have a feeling that she's playing games with me. When I get my hands on her files I should know more."

"Interesting. What else have you got?"

"Just a few pieces to the puzzle. Nothing solid."

"I told you this wouldn't be easy. Keep digging and try not to get discouraged, something will turn up. By the way, you've got an appointment to see that house with Skinner tomorrow afternoon. I wish I could be there to hear what he has to say but I've got to get back to Gainesville. Why don't you ask Lalo to join you?"

"I'd rather handle this by myself."

"I know you would, but I'd feel better if you didn't confront Skinner alone."

"Fine. Tell Lalo to meet me here at my house fifteen minutes early. If he's one second late, I'll leave without him."

Ben popped a piece of muffin in his mouth, a smile stretched across his bulging cheeks. He obviously was pleased that I agreed to let his investigator tag along when I met with Boyd Skinner. For the life of me I couldn't imagine what good that would do. There was no doubt in my mind that I could handle Skinner alone.

FOURTEEN

We arrived in Lalo's rusted pick-up truck posing as buyers of a million-dollar home. When I noticed Maya pressing her nose against the back window, I was grateful that Lalo insisted on driving. The thought of the dog's saliva on the leather seats of my car gave me the shivers.

A metallic blue Porsche was parked in the circular drive, sparkling in the Florida sun. It struck me that ten years after those three boys shared drinks at Snook Wallow, fate had dealt them radically different lives. Boyd drove a Porsche, Ty built a business to support his young family, and Logan sat in a cell on death row.

Lalo tipped back his Florida Marlins baseball cap and whistled. "Nice house. What are they asking for this place?"

"More than I can afford," I replied. Lalo turned off the engine. The temperature in the truck rose rapidly. I glanced at Maya, panting in the back seat. "Maybe you should leave the A/C running so she doesn't get overheated," I suggested.

Lalo got out of the car and rummaged around under the back seat. I watched as he pulled out a bright orange vest that he slipped over Maya's head. Letters stitched on both sides of the vest spelled, S-E-R-V-I-C-E-D-O-G. Lalo stood back and Maya jumped out of the truck.

"You've got to be kidding. What are you going to say when Boyd asks what kind of service dog she is?"

"Nobody ever asks. But if he does, I'm sure you'll come up with something."

When Boyd opened the door, I recognized his smiling face from the ads I'd seen on billboards all over town but nothing prepared me for the sheer bulk of the man towering above. A great block of a figure, Boyd Skinner wore a tailored jacket over a pair of dress slacks. His open collar revealed a well-tanned neck roughly the diameter of the columns out front. He glanced down at the dog, but accepted her presence without objection. Waving us into the house, he shook Lalo's hand. Turning to me, he took a moment to look directly into my eyes. Cool, dry, soft flesh pressed my palm. Standing close, I detected no smell of aftershave, no mouthwash, no nicotine, nothing at all. I couldn't get a read on the man.

"Pleased to meet you, Ms. Smith."

"Actually, my name is Stokes. Catherine Stokes."

The rictus of a smile remained on his mouth, but the crow's feet around his eyes disappeared.

He turned to Lalo, hopeful. "Are you Mr. Smith?"

"I am afraid not. We're here to talk about Logan Murphy."

Boyd twisted the band of his watch. "You should have called my office for an appointment."

"I've been leaving you messages for weeks. Why have you been avoiding me?"

"I've been busy," Boyd replied. "And frankly, I don't have anything to say to you, Ms. Stokes."

"That's Mrs. Stokes," Lalo said.

Boyd started gathering the brochures and listing sheets that he previously fanned out on the foyer table. "Well, Mrs. Stokes, the truth is I haven't thought about Logan in years."

"We won't take too much of your time. I've already spoken with Tyler Fox. I just want to hear your version of what happened that night."

Boyd stuffed the papers into a leather folder bearing his initials printed in gold. "If you spoke with Ty, then you already know what happened," he said, looking up at me. "Now if you don't mind—"

"I'd like to hear it from you."

Boyd stood staring at me, packed and ready to go. In his hand he jangled a set of keys. I didn't blink, determined to stand my ground until I got what I wanted. Lalo wandered into the dining room, taking a seat at the table. I noticed someone had set out eight place settings, crystal wine glasses catching the light from the chandelier above. Lalo picked up a fork and started tapping one of the china plates. Boyd looked at him in annoyance.

"Do you mind? That's vintage Wedgwood."

"The best way to get rid of us is to answer my questions," I said.

Realizing we weren't going anywhere, Boyd shook his head in resignation.

"I'll give you ten minutes. If you're not out of here by then, I'm calling the police."

Lalo put down the fork and leaned back in his chair. I nodded a silent thank you for his help.

"What do you remember about that night?" I asked.

"I remember Logan was beyond pissed when he took off to find that girl," Boyd replied. "Truth is, he never could handle his liquor."

For the first time since I introduced myself, Boyd appeared to relax a little. A small smile touched his lips.

"Something about that strikes you as funny?" I asked.

"Well, Logan wasn't exactly what you'd call . . . let's just say girls never gave him a second look. So yeah, when he bragged about getting that girl, it struck me as hilarious. Goes to show how drunk he was. She was hot. Way out of his league, if you know what I mean."

"What did he say to you when he left the bar?" I asked.

"He said he was hungry. It was his turn to pick up the next round of drinks but he found he only had enough money for an order of hot wings. That was Logan, always broke. Anyway, he gave me what little cash he had and asked me to get him some wings."

"Why would Logan ask you that, if he didn't intend to come right back?"

"I don't know, ask him. All I know is I didn't see him again that night."

Maya, who was lying at Lalo's feet, chose that moment to sit up and start scratching herself. In the stream of light coming through the sliding doors, I saw a cloud of dog hair rising around her. Boyd looked over, "I just had this place professionally cleaned. If we have to exterminate for fleas, I'm going to send you the bill."

"It's just an itch," Lalo replied. "Tell me, who ate the wings?"

Boyd glared at Lalo. "How would I know? We're talking ten years ago. And I'll be honest, I had a little too much to drink that night too so I can't say I remember everything clearly."

"Ty mentioned that you left before the band stopped playing," I said.

"That's right." Boyd began twisting the band of his watch again. "We didn't have any luck picking up girls and we had to get back to the work site early the next morning so we left early."

I was running out of time and needed to shift the discussion to Jane Doe before Boyd grew tired of my questions. "Ty told me that Jane Doe ordered two beers from the bartender. Did you happen to notice if she was with someone?"

Boyd stopped playing with his watchband and checked the time. "No. She was alone. And since Logan didn't come back, I assumed she was with him."

"A few minutes ago you told me she was out of Logan's league."

"Right, I did . . . that is, she was. Don't try to put words in my mouth, okay? Logan left Ty and me at the bar and went to find the girl. She gets killed, Logan's fingerprints are on the knife, and her blood is smeared all over his clothes. What am I supposed to think?"

I saw the color creep up Boyd's neck. He glanced at his watch again, "Time's up. What's it going to be?"

I thanked him for his time, and we left. Lalo reached the truck ahead of me, closing my door with a soft click after I climbed in. He started the engine and opened the windows, letting the sweltering heat escape while the air conditioner kicked in. Maya stood with her front feet on the armrest between us, lifting her face to the vent. At least the blast of cold air blew away the smell of the dog. I watched as drops of drool hit the padded leather between her paws.

"Doesn't that bother you?"

"What?" Lalo asked.

I reached into my purse and pulled out an alcohol wipe, cleaning the leather as best I could. Slimy though it was, I used the same wipe to catch a thin line of drool hanging from the corner of the dog's mouth. She rewarded me by leaning in and licking my face. Lalo pulled out his phone and began to read something on the screen.

"I wonder if he told us the truth." I cleaned my cheek with a new wipe. "He seemed pretty fixed on the idea that Logan went off to find the girl, but Ty clearly remembers Logan saying he went to use the bathroom. Of course the band was playing, so I guess Boyd might not have heard Logan above the noise. Aside from that, everything he just told us is consistent with Ty's recollection of events."

With Lalo still looking at his phone, I realized he hadn't heard a word I said. "Seriously," I snapped. "What is on that thing that is so important?"

"Text message from my ex," he replied, stuffing the phone back in his pocket. "She says the two of you have met."

"I meant to tell you. Our meeting got off to a rocky start but in the end Geri and I had a nice chat. She actually admitted that she might have been wrong about Logan."

Lalo closed the windows and put the truck in gear. "All the time we were married, that woman never once admitted she was wrong about anything. The first time she meets you, she admits she may have made a mistake with a murder case? That doesn't sound like the Geri I married."

"I'm telling you, she wants to know the truth."

"You're wrong there. She won't like it if you prove she screwed up somewhere. Geri is good at her job—one of the best—but she can't stand being wrong. On the other hand, if you can make Dick Hale look like a fool, she'll be your best friend for life. She hates that guy. More than me, and that's saying something."

"It sounded to me like her conscience is bothering her."

"Yeah right, her conscience. Let's get something to drink. I need a beer."

"Right now?"

"I want to have another look around Snook Wallow. Maybe find someone who remembers something."

"The bartender?" I asked.

"His shift begins in a few minutes."

"Drinks are on me."

On our previous visit to Snook Wallow the place was nearly deserted. This time Lalo and I arrived to find a group of banjo players loading folding chairs and music stands into their cars. I watched as one elderly musician wearing socks and leather sandals shuffled over to a vintage Jaguar convertible. He placed his banjo in the trunk and slowly lowered himself into the driver's seat. In a cloud of dust, he tore out of there like a teenager.

"What's going on here?" I asked.

"Banjo Society. They play every Sunday afternoon. Looks like we missed it."

The performance was obviously over, the crowd slowly dispersing. There were a few families with small children skipping ahead of their parents, but mostly the audience consisted of seniors who ambled in the direction of the parking lot, smiles on wrinkled, whiskered faces. We found Charlie, wearing a tropical print shirt, tending bar. He wiped the counter with a damp rag and dealt us two cardboard coasters with a flick of his wrist. "What can I get for you?"

I looked to my right and noticed a few stragglers perched on stools, sipping cold beer from frosted mugs. Glancing back at Charlie, I gave him my brightest smile. "Iced tea please, and my friend will have . . ." I turned to Lalo, realizing I didn't know what brand he preferred.

Lalo arched an eyebrow. He mouthed the word *friend* and wiggled his thick eyebrows, Groucho-style before turning his attention to the bartender. "Whatever you've got on tap."

Charlie nodded, scooped ice into a glass and poured my tea from a pitcher. I studied his angular face. Skin like tanned leather, coarse salt-and-pepper hair cropped short. There was something about him that reminded me of my father. After a few minutes, I realized it was the faint odor of cooked cabbage that rose from his skin. He set my drink on the coaster and thrust a pint glass under the tap with the Yuengling logo.

"Enjoy the show?" Charlie asked.

"We just got here," Lalo replied.

"Too bad. Folks come from all over to hear them guys play their banjos."

I let that sink in, wondering if we'd stepped through a time warp when we drove down the oak-canopied road to Snook Wallow. Banjo Society indeed.

"We'll come earlier next time." Lalo sipped the beer, and then wiped the foam from his lip with the back of his hand. "You work here long?" he asked.

"Twenty years, give or take," Charlie replied. "Took time off a while back when we was going through hard times. We're good now, though. New folks runnin' the place. They've done a pretty good job fixing up the buildings and keeping things running smooth. Used to get a little rough here some nights, but the new manager don't tolerate any of that nonsense."

"I heard there was a murder here a few years ago. Do you know anything about that?"

"Saw the girl with my own eyes. Pretty thing. Real pretty."

"You *saw* her?" I asked. There was no mention of a second bartender in the court transcript Ben sent me. At the trial another man, Lou Gravely testified that he served Logan and his friends that night. Gravely also remembered the girl and that Logan showed an interest in her. The prosecutor made the most of his testimony during the trial. But now I realized we had uncovered something new. I could feel my heart racing and it took every bit of self-control to resist placing a hand over my chest. *Breathe*, I told myself. Deep breaths like the doctor told me to take when I got worked up. I felt flushed, the blood rising to my face.

Charlie glanced at me. "Are you okay, lady?" he asked.

Lalo turned to me, a look of concern darkening his face. I nodded, giving him a weak smile. I motioned with my hand for him to keep talking while I took a sip of my tea.

"She's fine. You said you saw the girl that night?"

Charlie drew his eyebrows together, a look of suspicion crossing his face. "Who's asking?"

Lalo pulled out his investigator's license and placed it on the bar. Charlie glanced down and slid it back across the counter. "Thought it might be something like this. What are you doing, coming out here asking questions after all these years? Guy who killed that girl was caught a long time ago. Sent to death row, if I remember right."

"We're working for people who think maybe he didn't do it," Lalo said.

"You should have told me that right up front. I don't take kindly to people who play games. Enjoy your drinks."

With that he turned his back on us and started cleaning glasses. When the patrons at the other end of the bar called to him, he walked away to see what they wanted. They ordered another round and Charlie soon returned to where we sat in front of the beer tap.

"Do you think we could start over?" I sat up straight and tipped my head in what I hoped he might interpret as contrition. "You're right, we should have told you sooner. But now that we're here, I'd appreciate it if you could tell us what you remember about the girl."

Charming people was never my strong suit. Instead of getting the reaction from Charlie that I hoped for, I watched as he silently topped off two glasses from the tap and carried them back to the customers at the other end of the bar. He stayed there for a while, braced against the bar, chatting. Lalo reached into his pocket and pulled out a twenty-dollar bill, waving it in the air to get the bartender's attention.

"Put that away," I told Lalo. "I'll settle the bill and we can get out of here."

Charlie's eyes flicked over in our direction. Before I could reach into my purse, he came back and took the money from Lalo's hand.

"Nothing much to tell anyway. I never saw the guy who killed her. Lou worked the other end of the bar that night so he's the one you want to talk to. Only thing is, he's got the Alzheimer's. Some days he can't remember his own name, much less what happened ten years ago. Still, you can find him in Sunset Care if you want to track him down."

"About the girl," Lalo pressed. "What time was it when you saw her?"

"Oh, around ten, I'd say. Her and her friend."

"What friend?"

"Another girl. Kinda pretty, but didn't hold a candle to the one who got killed. They was hanging around here for a few days before the murder but I never saw the friend again."

"Do you remember anything else?" I broke in. "Did they speak to you? Did you overhear any conversation between them? Maybe a name? Whatever you can tell us would be a big help."

"They was speaking Spanish, going a mile a minute. I couldn't understand a word they said."

"Can you describe the friend?"

"Long time ago." Charlie shrugged.

Lalo pulled another twenty out of his wallet.

Charlie took the money with a smile. "She was pretty enough, I guess. But like I said, nothing compared to the one who got killed. The friend was a little taller, was maybe a few years older, too. And seems to me, she'd been used up a long time ago, if you know what I mean. The dead girl was just a kid really, but she wasn't what I'd call innocent either. She had this little silver ring in her belly button. Yeah, and I remember something else, now that we're talking about it. When she walked away I saw this tattoo on her back. Wings, or something like 'em."

A barking sound came out of Lalo's pocket. He pulled out his phone and brought it to his ear. A deep crease formed between his eyebrows. He spoke a few words of Spanish then paused to listen. As he gestured for me to hand him a pen, I grabbed one from my purse and passed it to him. He scribbled something on the palm of his hand and hung up.

Shoving the phone back into his pocket he pulled out a business card together with yet another twenty-dollar bill. He passed both to Charlie. "Sorry about that stuff earlier. Thanks for your help. If you can think of anything else about that night, give me a call."

He gave a low whistle and Maya jumped to her feet. Taking a hold of my elbow, Lalo quickly guided me back to the truck.

"This was supposed to be my turn to pay." I fished my wallet out of my purse and started pulling out some money.

"Put that away. I never once let a lady pay for my beer and I'm not about to start now." Lalo glanced at the dashboard clock. "Listen, there's something going on in Immokalee I need to take care of."

"What's the problem?"

"I don't know exactly, but it doesn't sound good."

He pressed his foot down on the accelerator. Gravel shot out from under the tires, a cloud of dust rising behind us. When we reached the end of the road leading out of Snook Wallow he didn't bother to brake before joining traffic on the main road.

"Immokalee is back the other way."

"I'm taking you home first."

"It'll save you at least half an hour if I come with you."

Lalo looked at me. I could almost see him tossing the idea around in his head. Without a word, he spun the steering wheel, tires screeching as he made an illegal U-turn. Roaring down the I-75 ramp, we flew south.

FIFTEEN

On the drive to Immokalee, Lalo explained that we were going to meet a girl he knew only by her first name, Luci. He drove through the streets of town like he knew exactly where we were. Rolling through one stop sign after another, he never paused to read the names of the streets. A little over an hour after we left Snook Wallow, Lalo turned the truck onto a side street and stopped. I followed his gaze as he scanned the area. Other than a few scraggly palm trees, all I saw was a mangy dog under a bus stop bench, his nose stuffed into a dirty McDonald's bag. I wondered if after driving through town with such purpose, Lalo had lost his way.

"She told me she'd be here," he muttered under his breath.

"You drove a little fast. Maybe we're early?"

Lalo shook his head, "I've got a bad feeling about this." He continued to scan the surrounding area with his eyes, searched the shadows.

We sat in the truck, engine running. Maya caught sight of the stray. Her lips curled back and a growl rumbled in the back of her throat. The stray looked up, shook the bag off his nose and wandered off. An empty rust-colored bus trundled by, black letters painted on the side, HERRERA'S HARVESTERS. After fifteen minutes and no sign of Luci, Lalo threw the truck into gear. We rode in silence. Lalo grew tense, his hands gripping the wheel. Despite the air conditioning, a bead of sweat broke out on his brow. He parked in front of a strip mall. A wooden sign hung over the end unit—El Rincón. Like everything else in the town, the place looked deserted.

"What are we doing here?" I asked.

"This is where Luci works," Lalo replied. "Wait in the truck. I'll be right back."

Maya whimpered as he walked away. I stroked her coat but with little effect as she continued to whine, keeping her eyes riveted on the door of the bar. I glanced around to see boarded windows in the building across the street, litter blowing through the parking lot, broken glass glittering in the afternoon sun. When Lalo emerged from the bar alone, Maya wagged her stubby tail.

"No luck?" I asked.

"She didn't turn up for her shift." Lalo drummed the steering wheel with his fingers. After what seemed like a long time, he made up his mind and put the truck in reverse.

"Where to now?" I asked.

"Luci's house."

It seemed to me that we should have started there instead of running all over town, but I kept my opinion to myself. We backtracked, passing the bus stop once again. The stray had returned, stretched out on his side, taking advantage of the dappled shade that the bench provided. Lalo slowed down to look as we passed, then took the truck around the next turn with wheels screeching in protest.

I could see the lights flashing three blocks ahead.

An ambulance, red strobes on the roof, was parked in front of the house where Lalo brought the truck to an abrupt stop behind a black Dodge that stood in the driveway. While Lalo sat staring at the front door, I noticed a blue-clad paramedic emerge from the back of the ambulance. The man pulled out a stretcher, taking his time to adjust the straps before retreating into the vehicle.

"He doesn't appear to be in a hurry. I hope that means whatever is going on inside isn't too serious."

Before Lalo could comment, a stocky man, face scarred by acne, came out of the house and headed toward us. Lalo swore softly under his breath. The man took his time, his necktie swinging to the rhythm of his gait. With every step, I could see the gaps in his shirt where the buttons strained around his belly. Lalo hopped out, pushed back his Marlin's cap and leaned against the hood of the truck. As the man drew close, I noticed how Lalo towered over him. The guy tipped back his head and scowled.

"What are you doing here?" he asked.

Lalo turned to watch the paramedic disappear into the house with the stretcher.

"One of Norma's girls called me."

"Which one?"

"The one who calls herself Luci. What's going on, Tom?"

"Wait here until we finish up inside," the man Lalo addressed as Tom said. "I'll be back in a few."

Lalo waited for Tom to enter the house before slamming the hood of the truck with his fist. "Damn!" he shouted. "Damn, damn, damn!" He looked up and when our eyes met he gave me a sheepish grin. He pounded the hood one last time—softer this time—before getting back into the truck. From the back seat, the dog nudged his shoulder. Lalo leaned back to rub her neck.

"Sorry about that. I don't make a habit of swearing in front of a lady."

"Who was that man?" I asked.

"Homicide Detective Tom Moreno," he replied.

A homicide detective. Things finally clicked. I understood why the paramedic was in no hurry. Why Lalo was so upset. My stomach twisted into a knot when I realized we arrived too late.

For the next thirty minutes we sat in the truck, windows open to let a light breeze pass through. I felt a change in the air, still warm but the cloying humidity of summer a thing of the past. Lalo spent the time bringing me up to speed on his previous visit to Immokalee, filling me in on the details of Ricky Castro's case.

"What exactly did Luci tell you when she called?" I asked.

"She offered me a deal. The name of the man who took Marcela in exchange for getting Luci out of here," Lalo replied.

"What are you going to tell Detective Moreno?"

As I said his name, Moreno emerged from the house, head bent as he lit his cigarette. Lalo got out to meet him and I followed so I could hear what they discussed. I inhaled, drawing the second-hand smoke into my lungs. Moreno tapped another cigarette out of the pack and held it out to Lalo who shook his head. I didn't hesitate when the detective offered one to me.

"What is going on in there?" Lalo asked as Moreno held the flame of his lighter to my cigarette.

"Call came in twenty minutes ago," Moreno replied, slipping the lighter back into his shirt pocket. "She was dead by the time the EMTs got here, so they followed procedure and contacted me. Norma called her doctor to make it official so the guys can remove the body. They're bagging her now."

"Who called it in?"

"Norma. As you can imagine, she's pretty upset so I suggested she stay in her room until we're done here."

"Cause of death?" Lalo asked.

Moreno took a deep drag on his cigarette and released the smoke slowly through both nostrils. "The girl was on her back, needle still in her arm, vomit spilling out of her mouth. Either she choked to death or the horse stopped her heart. The ME has the final say, but I'm reading this as your run-of-the mill overdose."

"I want to get a look at her," Lalo's eyes narrowed.

"You know I can't let you in there."

Lalo locked eyes with the detective. Moreno blinked first.

"You still haven't told me what you're doing here. Why did the girl call *you*?"

"What difference does it make?"

"Call it professional curiosity," Moreno replied with a cold smile.

"A trade. What I know for ten minutes inside."

Moreno took another drag on his cigarette and turned his back on us. "Make it five."

Crushing my own half-smoked cigarette under my heel, I fell in step next to Lalo. He took hold of my arm, yanking me to a halt.

"Wait in the truck, Cate."

"An extra pair of eyes can't hurt." He must have felt me trembling under his grip. My nerves were shot but I was determined to stand my ground.

Moreno stood by the front door, waiting. Lalo looked from him to me, realizing I wasn't going to give up without an argument.

"Don't say a word," he warned, releasing my arm. "If Moreno asks you a question, let me answer."

Luci's bedroom looked like that of any ordinary teenaged girl, pink bedspreads on all four beds, posters of rock stars taped to the wall, shoes and clothes strewn across the floor. As we entered, the paramedics hoisted a black body bag onto the stretcher. Moreno said something to them in Spanish and they stepped out of the room, leaving the three of us alone with the body. Lalo reached over and unzipped the bag, revealing the face of a young girl. Her head was turned to the side, her straight black hair pulled back in a ponytail revealing a tattoo on the back of her neck. The odor that rose from the bag made me gag.

"You okay?" Lalo asked.

I nodded and turned away, noticing that the contents of a canvas handbag were dumped on one of the beds. While Lalo reached for the girl's wallet I picked up a book from the nightstand and flipped through the pages.

"Was this stuff like this when you got here?" Lalo asked the detective. He dropped the wallet back onto the bed.

Moreno shook his head.

"Did you find anything of interest?" Lalo asked.

Moreno pulled a plastic evidence bag out of his pants pocket. Inside was a small packet of rose-gray powder.

"We see a lot of this stuff since the governor cracked down on the pill mills. The street price of heroin is lower than Oxy."

"What about her phone?" Lalo asked.

Moreno smiled and produced a second evidence bag from his other pocket. Though it was sealed in the bag, he pressed the green button on the cell phone twice. Lalo's phone began to bark.

"How did she get your number?" Moreno asked.

"I gave it to her," Lalo replied.

"When was that?" The smile faded from Moreno's face.

"Look," Lalo turned both palms upward, the picture of sincerity. "After we met you for lunch last week, Ben and I came to see Norma. Luci was here but she didn't want to talk to me. I gave her my number anyway and asked her to call me if she changed her mind."

"I didn't see your business card in there." Moreno motioned to the empty purse with his chin.

"What do you want from me, Tom?"

"I want to know why Luci called you."

"Said she wanted to see me."

"You expect me to believe you drove down here without asking her why?"

"Yeah, that's exactly what I expect you to believe because that is the truth." Lalo looked at the body bag. "If you want to know why, ask her."

"I'm going to let these guys wrap this up. You need to get out of here." Moreno held the door open. "*Adiós, amigo*."

Lalo called over his shoulder as we walked out. "*Hasta que la próxima vez*, detective. See you around."

The setting sun painted the sky in strokes of blood orange and maroon as Lalo backed out of the driveway and pulled away from the house.

At that moment, I would willingly give half my pension for another of Moreno's cigarettes. I kept my nerves under control while we were in the house, but in the aftermath of seeing the dead girl on that gurney, they were rapidly coming undone.

Lalo slammed his fist on the steering wheel. "Luci should have left with me."

"I noticed a tattoo on the back of her neck. What was that?"

"A bar code."

"That's strange, isn't it?"

"Not really. Human traffickers tag their girls. Luci literally belonged to the people who smuggled her into this country, just like every other girl that lives in that house."

I stared at him, my mouth slightly ajar. The idea turned my stomach.

"Does Detective Moreno know?"

"Moreno?" Lalo snorted. "Yeah, he knows."

"Why did you tell Moreno that Luci wouldn't talk to you the first time you came here?"

"What he doesn't know won't hurt him. And I wasn't the only one lying. Moreno knows what happened to Luci was no accident."

My thoughts exactly, but the undercurrents ran so fast back at the house that I couldn't sort out what went on between Lalo and the detective. While I mulled everything over in my mind, a long stretch of silence filled the truck.

"Remember that article you found in the paper?" Lalo asked. "The one with the sketch of Jane Doe?"

I looked at him, confused.

"What has our Jane Doe got to do with Luci?" I asked.

"Did you happen to see a copy of that sketch inside there?"

"No, why would Luci have—"

"I wrote my phone number on the back and gave it to her."

"Moreno thought she had your business card."

"An assumption I did not bother to correct."

"Is that why you looked through her wallet?"

"Yeah, I thought maybe she stuffed the sketch in there, or maybe that I would find an ID. Not that I expected she kept anything like that in there. Prostitutes almost always use fake names in case they get busted."

"Maria Luz Gutierrez."

"What?" Lalo asked.

"Maria Luz, that was her name."

"How do you know that?" He looked at me in surprise. In his eyes I could see a look of approval. I felt the blood rush to my cheeks.

"That book she was reading? Luci used an old envelope as a bookmark. It was addressed to Maria Luz Gutierrez. I figured Luz . . . Luci? Must be her."

"Was there a return address?"

I pulled the envelope out of my purse and put on my reading glasses.

"Based on the postage, I'd say Mexico. The handwriting is a little hard to read. I can't say exactly . . . looks something like Michigan."

He brought the truck to an abrupt stop and grabbed the letter out of my hands. I could almost feel the vibration of excitement rising from him as he held the envelope at arm's length to read it.

"Michoacán."

"That's it. Do you know where Michoacán is?"

"Yeah, I do." Lalo let the envelope fall into his lap. He tipped back his head and closed his eyes, deep in thought.

"What's the matter?" I asked.

"You shouldn't have taken this, you just removed evidence from a crime scene."

"I'm not the only one. I saw you slip that spoon in your pocket back there."

Lalo's eyes opened wide as he tried to feign innocence. "You never know when a spoon might come in handy."

"I don't get it."

"Did you see a cigarette lighter anywhere in that room?"

I shook my head.

"Me neither. Needle in her arm, spoon on the nightstand. Only lighter I saw was the one Moreno used to light your cigarette."

It hit me then. The spoon was part of Luci's drug paraphernalia, but she had to melt the heroin before injecting herself. So where was her lighter? And what did Lalo plan to do with that spoon? Before I could ask, he changed the subject.

"I need a favor."

"Something other than promising not to turn you in?" I asked with a smile.

"I need to leave Maya with you for a few days."

"Maya? That's not possible. I don't—"

"I can't take her where I'm going."

I found myself nodding. Before I knew it I was standing in my driveway with Maya, both of us watching Lalo drive away. The instructions he rattled off swirled in my brain. When to walk her, when to feed her, what brand of food she liked. I looked down at the dog. Maya returned my gaze with her liquid, gold-rimmed eyes. She leaned against my leg, the full weight of her body nearly knocking me over.

"Don't get too comfortable." I looked down at her. "He promised this is only for a few days."

Her stump of a tail beat the ground.

SIXTEEN

Ben stared at the file on his desk. He understood that the Project could not help everyone who came begging for help, but he wished his firm could do more. Even with the pro-bono work of local lawyers and eager law school interns, the Project only had enough resources to accept one out of ten petitioners. An hour earlier Greg rejected the petition sitting on Ben's desk. He faced writing a letter that would dash the hopes of yet another desperate convict.

A clearing of a throat brought him out of his trance. He looked up from the computer to see Stephanie standing in the doorway.

"That letter isn't going to write itself. Just tell the guy this wasn't his lucky day and move on."

Ben wanted to believe Stephanie was not as tough as she sounded. This was probably her way to remind him that he could not accept everyone who turned to the Project for help. On the other hand, it was possible that her skin was thicker than his. She developed an ability to depersonalize each situation. He made a mental note to quit on the day that happened to him.

"I'm going out for sandwiches. "What can I get for you?"

"Thanks, but I'm skipping lunch today. I have errands to run."

"The usual then, Reuben on rye," she smiled, hand on her hip. "Give me your laundry ticket and I'll pick up your shirts. That will give you a chance to finish the letter before you start collecting Social Security. Trust me, you'll feel better as soon as you get it off your desk."

That was Stephanie. One minute snarky, the next, surprisingly considerate. He reached into his suit pocket and pulled out the ticket.

"How did you know about the laundry?"

"Let me see, you've been tied to your desk for weeks, getting to the office before the sun comes up, turning the lights out as you leave. So every time you drive by the dry cleaners, he's closed. You've worn the same shirt two days in a row, and I'm guessing you'd like to have a clean one for tomorrow when you meet Castro at the State Prison."

"Is it that obvious?" He stuck his nose in his armpit and sniffed.

"Jelly stain on your left cuff." Stephanie snatched the ticket from his hand. "Yesterday's raspberry donut."

After Stephanie left, Ben turned his attention back to the unfinished letter. Greg was right, as usual. The case was a long shot and the client was a bad candidate since he was almost certainly guilty of the crime. On top of everything, the man was serving a twenty-year sentence while Greg preferred death row cases. With a sigh Ben set his mind to the task. As the printer started to spit out the letter, Stephanie reappeared.

"Forty-five bucks for five shirts and a pair of pants. Do the math. Fifty-two weeks brings that to two thousand, three hundred forty dollars a year. You could save enough to send your firstborn child through law school if you bought a washer and dryer for your apartment."

"Some things are worth it," Ben pulled a few bills from his wallet. "What do I owe you for lunch?"

"Greg told me to take it out of petty cash because you're having lunch with the new intern."

"What new intern?"

"In his infinite wisdom, our great leader is assigning an intern to you. I think he finally noticed that since he gave you the Castro case, the rest of your workload is backing up."

"You know as well as I do that interns don't *reduce* the workload," Ben groaned. "They just slow things down. And when they discover they can't get rich working in a place like this, they run back to school to figure out what other kind of law they can practice."

"Too late Shepherd, Greg says she's all yours. Her name is Kim Bailey, as in the Irish cream. Third-year at UF Law. She's waiting for you in the conference room."

"There's got to be a way for me to get out of this."

"'Fraid not."

He looked at Stephanie standing there, smiling at him. Orange hair pulled back in a ponytail, cheeks flushed from being outside in the sun, her eyes reflecting the emerald green silk of her blouse. For weeks he had been working up the courage to ask her something. Now seemed as good a time as any.

"Hey, Steph?"

"Yeah?"

"Do you have plans for Saturday night? I thought maybe we could—"

A blush crept up her neck. "Oh sorry, Shepherd. I do. Have plans, that is. Hot date."

"I thought you broke up with your boyfriend."

"New guy. I found this one online. Looks promising. Some other time, okay?"

"Right. No big deal. I just thought we could grab a pizza or something."

"Next time. Listen, you should get in there and meet the intern before your sandwich gets cold."

He waited for her to walk away before removing the letter from his printer and adding it to the fat manila folder on his desk. Deciding to make this a working lunch, he picked up the whole file and tucked it under his arm. This case was as good as any to show the intern the ropes. She might as well understand from the start that she could not save the whole world in this job. He would go through the case with her, page by page and explain the process. He just hoped she caught on quickly.

The following day, Ben arrived in Raiford with plenty of time to spare. He pulled into Millie's parking lot, scanning the area for Lalo's truck. Earlier that morning Ben texted Lalo, suggesting they meet for breakfast before going in together. He was a little surprised that Lalo didn't text him back, but he knew his investigator was a loose cannon, a maverick. With a sigh, Ben picked up his cellphone and tried once more. This time he went straight into voicemail. Instead of leaving another message Ben pressed Cate's number.

"I was just going to call you. Where is Lalo? I haven't heard from him since we got back from Immokalee."

"Immokalee? When did you go to Immokalee?"

"Last week. He didn't tell you?"

"No."

"Lalo and I were having drinks at Snook Wallow when Luci called. By the time we arrived, she was already dead."

Ben shook his head, thinking maybe he heard wrong. He and Lalo just saw Luci ten days ago. And he had no idea why Cate would have drinks with Lalo at Snook Wallow.

"Did you just say Luci is dead? Hold on, when exactly did you say this was?"

"Sunday. Like I said, Lalo and I went to speak with Charlie at Snook Wallow . . . Oh, if you haven't heard from Lalo then you don't know about Charlie either. Or the girl he saw that night with Jane Doe."

"Who's Charlie? What girl? Back up, Aunt Cate. Start from the beginning and tell me everything."

"Lalo and I went to see Boyd Skinner. You remember, right? You made the appointment for me. In the name of Smith."

While he sat in his car, Cate filled Ben in on what happened since he last saw her. The meeting with Skinner, the girl the bartender saw with Jane Doe, the discovery of Luci's body. She gave him all the salient facts, a summary as concise as any legal brief he'd ever read.

"I would have called sooner but I assumed Lalo kept you in the loop. I've been busy unpacking the last of my boxes and getting settled. It was a lot of work, but I'm finally starting to feel at home here."

"I haven't heard from Lalo all week, so I called to find out if you knew where he is."

"I have no idea. After he brought me home, he took off in a hurry. I had to contact Dix Powers the next morning to tell her I wouldn't be able to come in to take a look at Detective Garibaldi's files until I get rid of this dog. When you catch up with that man, remind him that he said it would only be a few days.

"What dog?"

"Maya. Lalo left her with me."

Ben did not know what to make of that. He couldn't imagine why Lalo left his dog with Cate and disappeared without telling anyone where he went.

"Aunt Cate, how would you like company? I'm in Raiford but after I meet with Ricky I can drive down and take you out to dinner."

"Sounds perfect, but I don't like the idea of you driving all the way back to Gainesville after a full day's work. Plan to spend the night. All the boxes are cleared out of the guest room and there are clean sheets on the bed."

"Great. I'll see you in a few hours."

Ben glanced at the clock on his dashboard and noticed the call had lasted much longer than he realized. He decided to skip the pancakes and go directly to the prison where his client waited for him.

Ricky Castro scowled at Ben. By law, death row prisoners were entitled to private meetings with their lawyers but prison regulations dictated that the prisoner remain in shackles. Ben recognized the expression on Ricky's face, the same one he saw every time he went to visit his client. He steeled himself knowing that look of anger would fade, and then turn to pleading by the time he left. A full month had passed since Ben took Ricky's case and although he had little to show for his efforts, there was plenty of reason for hope. Ben reminded Ricky of that several times over as he updated him on his progress with the case. He spoke about going to Immokalee with Lalo, the meetings with Detective Moreno and Norma Martin, and their brief encounter with Luci. What he didn't mention was Luci's unexpected death. He thought it best to wait until he caught up with Lalo before breaking that news to Ricky.

"Okay, so you got a copy of Moreno's files." The chains of his leg irons rattled as his knees pumped like pistons under the table. "So what? He's not stupid enough to give you anything that's going to get me out of here."

"I think we need to go over Salazar's statement." Ben reached into his messenger bag and pulled out a sheet of paper. Holding it up for the guard behind the two-way mirror to see, he placed the document on the table. Salazar's original statement was written on a legal pad, the blue lines visible on the photocopy Ben received from Moreno. Scrawled across the page were the words Salazar printed in block letters. Ben turned the paper around so Ricky could read it.

"Take a look."

"What for? I know what that liar said."

"Right here." Ben pointed to the paper. "He says that you recognized him when he came into the jail. Is that true?"

"Yeah, maybe. I knew him, all right? He was Marci's dealer." Ricky glared at him. Ben moved his finger down the page.

"According to this statement, Salazar asked why you were there."

"That sounds about right."

"And in response you told him Marcela was dead."

"I never said I killed her!"

Ben could see Ricky was agitated, but he needed to get past his client's emotional state to find out exactly what was said between him and the jailhouse snitch. Pushing back his chair, Ben reached into his messenger bag and pulled out a roll of mints. Holding them up to show the guard what he was giving his client, he waited to the count of ten. When he didn't hear the guard tapping on the other side of the two-way mirror, he passed the mints to Ricky. Ricky popped one into his mouth and slid the roll back across the table. Ben took one for himself before slipping the remainder into his bag.

"It's important that we cover this. We both know Salazar lied. But I need to prove it."

"Talk to Moreno." Ricky rolled the mint around on his tongue. "He's the one who put Salazar up to it."

"I think you're right. After meeting the guy I'd say Moreno is capable of cutting a few corners to get a conviction. But police misconduct is a serious charge. I need hard evidence before requesting a judicial review."

"You're missing the point," Ricky shouted. He jumped to his feet and bent over the table, coming face to face with Ben.

A tap on the window caused both of them to turn their heads. Ben waved, letting the guard know everything was okay. Ricky mumbled something under his breath and sunk back into his chair.

"I've told you like a million times, I didn't kill her. Stop spending time trying to get me out of here on a legal technicality. Shouldn't you be working to prove I'm innocent?"

"This is our best avenue of approach. I believe you when you say you didn't kill Marcela, but our goal is to get you out of here, no matter what it takes. You're going to have to trust me with this."

Ricky gave Ben a half-nod.

"What about the rest of what Salazar said?" Ben asked. He let Ricky take his time reading the entire statement.

"Pack of lies." Ricky dropped the page on the table. "After I told that *pendejo* Marci was dead, I turned my back on him and sat on my bunk. I was messed up, you know, pretty emotional and all. I didn't want Salazar to see me like that. He kept trying to talk about it, but I never said another word to that liar."

"Okay." Ben slipped the paper back into his bag. "Now let's talk about the people Marcela worked for. Starting with Norma Martin."

"Norma? I already told you everything I know about her. The cops said she had an alibi, but trust me, even if that bitch didn't kill Marci with her own hands, she sure knows what happened to her. Didn't Luci tell you Norma called someone to take Marci away?"

Ben nodded.

"Then it's obvious, isn't it? You have to get back down there and make Luci tell you who he was."

Ben paused before answering, knowing he should tell Ricky about Luci. But what could he say? That their most promising lead was dead? That his investigator had gone AWOL? He decided it was best to duck Ricky's demand—at least for now. "I don't think you should hold out hope that we're going to learn anything more from that direction. In the meantime, can you tell me who you think it might have been? Who are Norma's contacts in the smuggling cartel?"

"She keeps things pretty tight, but I know Norma made a weekly cash drop to someone named Angel. Marci told me he and Norma went way back but I never met him. I can tell you one thing, though. Marci was scared of the guy."

"About those drops . . . any reason to think Norma traveled outside of the area to meet with this Angel?"

"Probably not. Norma never left the girls alone for long."

"I'll get Lalo to search for people with that name who live in Immokalee. That'll give us a starting point."

"Good luck," Ricky shook his head. "There must be thousands of Angels down there."

"Let us worry about that. Now for the good news. I've been given approval to have DNA tests run on that stain on Marcela's skirt. With a bit of luck, we'll find out who she was with right before she died. You never know where that will lead."

"If you find out who he was, I'll kill the bastard when I get out of here."

"Don't joke about that sort of thing." Ben cast a nervous glance at the cameras mounted in the ceiling. While the law protected the privacy of their conversation, and the microphones were supposed to be turned off, he didn't want to take any chances. "Someone might think you mean it."

Ricky laughed. "You know I was kidding. Death row humor, that's all. Most of these guys here don't even bother to deny what they've done. Stories they tell . . . they're all a bunch of sickos."

Ben could not imagine how tough being locked up in this place could be for someone like Ricky. His client had spent his life outdoors working in the tomato fields. And just because he fell in love with the wrong girl he ended up trapped on death row with murderers and rapists of the worst kind.

"I'm working on it," Ben replied. "But remember, we're just getting started. We have a long way to go. Try to be patient."

"Patient?" Ricky leaned back in his chair. "Easy for you to say. You wouldn't last one day in this rat hole."

"Well, hang in there. Is there anything I can do for you?"

"You can give my sister a call, tell her I'm doing okay." Ricky's tone softened. "It's tough for her to get here to see me, what with her job and kids and all."

"Sure, I'll call her as soon as I leave. Anything else?"

"What you said about Moreno . . . about him cutting corners. What did you mean by that?"

"That Moreno might have traded Salazar's testimony for a favor. If he did, that would be what we call police misconduct and *that's* something worth proving. It could be your ticket out of here."

"Moreno was real friendly with the guy who ran the bar where Marci worked." Ricky stared at the iron cuffs on his wrist. "He came in all the time for free drinks. Marci always told me there was no risk of her getting arrested as long as Moreno was around. That's police misconduct, right?"

"Not the kind that will help us, I'm afraid."

"But maybe he had ties to this Angel guy. Maybe he was on the cartel's payroll."

Ben thought the idea that Moreno was linked to the cartel was absurd. The police sometimes acted foolishly and yes, some of them bent the rules. But while Ben believed the detective used Salazar to clinch his case, he had no reason to think the man offered protection to a prostitution ring. That would be going too far, even for the likes of Moreno.

"Let's stay focused. One step at a time. I'll let you know when I get the DNA results from Marcela's skirt and we'll take it from there."

SEVENTEEN

After hanging up with Ben, I put on my reading glasses, picked up my notepad and made a grocery list. I had no intention of letting my nephew waste his hard earned money taking me out to a restaurant. Living on donuts, pizza and hamburgers, the boy was overdue for a home-cooked meal. With the weather turning a bit cooler, I planned to cook a pot roast. To round it out, my famous garlic mashed potatoes, a side dish of green beans with sautéd mushrooms and a homemade apple pie for dessert.

I was cooking up a storm when the doorbell chimed. Maya beat me to the foyer, a ridge of hackles rising on her back. Thinking it must be Ben, I grabbed Maya's collar and opened the door. Annie Murphy took one look at the snarling dog and jumped back, her eyes wide in fear.

"When did you get a dog?" she asked.

Maya stopped growling and began to wag her stubby tail. I shook my head. "I'm minding her for a friend. She's harmless. I think." As I beckoned for Annie to come in, Maya thrust her nose into her flowing kaftan, hitting her squarely in the crotch. Annie froze.

"I'm so sorry." I hauled the dog inside. "She has absolutely no manners."

Annie remained outside, keeping her eyes fixed on Maya. "I can't stay. I just stopped by to ask if you wanted to come with me to the Drum Circle tonight."

"Drum Circle?"

"Every Friday some friends of mine get together on Nokomis beach and drum the sun down. We use bongos, empty five-gallon drums, tambourines, whatever. It's liberating. I think it would help you get rid of all the stress you carry around."

Sounded crazy to me, but I didn't want to offend her. "Sounds like fun, but I'm expecting my nephew for dinner."

Maya turned away and jogged down the hall in the direction of the kitchen. I was moments away from getting rid of Annie when I realized what the dog was up to.

"My roast!" I shouted.

I reached the kitchen just in time. Maya had her front paws on the counter, her nose lifted toward the pan on the stove. Swatting her away, I turned to see Annie right behind me, laughing.

"That guy must be a special friend for you to put up with his dog."

"He's not a friend exactly. He's an investigator with the Defender Project."

A thousand wrinkles appeared around Annie's eyes as her whole face erupted into a smile. "Does this mean the Project has accepted Logan as a client? That's why you're watching his dog, right? He's working on Logan's case."

"No, he's working on something else right now," I replied. "I'm just doing him a favor by watching Maya." Even though I had no idea what Lalo was up to, I felt it best to tone down Annie's expectations.

"Oh, I see." The disappointment in Annie's voice was unmistakable.

I wanted to say more, reassure her that I was doing everything possible to help her grandson. On the other hand, I didn't want to give Annie false hope. Though I'd been working on the case for several weeks, I hadn't found a thing that would convince the Project to accept Logan as a client. Still, Annie *was* Logan's grandmother and she had every right to hear about the small—very small—progress I had made with the investigation thus far.

"Don't be discouraged." I walked her back to the front door. "Lalo is helping me in his spare time. So I guess you can say there are two of us working for Logan now. As soon as we find anything new, I'll let you know. Thanks for inviting me to this drum circle thing. Perhaps another time."

"Not next week." Annie smiled, revealing her chipped tooth. "I'm going up to see Logan. But plan on joining the circle the following Friday. Wear something comfortable. Shoes are optional. I'll bring an extra tambourine in case you haven't unpacked yours yet."

I watched her walk away with a lift in her step, her untamed hair flying wildly, kaftan whipping around her legs as she headed back to her old Volkswagen Beetle. With a smile, I wondered what made her think I owned a tambourine. Even though I grew up in the sixties, I certainly wasn't cut out of the same cloth as Annie.

Ben ate like a starved dog. He shoveled down second helpings of everything before placing his napkin on the table and surrendering to a full stomach. When I brought out the apple pie he groaned, but he still accepted a scoop of ice cream on the side. After dinner I suggested we move to the living room for coffee. At this time of year, though the temperatures rose into the high seventies by mid-day, once the sun went down the air turned chilly. It was still nothing compared to the freezing weather up north where I came from, but it was too cool to sit on the lanai.

I set two steaming mugs on the coasters that protected my glass coffee table. Ben sat down on the couch and started to rub Maya behind her ears. The dog wore an expression that I had come to recognize as a smile.

"So Lalo never told you where he went?" Ben asked as he accepted the mug I handed him.

"No, just that he planned to be gone for a few days. I was supposed to meet Dix Powers last Monday—she's the administrative director at the Public Defender's office—to go through Geri Garibaldi's files. Problem is, I didn't want to leave Maya alone in the house so I called Dix and told her I couldn't make it. Those files have been sitting there for a full week now."

"Don't worry. They're not going anywhere."

"If I don't show up soon, I'm afraid Dix is going to send everything back to Detective Garibaldi."

"Do you want me to call Powers and ask her to give you more time?"

"No, I think that will do more harm than good. She sounded a bit prickly on the phone. If Lalo doesn't come back by Monday, I'll just have to take my chances and leave Maya alone in the house."

"Is there anything else?" Ben asked.

"Nothing that you don't already know." I picked up my coffee and cradled it between both hands. "I'm more interested in hearing about Luci."

Ben set his empty mug on the tray and studied his feet. "I called Tom Moreno this afternoon. He told me that Luci was a known addict and that there was no sign of a struggle at the scene. He believes she overdosed, and he doesn't see any reason to call it a homicide. But he reminded me that the final decision wasn't his to make. That will be up to the medical examiner. The autopsy results will be available early next week. Moreno promised to let me know the outcome."

Ben's apparent acceptance of Detective Moreno's lies rubbed me the wrong way. "I know Luci died from an overdose," I snapped. "But the real question is who stuck the needle in that poor girl's arm?"

"What does Lalo think?" Ben asked.

"That Luci was about to tell him who killed Marcela de la Vega. I gave Lalo an envelope I found in Luci's room. It had a return address from someplace called Michoacán. Lalo is probably there now, looking for answers."

Ben stared at me, his brown eyes unblinking under his dark eyebrows.

"You never fail to amaze me."

"I saw a barcode tattooed on the back of Luci's neck." I shuddered at the memory. "Did Marcela have one too?"

"She did. A tag that identified her as someone's property."

"But you don't know who that person is?"

"Not yet. All I have is the first name of a potential suspect, someone called Angel who may or may not have removed Marcela from Norma's house on the day she was killed. I need Lalo to chase this guy down to find out if he's the one we're looking for."

"Tell me something, why did the Project accept Ricky Castro as a client but not Logan?"

"Before we take on a client, my boss wants to see at least two of what he calls the Big Three." He held up his hand and counted on his fingers. "DNA evidence, jailhouse snitch testimony and police or prosecutorial misconduct. Logan's case didn't have any of those three. But with Castro we may have two."

"Those two being?"

"DNA evidence and a jailhouse snitch. The man or men Marcela was with used condoms but there was a stain on her skirt that could potentially yield a result. I just got approval from my boss to run the DNA tests."

"Didn't the prosecution check that out?"

"Moreno claims they didn't have enough of a budget to waste money on DNA testing when they had a slam-dunk case without it. With a bit of luck, the lab results will tell us who was with Marcela right before she died. And that may get me closer to discovering who killed her."

"What about the jailhouse snitch?"

"Moreno used a guy named Diego Salazar to offer false testimony."

"Can you prove it?"

"The snitch is dead. Murdered two months after the trial. Single gunshot to the head."

An involuntary shiver shook my body. Maya rose to her feet, her jowls vibrating as a whine escaped her throat. I reached out to give her a reassuring pat and she settled back down, resting her massive head on my feet.

"Do you want to hear my opinion about all this?" I asked.

Ben nodded, a slight smile on his face. He knew me well enough to realize I would give it to him regardless.

"So far you have two murders—Marcela and Salazar—and one drug overdose." I looked up to make sure he listened. "Three murders if it turns out Luci was killed too. I'm sure it has occurred to you that Moreno is the common denominator. If I were you, I'd start looking into his conduct."

"I already told you I can't prove Moreno coerced the snitch to lie. Ricky claims he hardly spoke to the guy when he entered his cell, but it comes down to his word against Salazar's. The prosecutor produced a photo of the two of them talking. That was enough for the jury to believe Salazar told the truth."

I thought about that for a minute. Seeing two people engaged in conversation—even if you didn't hear them—would lead one to believe that *something* was said between them. And given the circumstances, the topic would be obvious. I realized if I were one of the jurors, I probably would have come to the same conclusion. A thought popped into my mind.

"Wait. Who took that photo? If someone else was there, then maybe there's a witness who overheard them."

"I already checked that out. No such luck. The photo came from a frame off a surveillance tape. Cameras cover every square inch of that jail. Just today, when I was with Ricky I noticed two cameras mounted in the ceiling of the room. Standard practice. There's no sound, but the lens catches everything."

Ben turned to look out the window, squinting into the distance. I could tell something whirled around in his brain but decided to wait until he spoke.

"You might have just hit on something."

"What?"

"The video. The video *is* our witness."

"You just said there was no sound."

"I don't need sound. In Salazar's written statement, the one he wrote with Moreno looking over his shoulder, he claimed he had a long conversation with Ricky during which Ricky confessed to killing Marcela. But Ricky insists they only exchanged a few words. He told Salazar that Marcela was dead and then he turned his back on the guy. They spoke for two minutes, max. If the tape backs that up, then it suggests Ricky is telling the truth."

"Aren't you forgetting something?" I asked. "Even if you can prove Salazar lied, you have no way of proving Moreno coerced him."

Ben rolled his shoulders, took a deep breath and cracked his knuckles.

"My boss says my job is to find a legal route to get Ricky off death row. He doesn't want me to waste time or money spinning my wheels to prove Moreno is a bad cop."

"Your boss isn't part of this discussion. What do you say?"

"I'm thinking if Moreno crossed the line with this investigation, he's probably done it before. And he'll no doubt do it again until someone stops him. Which means I can't let this thing about Moreno go."

I smiled and leaned over to give him a kiss on the cheek.

"What was that for?" he asked.

"For making me proud." I replied.

EIGHTEEN

The queue for Courthouse security snaked all the way to the door. I stood behind an obese man who smelled like day-old sweat and fried catfish. When a shriveled up white-haired lady passed through the metal detector arch, the alarm sounded. The guard gestured for her to back up and pass through a second time. She shook her head, her curls bouncing. In a shrill voice cracked with age, she spoke loudly enough for the entire room to hear her say, "Do I look like a terrorist to you, young man? That's the pin in my hip tripping that alarm. Goddamn that Bin Laden. This used to be a free country."

Grabbing her purse off the conveyor belt she limped down the hall. A second guard who watched the x-ray machine looked up. With a shrug he gave a half-nod to his partner before going back to work. I saw my purse trundle down a set of metal rollers, pushed from behind by a plastic tray containing a wallet and a set of keys. Like my purse, I felt pushed from behind but I stood my ground, holding back a few paces as Fish Man advanced. He passed through the arch without sounding the alarm and soon I collected my things and made my way down the hall, heading for room 102, the Public Defender's office.

The door was locked, a number pad on the wall. I looked around, wondering if there was another way in. That was when I noticed what looked like a doorbell under the number pad.

"Yes?" the disembodied voice asked.

"Catherine Stokes to see Dix Powers."

"Fourth door on your left."

The door clicked. I turned the handle and entered what appeared to be a labyrinth of offices. Turning left, I passed three doors, discovering the fourth was open. Inside I saw an elderly man seated at one of the two desks crammed face-to-face in a small, windowless room. The smell of body odor gagged me and I realized the other man in the room—the one settling down behind the second desk—was none other than Fish Man. Both looked up as I rapped lightly on the door.

"I'm looking for Dix Powers."

"Next office down," Fish Man said. I nodded my thanks and moved on.

I found Dix in her office speaking slowly and deliberately on the phone sounding like she was trying to reason with a young child. She looked to be forty-something, darkly tanned skin, curly black hair, a minuscule diamond stud in her nose. Despite the slow pace of her speech, the drumming of her fingers on the desk suggested bottled-up energy, a teakettle gathering steam. She waved me in and gestured for me to take a seat. I sat with my ankles crossed, hands folded on my lap while I listened to her side of the conversation.

"You know the rules." The volume of her voice rose as she came to a full boil. Grabbing a water-stained slip of paper from her desk she waved it in the air as if the person on the other end of the line could see. "Expense forms must be accompanied by legible receipts and submitted in a timely fashion. This thing looks like it washed up on the banks of the Manatee River. There is no way the bean counters are going to cut you a check against this sorry piece of crap. If you want to get paid, then get yourself a new invoice. . . . What did you just say? Did you actually just tell me you're too busy? Do you think I sit around all day with my thumb up my— All right then, you do that. You are the best defense attorney I know John, but this is a government operation and we do not cut corners here. Do not pull this again, you hear?" She slammed down the phone and turned to me, lips pursed, a frown line creasing her brow.

"They never learn." She shook her head. "The idiots in accounting expect me to turn these guys into CPAs or something. Doesn't do a bit of good. I can threaten all I want, tell them I won't send any more business their way if they don't get the paperwork right, but they know I'm just blowing smoke. Not enough lawyers in this town who want to work for the money we pay."

She reached into the top drawer of her desk and pulled out a prescription pill bottle. Popping one into her mouth she sighed, her anger apparently spent. "All right then, what can I do for you?" she asked.

"Catherine Stokes. I'm here to have a look at Detective Garibaldi's files."

Dix cut me off with a wave of her hand. "Right. Geri said to keep you under the radar. Which will be no problem because I'm not expecting anyone from upstairs today. The only people here are a couple of volunteers organizing tomorrow's case files, so we're good."

"I'll try to stay out of their way."

Dix peered at me with blood-shot eyes. "If anyone asks, tell them you're a new volunteer. After you're gone I'll say the job wasn't right for you. No one will question that. Happens all the time. Got it?"

"Yes," I replied.

"Geri's files are in the conference room. Not ideal, but we're a little tight for space. You'll have to manage the best you can."

Dix stood and gestured for me to follow. The long hallway dead-ended with a wall of glass beyond which I saw a dozen plastic orange chairs set around a wooden conference table. She flipped the wall switch as we entered and the fluorescent tubes in the suspended ceiling flickered, flooding the room in a harsh, white light. On the table was a box marked State vs. Murphy.

"Coffee station is down the hall on your right. Twenty-five cents a cup. I think there are still donuts left over from Friday. They're free if you're desperate enough to eat one. Any questions?"

"I saw a key pad on the door?"

"Oh right. When you get back from lunch, just ring the buzzer and someone will let you back in. Make yourself at home. The conference room is yours for the day."

My eyes fell on the box. "I may need more time."

"Well, today is all you've got." She gave me a humorless smile. "Geri didn't say anything about letting you move in. As I explained, we're kind of short on space here."

I decided not to push it.

"All right then." Dix pinched the bridge of her nose. "You know where to find me if you need anything."

After she left the room I got to work. The box was two-thirds full of file folders stuffed with papers. Crammed behind the folders was a large manila envelope marked Crime Scene Photos and behind that I discovered a shoebox containing a dozen or more cassette tapes. I lifted one of the tapes out of the box and held it at arm's length so I could read the label identifying them as tip line calls. I didn't think to bring a tape player with me so I dropped the cassette back into the box, pulled out my reading glasses and began with the first folder labeled "30 Flamingo Avenue, Suspect's Home Address."

The transcript of Annie's 911 call pretty much confirmed what I already knew. Her sense of urgency, even on paper, came through. *Something terrible has happened. My son found a dead girl in the woods.* As I scanned the pages I saw the operator kept Annie on the line until a uniformed deputy arrived at her house and the call was disconnected. I read the deputy's report—written in terrible penmanship—then moved on to the search warrant return and list of evidence collected there. The list included Logan's bloody clothes, jeans, shirt, socks and shoes.

Within a few minutes I gained a solid appreciation for Geri Garibaldi's attention to detail. Call it obsessive-compulsive disorder, or call it competence. Whatever it was, no one could accuse the detective of doing things halfway. Her reports left nothing open to interpretation. The name of the responding uniformed deputy, his statement that Logan was in the shower when he arrived, the discovery of Logan's bloody clothes in the outside trash. Geri documented everything meticulously. After returning the folder to the box, I paused to reflect on how all this must have appeared to the homicide detective. Little wonder Logan was Geri's prime suspect right from the start.

What followed was a thicker file labeled INTERVIEWS. Leaning back in my chair with the stack of papers on my lap, I adjusted my reading glasses and dug in. Finding nothing unusual in Annie or Logan's statements, I moved on. Picking up Geri's summary of her interview with Boyd Skinner, I made notes as I read.

> Witness states he and Tyler Fox remained at the bar until est. 23:30 hours. At that time witness believed Murphy was with the victim. The witness proceeded to the parking lot with Fox. He recalls seeing Murphy's Harley Davidson parked next to his own motorcycle. Skinner had trouble starting his motorcycle so there was a delay in his departure. By approximately 00:15 hours witness arrived home. He states his parents were asleep and did not hear him come in.

I put my pen down, set the sheet to one side and picked up Tyler Fox's interview summary. His story confirmed Boyd's statement with only one minor variation. Tyler was specific about the time they left the bar, saying it was 11:35 pm. His statement confirmed Boyd had a problem with his motorcycle. He mentioned seeing Logan's Harley in the parking lot when they left. Like Annie and Logan's interview summaries, I didn't find anything unusual. Still, I flagged all four summaries with sticky labels in case Dix let me use her photocopier.

The final interview I flagged was toward the bottom of the stack. Long after the murder, Geri spoke with one of Logan's ex-girlfriends, Bibi Marks. Logan's relationship with Bibi ended a full year before the murder. On the night Jane Doe was killed, Bibi was miles away from Snook Wallow, asleep in her bed. She knew nothing about what happened out in the woods, but that was not what interested Geri. Months into her investigation, the police still lacked motive. Geri resorted to fishing for anything that would expose a character flaw in her main suspect. The search led to Bibi. I read the single-page summary, knowing full well how damaging the girl's comments were to Logan's defense.

Making a note to find out if Bibi testified at the trial, I knew before the ink dried that she did. In Bibi Marks, Geri found exactly what she needed.

> The witness stated she and Murphy dated for a short time during their junior year in high school. They were sexually active, and the witness recalls Murphy used the Trojan brand of condoms whenever they had intercourse. When the witness decided to end the relationship, Murphy threatened her with violence.

Though Geri still didn't have her motive, she settled for the next best thing—a suggestion that Logan had a violent streak. I returned the folder to the box and stood, arching my stiff back. With a quick glance at my watch I realized I had covered a quarter of the files in just over two hours. The remainder promised to be more tedious. The crime scene report, lab data, police reports and autopsy results were loaded with technical details. I craved a cigarette, but signs posted on every door identified the building as a no-smoking zone. Before tackling the next folder, I needed a cup of coffee to get my blood flowing. I made my way down the hall and filled a Styrofoam cup with the syrup-thick remains from the morning. After poking around, I found a new packet of coffee and started a fresh pot. Before returning to the conference room, I stopped in front of Dix's office and rapped on the open door.

"Would it be possible for me to make a few photocopies before I leave?" I asked.

"How many pages are we talking about?" She gave me a guarded look.

"Not many. Just interview summaries. Maybe six pages in all."

"In that case, use the machine in the front office. When it asks you for the case code, enter 999. I gave up long ago expecting the volunteers to actually look up codes before they run copies so they all use 999. What am I going to do, fire them?" She laughed and I smiled to humor her. "The guys went out for lunch so if you want to use the machine, now would be a good time."

"No problem. I planned to skip lunch today anyway."

Not that I wasn't tempted to take a break. My vision blurred from reading under the fluorescent light and the arthritis in my fingers screamed in protest from my note taking. Not to mention my craving for nicotine. Still, there was a lot of material to cover by the end of the day. I had to depend on the coffee to power me through.

Dix stared at me for a few seconds, as if to make up her mind about something. A tilt of her head and the light caught the stud in her nose. "I checked the schedule. The conference room is yours tomorrow if you want it."

"I appreciate that, thanks."

"All right then."

With that she dismissed me, turning her attention to the papers on her desk. Coffee in hand, I returned to the conference room, picked up the pages I had flagged to be copied, and headed for the machine. Halfway down the hall, I stopped. Returning to the conference room I gathered up several other folders. Since I had the chance, I thought it might be nice to have copies of the crime scene and autopsy reports for my own file. Lab results too. If Dix ever took the time to check, she would never know how many of the 999 copies were mine.

Maya greeted me at the door, placed her paws on my shoulders and gave my face a tongue bath. As I reached into my purse for the disinfecting wipes, she raced to the kitchen, returning with her leash hanging from her mouth. We walked around the block to the sound of palm fronds swishing in the breeze they caught from the Gulf. The jacaranda trees were in full bloom, blossoms dropping, lining the sidewalks with a purple carpet. I drew in a deep breath of sweet, perfumed air as a flower landed on Maya's head. She shook it off and looked up at me with a smile.

Returning home I fed the dog, refilled her water bowl and then poured myself a glass of Chablis. I stretched out on the chaise lounge and took a gulp. Gazing at the back yard I noticed the hibiscus plants at the edge of my property rose above the fence. I made a mental note to get out the hedge trimmers as a reminder. The wine went down cool and easy, just what I needed to help me unwind after the long day. My eyes still burned, unaccustomed to the harsh office light. I thought perhaps I should close them for a few minutes before getting up to fix dinner. The sound of Maya drinking water from the toilet reached my ears. I felt her wet nose nudging my hand before I drifted off.

An incessant ringing woke me from a deep sleep. I bolted out of the lounge chair, knocking over the empty wine glass and stubbing my toe on the table. Hop-skipping to the kitchen where I left my phone, I picked up. Lalo's voice came through the line.

"Are you going to let me in or not?"

"Lalo?" I went to the front room and peered through the plantation shutters to see him standing out front.

"Why didn't you ring the bell?" I asked as I yanked the door open. Maya pushed past me and wiggled in joy, leaning against her master's leg as he reached down and rubbed her head.

"I did. Twice. I brought dinner." He held up a clear plastic bag. Inside I saw a fish covered in dull gray scales, its dead eyes staring back at me.

Annoyed, I swatted the bag dangling from his hand.

"Get that smelly thing out of my face."

"I thought you liked fish." Lalo lowered the bag and tilted his head to one side.

"No . . . I mean yes, I do, but . . . would it have killed you to call first?"

"At least one of you is happy to see me." He bent down and ruffed the fur around Maya's thick neck. The dog responded by whining and curling her massive body around his legs. Lalo grinned at me from under the brim of his fishing hat. The smell of the sea rose from his clothes, salty and ripe.

"You said you would only be gone for a few days. You could at least have called Ben let him know you wouldn't be able to meet him at the prison when he went to see his client."

"Phone reception wasn't great in Mexico." Lalo shrugged, as if that explained everything. He stepped past me, heading for the kitchen. "I'll talk to Ben tomorrow. Let's eat."

I watched Lalo turn my kitchen upside-down as he pulled out a frying pan and proceeded to gut the fish on my granite counter. Anyone else would have been out of there with that dead fish wrapped around his neck in under ten seconds. Seething at his lack of remorse and his inability to sense that I was piqued, I banged the cabinet doors as I searched for something to add to our meal. Pulling a bag of Arborio rice and a can of chicken broth from the pantry, I slammed them both on the counter. Standing wordlessly next to him I measured a cup of rice into a pot, added butter and stirred, watching as the grains turned a shade of gold.

"Risotto?" Lalo asked.

I responded with cold silence.

"I always throw in a little wine before adding the broth."

"Who asked you?"

"It tastes better that way."

I passed him the wooden spoon and went in search of the wine. Finding the half-empty bottle on the lanai I took a swig before returning to the kitchen. Lalo took the wine from me and added a splash to the rice, then filled two glasses with what remained. We cooked in silence, sipping our drinks as an incredible aroma rose from the stove. Basil, melted butter, white wine, the sea. Maya, who all this time watched us with her intelligent eyes, rose to her feet and left us alone. She soon reappeared, jowls dripping. With a sigh I reached under the sink for the paper towels and bent to mop the trail of water that led back to the toilet. When I returned, Lalo spooned the rice onto our plates.

"Admit it, you missed me."

"Don't flatter yourself," I shot back.

He tossed Maya a tender morsel of fish. The dog snapped her jaws, catching the fish in mid-air. Lalo looked at me, a wide grin on his face. Despite my resolve to stay angry, I smiled back.

NINETEEN

As I sat across from Lalo at my dining room table, the musky smell of his cologne triggered a memory of when we first met. I recalled how uncomfortable I felt next to him in the cramped, dark cabin on his boat. Being that close made my heart pound, and I—a person who prefers to be in control—instinctively knew this man was uncontrollable. His subsequent behavior proved me right. Sudden appearances and disappearances, total disregard for time, the way he looked at me with that half smile. In short, he drove me crazy. Not to mention his intolerable old-fashioned machismo that made me want to slap him into the twenty-first century. And yet . . . there *was* something appealing about him. After being gone for ten days, the guy acted like it was the most natural thing in the world to show up with a dead fish for supper. If he wasn't so clueless about why that struck me as odd, I might have been genuinely annoyed.

Over dinner he asked about Arnie. How he knew I was widowed was beyond me but for once I could talk about my husband without breaking down in tears. I smiled, remembering the good times we had together. Lalo told me about his first wife, his high school sweetheart. Geri came later, and while the marriage ended in a spectacular display of animosity, he admitted that they were once happy together.

We came from different worlds. While I grew up in a middle-class family in New Hampshire, he was the son of migrant agricultural workers. Lalo's childhood offered none of the stability and comfort that I took for granted. And though he spoke openly about his time on the police force, I sensed he held something back. There was more to the man's past than what he was willing to share.

When I brought out a fresh bottle of Chablis, Lalo took it from my hand and removed the cork. I took a sip and smiled at him across the table. Somehow I lost track of the amount I had to drink. As soon as my glass was half-empty, Lalo refilled it. Three glasses? Four? I couldn't remember the last time I drank more than two in a single evening.

With the sun going down, the evening breeze brought a chill into the room. When I stood to close the window, Lalo said, "It is a beautiful night. Let's go out to the lanai where we can get a little fresh air."

"I need a sweater." The falling temperature raised bumps on my arms. "I'll meet you outside."

When I left New Hampshire I foolishly gave my warm clothes to charity thinking I wouldn't need them in Florida. After rooting through my closet, I found an old sweater that I slipped over my blouse. Taking a quick look in the mirror, I noticed a small hole near the collar. On an impulse, I grabbed my good silk scarf and draped it over my shoulders to cover the damage. I found Lalo seated comfortably on the lanai holding his empty wine glass in one hand while rubbing Maya behind her ears with the other. It didn't take long for him to make himself at home.

"You look nice." He fixed his gaze on me. "The color of that scarf matches your eyes."

I felt the blood rush to my cheeks and turned away quickly. "Can I offer you coffee?"

"It is still early. You haven't finished your wine yet."

I glanced down to see my glass filled to the brim. With a nod, I reached for the wine and sat down.

"The wind is coming from the west." Lalo watched me closely. "Can you hear the waves hitting the beach?"

I nodded, listening. "I love living near the sea. But being *on* the water makes me nervous. I honestly don't understand why you choose to live on a boat."

He shrugged. A moment of silence followed. "I don't like being tied down. This way I can raise the anchor and move whenever I want."

Taking another sip, I closed my eyes and felt the room spin. I looked up with a start. "Why are you smiling at me like that?"

"I'm thinking about the first time we met. You acted like a scared rabbit, desperate to get away."

"The boat frightened me."

The way he looked at me, the suggestion that he noticed everything about me made my heart race. I set my glass down and stood, praying I wouldn't sway as the wine went to my head.

"I think I'll make that coffee now. When I come back I'll tell you what I found in Geri's files today."

I felt his eyes on my back as I made my way to the kitchen.

When I returned to the lanai we discussed the case over steaming mugs of black coffee. I told him about Bibi Marks, that I intended to find her and ask about her accusation regarding Logan's threat of violence. Lalo suggested I speak with Logan before tracking the girl down. If her statement were true, then there would be no gain in confronting her. Though I was a little irked for not thinking of that first, I saw the wisdom in his advice.

"Now it's my turn. The bartender at Snook Wallow called me today." He picked up one of the fancy waffle cookies that I set out with the coffee and tossed it to Maya. She snapped her jaws shut and swallowed without chewing.

"Charlie?" My pulse quickened. "What did he say?"

"He said he remembered something. On the night of the murder, when he locked up he heard someone having trouble getting his motorcycle started."

I was suddenly wide-awake. "Boyd had engine trouble that night."

Lalo took a sip of his coffee and nodded. He looked at me over the rim of his mug, waiting for me to say more.

Something wasn't adding up. In my fuzzy mind I tried to reconstruct the events during those early morning hours. Charlie working in the bar, Logan passed out in the woods, the girl's naked body lying cold on a bed of leaves while Boyd struggled to start his motorcycle . . . then it hit me. "Boyd and Ty left long before the bar closed."

Lalo put his cup down without breaking eye contact. "The bar closed at one."

"So Charlie must have heard someone else."

Lalo held my gaze. "What if the boys lied about the time they left?"

I felt that he was prompting me to come up with answers that he already had.

"Why would they?"

Lalo shrugged. "Could have been someone else Charlie heard."

He stood right in front of me. Bending at the waist he brought his face uncomfortably near to mine. I looked up, smelling the wine on his breath as he drew even closer. My heart pounded in my ears, my mind racing. I closed my eyes, waiting for the press of his lips against mine. Instead, I felt the tickle of his breath as he whispered in my ear.

"I should go. Thanks for taking care of Maya while I was gone."

He pulled away, smiling. I nodded dumbly, blinking twice, feeling the heat creep up my neck, wondering why I thought he was about to kiss me.

With a soft click of the door he was gone. I retreated to my bedroom and sat down in front of the dressing table. Reaching into the top drawer I grabbed a pack of cigarettes. Lighting up, I blew smoke at my image in the mirror. Lalo was right, the color of the scarf did bring out the blue in my eyes. Wisps of hair had pulled free of the French twist, falling softly around my face. I noticed for the first time that under the Florida sun my skin turned a golden brown. In all honesty, I didn't look too bad for a woman my age.

I drew in a lungful of smoke, holding it a moment before exhaling. The woman in the mirror stared back at me through the haze. Suddenly, the house felt unusually still, not even the sound of Maya's snoring to break the quiet. I twisted my wedding ring around my finger, then closed my eyes and listened to the silence.

TWENTY

Come morning, I vowed to never touch wine again. I closed the shades against the blazing sun and stood under the shower until the hot water ran out. Despite the aspirin I took with my first mug of coffee, my head pounded. My eyes were still dry as dust when I arrived at the Courthouse.

The moment I entered her department I heard Dix on the phone, her sharp voice drilling into my brain as she chewed out the poor soul on the other end of the line. There was no sign of the elderly gentleman or Fish Man. Their two chairs behind the desks in the small, cramped office sat empty. I dropped a quarter in the box, poured myself a cup of coffee and proceeded directly to the conference room. When I reached the end of the hall I stopped short. Behind the glass wall I saw two gray-haired ladies surrounded by stacks of papers covering the table. One of the women looked up at me and smiled before going back to work sorting through the piles. I turned around and laid a direct course for Dix's office.

As I entered she slammed the receiver down, the sound reverberating in my head. The scowl on her face reflected her bad mood, but I was too annoyed to pave the way with pleasantries.

"There are people in my conference room."

"*Your* conference room?"

"You know what I mean. You said I had the room all day."

One corner of her mouth curled up. "You look awful. Rough night?" She reached into her desk and withdrew the prescription bottle. Shaking two pills into the palm of her hand she popped them into her mouth and swallowed. When she held the bottle out to me I shook my head.

"Suit yourself," she growled. "Seems to me you could use *something*. Sit down and drink your coffee."

I slid into her visitor's chair, setting the heavy canvas bag that contained a growing volume of case files on the floor. The coffee was so weak I suspected whoever made it—probably one of the worker bees in the conference room—forgot that rationing ended more than four wars ago. I gulped greedily. As the hot fluid worked its way into my bloodstream I felt marginally better.

"Change of plans," Dix began. "We're getting visitors today. The prosecutor's office is sending someone down to pick up a set of discovery documents that the volunteers in the conference room are preparing. That makes two problems for me and I need more problems like the devil needs a barbecue grill. First, there isn't enough room in that little office for the ladies to work. Secondly, I can't have anyone from the DA's office catching you plowing through Geri's files or she will skin me alive. So here's what we're going to do. The volunteers get the conference room and you get the office. You'll find the box is already there. Just be sure to close the door and keep it closed. All right then?"

"All right then," I replied with a grin. She scowled. Apparently whatever pill she swallowed didn't improve her sense of humor.

When I stepped into the small office I gagged at the lingering smell of Fish Man. The ladies in my conference room probably took one whiff and told Dix they needed more space for the day, thus relegating me to this dreadful office. I closed the door and flipped the light switch, wondering how long I could stand the odor. As I heaved the box onto the desk, I collected my thoughts.

My overall impression was that Geri had done an amazing job of observing the crime scene and documenting what she saw. It was up to me to analyze everything to see if I could poke holes in her case.

I lifted the lid of the box and stared at the contents. The prior day I made copies of all the technical reports so I dismissed those folders, knowing I could dissect their contents at home. My gaze landed on the shoebox containing the hotline tapes. I wondered how many calls were recorded on those cassettes. Reaching in, I pulled out a piece of paper tucked against the side of the box. After a quick glance, I realized I held a spreadsheet itemizing the date and time of each call as well as the incoming phone number and name of the caller.

A brief comment described each call. *Saw victim at mall. Old girlfriend from high school. Works at Wal-Mart*. The next column ranked the call according to potential. I figured out that the few calls graded as a '5' were considered important enough for a personal visit from a uniformed officer. At the other end of the scale were the dead-end calls. Despite my headache I had to smile when I read, *Caller believes victim is alien from Mars*. I pitied the officer who manned the phone. Six hundred and thirty-eight calls leading nowhere. Even if I started right away, it would take me the whole day to listen to them all. And given the age of those tapes, I doubted anything on them would help me now.

Running my finger down the list, nothing jumped out at me. But as long as I brought my cassette player, I figured it wouldn't hurt for me to pick a few calls and listen. Fortunately, the list identified the location on each tape where the calls were stored, making it possible for me to skip around. Deciding to start with the most promising leads, I unpacked the machine from my canvas bag and got to work.

It took me a while to get the tapes in order but soon I fast-forwarded to the first call of interest. The caller's voice cracked as he identified himself as Bill Woodward of Venice. Woodward said the victim was someone he worked with at a fast food chain in town. His co-worker had disappeared without notice a few days before the murder, but until he saw the sketch in the paper he didn't give her a second thought. The officer taking the call did a professional job of getting all the pertinent information—the girl's name was Sharon Farley—and assuring Woodward that if the tip panned out, the Sheriff's department would be in touch regarding the reward.

Feeling a ping of excitement, I dove into the folder containing the follow-up reports to see if Sharon Farley had slipped through the net. It turned out she was alive and well, working as a clerk for a major grocery chain. She told the officer that she quit the fast-food chain without notice, trading in her paper hat and all the greasy fries she could eat for a better paying job with benefits.

The next five calls followed a similar pattern. All the callers seemed more concerned about how and when they could collect the reward money than anything else. Not one of the tips resulted in a solid lead. I spent a lot of time looking for the location of the calls on the tapes, sometimes over-shooting by a few minutes and sometimes having to listen to a few other calls before finding the one I sought.

I loaded a new cassette into the machine and searched for call number seven. Fast-forwarding to the noted location I pushed 'PLAY' only to hear a woman mid-call speaking rapid Spanish.

Intrigued, I paused the tape and checked the spreadsheet, discovering the call came in fourteen minutes after the one I wanted. The description simply read, *Call disconnected, no follow-up required*. My first inclination was to simply go back to where I wanted to be but with my curiosity piqued, I listened to the caller from the start. With a soft click, the call began.

"Tip line," a male voice answered.

The caller replied in Spanish. I didn't understand a single word of what she said and apparently, the officer manning the phone didn't either.

"Do you speak English?" he asked, the volume of his voice rising with each word.

More Spanish. A heightened level of frustration in the caller's voice.

"What. Is. Your. Name?"

"*Nombre? Su nombre es Juliana Martínez*."

Sure enough, when I checked I saw the officer wrote this down as the name of the caller.

"Okay, Juliana, stay right there on the line while I find someone who can speak Spanish and then we'll take your statement. Comprendo?"

Apparently, Juliana *didn't* understand because she launched into a tirade of more Spanish. A pause, an inflection in her voice like she was asking a question, but when no one answered, she hung up and the line went dead.

Under normal circumstances I would have simply let the machine run until I got to the call I was looking for. But in the final burst of Spanish, I caught a word that started a buzzing in my brain. I rewound the tape and ran it again to see if I heard correctly. After the second try I was certain but I ran it one more time, my heart pounding as I listened to Juliana say something about a place that up until a few days ago I never knew existed.

Michoacán.

A breath of fresh air caused me to look up. Geri Garibaldi stood in the open doorway wearing a tangerine T-shirt, matching lipstick and no jacket. Her nose wrinkled. "Smells like something died in here. Grab your bag, we're leaving."

"Where are we going?" I asked, reaching for my purse.

"There's a place on the bay front, a real tourist spot where we can talk without risk of anyone from my office seeing us. It's time we have a talk."

Detective Garibaldi and I sat on a bench overlooking Sarasota Bay, our backs to a fountain with three magnificent dolphins flying through a spray of water. The landmark drew a constant parade of dog walkers and tourists. I couldn't hear anything they were saying over the noise of the fountain. Presumably they couldn't hear us either which is why I figured Geri picked the spot. As a group of children jumped up and down pointing at something, I turned. A real dolphin appeared in the gray-green water of the bay, his dome-shaped head breaking the surface to suck fresh air through his blowhole before diving back under.

Geri took a bite out of her hot dog. On our way through the park we stopped at a Tiki Hut to buy lunch. I was skeptical about the choice, but she promised it would be the best hot dog I ever ate. After the first nibble, I agreed.

"Beautiful animals," Geri said, following my line of sight. "The folks at Mote Marine figure we have six hundred dolphins in this bay. I never tire of seeing them play out there."

I knew we didn't come to discuss marine life. "Why did you bring me here, Geri?"

"You have someplace better to be?" Swallowing the last of her hot dog, she tucked a lock of blond hair behind her ear before turning toward me. Her eyes were invisible behind the reflective lenses of her black-rimmed sunglasses. "Listen, I'm on your side, remember? Those are my files you've been pawing through. I already explained that we can't discuss this case in my office, so I thought I'd invite you to lunch and ask how it's going."

Before leaving the office I turned off the cassette player, leaving the last tape in the machine. My thoughts revolved around Juliana Martinez. I wondered if she called the hotline again in an attempt to connect with someone who spoke Spanish.

"I do have a question about the hotline calls."

"Shoot."

"There was a Spanish speaking caller, Juliana Martinez. Does that ring a bell?"

Geri furrowed her brow, glancing at me over the rims of her sunglasses. "No, why?"

"She hung up before the guy who answered could get someone who spoke Spanish. I would like to know if she ever called back."

"Did you check the list?"

"No, I'll do that as soon as I get back. But I noticed something else. A lot of callers said they thought the victim was a prostitute who worked the Fish Camp on the weekends."

"Yeah, and?"

"Those calls were never followed-up."

Geri popped the last of her French fries into her mouth, washing them down with a swig of soda before answering. "Obviously you haven't seen the autopsy report yet."

An image of the first page of the coroner's report flashed into my mind. A headshot of Jane Doe, eyes closed, painted lips, jet-black hair falling away from her face, ashy-white in death. Rather than take the time to read the entire thing in Dix's office, I decided to make a copy and add the report o my files for later study at home.

"I haven't got that far."

"Yeah, I figured as much or you wouldn't be asking about those calls. The medical examiner said the girl was a virgin before she was raped that night."

The news took me by surprise. I had assumed all along that the provocatively dressed girl was not as pure as the driven snow. It took me a moment to process the information.

"A virgin?"

Geri nodded. "There's no way to know for sure, but the ME said it looked that way to him. We kept that bit out of the press. It was one way to sort out the bounty hunters from the real deal." She pointed at my untouched fries. "You gonna finish those?"

Suddenly I had no appetite. "Help yourself."

"So tell me." She stuffed a fry into her mouth. "Do you still think Murphy is innocent?"

"I do. But I'm no closer to proving that than when I started."

"You've had time to work on this. Any theories?"

"Not really. A suspicion, maybe. Do you remember Boyd Skinner?"

She pushed her sunglasses to the top of her head and leaned forward. Her eyes narrowed and I could tell by her focused attention that she wasn't surprised at the mention of his name. "The big one. Yeah, I remember. What about him?"

"I get the feeling that he wasn't totally honest with me."

"You think?" I saw a spark in her eye, a look of respect.

"Don't get me wrong, I can't put my finger on what bothers me about the guy." I struggled to put my feelings about Skinner into words. "He was with Ty that whole night, right up until they left Snook Wallow. But he said his parents were asleep so there's no way to prove what time he got home. I'm thinking maybe he turned around and went back—"

"Maybe. There was something about Skinner I never liked."

"You went to his house that night, right?"

"Yeah, but not until after I saw Tyler Fox. Got Fox out of bed. When I asked his parents for permission to look around, they gave me free access to the whole house. I started in the kid's bedroom, looking for his shoes and dirty clothes. They were tossed into a pile on the floor but there was no sign of blood spatter or mud on them. Fox couldn't have stabbed the girl and come away that clean so I figured he wasn't involved. I searched the rest of the premises for the victim's clothes but came up empty."

"After that you went to see Boyd?"

"You should have seen the look on Skinner's face when I flashed my badge. I know the look, saw it all too many times. He was spooked about something, even before I told him why I was there."

"I didn't see anywhere in your files that he was ever considered a suspect."

"Here's the thing. Skinner lived in one of those McMansions on Dona Bay. His parents weren't exactly cooperative. The father knew his rights. Told me I didn't have reasonable cause for search or seizure and if I wanted anything more I could come back with a warrant. Then he grabbed his son by the collar, yanked him back into the house and slammed the door. By the time I tracked down a judge and returned with the warrant Skinner could have bathed and bleached himself to the bone. And his clothes were washed, dried and folded on his dresser."

"So you had nothing on him."

"Right. But from the start I had a bad feeling about that kid."

"Me too." I nodded agreement. "He's not a kid anymore. With his money he'll lawyer up in a heartbeat if we start pressing for more information."

Still, it may be worth grilling Fox to see what else you can learn about Skinner. Or better yet, ask Lalo to do it. He's good at that sort of thing."

Geri pulled her glasses back over her eyes and slurped the last of her soda through the straw. While I took another sip of my drink she dug a compact out of her purse. A quick flick of her fingers through her hair, a swipe of tangerine lipstick and she flashed me a smile.

"Speaking of Lalo, how are you two getting along?" she asked.

Remembering the previous evening, how I had a little too much to drink, I couldn't stop the heat rising to my face.

"Ah, so it *is* like that between you. What happened to his sweet young thing? *She* didn't last long."

"I have no idea."

"Um hmm."

"Not that it's any of your business," I shot back. "But there's *nothing* going on between us. He came over for dinner last night to discuss the case."

"My bad," Geri laughed. "But you can't blame me for jumping to conclusions. Don't forget I know the man. We met when he was still on the force. There was a case we worked together and . . . well, one thing led to another. We had a few good years before things fell apart. But I gotta say, there will always be a soft spot in my heart for him." She gave me a pointed stare over the top of her sunglasses. "Just don't tell him I said so."

A large yacht sailed past on the way to the marina. An elderly couple sat on the back deck sipping drinks while a younger man wearing a captain's hat stood at the helm. I watched in fascination as the man expertly maneuvered the boat into a tight slip. A crew of bronzed teenagers dressed in matching T-shirts appeared from below deck and threw lines onto the floating dock, securing the boat before the captain cut the engine.

I glanced at Geri who seemed lost in thought, a lingering smile on her lips. Perhaps she was still thinking of Lalo, the years they spent together on his old trawler.

"Right up front you advised me to concentrate on discovering the identity of Jane Doe. And the more I get into this, the more I'm convinced you were right. I keep wondering why her family didn't report her missing."

"Keep digging." Geri's smile melted away. "You never know when you're going to catch a break."

"I hope so, for Logan's sake. I'll be finished with your files by the end of the day. Shall I bring everything to your office when I'm done?"

"Dix will take care of getting the box back into storage." She pulled out a business card and wrote a number on the back. "That's my private number. Call me if you need anything," she offered, handing me the card.

"Thank you, Geri. I appreciate your help."

"Don't thank me. I'm doing this for my own peace of mind. I still say something wasn't right with this one. You seem bright enough. Figure this one out, and we'll call it even."

We parted ways, Geri walking briskly down Main Street in the direction of the Courthouse while I lingered to smoke a cigarette. I watched the couple still sitting on the back of the yacht with their drinks. The crew buzzed around the deck, washing down the boat and polishing the chrome trim. I tried to process everything I had learned in the past few days. A bartender's dusty memory, Boyd Skinner's engine trouble, the ex-girlfriend's testimony, calls to the hotline that went nowhere. Despite all that, I was no closer to knowing who killed Jane Doe than when I started. With every lead turning into a dead end, I began to think I never would.

TWENTY-ONE

The girl in the coffee shop looked up, flashing Ben a smile as he approached and peered at him from under her long eyelashes. "Your secretary just left."

"You mean Stephanie?" Ben asked in surprise. During his time at the Defender Project, his paralegal never once bought her own coffee.

"No, the new girl. Long brown hair, brown eyes, freckles across her nose?"

"That must have been my intern, Kim Bailey."

"Oh, well she specifically asked if I knew how you took your coffee. I told her black, and that you always buy a tall, double-shot latte for Stephanie. She left with your coffee and a vanilla cream decaf for herself."

"Did she buy anything else?"

"Nope, just the two coffees."

Ben glanced at the clock on the wall. Ten to eight.

"Okay, give me Stephanie's latte and two jelly donuts."

She counted out his change and as usual, let her fingers rest in his palm longer than necessary. With a smile, Ben grabbed the bag and left, pausing on the sidewalk to look at the cloudless sky. He marveled to think that while his folks up north raked frostbitten leaves from their lawn, the weather in Gainesville was warm enough for him to remove his suit jacket as he walked the two blocks to the office.

Kim stood outside the small, one-story building waiting for him.

"You're early," Ben pulled his keys out of his pocket.

"I stopped for coffee on the way in." Kim held up the orange and pink bag. "I picked one up for you too."

"What do I owe you?" Ben slid a key into the lock and opened the door. His eyes moved from her freckled face to the coffee clutched in her hand.

"This one is on me." Kim glanced down at the matching bag in Ben's hand. "I guess the girl in the coffee shop forgot to mention I bought yours."

"No, she told me. This is for Stephanie."

He held the door and gestured for her to enter his office. After accepting his coffee he watched her peel off the plastic lid on her own cup. With the cup raised to her lips, her eyes scanned the white board mounted on the wall.

"What is all this?" she asked.

Ben opened the bag with the donuts and held it out to her. When she shook her head he reached in and pulled one out for himself. He left his favorite, raspberry, in the bag.

"A case I'm working on." Ben wiped the sugar from his mouth with a napkin.

"This looks like a timeline." Kim moved closer to read the board.

"It is."

"What are you going for here, exoneration?"

"I don't know yet. It's a death penalty case so even if we get the client's sentence commuted to life that would be a win."

"Let me help you with this."

Ben looked at the case files sitting on his desk. Kim impressed him by catching on after only three days on the job. But it was clear that her internship was not going to reduce his workload any time soon. It would be weeks before he could trust her to review a petition on her own, and even then he needed to check her work before submitting anything to the boss. Not to mention that Greg told Ben to limit Kim's activity to learning the ropes as an entry-level worker. Letting her get involved with his case would be going against instructions.

"Thanks for the offer, but I want you to stick to the petitions for now." He waved his hand in the direction of the files on his desk. "Greg's orders."

Ben watched Kim closely while she studied the board. She nodded slowly, and turned to meet his gaze.

"You don't know me well, and coming from that fancy school in New York you probably think I'm just a country hick. But I want to tell you, I'm a fighter. I didn't come here to review petitions and fill out forms. What I want is to get appeals experience. I don't care what the boss says. I want to work on this case."

Ben smiled, amused by the look of determination on her face. "Let's see how you're doing after a few weeks."

"Can you at least give me the highlights?"

Ben glanced at the clock again. Plenty of time before Greg came in. He stepped up to the picture of a dark-eyed Latina on the board and explained, "This is our murder victim, Marcela de la Vega. She came to the country illegally about five years ago and landed a job waiting tables at a bar in Immokalee." Ben pointed to the photo next to Marcela's picture. "That's our client, Ricky Castro. The victim was his girlfriend. Just over two years ago Ricky discovered Marcela's body in an alley behind the bar where she worked. Turns out she was strangled to death. When the police arrived at the scene, they found Ricky kneeling next to the body, crying his heart out." Ben nodded with his chin at the official photo of Moreno that he found on the Collier County website. Moreno was dressed in his uniform, posing for the camera with arms folded over his broad chest. "And that guy is the homicide detective who investigated the murder, Detective Tom Moreno. He was a first responder, getting there before anyone else. Ricky was his prime suspect. He based his case on the testimony of a jailhouse snitch, a guy by the name of Diego Salazar." Ben pointed to the only other photo on his board, the mug shot of Salazar looking disheveled, eyes bloodshot, his greasy hair plastered to his scalp.

"That's why Greg approved Castro's petition." Kim's eyes glittered. "The jailhouse snitch. One of the red flags you told me to look for."

"I see you were listening. The snitch was the first thing that caught my attention. Unfortunately, Salazar is unavailable for questioning. As it happens, he was killed two months after the trial."

"You must have something else to go on or you wouldn't still be working on this."

"Potentially, yes. But it's too soon to tell if anything will pan out."

"Email me the Court Summary, and a copy of the trial transcript so I can get up to speed."

Ben arched an eyebrow, glanced at the folders on his desk then back at her.

"Background," she said quickly. "I'll read it on my own time."

"I guess there's no harm in that. After I log into the system I'll shoot you a link to the files."

"I have a confession to make, Ben." Kim bent over to toss her empty cup into the trash. Turning around, she leaned against his desk, "I looked you up on the Internet last night."

He was about to ask what she meant when the sound of someone clearing her throat caused him to spin around with a start.

"My coffee?" Stephanie asked, aiming a fire engine red fingernail at the bag on his desk.

"Right here. I guess I forgot to put it on your desk."

"Um hmm." Stephanie looked past Ben at Kim who was still leaning against the desk, smoothing her skirt.

"Am I interrupting something?"

"I was about to tell Ben that I went online and found a paper he published in his school's law review. Impressive."

"Do you make a habit of poking around, spying on your co-workers?"

Ben stole a glance at Kim. He couldn't see any harm in what she had done. After all, everything on the Internet was public information.

"Only those who count." Pushing herself away from the desk she brushed by Stephanie on the way out.

"What a bitch," Stephanie hissed under her breath.

"I don't think she meant anything by it."

"No? Come on, open your eyes."

"She's just a kid. In four months her internship will be over and she'll be out of here."

"Don't be so sure," Stephanie picked up her coffee and headed for the door. "I know the type. Watch your back, Shepherd. She's probably angling for your job."

Left alone in his office, Ben stared out the window, watching as his boss pulled up in a white Audi. With a click of his key fob, Greg locked the car, headlights flashing in confirmation. Ben wondered why, out of all the applicants he interviewed, Greg offered Kim an internship with the firm. The legal profession was filled with people driving hard to get ahead and Kim was just one more. Greg must have seen something behind that small-town-girl image Kim projected.

He turned on his computer and with a few quick clicks of his mouse he found the documents his intern requested. He hesitated, hands poised over his keyboard as he wondered if he was making a mistake by letting Kim get involved with the Castro case. On the other hand, he could use all the help he could get and Kim was obviously motivated to do a good job. With a push of the button, he sent the files.

Ignoring the petitions piling up in his in-basket, Ben pulled out Moreno's blue binder. When Cate suggested he should focus on the detective, she was right on the money as usual. Ben decided to put all his efforts into determining if Moreno had conducted his investigation within the boundaries of the law. From the start, Lalo cautioned him that Moreno might be holding something back. Ben was not surprised to find the information in the binder contained insufficient evidence to charge Castro with a traffic violation, let alone first-degree murder.

Ben wondered if Moreno played him. There was no apparent order to the file, no table of contents, no index. Everything seemed to be shoved together haphazardly with at least half of the pages loosely stuffed between the few ring-bound sheets. Ben decided to put things in chronological order and read through everything again. Reaching for his second donut, he put his feet up on the edge of his desk and took a look at the Crime Scene Report.

The form was filled out by hand, the scrawl hard to read. Having seen many other crime scene reports, Ben guessed he was looking at a copy of Moreno's rough notes taken at the scene and not the official, typed version of the report.

At the top of the form the detective scribbled the date, weather, and time he arrived at the scene. A list of responders included Deputy L. Lamb and Deputy M. Swift of the CCSD, the Collier County Sheriff's Department. Also responding was the Lehigh Regional Medical Center ambulance crew, no names provided. Time of arrival was noted as between 13:45 and 13:52. On the line titled, "Summons" Moreno wrote, "Hector Navas, 13:35." Ben seemed to remember Moreno greeting the El Rincón bartender as 'Hector' so presumably he was the person who made the initial call to the 911 operator ten minutes before the police arrived at the scene.

Ricky Castro was listed as the sole eyewitness.

What followed was barely legible. For his own benefit, Ben decided to open a new document on his computer and type the information as it appeared on the form in Moreno's binder, spelling mistakes and all.

> Victim, Marcela de la Vega, DOB. 8/5/92 (20 yrs.), approx. 5'4" 105 lbs, blk hair, found lying on her back, face up in alley behind El Rincón. Wound on left cheek, gravel and dirt stuck to victim's knees. Victim wearing pink T-shirt, black skirt, no underware, high heel shoes. Thin gold band on victim's right ring finger, gold hoop earings in both ears and small diamond (?) stud in nose. Body discovered in same location by the witness, Ricky Castro. Castro found kneeling next to the victim. Appears distressed. Castro resists efforts of L. Lamb to check for victims pulse. M. Swift removes Castro from area. L. Lamb checks for pulse in neck and listens to chest and mouth for breathing. L. Lamb determines body still warm. A pink, beaded handbag is on the ground near the victim. Inside the bag is lipstick, cell phone, plastic sunglasses, a pair of pink panties and one-hundred fifty dollars in cash, as follows: Four twenties, two tens, one fifty dollar bill. Coroner David Graves, MD arrived on scene 15:35 hours. Removed victim at 16:50 hours to Lehigh Regional morgue. Preliminary finding, homicide due to strangulation. Time of death approx. between 12:45 and 13:45 hours.

The remainder of the report included crude crime scene sketches placing Marcela's body next to the dumpster behind the bar. Moreno found a vehicle registered to Ricky Castro parked at the end of the alley. A separate sheet itemized Marcela's beaded bag and the items found inside. According to the report, no additional evidence was removed from the scene.

At the bottom of the form Moreno noted that Deputy Lamb logged the evidence chain into the CCSD locker. Moreno secured the scene at 18:00 hours.

Ben rubbed his eyes and leaned back in his chair to gaze at the white board. Something about the evidence in the victim's purse bothered him. Struck by a thought he opened a file on his computer titled, "Castro trial transcript" and scrolled through the pages until he found what he was looking for. The money from the purse was entered into evidence as exhibit 75B. Included in the list were four twenties and two tens. One hundred dollars in total. The fifty-dollar bill was not listed anywhere.

Ben then went to the CCSD website and searched for Deputy Lamb. In a matter of seconds Lamb's image stared back at him from the screen, arms folded, unsmiling, mustache trimmed above his upper lip. With a click of his mouse, Ben sent a copy of the deputy's career summary and contact details to his printer. He then grabbed the printout and wrote with a red marker, CHAIN OF EVIDENCE? under Lamb's image. After taping it to the white board Ben stood back, his mind racing. The crime scene report, bad as it was, had given him something to work with. He knew calling Moreno at this point would be useless but Ben wondered if Deputy Lamb could explain what happened to the missing fifty. Deciding he had nothing to lose, he sat down at his desk, picked up his cell phone and checked the number on the screen.

Poised with his finger on the phone, something on the website caught his eye. Lamb was no longer based in the Immokalee substation. The deputy now worked out of the South County sheriff's office in Ochoppee. With a burst of adrenaline, Ben searched until he found what he was looking for, Lamb's transfer date. His heart pounding, he grabbed a stack of papers from his desk drawer and paged through them, stopping when he found the date Diego Salazar's body turned up in the dumpster. Leaning back in his chair Ben blew a low, whistling sound through his pursed lips.

The dates matched.

TWENTY-TWO

A chilly silence came through the line when Ben explained why he called. If Deputy Leroy Lamb had any recollection of Marcela de la Vega or Ricky Castro, he did not let on.

"The murder occurred during your time in Immokalee," Ben prompted.

"I remember," Lamb replied. "I'm just wondering why you're asking."

"I'm an attorney with the Defender Project."

"So you said, Counselor."

"And I hoped you could answer a few questions I have regarding the chain of evidence recovered at the scene. I understand there was a problem with one of the bills found in the victim's purse."

"I've been all through that stuff about the serial numbers with the DA's office," Lamb replied. "You can look it up in the court records for yourself. I don't have nothing more to say on the subject."

"I'm not looking to make any trouble for you, Deputy Lamb. I just want to understand what happened. Did you make a mistake when you wrote down the number?"

"Why don't you ask Detective Moreno? Castro was his collar."

Ben hesitated. He knew his next move would be critical. One misstep and he risked shutting down the conversation with Lamb for good. On the other hand, if he played his cards carefully he could potentially get the break he needed in his case. All he had to go on was his instinct. That and the coincidental timing of Lamb's transfer occurring immediately after Salazar's body was found. And Ben didn't believe in coincidences.

"I don't trust Moreno," Ben replied, rolling the dice. "And I'm beginning to suspect you don't either."

Now it was Lamb's turn to hesitate. After another long stretch of silence Ben spoke again. "Look, you don't know me and I don't know you. Can we meet somewhere to discuss this in private? I'll buy you a drink and we can see where this goes."

"Yeah, maybe we could do that. Where do you have in mind?"

"You pick the place. I'll be driving down from Gainesville."

"I'd rather not do this anywhere near my station. I can drive a bit north and meet you part way."

"Can you make it to Bradenton tomorrow?"

"Tomorrow's not good. How about Friday, say eleven o'clock?"

"Perfect. I'll text you the address."

With a sigh of relief, Ben disconnected the call.

Leroy Lamb was not a heavy man, but as they faced each other on the pier at the Twin Dolphins Marina, Ben figured the lanky deputy towered a good six inches above him. Lamb showed up in civilian clothes, chinos and a polo shirt. Removing his suit coat, Ben loosened his tie and unfastened the top button of his shirt. Rolling up his sleeves, he gestured for Lamb to follow him onto Lalo's trawler.

Lamb ducked under the low threshold as they entered the cabin. He looked around. "Nice boat. Is it yours?"

"Belongs to a friend of mine," Ben replied.

Before they arrived Lalo had set out a few cans of soda, a bucket of ice, and two semi-clean glasses. An unopened bottle of rum stood on the table.

"This is all off the record, right Counselor?"

"If that's the way you want it, Deputy. I promise this conversation will be confidential. No one will ever know you're my source. But I have to warn you, if you tell me something that will help my client, I will use it to the best of my ability."

"Fair enough. Let's say you start by calling me Leroy."

"Okay, Leroy. Would you like something to drink?"

"A soda sounds good." Lamb licked his lips, eyeing the bottle of rum.

After dropping a fistful of ice into both glasses, Ben popped open a can and filled them to the brim. The boat rocked gently as Lamb took a sip.

"Obviously you called me because of the problem with that fifty." The deputy set his glass back on the table.

"I looked up the court record as you suggested. The serial number on the bill didn't match what you wrote on the evidence bag."

Ben slid a new can of soda across the table. Lamb ignored it.

"Castro's lawyer made a big deal over that. Because of the problem with the money, he wanted to get all the evidence in that purse tossed out. In the end, like everything with the law, the judge told the lawyers to compromise. The fifty was thrown out, everything else, including the rest of the money, stayed in."

"Walk me through this." Ben sipped his drink slowly. "Tell me exactly what happened."

"I picked up the victim's purse from the ground and opened it. 'Course I put gloves on first, you know, SOP, standard operating procedure. First thing I saw inside was a few folded bills, fifty on the outside. Didn't know exactly how many until later when I had it all spread out on the bar."

"You brought the evidence into the bar?"

"Yeah, it was August, stinking hot in that alley. Stunk to high heaven too, what with that dumpster right there. Body was still warm but the flies already started to show interest." Lamb reached for the bottle of rum and topped up his glass. He passed the bottle to Ben who hesitated before adding a drop to his own soda. Taking a polite sip he told Lamb to continue.

"So Moreno, he says let's go inside where it's cool and we can get this paperwork done. He tells Mikey—that was my partner, Mike Swift—he tells Mikey to stay outside with the suspect."

"The suspect being Castro?" Ben asked.

"Right, Castro. So I go out front and get an evidence bag out of my patrol car, then come back in and spread everything on the bar so's I can inventory the contents of the victim's purse."

"Did you bring the purse with you when you went to the car?"

"Yeah, SOP. You don't let the evidence out of your sight until you seal the bag. So I go back inside and empty the purse on the bar. I start with the fifty, write the serial number down and pick up one of the tens when suddenly Moreno looks up from his paperwork and says, 'Hey Leroy, go out back and make sure your partner Mirandized the suspect.' Like we were a pair of rookies. I say Mikey knows enough to read the guy his rights, but Moreno, he insists. And he's the senior officer on the scene so I do what he tells me to do. I go out back and check with Mikey. 'Course he looks at me like I'm crazy or something, then he says sure, he already took care of it. I was out there for two minutes, max. When I get back everything is exactly as I left it. Moreno is still writing his report and I finish inventorying the evidence."

"I thought you stated it was standard operating procedure to keep the evidence in sight until the bag is sealed."

"Yeah," Lamb finished his drink, the ice cubes rattling against his teeth. Opening up the new can of soda he filled his glass half full and added another splash of rum. "I probably should have told Moreno to go out and check with Mikey himself. I tell you Counselor, I screwed up big time that day."

"Listen, if I'm going to call you Leroy you should call me Ben."

"Okay, Ben," he took another swallow. "Anyway, where was I?"

"Back in the bar. Everything was as you left it and you went back to writing the serial numbers of the rest of the bills on the evidence bag. Tell me, was there anyone else in the bar at that time beside Moreno?"

"Yeah, the bartender. Hector was there. When the Collier County prosecutor decided to blame me for the screw-up, they called Hector in as a witness. Both he and Moreno swore that neither of them touched any of the evidence when I went outside."

"So how do you account for the mistake?"

Lamb gave Ben a sickly smile and raised his glass to his lips. "It wasn't no mistake, Counselor. I can promise you that." He drained his glass and set it down carefully. "I wasn't off by one or two digits. The whole serial number was different from what I wrote down. Eleven years on the force and I never once made a mistake like that. You can check. 'Cept for this one time, my service record is clean."

"So what happened?"

"It's obvious, isn't it? Someone switched out that fifty."

"Who?"

"I'm not saying that . . . Listen, Immokalee is a hard beat. You can't believe the stuff that goes on in that place. Don't get me wrong, there are lots of good people, hard working people there. But they come here looking for the American dream and they end up living in a nightmare. The conditions some of them live in . . . ten, twenty people crammed into a trailer with no running water and sewage backing up into their yards. Places like that, everyone struggling to make ends meet, drugs, gangs, the cartel . . . All I'm saying is that being a cop in that kind of place is tough. Sometimes you have to go along to get along, you know what I mean?"

"I'm not sure I do."

"For the better good. To keep the peace. You make your choices and do the best you can."

"I still don't get it. Why don't you just come out and tell me what you're trying to say?"

"Off the record, right?"

"Off the record."

"Moreno, he sometimes does things to help people he maybe shouldn't. And if those people show their appreciation in a certain way—say a contribution to his retirement fund—he doesn't argue."

"You think *he* switched the fifty when you went out to the car? Why would he do that?"

"Who knows? Maybe he was protecting the girl's john. You know, fingerprints and all that. All's I know is I wrote down the serial number of a certain fifty dollar bill, and when the county prosecutor opened the envelope, a different fifty was in there. What difference does it make anyway? The jury convicted your guy without even knowing about that money."

Lamb picked up his empty glass and stared at the melting ice. Ben reached for the bottle of rum and started to pour when the deputy waved him off. "I gotta be going. Thanks for the drink."

Ben's mind ran down the list of things he wanted to cover with Lamb. He knew he may never get another chance to speak with the deputy and he might have missed something. Lamb slid to the edge of the bench, getting ready to leave.

"One more thing." Ben rested his hand on Lamb's arm. "The crime scene report showed Moreno was first to arrive at the scene. Is it normal for a detective to be called out before the uniforms?"

"No. But Moreno said he was having lunch next door at Chaparrito's when the call came over the radio so he got there first. Mikey and me arrived maybe five minutes later."

Ben felt there was something important in that small detail, but he could not get his hands around it. Reaching into his pocket he pulled out his business card and passed it to the deputy.

"Thank you for meeting me, Leroy. If I can ever return the favor, let me know."

"I can't imagine that happening, what with you being on the other side of the table, so to speak. But there is one thing you can clear up for me."

"What's that?"

"When you called, you mentioned something about not trusting Moreno. What made you say that?"

"I noticed the date on your transfer request form," Ben replied.

"Yeah, so?"

"You asked to be reassigned on the same day Moreno's snitch turned up with a bullet in his head."

The only sound in the cabin was the purr of an engine as a boat passed by. Lamb stood, swaying unsteadily. Ben saw him grab the table to keep from falling.

"Yeah, Salazar. Did you know I brought him in the day that girl was murdered?"

"I read the arrest report," Ben replied.

"Well, what you don't know is that right after Moreno threw your client in jail he told me to find Salazar and arrest him. When I asked him what for he said I could be creative. Well, it wasn't a great stretch. Salazar had enough Oxy in his pockets to charge him with possession of a controlled substance with intent to distribute."

"Were you involved with the deal to get him to snitch on Ricky Castro?"

"No, that's the thing. Salazar was my collar but the minute I brought him in Moreno dismissed me and he directed it from there. I was pissed off at the time but looking back I guess he did me a favor by keeping me out of it."

"Do you have any idea who might have killed Salazar?"

"The crowd he ran with, could've been anybody. But when I heard the news, I figured it was time to get out of Dodge. Watch yourself, Counselor." Lamb gave Ben a cold, hard stare. "You're swimming with the sharks down there."

TWENTY-THREE

The melting ice shifted in Ben's glass when someone stepped onto the deck above. Heavy footsteps together with the patter of Maya's paws announced Lalo's return. Ben looked up as the dog scrambled down the stairs and leapt onto the bench next to him. Face-to-face with the panting Rottweiler, he slid over a few inches to give her room. Maya flopped down with a grunt, resting her head on his lap.

"How did it go?" Lalo asked as he grabbed the handrails and swung down into the cabin. His feet never touched the stairs.

"I'm not sure what to make of Deputy Lamb," Ben replied.

"Did he know anything about Moreno's snitch?"

"Nothing that helps. We did have an interesting conversation though."

Lalo poured a shot of rum and downed it in one swallow. "What's bothering you?" he asked.

"Who said something is bothering me?"

"Everyone has a tell, a nervous habit. You? You crack your knuckles."

Ben made a fist and stretched his fingers wide.

"Aunt Cate is always on my case about that. Just like my mother, warning me that I'm going to get arthritis when I'm old."

"Yeah, well Cate has her own tell, doesn't she?"

"Cigarettes, right?"

Lalo chuckled. "Right."

Ben watched Lalo's face, reading something in the investigator's smile. "You like her, don't you?" he asked.

Lalo poured himself another shot, ignoring Ben's question and asked, "So what did Lamb say?"

"We mostly talked about the problem with the serial number on the money in Marcela's purse. I promised to keep our conversation confidential so I can't go into detail."

"Then let me ask another way. Did the guy give you anything useful?"

"Maybe." Ben paused, reaching for the answer. It was the question he had asked himself since Lamb left the boat. "Tell me, can a fingerprint be lifted from a fifty-dollar bill?"

"That depends," Lalo replied. "These days lab techs have chemicals that work pretty well, even with paper. But the main problem with cash is there are too many prints. They overlap, making it difficult to isolate one with enough points."

Ben knew that forensics experts ran fingerprints through their local databases, hoping to find a match. The system compared fingerprints at various points on the whorls and grooves. Twelve points was the minimum necessary for most systems to come up with a positive identification.

"So theoretically speaking, if someone handled the money and it didn't change hands again, the forensics guys could lift a print."

"I'd say that was a good possibility."

"Then that's why Moreno switched the money," Ben murmured. "He knew the person who gave Marcela that money."

Lalo stared at Ben, his dark eyes unblinking. "Are we still speaking theoretically? Because I think you just accused Moreno of evidence tampering."

"Yeah, I guess I did. Problem is I can't prove it."

"What about witnesses? Was Moreno alone when this switch *allegedly* occurred?" Lalo asked.

"Lamb said the bartender was there, Hector Navas."

Lalo pressed his lips together. "Don't waste your time talking to Navas. I'm guessing he'd lie rather than get his friend in trouble. But let's assume you're right and Moreno did switch the money. Why would he do that?"

"Lamb suggested Moreno was protecting someone, maybe Marcela's john." Ben parsed his words carefully. "But Moreno's motive doesn't matter. If the investigating officer didn't conduct himself within the boundaries of the law, we could accuse him of misconduct and request a judicial hearing. That brings me back to what I said earlier. We need proof."

Ben's phone pinged. He glanced down and tapped the screen, scrolling down to read the message. With a smile he slipped the phone back into his back pocket.

"Anything important?" Lalo asked.

"Stephanie is going ballistic. I think she's ready to strangle my intern."

"Do you need to call the office?"

"That's the last thing I want to do. Tell me how your trip to Mexico went."

Lalo reached into his pocket and pulled out a set of keys. "I make it a rule not to talk on an empty stomach. There's a little place down the river where we can get something to eat. Maya likes their fish tacos."

The *Chilanga* sailed beyond the sea wall and cut across the choppy river with hardly a tremor. Once Lalo steered the boat to the far bank he headed west. After about thirty minutes the river grew wider, the waterway broken up by small islands inhabited by hundreds of brown pelicans. Though Lalo held the boat steady, the *Chilanga* rocked on the waves. In the cabin below one of the cans of soda rolled off the table and hit the floor with a thud.

"We just entered Tampa Bay," Lalo yelled above the roar of the engine. "That's why it's a little choppy here."

"Is that the Skyway Bridge?" Ben asked pointing to the structure on the right. Rays from the late afternoon sun illuminated the yellow arches against a cloudless sky.

Lalo nodded as he spun the wheel hard, turning the boat away from the bridge. "We'll be passing between Anna Maria Island and the mainland. Things will get quieter soon."

As soon as they entered the inland waterway the boat stopped rocking. Traffic was heavy in either direction, small pleasure boats speeding by as they headed out to the bay. Lalo steered the *Chilanga* behind a large commercial fishing boat, its nets spread like wings. Ben noticed they once again rode with the current, the surface of the water untroubled by the wind.

Lalo reached into his shirt pocket and pulled out an envelope that he tossed to Ben. "Take a look."

Ben glanced down, recognizing the name on the envelope. Inside he found a letter written in Spanish.

"Is this the letter Aunt Cate took from Luci's room?"

Lalo had the same amused look on his face as when Cate's name came up earlier. "Your aunt stole that right from under Moreno's nose. The return address on the envelope led me to a small fishing village in Michoacán where Luci's mother lives. How good is your Spanish?"

Ben passed over the words he did not recognize but managed well enough to understand the gist of it. He looked up at Lalo in surprise.

"Do I understand this correctly? It sounds like Luci's mother thought her daughter found a good job waiting tables at a fancy restaurant in Immokalee."

"Yes. And that Luci planned to get married and start a family soon. All lies, of course. I didn't have the heart to tell the woman her daughter was a prostitute."

"But Luci's brother also lives in Immokalee. He must have known the truth."

"I suppose he kept her secret to protect her honor. When he called to tell their mother Luci died, he didn't say anything about how she lived."

Ben shook his head, remembering the young Latina. The image of her walking down the street in her high heels remained etched on his brain.

"Luci's mother is under the impression that Norma Martin is a saint," Lalo continued. "Every time she mentioned her name she made the sign of the cross. By the way, Norma's last name is actually Martinez, not Martin. She came from the same village and left with her sister about twelve years ago. They crossed the border with the help of a *coyote*. Since then Norma has become something of a legend down there. Girls risk crossing the border knowing that once they get to Immokalee Norma will take them in, find them jobs and protect them from immigration officials."

"You're kidding, right?"

Lalo shrugged. "As they say in Mexico, *me temo que no*. I'm afraid not. Luci assured her mother that there was no risk of being deported because Norma paid for police protection."

"And she believed that?"

"Hey, for all I know it's the truth. I'm guessing Moreno was on the take."

"So what happened to Norma's sister? Is she involved in this human trafficking ring too?"

Lalo shook his head. "The sister, Juliana apparently fell victim to the evils of *el norte*. About one year after coming to the States she became pregnant, ran away with her boyfriend and never contacted her family again. Every day the mother lights a candle in the church for her younger daughter, but the father has disowned her."

Ben stared at the birds circling the fishing boat. The details behind Norma's operation were taking shape, but so far nothing Lalo told him—aside from the possibility Norma paid Moreno for police protection—seemed to help his case.

"Did you look up Marcela's folks while you were down there?" Ben asked.

"I spoke with her father. He believes what Norma told him, that Ricky Castro killed his daughter in a fit of jealous rage. As soon as the man realized who I worked for, he threw me out. I'm afraid I didn't get anything that could help with the case. Not from him anyway."

Up ahead the fishing boat left the channel and turned into a marina. The *Chilanga* continued straight under a bridge, the rumble of cars driving over the metal grate above breaking the silence on board.

Ahead Ben saw a fishing pier jut out from shore. Pulling back on the throttle, Lalo turned to him and directed with a wave, "I need you to get on the bow. When we get close enough to the pier, cast a line to the guy on the dock so he can tie us up."

Ben saw a thin, bewhiskered man put down his fishing pole and wave. He threw short on the first try but the old man caught the rope on the second attempt. When the line went tight, Ben felt the boat shift under his feet as it bumped against the old tires nailed to the boards of the dock. Lalo cut the engines and whistled for Maya. The dog came bounding up the stairs and made a flying leap onto the pier where she ran directly to the fisherman and sniffed his crotch.

The guy smiled a toothless smile. "Crazy dog." He gently pushed Maya away, reaching down to scratch the dog behind her ears. Maya closed her eyes, and wagged her tail.

"I see you got a new crew member there, Lalo," the old man called out.

"Friend of mine," Lalo called back from the stern of the boat.

Ben turned to Lalo. "Right before you docked the boat it sounded like you wanted to tell me something."

"Oh, right. While I was down in Mexico I took the opportunity to track down information about the smuggling cartel Norma works for."

"That's straying a bit far from the point. My job is to find a legal solution to get Ricky Castro off death row. And from everything we've learned so far, it looks like Moreno is the key to getting that done. We need to concentrate on him, not the cartel."

"So you don't want to hear what I found?"

"That's not what I mean. My point is, you know . . . we should stay focused."

Lalo gave Ben a wide smile, exposing the gap between his front teeth. "Remember when Castro mentioned Norma's boss? The guy she channels all the money through?"

"Ricky said his name was Angel. But he didn't know the guy's last name."

"It just so happens that the *coyote* who brought Norma across the border is her boyfriend, Angel. He's a small fish in a giant operation, but in the past ten years he's done a good job of growing the business in Immokalee. The big boys in Mexico are starting to take notice."

"Stop grinning like a fool and just tell me his last name."

"Abarco. The guy's name is Angel Abarco."

Lalo stepped off the boat, shook hands with the fisherman and headed toward shore. Maya trotted by her master's side with Ben running to catch up. They turned down a side street, stopping in front of a building that looked like it was about to slip off its pilings and fall into the water. A board outside listed the lunch specials.

"Fish tacos, huh?"

"The best around." Lalo stopped and faced Ben, all trace of his smile gone. "Listen, if I find Abarco had anything to do with Marcela's murder, you'll be the first to know. But this thing could get tricky. I need to run this angle of the investigation alone."

Ben slowly nodded. By the tone of Lalo's voice, he suspected his investigator's interest in the cartel ran deeper than his search into Marcela de la Vega's death. He knew the man well enough to know that no matter what he said, Lalo was going to work his own agenda. Ben only hoped that Lalo didn't waste too much time on this Abarco guy before he turned his attention back to what mattered—nailing Moreno.

TWENTY-FOUR

Glancing down at his speedometer, Ben eased his foot off the gas pedal of his old BMW. The blue lights rode up on his bumper showing no sign of passing. Ben pulled over. In the time it took for the trooper to get out of his patrol car, Ben had his license and registration ready to hand over.

"Please remain in your car, Mr. Shepherd. I'm going to run your information through the system. Won't take but a minute."

Ben drummed his fingers on the steering wheel, wishing the guy would be quick about it. Checking his watch, he figured there was still an outside chance he could make it back to the office in time to catch Stephanie before she left for the day.

Driving two hours north on I-75 had given Ben time to think. After the meetings with Deputy Lamb and Lalo, he felt he had a solid picture of what happened to Marcela de la Vega. Soon he could sit down with his boss and lay it all out for him. But Greg did not suffer half-baked theories. Ben still had to nail down a few details.

The trooper reappeared, a pink slip clutched in his hand.

"I clocked you going eighty-three back there," he said.

"Sorry officer. I'm in a hurry to get back to my office and I guess I wasn't paying attention to how fast I was going."

"Okay, well, slow down, drive carefully and have a good day.

Ben waited for the trooper to pull out before he rejoined the stream of cars heading north. As soon as the patrol car turned off the interstate and stopped behind a stand of trees on the median, Ben pressed down on the accelerator. His car jumped ahead as he reached for his phone. Keying in the passcode with his thumb he saw he had four missed messages from Kim. Ignoring them, he pressed Stephanie's cell phone number. The call went directly into voicemail.

"I'm running late, but if you can wait for me, I could use your help with something."

With another glance at his watch, Ben figured he might just catch her in time.

Stepping into the dark building, he saw Stephanie's desk was clean, everything put away for the weekend. As he reached for the light switch he noticed a glow coming from under his office door at the end of the hall. At least Stephanie thought to leave his desk lamp on, knowing he was coming back to the office.

"Is that you, Ben?" a female voice called.

"Stephanie?" he called back.

A freckled face appeared in the doorway. "No, it's me, Kim, I've been waiting for you. How was your day?"

"What are you doing in my office?"

"Putting a file on your desk. I finished processing my second petition today. I've got time if you want to take a look at it now."

Finished? That sounded improbable to Ben. When he began working at the Project it took him three weeks to process his first petition. And another two for the second. Either she was a genius or Kim had cut corners in an effort to impress him with her output.

"You probably have better things to do than hang around here. I'll look at it on Monday."

"If you say so. By the way, when I went through the stack of open petitions I found a rejection letter you forgot to send. I gave it to Greg for his signature." She looked at him, a big grin spreading across her face.

"What letter are you talking about?" Ben tried to keep his voice steady.

"Logan Murphy."

"Has Greg signed the letter yet?"

"No, I put it on his desk after he left. Why? Is there a problem?"

"You should have checked with me first."

Kim put her hands on her hips and looked him straight in the eye. "I tried to call you. Several times, as a matter of fact. You didn't answer so I made a decision. When I first started here you told me that you don't have time to check every little thing I do and that I should use my own judgment."

"There's a reason that case is still open," Ben replied, pinching the bridge of his nose between his thumb and index finger. "But as long as Greg hasn't seen the letter I guess there's no harm done."

He looked at Kim, trying to read the expression on her face. She broke contact, her eyes focusing on something behind him. He turned around to see Stephanie holding a large pizza box in one hand while she shoved her keys into her purse with the other.

"I brought dinner."

Stephanie dismissed Kim saying she and Ben had work to do. After Kim left, Ben retrieved the letter from Greg's desk and ran it through the shredder. When he returned to his office, Stephanie told him the other interns were starting to complain about Kim.

"I'm telling you, Shepherd, she's got to go."

Ben shook his head. He knew firing Kim was not an option. Greg expected him to give her every opportunity to complete a successful internship with the Project. The boss wanted to get as much free work out of the deal as possible. For better or worse, Ben was stuck with the girl for the next few months.

"She rubs me the wrong way too, but she's getting the work done."

"I've seen loads of interns come and go, trust me, I know trouble when I see it."

Ben thought about Kim giving Logan's rejection letter to Greg without consulting him. But now that the letter was destroyed, he could relax. Kim's intentions were good even if her judgment was bad. After all, she had no way of knowing that he intentionally kept Logan Murphy's case open and hidden from the boss. He looked down at the completed petition on his desk and shook his head.

"I'll ask her to make an effort to get along with the other interns." He glanced up at Stephanine.

"You left me a message. Something about needing my help?"

"When I came in and saw your desk I figured you were out with your date."

Stephanie wrinkled her nose. "To be honest, I was glad to have an excuse to cancel our date. He's a bit too desperate, if you know what I mean. I figured we needed to take a break."

Ben waited, wondering if she was giving him an opening. Deciding to play it cool, he let it go. If her new romance ran the same course as all her others, in a month or two this guy would be history and Ben could try again.

Stephanie stared at him with her green eyes. "So tell me, what do you want?"

Another opening? He looked at her, searching for a clue. Nothing in her expression suggested she was flirting so he got straight down to business.

"Well, since I started here I've only worked the incoming desk," he began.

Stephanie nodded, one corner of her mouth turning up in a smirk.

"Ricky Castro is my first real client. I want to show Greg I can handle the case without running to him every time I need advice."

"Come out with it, Shepherd. This isn't the first time a rookie lawyer asked me to explain something."

"I haven't got a clue how to go about issuing a subpoena."

"And you don't want Greg to know how clueless you are. Sure, I'll help. But it'll cost you."

"How much?"

"Dinner at Chouko's tomorrow night."

"Deal."

"Okay, so what's this subpoena for?"

"Norma Martin's telephone records. On the day Marcela de la Vega was killed Norma made a phone call around eleven o'clock in the morning. I want to know who was on the other end of that call."

"Then what you need is a judicial subpoena *duces tecum.*"

"A what?"

"They don't teach you anything about actually practicing law in law school, do they? Subpoena *duces tecum,* a subpoena to produce evidence. In this case, you want the phone company to produce the records of one of their customers. They won't do that without a judge's signature. Do you have enough cause to get one?"

"An eye witness told me she overheard Norma tell someone to come and get Marcela. That was the last time she was seen alive."

"That should be good enough," Stephanie said. "I'll help you fill out the form so you can take it to the Court Clerk's Office on Monday. If the judge questions you, keep it vague. Say you need the phone records to identify a potential new witness."

"Great. I think this is going to give me all I need to make the case."

"You're talking like you already know what the record will show."

"Yeah, I do. Norma called Tom Moreno."

"A cop? Are you out of your mind? You need to tell Greg before you go poking that hornet's nest."

"Not yet. I want to be sure first. I'll fill the boss in as soon as I can confirm that it was Moreno."

Fifteen minutes later Stephanie sent the completed subpoena request from her computer to the printer. She handed the paper to Ben with a smile.

"I can't wait to see Billy's face when I tell him we're going to Chouko's tomorrow. I wanted him to take me there last weekend, but he says the place is way out of his budget."

Ben just stared at her.

"What? You didn't think that . . . wait, you thought that you and I . . . Seriously?"

"No, of course not," Ben replied. "Just go easy with the wine list, okay? You know what a rookie lawyer earns around here."

After she was gone, Ben sat in the silence of his office, his mind running in several directions at once. He was usually pretty good at reading people, especially women. But Stephanie was sending mixed signals. Obviously, he got it wrong this time.

His thoughts turned to the subpoena safely tucked away in his messenger bag. If he were right about Moreno, then Norma Martin's phone records would support his suspicions. He believed that Norma called Moreno, telling him to come and take Marcela away. Whether or not she had anything to do with the death of the girl was immaterial. If Ben could prove the homicide detective investigating the case transported the victim right before her death, then the prosecution's case was, by definition, contaminated. His client's chances for a reversal were excellent.

Smiling to himself Ben started to thumb through his in-basket, checking to see if there was anything that couldn't wait until Monday. His hand froze when he caught sight of the envelope on the bottom of the pile.

With everything else going on, Ben nearly forgot about the DNA test he had ordered weeks ago. His hand trembling, he ripped open the envelope from the private forensics company that provided lab services to the Project. A packet of paper landed on his desk. Ben scanned the documents. A preliminary test at the lab confirmed the stain found on Marcela's skirt was indeed dried seminal fluid. His spirits rising, Ben skipped through all the technical jargon regarding testing procedures and probabilities. He paused, slowing down when he got to the results. The skirt had provided enough of a sample for the lab to get an identifiable strand of DNA, the unique genetic fingerprint they searched for. The lab technician then ran through the DNA Index System looking for a hit. Ben stared at the last line of the report. *No match.*

With a shake of his head, he let the page float back onto the surface of his desk. Over the course of his investigation he began to realize the DNA evidence might not be as helpful as he once thought. Since Marcela was a known prostitute, the seminal fluid could have been left by any one of her customers. And since there was no way to date the sample, he could not prove the stain was left on the day of her murder. Still, it would have been nice if the results shed light on Marcela's last moments on earth. After all, DNA evidence was one of the key factors he used to persuade Greg to accept Ricky Castro's petition in the first place. He could only hope that when he shared the results with the boss on Monday morning, Greg would not tell him to drop the case.

Ben consoled himself with knowing he still had other leads that looked promising. Norma's phone records for one. And Ben had high hopes for the video recording of his client speaking to Moreno's snitch. Getting a copy of that tape proved difficult but after Ben made multiple phone calls and submitted a mountain of paperwork, he was assured one would be sent to him. It was only a matter of time before he could pull everything together and file his petition with the court.

With his messenger bag slung over his shoulder, the subpoena request safely tucked inside, Ben turned off the lights and closed the door behind him. Brimming with confidence, he felt he was on the cusp of freeing an innocent man.

TWENTY-FIVE

I leaned back on my heels to survey the weed-free rows between tomato plants. Wiping a bead of sweat from my brow I could feel the smudge of grit that my glove left behind. The plants had been in the ground for less than two months, growing like Jack's beanstalk. Between Annie's organic mulch, the Florida sunshine and a daily dousing of water, they were almost ready for a second tie. The plants were covered with small, star-like flowers. Soon I would have more tomatoes than I could ever eat.

In recent weeks I added peas, radishes and potatoes to the garden. I tried growing lettuce, but within days the pale green leaves turned to lace. Instead of fighting an impossible war with the snails, I went back to the garden center for something different. As I wandered between rows of potted herbs under the mesh canopy, a man with a distinctive Cracker accent gave me unsolicited advice. He assured me that rosemary did well in the Florida climate. And truth be told, I liked the idea of having the herb around in case Lalo happened to stop by with another fish. Those fragrant herbs now thrived in my garden. I nipped a small piece from the sturdy stalks and crushed the needles between my fingers. Holding them up, the pungent aroma filled my nose.

I stood, brushed the dirt off my knees and headed back to the house. My smoking habit was back to a pack-a-day. I wasn't happy about it, but I figured I had plenty of time to quit again before my next appointment with my doctor in a few months' time.

As I grabbed my Lights from the kitchen counter the phone rang. I hadn't heard from Lalo in weeks, not since that evening when he came to pick up Maya. More than once I considered calling him to ask if we might visit Tyler Fox together. Yet every time I reached for the phone, I recalled how the evening ended. How I closed my eyes and waited for the kiss that never came. I had acted like a drunken schoolgirl and was too embarrassed to call him.

"Hello?" I asked, hoping to hear his voice at the other end of the line. The words I'd practiced in my head. *Oh, it's you. Funny you called, I wonder if we could . . .*

"Hi Cate," Annie's greeting broke into my reverie. "Just calling to make sure you're still coming to the Drum Circle tonight."

I hadn't seen Logan's grandmother in two weeks. Two weeks during which I had made little progress on her grandson's case. I glanced at my wall calendar. The Drum Circle on Nokomis beach was the only thing written there.

"I don't know," I replied, struggling to come up with an excuse. "I'm in the middle of something right now."

"You work too hard. You need to relax. Let your soul fly free. Trust me, you'll love this. And I have a surprise for you. I'll swing by your house to pick you up at five. Remember, dress comfortably."

Unlike Annie, I didn't own a closet full of kaftans. Jeans and a T-shirt would have to do.

With a few hours remaining until Annie showed up, I decided to pull out my copy of Geri Garibaldi's police files and get back to work. I hadn't looked at the papers since vacating the windowless room at the Public Defender's office. Starting fresh, I picked up a pen and flipped through the pages of my notebook until I found a clean sheet of paper. Drawing a line down the center of the page I titled the left side, "Innocent." On the other side I wrote, "Guilty."

Perhaps it was my state of mind, perhaps the pressing weight of Geri's files on my lap but the right side of the page filled quickly. The evidence for conviction was strong. Logan's fingerprints on the murder weapon, his clothing soaked with the victim's blood, his shoe prints found in the mud at the scene, the statements made by his friends who believed he went to find the girl and never came back. And then there was the testimony given by his ex-girlfriend who claimed he had a nasty temper.

I stared at the blank lines on the "Innocent" side, willing myself to come up with something. It seemed that each time I thought I was on to something, success eluded me. I remembered Logan told me about his chance for a reduction in sentence due to his age at the time of the murder. He had refused to confess, even to save his life. That counted for something, I reminded myself. That was the reason I got involved in the first place. In blue ink I made my first entry for innocence.

The thoughts came quickly after that. The prosecution never found the victim's clothes. Or the condom used by the man who raped her. In fact, all the damaging evidence was gathered as a result of Logan going home and telling his grandmother that he discovered the girl's body in the woods. A terrible thought crossed my mind. If Annie hadn't called the police, Logan would certainly be a free man.

Setting my notebook aside I opened the folder containing the autopsy report. I stared at the girl's face. So young, so beautiful. Under the white lights in the pathology lab her face was ashen, her jet-black hair pulled away from her face so the photographer could capture her image. The stab wounds in her belly and the bruises on her wrist were violations of an otherwise flawless body. A series of photos showed her back, the tattoo of folded wings standing out starkly against her bloodless skin. The report, written in dry, clinical language stated the reason her heart ceased to pump life through her body. Knife wounds to her liver, her stomach, her spleen. Cause of death, exsanguination. She bled to death, plain and simple.

The toxicology report showed alcohol in her bloodstream. Though she was drunk, there were no illegal drugs in her system at the time of death. There were traces of the lubricant from a Trojan, a common condom on the market. No skin under her fingernails, no abrasions on her body other than the bruises on her wrist. Despite the prosecution's theory that Logan had raped and killed this girl, there was absolutely no DNA evidence to link the victim to my client.

So where did that leave me? Geri Garibaldi told me her conscience bothered her about this case. Though she had doubts about Boyd Skinner too, I didn't think that was at the root of the detective's sleepless nights. She was troubled by the lack of motive. Picking up the pen, on the right side of the paper I wrote in block letters, WHO WAS THE OTHER GIRL AT SNOOK WALLOW? Then, as an afterthought I wrote the same thing on the left.

The doorbell rang. Annie Murphy, her face framed in a mass of wild gray hair, smiled at me.

It was time to beat the drums.

TWENTY-SIX

People of all ages crossed the dunes, sea oats brushing their legs as they made their way to the shoreline. When we arrived, there were perhaps two dozen seated on the beach in the form of a crescent, leaving an opening that gave everyone a clear view of the Gulf of Mexico. Some cradled plastic five-gallon paint pails between their knees, others sat on stools behind large sets of drums. Annie nodded at a tall, bearded guy who waved us over. As he took my hand and welcomed me to the circle I caught a whiff of stale cigarette smoke. Everyone shifted to one side, creating a space for us to squeeze in. My knee joints felt stiff from working in the garden all afternoon but I managed to lower myself to the sand. Annie, who dropped to the ground and adopted the lotus position like a yogi, watched as I tried to get comfortable.

"I'll bring you ginseng root. Works wonders on arthritis." She reached into the large, macramé bag that hung over her shoulder and pulled out a tambourine.

I accepted the instrument with thanks, but was too busy looking around to worry about what I was supposed to do with the thing. The strangest people were drawn to the event. Men with gray ponytails halfway down their backs wore tie-dyed T-shirts and peace medallions. Children ran laughing around the circle, kicking up sand as they went. A woman I judged to be in her forties approached us, her blond hair in dreadlocks, matted and dirty. Annie jumped up and gave her a hug, introducing her as Glenda. My fingers itched to shear the woman's head to give her a fresh start on looking human.

There were plenty of normal—or what *I* would call normal—people gathered there too. They came to observe, the majority of them senior citizens like myself but with the better sense to hang back. They kept their distance on the outer edge of the circle in their cargo shorts and sandals as they waited for the show to begin.

An old, familiar smell reached me. Out of the corner of my eye I saw Annie accept a reefer from Dreadlock Glenda and take a drag. She passed it to me, and somehow I found myself staring at the smoldering roll-your-own cigarette in my hand. The last time someone offered to share was a hundred years ago in my college days. Deciding I was too old for this nonsense I passed it back untouched.

The tall bearded guy who first greeted us began with a slow, throbbing rhythm on a large drum. Others joined in. Annie closed her eyes and caressed her set of bongos with the palms of her hands. Right, left. Right, left. I soon found myself rocking, tapping my tambourine lightly. A few belly dancers draped in sequined veils jumped into the center of the circle, arms weaving above their heads, hips moving to the pounding rhythm. The pace quickened. The sun dropped on the horizon.

If all this wasn't weird enough, a few bikini-clad girls with hula-hoops joined the fray. Soon the inner circle was full, people dancing, swaying and gyrating against the backdrop of the crimson-edged clouds hanging over the darkening waters of the Gulf. The crowd behind us applauded. While the drummers and dancers appeared to be taking all this seriously, the people in the audience laughed, shaking their heads in amazement. The air was infused with the sweet aroma of marijuana. I decided I should ask for Annie's keys and offer to drive us home.

As the sun melted into the Gulf, the drums reached a frenzied hammering, everyone banging away. I played along on my borrowed tambourine, albeit less enthusiastically than most. Suddenly it was over. I don't know how everyone knew to stop, but I gave a final tap and the cymbals rang out one second after the drums went silent. The crowd started to shuffle away. Annie opened her eyes and looked at me.

"What do you think?" she asked.

"Interesting." I didn't know what else to say.

"Did you feel it? That primal beat, taking you back to the womb?"

Actually, no. But I nodded agreement.

"I'm so glad you came tonight. Are you ready for your surprise? She's going to meet us at Pop's Sunset Grill."

"Who?" I asked.

"Bibi Marks."

I looked at her, speechless. In a matter of minutes, I'd be meeting Logan's ex-girlfriend.

The veils and sequins were a dead giveaway. As Bibi approached our table, I recognized her as one of the belly dancers on the beach. Logan's high school sweetheart bent down and planted a kiss on Annie's cheek before settling onto the seat opposite me. The waiter, a tall, thin man wearing a *Salt Life* T-shirt appeared and asked what we wanted to drink. We each ordered a glass of the house Chablis and as soon as he left, Annie made the introductions.

On the way to the restaurant Annie revealed that Bibi Marks was married to Logan's best friend, Tyler Fox. After my initial surprise, I realized this wasn't as strange as it seemed. Annie explained that Bibi and Ty started dating after Logan's trial. An unplanned pregnancy cemented the relationship. Ty dropped out of college and moved back to Venice to marry the girl, start his construction business and raise a family.

Bibi was only sixteen at the time of the murder. To see her now, other than the small mole on the crest of her cheek, she only faintly resembled the photos in Geri's police files. Thanks to years under the Florida sun, her face was covered with premature wrinkles. Her body, of which I could see far too much through the veils, was lean and sinewy. She smiled and in her clear eyes I detected a serious expression.

"I'm so glad to meet you, Cate. Annie told me you're going to get Logan out of jail."

I had no idea how to respond. My initial reaction was to snap back, remind her she testified against him. But there was something about her manner that held me back. When she reached for the silver ball hanging on a thin chain around her neck, I heard a soft chiming sound. The gesture told me Bibi was nervous. Annie must have noticed too because she placed her hand on Bibi's arm before turning to me. I looked into the enlarged pupils of her red-rimmed eyes.

"Bibi and Ty have been so good to me over the years. They always remember me on my birthday. Mother's Day too. And I don't know how I would manage around the house without Ty. Whenever I need something fixed he comes right over. They know Logan didn't kill that girl. Bibi is here because she wants to help."

"I still feel guilty about what happened at the trial. That lawyer, you know, he twisted everything I was trying to say."

"Did you lie under oath?" I asked.

Bibi stole a quick glance at Annie.

"Go ahead, tell her. I've heard it all before."

"You're talking about Logan threatening to hurt me, right?" Bibi asked me.

I decided to play it straight and not hold back. "Well, that was the reason the prosecutor put you on the stand. He used your testimony to show Logan was capable of violence against women."

"I did tell the truth about that stuff, but the lawyer, he didn't give me a chance to explain."

"What do you mean?"

Just then the waiter appeared with our drinks and set them on the table. He asked if we wanted to order some food. Annie told him we needed a little more time but that he could bring us a basket of nachos for starters. As he turned to leave, Bibi picked up her glass and swallowed half her wine in one go.

"I lost my virginity to Logan in my sophomore year, she said. "He told me I was his first, too but I always thought he just said that to make me feel, you know, special. Anyway, Logan was the jealous type. He got angry when other guys looked at me."

"I read the trial transcript."

"With all respect, you weren't there. That lawyer, he made it sound like Logan was a monster. And I kept trying to tell him it wasn't like that at all. I loved Logan."

The waiter reappeared, placing the basket of nachos on the table.

"Have you ladies decided yet?" he asked.

"I'll have the veggie burger," Annie replied. "With a side of quinoa salad."

"Just the house salad for me," Bibi chimed in. "No dressing."

The unopened menu was still on my plate, so I had to make a quick decision. I ordered a cheeseburger, medium rare. When the waiter left us alone I turned back to Bibi.

"If you loved Logan, then why did you break up with him?"

"Well this other kid in my class, Freddie Kindle started flirting with me and, you know, we went out on a few dates. When Logan found out he went wild. That's when he said those things that I repeated on the stand. But I never, ever thought he would actually hurt me."

She sighed, picked up her glass and took a smaller sip this time. I stared at the empty basket of nachos, believing her every word.

"What happened to Freddie?"

"Oh, Freddie. I can't believe I lost Logan because I went out with Freddie Kindle of all people. Can you imagine if I had stayed with him what our kids would look like? All pimples and all. Thank God Ty came along and saved me from that."

"That was after the trial?" I asked.

"Yeah. We got together a few times, you know, because we both felt so bad about what happened to Logan. One thing lead to another and well . . . Ty was supposed to go back to school at the end of the summer but we decided to get married instead."

I noticed she left out the part about getting pregnant, but I couldn't see how that had any bearing on the subject of Logan Murphy's innocence. In fact I had a hard time understanding how any of her story mattered as far as Logan was concerned.

"If you had the chance to speak with the prosecutor today, what could you tell him that might make a difference?" I asked.

"Don't you see? That police detective made a big deal out of nothing. Sure, Logan went ballistic when he found out about Freddie, but that was just, you know, boy talk. Believe me, Logan never hurt a fly. *That's* what I wanted to say at the trial. Logan would never, ever do what they accused him of."

The food arrived and Annie dove right into her veggie burger before I could put the ketchup on my fries. When I asked Bibi if she wanted another glass of wine she nodded gratefully. Annie told the waiter to make it two. As I took a bite of my burger, I watched Bibi pick at her salad. She must have sensed me watching as she turned and caught my eye.

"It's not enough, is it?" she asked. "It doesn't matter what I say now. Those people won't let Logan go."

"You've heard the expression, 'innocent until proven guilty,' right?" I asked.

Bibi nodded.

"Well, once a person is convicted of a crime, everything gets turned around." I adopted my professional, lawyer's voice. "Right now it's up to us to prove Logan is innocent. And while I appreciate what you've told me, I'm afraid it doesn't help."

"That's what Ty said. He didn't want me to see you tonight. Said it wouldn't change a thing."

Her eyes welled up, a single tear spilling out and rolling down her cheek. This time it was me who reached out to place a comforting hand on her arm. We sat there for a few minutes, saying nothing.

She cast her eyes downward, spearing a bit of lettuce with her fork. "It's all my fault."

"No, Bibi. Don't say that," Annie said. "The real blame lies with the animal who killed that poor girl. Some nights I lie awake thinking he is still out there somewhere. But Cate here, she's going to find a way to bring Logan home. Isn't that right Cate?"

I forced a weak smile, a sad attempt to convey a confidence I didn't feel.

TWENTY-SEVEN

I dreamt I was in the woods, pinned under a hulk of a man, my body slick with sweat. The more I squirmed beneath him, the more his weight pressed me down. Thunder rumbled above. I caught a glimpse of his face as a bolt of lightning lit the sky.

As I slowly rose to consciousness, a clap of thunder—real enough this time—woke me. The weather forecast called for bands of wind and rain throughout the night. We were on the edge of a tropical storm that was barreling through the Caribbean. Rain hammered my roof as I turned onto my back and threw off the covers. I counted the revolutions of the ceiling fan above. My heart gradually stopped beating a thousand times a minute and returned to a rate that didn't threaten cardiac arrest.

The remnants of the nightmare lingered in the corners of my brain. I left the bedroom and shuffled to the kitchen. Pulling a carton of milk from the refrigerator, I kept the door open while I poured myself a glass. The soft glow of light reassured me. I was home, alone, safe. A dream, nothing more. Another thunderous boom rattled the windows and I felt my pulse spike again. If this was only the fringe of Mother Nature's fury, I shuddered to think what the heart of the storm looked like. Feeling daring, I stepped out to the lanai. The rain came down in sheets now, my tomato plants laid flat. Lightening ripped through the air, turning night to day. Craving a cigarette, I reached into the pocket of my robe and pulled out a pack of nicotine gum. Popping one into my mouth, I drew in a deep breath. Two days free of the habit, I still needed something to bridge the gap between determination and addiction.

The air smelled of earth, clean and good, a trace of the organic fertilizer in my garden. The odor triggered a recollection of my dream. In my mind's eye, I saw the face of the man pinning me to the ground. Boyd Skinner. Not the cocky real estate broker that I met a few months ago, but a younger, rougher version of the man. My subconscious brain tried to tell me something. Or maybe it was just indigestion from the cheeseburger at Pop's. Whatever the cause, I didn't feel like going back to bed. Not yet.

I went inside and headed to my office. Sitting at my desk, I inhaled the scent of old oak. The desk and glass-front bookcase were the only pieces I'd kept from our home in New Hampshire. I chose to decorate my beach house in a contemporary style in an effort to make a clean break with the past. But somehow I was more at home here than anywhere else in the house. Beneath the overhead light, the furniture shone with a golden hue, warm and comforting.

I reached for my canvas bag bulging with all the material I had gathered for Logan's case. As I lifted my notebook from the top I noticed the cassette player beneath. Since I didn't plan to listen to any more of Geri's hotline tapes, I picked the machine up and set it on a shelf in the closet. Then I remembered the tape.

Leaving the cassette in the player was not intentional. When Geri dropped by the PD's office and invited me to lunch, I was listening to a caller named Juliana Martinez. Remembering I promised Geri to check and see if Juliana ever called back, I scanned the call list. Nothing. I decided to push the PLAY button and listen one more time. Once again, I only caught one word of her machine-gun Spanish. *Michoacán.* There was no doubt in my mind that I should get the tape back to Geri as soon as possible, but my curiosity was aroused. I popped the cassette from the machine and placed it in the top drawer of the desk, planning to give it back to Geri after I had the chance to ask Lalo to translate. Assuming, of course I ever heard from him again.

Wide-awake now, I made a few notes to document my conversation with Bibi. She didn't give me much information that I found useful, but as I wrote, the image of Boyd Skinner's face once again flashed in my mind. What was it Geri said?

From the start I had a bad feeling about that kid.

Reaching back into the canvas bag, I pulled out Jane Doe's autopsy report. Among the photos of the girl's naked body, the report included a series of close-up shots. I studied them now, wondering why the pathologist zoomed in on the red smudges of blood on Jane Doe's hips when clearly the fatal stab wounds were higher up on her abdomen. Finding the transcription of his recorded observations, I skipped ahead to the part where he described the area in the photos.

". . . the skin on both hips exhibit what appear to be blood smears . . . hang on a minute, that color doesn't look right . . . what is this stuff? Let's take some close-ups and send a scraping to the lab for analysis."

Though I read through the entire autopsy report earlier, I never assigned any importance to these close-up shots. The feeling that I was onto something was like an electric current flowing through my body. I rifled through my files, urgently searching for the lab results, finally finding what I sought. At the back of the toxicology report, behind the cross-section photos of organs, I saw the analysis of the material found on Jane Doe's skin.

Using analytical chromatography, the lab technician separated the components of the sample. What he found was lycopene, acetic acid, capsaicin, fructose, glucose, raffinose, and sodium chloride. None of that meant anything to me so I looked the words up, one-by-one on the Internet. Tomato, vinegar, chili pepper, sugar, salt. The results set alarm bells ringing in my head.

My hands shaking, I picked up my notebook and flipped back to the beginning, stopping to read the notes I made after Lalo and I met with Skinner.

As the rain pounded the windows, I stared at the page, knowing what I had to do.

Stacy, pink glitter eye shadow and all, answered the door to Tyler Fox's construction company. She smiled and popped her gum as she waved me in. When she bent over to retrieve a bottle of water from the refrigerator, I noticed the baby bump. Early yet, but unmistakable.

"How are you doing, Stacy?" I asked as I accepted the water from her.

"Oh, great Mrs. Stokes. Look, I'm getting married!"

She extended her left hand for me to admire the ring. Cubic zirconia if I was any judge of these things. Her fiancé, Randy I assumed, had gone all out.

"Good for you." I forced a smile. "You must be happy."

"Yeah, yeah I am. My dad isn't real thrilled, but my mom, she says Randy is doing the right thing. She even said we can live with them until we find our own place which I don't think will take too long because Randy says he's due for a raise and we'll be gettin' money for wedding presents, right? Hey, it's weird, you showin' up like this. Bibi came in this morning and told me she saw you at the Drum Circle. She's somethin' isn't she, with her belly dancing and all? She said you were like, getting into it with your tambourine, which I thought was kinda funny. No offense, but I can't picture you with a tambourine."

"No offense taken. Is Ty in? I'd like to speak with him."

"Oh, yeah. He's out back. Do you want me to tell him you're here?"

"That would be nice, thanks."

She keyed the microphone on her desk and shouted, "Ty, you got a visitor!"

"May I wait for him in his office?" I asked.

"Sure, he won't be long. Do me a favor and tell him I remembered the water."

Assuring her I would, I made my way to Ty's cluttered office. Setting aside a box of screws from the lone visitor's chair, I made myself comfortable. After placing my handbag on the floor I took a look around. The wall calendar was turned to October but other than that, everything appeared unchanged from the last time I was there. Since that first meeting, I had learned quite a bit about the night Logan and his friends went to Snook Wallow. I felt I was getting closer to the truth, but so much depended on what Ty could tell me now. When the young man came through the door, I stood to meet him. Though the office area was air conditioned, it must have been hot in the workshop out back. Sweat trickled down his brow, his damp shirt stuck to his chest. He gave my hand a firm shake, his damp palm pressed to mine.

"Bibi mentioned she met you Friday night."

"Yes, she's still feeling bad about her testimony. She wanted to clarify something for me."

A crease appeared between his brows. "What did she say?"

"Nothing important." I waved my hand in the air as if to brush away his concern. "She wanted to help, but I'm afraid it's a little late for that."

"That's exactly what I told her," Ty replied.

"Yes, well I have made progress with the case. I hope you don't mind answering a few more questions for me."

"Um, yeah, but I'm busy right now. Can we do this another time?"

"This won't take long," I sat back on the visitor's chair to signal I wasn't going anywhere soon. After a slight hesitation, Ty sat behind his desk and faced me.

"Fire away."

"Well, as you may know, I spoke with Boyd Skinner about the night of the murder."

"I don't see much of Boyd these days. If you have any questions about something he said, you should ask him, not me."

"But I'm not sure he's being completely honest with me. Since you were there that night, I thought you might be able to help."

A wary expression crept into Ty's dark features, his eyes slightly closed, his lips pressed together. He remained silent, waiting for me to continue.

"I understand that Logan gave Boyd money to buy hot wings right before he left to use the men's room."

"Maybe. To be honest, I don't remember that."

"Well, Boyd and Logan both mentioned the wings so we can assume that's what happened. I wonder who ate them."

Ty's eyes darted from side to side as he searched his memory.

"I'm sorry, but I can't remember. What's so important about an order of wings?"

"You and Boyd were all good friends back then, weren't you."

"We hung out together but I wouldn't say we were tight. It was more Logan and me. Boyd just kinda tagged along."

"I have reason to believe Boyd returned to Snook Wallow that night after the two of you parted ways."

"What are you talking about?" Ty leaned forward, both hands gripping the edge of the desk.

"I have an eyewitness who saw Boyd leave the parking lot after one o'clock in the morning."

Ty's eyes opened wide. "What the . . . who?"

"One of the bartenders."

I hoped he didn't see through my white lie. Charlie heard someone trying to start his motorcycle that night but he admitted that he didn't see anyone. Ty ran his fingers through his hair and shifted his weight in the chair.

"That's not possible."

"Why not? Is there something you're not telling me?"

"Logan was my best friend. If I knew who killed that girl I would have said something long ago."

The muscles bulged in his upper arms, his jaw working overtime. Judging from the sweat on his brow, I knew Ty was worried about something.

"I imagine the police will want to speak with Boyd."

It was an empty threat but I accomplished what I set out to do, tip Ty off to my theory about his friend, Boyd. Now that I set things in motion, I needed to get out of there.

I stepped into the reception area and Stacey looked up, gum snapping in time to the rock music blaring from the radio on her desk. Returning her smile, I noticed again how her stomach bulged under her too-tight jeans. As the door closed behind me, I silently vowed to send her a card with money as a wedding gift.

Ten minutes later, Ty got into his pick-up truck and flew out of the parking lot in a spray of gravel. My car ran silently on its battery as I followed. Ty seemed unaware that I tailed him. I maintained my distance, keeping him in sight with two cars between us. He turned left and crossed the bridge, heading downtown. I drove right by when he parked in front of a brick building on Venice Avenue. The sign, in gilt letters read Skinner Premier Real Estate.

Turning onto Harbor Drive, I brought my Prius to a halt. Under the canopy of live oaks, I pulled out my phone and pressed Ben's number. He answered on the first ring.

"We need to talk. If I come up on Friday will you have time to meet with me?"

"Sure," Ben replied. "What's going on?"

"I'll tell you when I get there."

"You're driving a long way just to talk."

"I planned to meet Logan at the prison on Saturday anyway," I replied. "I'll book a hotel room for Friday night so I don't have to drive back and forth."

I could hear the click of his keyboard as he checked his schedule. God only knew that at my age I sometimes had a bit of trouble keeping track of things, but I swore to myself that I would never resort to letting a computer manage my life.

"I just cleared my calendar so I can get out of here early on Friday," he replied a few seconds later. "Forget the hotel. You're staying at my place."

"That would be nice, thanks." I tried to picture Ben's apartment. An image of a student dorm came to mind. Dirty clothes strewn about, a refrigerator containing a six-pack of beer and moldy cheese, the pantry stocked with Ramen noodles and Pop Tarts.

"Do you know any good restaurants in the area?" I asked. "My treat."

"There's a place near here called Chouko's. I hear it's pretty good."

"Sounds perfect. Go ahead and make a reservation."

Minutes later I was home, pulling a map of Florida from my desk drawer. A straight run up the interstate would take me from Venice to Gainesville. Folding the map so the appropriate section was readily visible, I tucked it into a side pocket of my overnight bag.

Though I vowed not to call Lalo, I was tired of waiting for the man to make the first move. If he was going to be home on Friday, it would be an efficient use of my time to stop on the way and get him to translate the hotline tape, so I could get it back before Geri discovered it was missing. Picking up the phone I dialed his number. After only two rings a recorded voice cut in, informing me that his mailbox was full. I wondered where the man could be. Geri's cassette would just have to wait. With a sigh, I picked up my gardening gloves and headed out to see if I could salvage my tomato plants from the damage done by the storm.

TWENTY-EIGHT

When I opened the door to the Defender Project, I found myself facing a stunning redhead dressed in a tight-fitting business suit. Her green, cat-like eyes met mine, one ginger eyebrow arched in question.

"May I help you?"

"Catherine Stokes to see Ben Shepherd. He's expecting me."

She looked me over, a crooked smile on her lips. Almost immediately Ben appeared from around the corner.

"I see you found us."

"Rand McNally got me here."

"Doesn't your car have GPS?

"I don't trust a stranger's voice to give me directions."

Ben gave me one of those patronizing grins that young people give senior citizens. I wanted to smack him.

"Come and wait in my office while I shut down my computer." Turning to the redhead, he said "I'll be leaving a little early today, Stephanie. If Greg asks where I am, tell him I'm working from home."

Manila folders were stacked on every surface in Ben's office, a tower of law books on the floor in one corner, a dead plant in another. All the filing cabinet's flip-doors stood open to reveal hundreds of files jammed together. On the wall behind Ben's desk was an old picture of Manhattan, the twin towers of the World Trade Center standing proudly on the skyline. Hanging on the opposite wall was a white board covered with photos and colored sticky notes bearing Ben's familiar scrawl.

Of all the photos on the board, the only faces I recognized were those of Detective Moreno and Luci. I studied Luci's photo. The shot was obviously taken at the time of the autopsy, her eyes closed, her skin ashen.

"How's this going? Have you made any progress?"

"I'll fill you in when we get home," Ben replied as he glanced down at a pink message slip and picked up the phone on his desk. "Give me one minute and then we can get out of here."

Before he could punch in the number, Stephanie stepped into the office. She closed the door behind her and gave Ben a coy smile as she waved a brown envelope in front of him. Seeing what she held, he slammed down the phone.

"Is that what I think it is?" he asked.

"The phone company's response to your subpoena. A courier just dropped it off."

Ben grabbed the envelope from her hand and ripped it open. Running down a list of numbers with his finger, he stopped in the middle of the page and reached for a yellow highlighter.

"Is that what you were looking for?" Stephanie asked.

"This is the only call that falls within the timeframe that Luci gave us. If I'm reading this right, the record shows Norma didn't use her phone in the hours preceding or after. This has to be the one."

"Are you talking about Norma Martin?" I asked.

Stephanie gave me a sharp look before turning back to Ben. "I thought Mrs. Stokes was working for Logan Murphy. How does she know about Norma Martin?"

"She was with Lalo when Luci called him. But how did you know Cate is working on Logan's case?" Ben asked.

"Don't you remember? You said you handed the case over to another lawyer. Then I saw Mrs. Stokes' name on your email and . . . well, when you didn't close out Murphy's file, I figured she was working for you behind the scenes."

My eyes darted between Ben and Stephanie. Ben wore that childish smile I knew so well. She smiled back with a challenging smirk. I wondered why he never mentioned Stephanie to me before. Their chemistry was almost fluorescent.

"I'm here to give Ben an update."

"Well this should be interesting. Just this morning Ben's intern asked what I knew about the case. Ben reacted a little too strongly when she tried to send Murphy a rejection letter. She suspects something isn't kosher."

Ben looked up at her. "What did you tell her?"

"Come on, Shepherd. Do you actually believe I'd share anything with that sneaky weasel? I told you, I've seen her sort pass through here before. Mark my words, the minute Kim finds dirt on you she'll run to Greg and rat you out, hoping to worm her way into a permanent job here. I'll be happy when her internship is over and she's gone."

Ben let out a visible sigh.

"When Mrs. Stokes showed up just now, Kim went into overdrive. It kills her not to know what's going on."

"Please stop calling me Mrs. Stokes. My name is Cate. And I wish the two of you wouldn't refer to me in the third person. I'm standing right here."

Stephanie acknowledged me with a grin and a nod. Turning back to Ben she asked, "So whose number did Norma call the day Marcela was killed?"

Ben looked back at the list of numbers on his desk and ran his finger across the page. From where I stood I could read the name he pointed to. The highlighted phone number belonged to Chaparrito's Restaurant in Immokalee. Ben looked at Stephanie, an excited light in his eyes.

"That restaurant is located in the strip mall where Luci worked," I said.

"Marcela de la Vega was killed in the alley behind the bar, and Tom Moreno happened to be at Chaparrito's on that day."

"Coincidence?" Stephanie gave Ben an incredulous stare.

"I for one don't believe in coincidences," I said.

I heard a soft click and turned to see a diminutive, freckle-faced girl pushing the door open. She leaned forward without actually stepping in. Her eyes flitted between the three of us, coming to rest on Ben.

"Sorry to disturb you, but when you get a minute I could use your help with something."

That fresh-scrubbed face could have come straight out of an Ivory soap commercial, a pure, innocent, girl-next-door face. Ben pressed his lips together, shooting her a look of annoyance. Stephanie looked like she wanted to devour the girl and spit out the pieces. I figured this must be Kim.

"Can it wait until tomorrow?" Ben asked. "I'm in the middle of something right now."

"Then I guess I have to figure it out for myself," Kim replied with a childish pout. Her eyes swept the scene again as if she wanted to memorize every detail. She slammed the door behind her.

"I need to call Lalo," Ben said.

I threw up my hands. "Good luck with that. I haven't heard from him all week."

Stephanie turned to Ben. "Careful, Shepherd. If Greg catches you charging the Project for an unsanctioned case, you'll be out on your butt in a New York minute."

Ben laughed. "Lalo and Cate are working pro bono. Last I knew he went to Immokalee to chase down someone named Angel Abarco." Ben removed his suit jacket from the back of his chair. "I'll try calling again from the car. It would be good to catch him while he's down there. I'd like him to have a word with the restaurant's owner to see if he can learn more about that phone call."

I turned to Stephanie and said, "It's getting late. Why don't you join us for dinner? My treat."

"I'd love to." Stephanie tipped her head toward Ben and flashed him that crooked smile.

I was right about these two. Chemistry.

Ben's furniture looked like it came straight out of an Ikea showroom. Bookshelves covering one wall were filled with research books, classic literature and popular crime fiction. A few law review magazines lay scattered on the glossy white coffee table, photos of Ben's parents stood on the credenza next to the television. Hanging on the wall over the leather sofa was another framed print of New York, this one post-911. From the twin spotlights reaching up to the sky I knew the photo was taken on an anniversary of the attack.

Crossing the living room, Ben pushed the drapes aside to reveal a small balcony with a clay pot containing the dried remains of an azalea. The day outside was cool, a bright, cloudless sky overhead. When Ben opened the door a slight breeze blew a few dead leaves into the apartment.

Stephanie agreed to meet us at Ben's so we could drive to the restaurant together. Before we left the office, Ben called to request a private room so we could discuss business over dinner. Ever the good lawyer, he didn't want our conversation overheard, no matter how unlikely it would be that anyone cared.

"I'm proud of you, Ben." I stared at a photo of Ben standing on the steps of the courthouse in a black robe on the day he graduated from law school. "I always knew you would make a great lawyer."

"Not great," he replied. "I'm just trying to do my best. It kills me to know there are two men on death row that don't deserve to be there."

The doorbell rang, announcing Stephanie's arrival. She had changed her outfit, casting aside her business clothes in favor of a short cocktail dress. A gold thread ran through the material, catching the light with her every move. Her three-inch heels brought her to within a hair's width of Ben's height. In my loafers and jeans I felt painfully short and seriously under dressed.

"White or red," Ben asked as he went to the kitchen and pulled three wine glasses from the cabinet.

"Whatever's open," Stephanie replied. "Any luck reaching Lalo?"

"Nope. And his mailbox is still full so I couldn't leave him a message."

"I think I'll go and change for dinner." I glanced down at my jeans. Not that I had anything with me to rival Stephanie's attire, but I did pack a pair of black dress pants and a white blouse for my visit with Logan. Nothing I could do about the one-and-only pair of the sensible loafers on my feet.

"No need, you look perfect," Stephanie said.

Ben handed Stephanie her glass. "She's right, you look fine. As a matter of fact, I planned to get out of this suit and put on chinos before we go. You can bring Stephanie up to speed on your investigation while I'm changing."

It didn't take long for me to hit the highlights. Stephanie was familiar with Logan's case but of course she didn't know anything about the discovery of a second girl who was with Jane Doe that night. Or that the bartender heard someone—possibly Boyd Skinner—having engine trouble around one o'clock in the morning. I told her Skinner left Snook Wallow earlier with Ty Fox but that I was working on the theory that he returned. I was just getting to the part about the tip line calls when Ben returned to the room.

"So what is so important that you couldn't tell me on the phone?" Ben asked. He settled on the couch next to Stephanie, his knee lightly touching hers. She didn't pull away.

"I want you to see this." I handed Ben a copy of Jane Doe's autopsy report. "At first the pathologist thought they were blood smears, but it turns out it was hot wing sauce."

Ben studied the photo of three streaks on both sides of the girl's hips. They started out heavy then faded to almost nothing as if someone grabbed a hold of her and pulled. "Hot wing sauce?" A deep crease formed in his brow.

"The gas chromatography results are included at the back of the report. When the lab broke down the components of the substance they found lycopene, acetic acid, capsaicin—"

"Okay, okay. I'll take your word for it. Hot wing sauce. But what does that mean?"

"I'm pretty sure Boyd Skinner ate hot wings that night."

Ben paused to look at me. I could tell from the expression on his face that he wasn't buying my theory.

"So there are three items on the menu of every bar in the country, burgers, fries and wings. There's a pretty good chance lots of people ate wings that night. This doesn't make Skinner a suspect."

"Don't get sarcastic with me, young man."

"You're saying Skinner went back to Snook Wallow later?" Stephanie looked back and forth between us.

I nodded.

"Okay," Ben said. "If Skinner ate the wings he bought with Logan's money, it was before he and Ty left. And even if he still had sticky fingers more than an hour later, how do you explain there wasn't any trace of the sauce on the knife?"

He held me in his steady gaze.

"I haven't worked out all the details yet."

"Hold on," Stephanie chimed in. "Maybe Cate didn't get it exactly right, but she raises some good questions. Maybe it *was* Skinner's motorcycle that the bartender heard late that night."

I was starting to like Stephanie more and more.

"What else have you got?" Ben asked with a sigh.

"Well, I went to see Ty on Monday and told him the bartender saw Boyd back at Snook Wallow long after the two of them left."

"Why?"

"I wanted to see his reaction. I'm pretty good at reading people and I'm telling you, Ty is hiding something. After I left, I waited in my car for a few minutes and sure enough, he came out of that building like his hair was on fire. I followed him downtown to Boyd Skinner's office. I'll admit, there may be a few holes in my theory but there's something fishy going on. I can feel it in my bones."

"Did you say anything to Ty about the hot wing sauce on the body?"

"I asked him who ate the wings. He doesn't remember."

Ben ran his hand over his face and groaned. Stephanie started to laugh.

"Come on, Shepherd. Cate is working the case."

"Aunt Cate," Ben said, ignoring Stephanie. "Let's just say, hypothetically, that you're right about Boyd. What did you gain by telling Ty?"

"Wait, did you call her *Aunt Cate*?" Stephanie stared at me with her mouth open.

"Didn't he tell you? My sister is Ben's mother." I turned back to Ben. "You know me well enough to realize I won't let Logan rot in jail for a crime he didn't commit. I am not going to stop digging until I find out who killed that girl."

Ben paused, cracking the knuckles on both hands. At length he shook his head. "I'll speak with Lalo about Boyd. But as of now, you're officially off the case."

I met his serious brown eyes straight on. We were locked in a battle of wills, neither one ready to back down. No matter what Ben said, I was determined to see this through to the end. And he knew it.

"Listen Shepherd," Stephanie said, breaking into our silent stand-off. "Cate was never officially 'on' the case. Murphy doesn't even exist as far as the Project is concerned. You can't expect her to drop everything now that she's come this far."

This girl was a keeper. I wondered if Ben realized what stood right before his eyes.

"Okay, here's the deal, you can keep going with the investigation but I want you to swear that you will not have any further contact with either Tyler Fox or Boyd Skinner. Let Lalo handle this aspect of the investigation."

"Lalo is AWOL."

"Those are my terms. Take them or leave them."

Stephanie nodded slightly.

"Deal," I promised.

"Aunt Cate," Stephanie smiled. "I should have known. Ben must have inherited his stubborn streak from your side of the family."

TWENTY-NINE

Chouko's was full, the potted bamboo between the tables doing little to mute the noisy chatter of the diners. I was glad Ben thought to reserve a room. That gave us the privacy we needed to discuss Ricky Castro's case.

"Let me see if I have this straight." I went on only after the kimono-clad waitress left with our sake order. "Ricky and Marcela had a big fight the morning she was killed. She left his apartment in a huff and went home to . . . to do what?"

"Depends on whose story you believe, Ricky says she went home to pack so they could run away together. Luci said Marcela was looking for cash to buy drugs. Maybe both are right."

"And now you know Norma called Chaparrito's right after she caught Marcela going through her things."

"Right," Ben replied. "We know where she called, but we can't be sure who she spoke to. Or for that matter, who came to Norma's house and took Marcela away."

The image of the short detective standing toe-to-toe with Lalo in front of Norma's house sprang to my mind. "My money is still on Moreno."

"Well, whoever it was, we still don't know how Marcela ended up in the alley behind El Rincón," Stephanie said.

"True," Ben agreed.

Our conversation was interrupted by the return of the waitress. She bowed her head, poured sake into each of our thimble-like cups and set the tokkuri on the table. After Ben ordered a variety of dishes for us to share the waitress backed away with another bow.

"So what are you going to do?" I asked, taking a sip. The hot rice wine went down smoothly, evaporating in the back of my throat. Stephanie knocked hers down in one gulp.

"None of the potential I saw in this case is panning out." Ben reached for the tokkuri and refilled Stephanie's glass before taking a sip of his own. "Initially I thought I could use the jailhouse snitch angle. Proving Salazar lied in return for a favor from the police would get the verdict thrown out. But Salazar is dead and Moreno denies any favors were traded for his testimony. I thought I was on to something with the security tape from the jail. But when I finally got my hands on a copy it turned out to be another dead end."

"What did the tape show?" I asked.

"The video did more to support Salazar's version of events than my client's. Based on what I saw, those two guys knew each other pretty well. When Salazar showed up, Ricky spoke with him for about ten minutes. In the eyes of the court, that would give Ricky plenty of time to confess to killing Marcela."

"There must be something else. You said Lalo is in Immokalee chasing down another lead?"

"I'm not exactly sure what he's up to. Whatever he's doing, I hope it will help. Frankly, I'm running out of ideas."

When the food arrived, Ben ordered another tokkuri of sake and we dug into plates heaping with rice, shrimp, vegetables and chicken. Ben and Stephanie used chopsticks. I used a fork. After our plates were cleared, the waitress returned with our fortune cookies.

"You first." Stephanie pointed at Ben.

"Aren't fortune cookies a Chinese thing?" I asked.

"Doesn't matter." Ben broke open his cookie and pulled out the small strip of paper. "Your everlasting patience will soon be rewarded," he read.

"There you go," Stephanie said with a grin. "Maybe Lalo will come back from Immokalee with all the evidence you need to file a wrongful conviction motion for Ricky." She looked down at her own fortune. "Love is for the lucky and the brave. Well, I haven't had much luck in love lately, that's for sure."

"What happened to the guy you found on the Internet?" Ben asked as he bit into the crisp almond shell.

"That lying creep? Turns out he's married," Stephanie replied.

I pulled my glasses out of my purse so I could read the slip of paper in my hand. After a while I realized both Stephanie and Ben stared at me, waiting to hear what it said.

"This is silly." I crumpled the paper in my hand and tossed it on the table.

"Oh no you don't." Stephanie snatched my fortune and smoothed it out. "A thrilling time is in your immediate future."

"Well at my age, thrills are few and far between."

My two young companions laughed at that, and I thought once more how well suited they were for each other. I hoped their fortunes would come true. But as far as I was concerned, I wasn't looking for any more thrills in my life. Once I finished helping Logan Murphy, I would be happy to spend the rest of my days working in the garden and walking on the beach. Not to mention getting a start on writing my novel. Unfortunately, I didn't seem to have much time for any of those things lately.

I arrived at the prison mid-morning. It simply wasn't worth skipping breakfast just to wait in a holding pen with a crush of visitors, all of whom wanted to be first in line. The officer peered at my driver's license and looked up at me for an uncomfortable amount of time as he verified I was the person I claimed to be. He then cross-referenced the visitor's list and made a mark next to my name. As he stared at a spot on the wall behind me, he ran through all the regulations by rote, a monotone litany of words I assumed he recited to hundreds of visitors every weekend. I nodded mutely as he covered everything from the no-contact rule to what to do in the "unlikely event" of an emergency lock-down. I gathered that when alarm bells started ringing I should hit the deck and keep my head down. Basically, I was supposed to play dead which hopefully would save me from the real thing.

He then confiscated my pocketbook, cell phone, reading glasses, wallet and nicotine gum. With a sweeping glance he checked to see that the outfit I wore wasn't going to start a riot. As if the sight of a sixty-something woman would turn the prisoners into sex-starved animals. The security guards eyed me suspiciously as I passed through the x-ray arch. No bells rang but a female guard used her wand to pat me down just to be sure I wasn't smuggling any contraband under the folds of my loose blouse. Satisfied that I didn't have bags of heroin taped to my midriff or a knife stuck in the waistband of my pants, she handed me over to another officer who led me through a maze of gated corridors until we reached the death row visitor's room. I spotted Logan in his orange T-shirt and blue work pants already waiting on the other side of the partition.

"It's good to see you again," I said.

In truth, he didn't look as well as the first time I saw him. A few short months ago he appeared relaxed, his legs stretched out in front of him, chatting with me like it was normal for us to be separated by a plate of Plexiglas. Now he sat erect in his chair, knees pressed together as he gnawed at a cuticle on his thumb.

"It's good to see you too, ma'am," he responded in his slow, Florida drawl. "Thank you for coming."

I smiled, trying to put him at ease. Since we first met, I had learned quite a bit about that fateful night at Snook Wallow. I got to know the people whose lives were affected by Jane Doe's murder. Annie Murphy, Geri Garibaldi, Boyd Skinner, Tyler Fox and his wife, Bibi. And in some ways I felt I knew Jane Doe, the victim of that tragic crime, though her true identity was still a mystery.

"How have you been?" I asked. "Your grandmother worries about what you're eating."

"I do miss her cooking," he replied with a small smile. "But to be honest, if I never have to drink another cup of that stuff she calls tea, that would be fine with me."

"I'm sure you want to hear where we are with your case. For starters, I went to Snook Wallow with our investigator and spoke to a witness who remembers seeing Jane Doe speaking Spanish with another girl. This other girl was a little taller than the victim, maybe a few years older and not quite as pretty. Do you recall seeing anyone who fits that description?"

"No ma'am," Logan replied, leaning forward in his chair. "Can you find out who she is?"

"I don't know. But if we can locate her we might be able to identify the victim. The bartender said the girls were hanging around for a few days before Jane Doe was killed, but they weren't what he'd call locals. Lalo is passing the sketch around the Hispanic community in the area but so far he hasn't found anyone who recognizes her. These things take time. Try to be patient."

"Well, time is one thing I don't have a lot of," Logan replied. Leaning back he started to pick at a bleeding cuticle. "I got word yesterday that the State Supreme Court denied my final appeal." He looked up at me, a crease on his brow. "I know you're friends with my grandmother and all, but please don't say anything. The news will kill her."

I was pretty sure Annie would survive, but his concern for her touched me. The news was bad. The fact that Logan's appeal had reached the Florida Supreme Court and been rejected meant that he was almost out of options.

"What was the nature of the appeal?" I asked.

"That the State's case was based on circumstantial evidence. And while we were at it, we threw in a challenge to the constitutionality of Florida's death penalty and the proportionality of a death sentence in my case."

With his soft southern accent, Logan sounded more like Atticus Finch than a convicted murderer. Obviously he had spent time in prison becoming familiar with appellate law.

"Remind me, what does 'proportionality of a death sentence' mean?" I asked.

"Aren't you a lawyer?"

I didn't want to shake his confidence in me by telling him the closest I ever got to the inside of a courtroom was when I showed up for jury duty thirteen years ago. "I practiced law in New Hampshire but we don't have the death sentence there so some of this is new to me. Ben is coaching me on the nuances of the law down here."

"Oh." Logan gave me a sideways glance. Though I could see my qualifications gave him pause, he seemed to make up his mind quickly. "Well, it means we requested a review of other death sentences in the state to determine if mine was comparable. And believe me, it was not. Most people, they get life without parole for something like this and that's what my lawyer tried to show. But the court didn't see it that way. The original conviction stands."

"So what happens next?"

"There is a new case before the US Supreme Court that we're following pretty close. It has to do with the court accepting the recommendation for the death penalty by a divided jury."

"In your case the jury voted seven to five."

"Yes, ma'am. The U.S. Supreme Court is going to decide if that violates the Constitution. Believe me, I have a lot of friends here on The Row who are holding their breath just like me. We're waiting to see what happens."

"Then there's hope."

"There's always hope, Mrs. Stokes. But I've had more ups and downs in here than I can count. To be honest, I don't know how much more I can take. There are times when I think someone will find the real killer and the doors will fly open so I can go home. Then something like this comes along and I just want it to be over with."

"Don't give up. We're doing everything we can to find out who killed that girl."

"I appreciate that, ma'am, and no offense, but others have tried and they all came up empty."

"Can you think of any reason Boyd Skinner might have returned to Snook Wallow that night?"

It seemed Logan's eyes grew a shade darker as he peered at me. "What makes you ask?"

"You don't look surprised."

"Let's just say Boyd wasn't one to go home before the band stopped playing, so when I heard he left early I wondered." Logan stared at the wall behind me for a few minutes before adding, "But then again, Ty left with him."

"Is there any chance Ty is protecting Boyd for some reason?"

Logan shook his head. "No, ma'am. Ty and me were like brothers. He would never let all that stuff rain down on my head if he could stop it. I'd bet my life on that."

I thought about mentioning the smears of hot wing sauce on the victim's hips but since I didn't want to raise false hope, I decided to keep that information to myself for now.

Before leaving, I asked Logan if I could bring him something the next time I visited. He thanked me for the offer, but reminded me that visitors were not permitted to give anything to the inmates. To keep him occupied he had a radio, several magazine subscriptions and access to all the books in the prison library. We spoke for a while about the PBS programs that we both watched. Remembering Annie once mentioned Logan was an avid Tampa Rays baseball fan, I asked how they fared this past season.

"Not so good," he replied with a frown. "But there's always next year. We don't have cable in here so I can't watch them play but I do catch the games on the radio. Did you know they have a new guy on the team with the same name as me?"

"Logan Murphy?"

"No ma'am." Logan smiled. "Logan Forsythe. Second baseman. Hit seventeen home runs this season. If I ever get out of here, the first thing I'm going to do is buy a ticket to Trop Field so I can see him knock the ball out of thc park."

Simple pleasures. Watching a baseball game. That was what Logan missed the most. After ten years on death row, I wondered if he understood how much the outside world had changed. If he had any idea of all the new technology intruding into our daily lives. On the other hand, looking at him smiling at me, dreaming of the day he could watch his favorite team play, I suspected it didn't matter. Logan would be just fine.

Vowing to find a way to get him out of this place, I said goodbye.

He lifted one manacled hand and waved before rising from his chair and turning to face the officer standing behind him. I watched his back as he shuffled out the door.

Leaving Raiford, I popped a CD in the player and let Billy Joel transport me from the grim atmosphere inside the prison walls to fond memories of my youth. As I headed west, the landscape morphed from flea markets and abandoned citrus stands to sprawling farms with white rail fences. Mile after mile through Ocala I passed thoroughbred horses grazing in lush green pastures. Humming along with Billy, I hit the interstate and set the cruise control. A few hours later I arrived at the Venice drawbridge. When I rolled down my windows the smell of low tide filled the car. I waved to the bridge tender and he waved back. Smiling, I counted down the minutes before I reached home. My plan for the evening was to kick off my shoes, pour myself a glass of wine and curl up with a good book. As I turned onto my street, the setting sun blinded me in a brilliant blaze of light.

I raised my hand, blinking twice to clear the black spots in my field of vision. One of those black spots took shape. Lalo's truck was parked in my driveway.

THIRTY

A hazy film of dog slobber ran down the tinted windows of the truck. Peering inside, I saw a tattered suitcase and a brown paper bag on the back seat. No sign of Lalo or Maya anywhere. As I stepped into the house, the faint smell of Lalo's musky cologne greeted me. I caught sight of empty beer bottles and an open package of pretzels on my kitchen counter. Following the sound of Lalo's deep voice to the lanai, I found him wearing a Tampa Ray's baseball cap and speaking into his cell phone. There was something about him, something different. It took me a full minute to realize in the weeks since I had seen him, he'd grown a mustache.

Maya rose to greet me, her entire body wagging. My eye caught a slight movement to my left and I spun around. A girl with hazelnut skin and a round face sat on my chaise lounge, her knees pulled tight to her chest. She stared at me, unblinking.

I judged her to be seventeen, maybe eighteen years old. She wore a tight pair of denim shorts and pink flip-flops. Her T-shirt fit like a second skin telling the world she went braless. Straight, jet-black hair fell halfway down her back. Despite the angry red scar on her chin, she had a beautiful face. Getting a better look, I realized she might be a few years younger than I originally thought. Layers of makeup, blood-red lipstick and kohl eyeliner masked her youth, but the hard look in her eyes spoke of experience. Those eyes, the color of black coffee, scanned the length of me. I got the impression she was trying to make up her mind about something.

Seeing me, Lalo pinched his thumb and index finger together to tell me he would only be a minute. Listening to his side of the conversation, I surmised he was speaking with Ben.

"She just walked in . . . Yeah. Okay, thanks. See you tomorrow."

He ended the call and looked at me. The gap in his front teeth showed through the wide grin on his face. I wasn't smiling.

"How did you get into my house?" I asked.

"This is Valentina," he replied with a wave in the direction of the teenager.

As if that answered my question. I figured he probably found the key I kept hidden under a flowerpot by the front door. It would have been nice if he apologized for entering without permission. Or maybe offered a word of thanks for the beer and pretzels. Obviously, I expected too much.

At the mention of her name, Valentina shifted her gaze to Lalo. When she unfolded her body I caught a glimpse of a silver heart hanging from a chain around her neck. She flicked those eyes back toward me, a feral cat ready to spring.

"Her English isn't so good, but I expect you'll manage okay."

An uncomfortable feeling crept up my spine. A far-off warning bell started ringing in my ears.

"What do you mean, I'll manage?"

"She's staying with you for a few days."

"What in the world do you . . . you think you can waltz in here and turn my home into a half-way house for any stray you pick up off the streets?"

I looked back at Valentina. Her face wore an indifferent stare but everything about her body language suggested a nervous current running through her. A bead of sweat bloomed on her forehead. Fingernails dug into bare thighs, her jaw clenched. She curled and relaxed her toes like she was ready to run.

"Sorry Valentina, nothing personal."

Her eyelids closed, re-opening in a slow-motion blink. Her jaw remained fixed but she relaxed her hands, revealing small red crescents where her nails cut into her skin.

"I needed a place to stash her," Lalo said.

"What's wrong with your boat?"

"My boat is the first place they'll look."

"They? Who . . . wait, I want to have a word with you. Inside. Now."

Lalo nodded and made a downward motion with his hand. Maya, who leaned against my leg, walked over to Valentina and sat. When the girl reached out to pat her head, the dog lay down next to her.

I led the way into the kitchen and poured myself a glass of wine. After taking a healthy swallow I counted to ten, trying to calm down. I popped two pieces of gum in my mouth and kept counting to twenty. The heat of anger burned my cheeks. Or maybe that was the wine. Either way, I was fired up and prepared to stand my ground.

"She can't stay."

"Calm down, Cate."

"Don't tell me to calm down. You have a lot of nerve breaking into my home uninvited." I waved my hand at the mess on the counter. "Let's get one thing straight. You can't keep dropping in and out of here, thinking I have nothing better to do than take care of your problems. Bring that girl back to wherever you found her. I mean it. I've had enough of your games."

"You're saying you won't let her stay?" The wide eyes, the arched brows a picture of pained disbelief.

"You're not listening."

"I only need you to watch her until the police take her statement."

Curiosity pulled me back from the brink of tossing them both out on the sidewalk.

"What statement? What's going on?"

"You remember Luci?" Lalo said quietly.

I nodded.

"Valentina knows who killed her."

"Then bring her to the police."

"I need to get a few things sorted out before I can do that."

He had my attention. "So you were right about Luci? It wasn't an accident? Where does Valentina fit in?"

"She's one of Norma's girls. And she claims she saw everything."

"Let me guess. You don't want to bring her to the police because Moreno is somehow involved."

"No . . . listen, it's more complicated than that."

"If you expect me to take her in, then you'd better start uncomplicating things right now."

"Valentina's boyfriend killed Luci. Valentina didn't go to the local police because she knows Moreno is dirty. That, and the fact that she is afraid of the boyfriend. When I heard all this, I offered to take her to Geri. All I'm asking is for you to keep an eye on her for a day or two until I have a chance to run a few things by Ben."

I didn't buy the whole story. Something still didn't feel right but despite everything, I believed Lalo was trying to do the right thing.

"What does Ben have to do with this?"

"There's a connection between Valentina and Ben's client, Ricky Castro."

"Is that what you were talking about when I came in?"

"Ben agrees that Valentina should stay here for the time being."

"Let me speak with him, then I can decide."

Lalo pulled out his phone and after tapping the screen twice he passed it to me.

"Hey, Lalo. How did Cate take it?"

"Cate didn't take it well," I shot back. "But thanks for asking."

"Aunt Cate? I thought you were . . . what are you doing with Lalo's phone?"

"Are you crazy? I will not harbor your murder witness. In my opinion, you should call Geri Garibaldi right this minute. I don't understand why you can't—"

"Hang on, Aunt Cate. I don't know exactly what Lalo told you, but things are a little complicated."

"Complicated my eye. What's so complicated about this? The girl knows her boyfriend killed Luci. Tell Geri to arrest the guy. End of story."

"You have to trust me on this one, okay?"

"Oh great."

"Listen, there's a risk that Valentina will get cold feet and run. If that happens, her boyfriend will literally get away with murder. Lalo can't keep her on the boat and I certainly can't watch her while I'm at work."

"Well, if she wants to leave I can't stop her."

"But if she decides to stay at least she'll be safe."

"I don't know . . ."

"Lalo says the girl knows something that will help Ricky."

I could hear the pleading in his voice. But the ringing in my ears was as loud as ever.

"Aunt Cate?"

"Okay, you win. But I'm telling you, I've got a bad feeling about this."

When I passed the phone back to Lalo, he assured Ben that everything was under control. Lalo gave me an approving nod and left me standing there, sipping my wine while he returned to the lanai. I heard him speaking in low tones with Valentina. She answered in something just above a whisper, but since they spoke Spanish I couldn't understand anyway. After a few minutes Lalo reappeared in the kitchen, picked his keys off the counter and headed to the front door. As I watched him walk toward his truck, I realized he left without the dog.

"Wait," I called. "You forgot Maya."

"Let her sleep in Valentina's room," Lalo shouted back. "She'll raise the alarm if Valentina decides to cut anchor and run." He paused, as if something new occurred to him. "Keep your cash and credit cards under your pillow at night. Your car keys too. And I almost forgot . . ." He reached into his pocket and pulled out a business card. Coming back to the front door he pressed it into my hand. "Don't forget to take her to the clinic in the morning."

"What clinic?" I looked down to see the card was from a place called the Detox Center on Tamiami Trail.

"We stopped on the way here and registered Valentina as an outpatient. They started her on 60 milligrams of methadone this morning."

"You might have mentioned she's a drug addict." I stared at the card in my hand, ready to throw it back at him together with Valentina and the dog.

"But then you wouldn't have agreed to let her stay," Lalo smiled. "Listen, it sometimes takes a day or two for the methadone to kick in so she may experience some . . . a little discomfort until she stabilizes. After that she'll be fine. I have a sheet with instructions for you somewhere here."

He fumbled around for a minute before fishing a crumpled paper out of his pocket. At the top of the page it read, "Home Options for Opiate Withdrawal." Scanning down I read the words anxiety, sweating, irritability, nausea and muscle pain. For each symptom there was a suggested home remedy, all of which I had in my medicine cabinet. At the bottom of the page, in large, bold letters was a warning to contact the Detox Center if symptoms persist.

"I still can't believe you brought a drug addicted prostitute into my house and expected me to . . ."

Lalo reached up and peeled his baseball cap off his head. With a sharp intake of breath, I noticed his thick, black hair was completely gone. Salt-and-pepper stubble covered the dome of his head.

"What happened to you?" I asked.

"Shaving my head seemed like a good way to blend in."

"Blend in where?"

"I've been working as a migrant farm hand for the last few weeks."

"You look so different. You're hair, that mustache . . ."

"Listen, I'm trying to make a point here. Appearances can be deceiving. Those folks in the tomato fields took one look at me and assumed I was one of them. You don't know Valentina's story. In your eyes she's a lost cause, a junkie hooker. You want to know what I see? I see a victim. Her family back in Mexico probably has no clue about the life she leads. And even if they do, they're too far away to do anything about it. Right now I'm all she's got."

I let his words sink in. Recognizing the truth when I heard it, I felt ashamed. I had prejudged Valentina without a second thought as to what circumstances brought her to this end.

"Well," I said at last. "You're wrong about one thing. She's got me too."

THIRTY-ONE

Lalo sat on Ben's couch, looking up at the ceiling as he rubbed the top of his closely cropped head. Ben thought the new haircut combined with an unexpected appearance of a mustache and three days of gray beard stubble made his investigator look ten years older. He shifted his attention to the paper bag on the coffee table.

"So I'm gonna ask again. What's in the bag?"

Lalo dismissed Ben's question with a wave of his hand. "I'm getting to that."

Ben knew Lalo spent the last three weeks in Immokalee investigating Luci's murder but despite his investigator's promise that there was a connection between Luci and Marcela de la Vega, he still didn't know what it was.

Lalo reached for his beer and drained the last drop.

"Are you ready for another beer?" Ben asked.

"Later. Where was I?"

"You were giving me your report on how you went to Immokalee to track down Angel Abarco."

"Yeah. You remember his name popped up when I went down to Michoacán last month, right? He's the guy who crossed the border with Norma and her sister."

Ben nodded.

"Well, he works for a smuggling cartel. He specializes in recruiting young girls from his old village and bringing them to Immokalee. Once they get here, Abarco finds them jobs, gets them a place to live and paves the road to the American dream. At least that's what he promises to do. Marcela, Luci, Valentina, they all came from that village. And one way or another, Abarco is responsible for what happened to them."

Ben sat up straight in his recliner. "Are you saying Abarco killed Marcela?" he asked.

"Patience, *amigo*. Where was I? Oh yeah, after I arrived in Immokalee, I took a day or two to figure things out. I wanted to blend in and get the lay of the land before making any moves. And I figured the best way to do that was to get a job in the tomato fields. So I shaved my head, put on an old pair of jeans and a straw hat. Everyone assumed I was just another migrant Mexican looking for work. As long as I kept up with the other field hands, no one questioned where I came from or what I was doing there."

Lalo picked up his bottle and peered through the brown glass.

"Now do you want that second beer?" Ben asked.

"Not yet."

"So how did you find Abarco?"

Lalo shook his head and his mustache curved downward. "I did my job, kept my head down and my ears open. Before long his name came up in conversation. I heard someone say he's the owner of a restaurant in town, a place where a hard-working man can get a plate of real Michoacán food for a fair price. Chaparrito's."

"Chaparrito's? Are you saying the short guy we met when we had lunch with Moreno is Angel Abarco?" Ben asked.

"One and the same. Abarco was right in front of us the whole time."

Ben's mind raced. He remembered the bear hug Abarco gave Tom Moreno when they met at the restaurant. Deputy Leroy Lamb suggested Moreno sometimes "went along to get along" with people who ran illegal operations in the town. And then there was the connection to Norma who crossed the border with Abarco in the first place, both of them from the same village in Michoacán as Marcela, Luci and Valentina. Phone records indicated Norma called Chaparrito's on the day Marcela was killed. Though Ben suspected Lalo knew something about that call, his investigator took his own sweet time getting to the point.

"And you said Valentina is Abarco's new girlfriend?"

"*Was* his girlfriend." Lalo shrugged, palms turned upward. "Abarco likes his girls young, very young. Valentina was fourteen when he took her for his own but it's been two years and . . ." Another shrug. "I guess he got tired of her. Remember the waitress we saw at Chaparrito's? That was Valentina. With Luci gone, Norma was down one hooker so Abarco decided Valentina could turn in her waitress uniform and start turning tricks for a living. I found her in one of Abarco's bars, selling customers more than the piss they pass as beer in that place."

Lalo shook his head and stared out the window. "I got the full picture of how Abarco's operation works. He pays Norma to control the prostitutes. She keeps them buried in debt by charging an arm and a leg for room and board. Abarco's side business, or maybe his main business, is drugs. He started out as a coyote, transporting both girls and drugs across the border for the cartel but now Abarco runs the whole operation in Immokalee for them. He even launders the cash through his bars and restaurant."

"What did you say to convince Valentina to leave?"

"What's that expression about a woman scorned? Hell hath no fury, right? After I rolled into town, it didn't take long for me to get wind of her story. I needed to be careful not to let her know I was one of the guys who showed up at Chaparrito's to meet with Moreno but she never recognized me with my new look. I made it a habit to hang out in the bars she worked. At first I think Valentina pegged me for a narc, but after a while, she began to realize I was her ticket out of there."

Ben nodded, impressed. Lalo explained that once he gained her trust, Valentina began to confide in him. One night, eyes scanning the bar to be sure no one could hear her, she whispered in his ear that she was in the room when Luci died. Breathlessly, she told him Angel Abarco killed her.

"And she's willing to testify?" Ben asked.

Lalo nodded. "Yeah. But for a little insurance I recorded everything she said." He reached into his pocket and pulled out a set of keys. When he pressed a button on the fob, a girl's voice whispered in Spanish against the backdrop of Latin music.

"Did she give you consent to record that conversation?"

"Are you crazy? 'Course not."

"Then it's not admissible in court. Florida statute."

"I know that," Lalo replied with a grin as he stuffed the keys back into his pocket. "Just wanted to try out this new gadget. Nobody pays any attention to a set of keys on the table. When I get back to the boat, I'll send you a copy of everything I got down there."

"You have more?"

"Yeah, lots. First time I used this baby was when I spoke to Luci's brother. I figured it wouldn't hurt to get him on record in case there was any question down the road about how I got my hands on Luci's autopsy report. When I told him what I was up to, the brother was happy to help. Within a week I had everything I needed."

"Weren't you running the risk that Moreno or Abarco would find out you were poking around?" Ben asked.

"Not really. The medical examiner ruled Luci's death an accidental overdose. We've got a heroin epidemic here in Florida. If the sheriff's office opened a criminal investigation every time a junkie went belly-up, the courts would be jammed for years. When Luci's brother asked for the report, no one at the ME's office batted an eye."

"I assume the cause of death was drugs?"

"China White."

Ben tipped his head and arched an eyebrow.

"Fentanyl-laced heroin," Lalo explained. "Fentanyl is a synthetic opiate. It packs a punch for the user and the suppliers love it because it's cheap. Win/win, right? Problem is China White kills. Luci's system was loaded with the stuff."

Ben cracked his knuckles, recalling a lecture in law school that concerned the case of a one-armed homeless man who asked a friend for assistance in getting his fix. As a result of the injection, the man died of an overdose. A first-degree murder charge was brought against the dead man's friend. The defense argued that the addict wanted his friend to inject him. In the end the charge was reduced to manslaughter and the accused went to jail for only a few years.

"Did Luci ask Abarco to shoot her up?" Ben asked.

"I know what you're thinking," Lalo replied. "There's no way Abarco will be able to plea this down to manslaughter by saying Luci asked for it. Valentina said Luci tried to fight him off, but he had Valentina hold her down while he shot her up."

"Then technically Valentina was an accomplice."

"Yeah, that's why you need to negotiate a plea deal before we turn her over."

"I think I can make that work. Valentina's testimony, in exchange for immunity from prosecution."

"Are you volunteering to represent her?"

"I can't sign her with the Project but I can take her on as a private client, pro bono, of course."

"I hoped you'd say that." Lalo took another look at his empty bottle. "But there's more. I'm guessing Luci wasn't Abarco's only victim."

"What do you mean?"

"Get me that other beer and I'll tell you what I've got in the bag."

Ben went to the kitchen where he pulled two cold bottles from the refrigerator. As he unscrewed the tops, his mind churned through everything Lalo had told him. He returned to the living room and sat down. He stared at the bag on the table, "Tell me you have something in there that's going to help me prove Ricky Castro didn't kill Marcela de la Vega."

Lalo took a deep drink and set the bottle down on the table. "One night, after a long day in the field I stopped to see Valentina. She joined me for a drink at a table in the back. The drunker she got the more she felt inclined to tell me what a *pendejo* Abarco was. She said that the day he kicked her out of his house, she threatened to leave town. Said she was going to start a new life, maybe even go back to Mexico. If she expected a kiss goodbye she was off by about a mile. Abarco slapped her hard across the face. While she checked to see if she still had all her teeth, he went ballistic, screaming that no one leaves him, not ever. Just to make sure she got the message, he sucker punched her in the stomach. As she puked her guts up on the floor, he told her that was the only warning she was going to get."

"What did he mean by that?"

"Valentina said Abarco spat in her face, saying the next time she thought about leaving, she should remember what happened to Marcela."

Ben leaned forward in his chair. He sensed Lalo was finally ready to connect the dots between Valentina, Luci and Marcela. He searched the face of his investigator, looking for a clue. Lalo only gave him a half-smile and raised his bottle to his lips.

"Valentina was with Abarco for two years," Ben thought out loud. "So she must have known Marcela. Were they friends?"

"Not friends. Abarco keeps his private property isolated from the other girls. But Valentina was at Chaparrito's when Norma called. Abarco grabbed the phone and waved Valentina away but she ducked around the corner long enough to get the drift of the conversation. When he hung up she slipped into the ladies' room. By the time she came out, Abarco was gone. Twenty minutes later he was back, dragging Marcela behind him."

Ben waited for Lalo to finish his beer. When the bottle hit the table, Lalo continued.

"That's everything. When I pressed Valentina for more she said if I wanted to know what happened in that alley it would cost me." Lalo snorted a laugh. "We got down to business real quick. I told her you were the guy in charge of the reward."

"What reward?"

Lalo shrugged. "Do you want to help your client or don't you?"

"How much are we talking about?"

"That . . ." Lalo belched. "That is negotiable. I doubt Valentina is stupid enough to run back to Abarco but I wouldn't count on her waiting around forever. Take a look in that bag I brought in with me. We need to talk about strategy."

Ben reached for the bag. As he lifted it off the table, the contents made a clinking noise. Peering inside, he saw two glasses. Nesting in one of them was a spoon sealed in a plastic sandwich bag.

"What is this?"

"What you've got there is evidence, *amigo*. Abarco's fingerprints and DNA."

"Why does one glass have a red mark on the bottom?"

"Valentina worked at the bar a few nights ago when Abarco came in with a friend. After they left, she took both glasses and brought them to the kitchen. Unfortunately, she got them mixed up and couldn't remember exactly which glass was which. So she used her lipstick to make an X on the bottom of the one she thinks Abarco used. Just in case she got it wrong, she stuck the other one in the bag and smuggled them both out of there. One of those glasses—hopefully the one marked with lipstick—will give you Abarco's prints and DNA."

"The chain of evidence won't hold up with any of this stuff."

"I know. But with Valentina's testimony, you have enough to nail that son-of-a-bitch for killing Luci."

"What's with the spoon?" Ben asked.

"Yeah, you might want to send that to the lab too."

"Why?"

"I picked it up from Luci's nightstand. I'd bet my boat that Abarco's prints are on it. And I can tell you for a fact that the residue in the bowl will match the China White they found in Luci's bloodstream."

The two men sat in silence, Ben absorbed in his own thoughts while Lalo sat with his legs crossed, blowing into his empty bottle. Despite the relaxed atmosphere in the room, Ben felt wired. In the course of the last few hours, Lalo gave him everything he needed to open an investigation into Luci's death. But what he really needed was information to help his client, Ricky Castro. If Valentina was telling the truth, she had information about Marcela's murder. Ben had to figure out how to get her to talk.

Lalo stood and stretched.

"I'm thinking about ordering pizza."

"Thanks, but I want to get back to the boat before dark." Lalo played with the keys in his pocket. "When you send those glasses to the lab, don't forget to have them check Abarco's DNA against the stain on Marcela's skirt."

"I can't believe I didn't think of that. I sort of discounted that stain because we can't pinpoint the time when it landed on her skirt, but you never know, right? Listen, I've been thinking . . . we have a jurisdiction problem. We can't bring Valentina to Geri. She's with the Sarasota County Sheriff's Office and this is a Collier County issue."

"Yeah, well if you go to Moreno, he's sure to tell Abarco. And if Abarco finds out Valentina is willing to testify against him—"

"He'll come looking for her." In his excitement, Ben almost forgot their key witness. "I never thought about that. By asking my aunt to watch Valentina, I've put her life in danger."

"I don't think so. The trail will lead to me, not Cate."

Ben nodded. "I agree we need to keep Moreno out of this. But getting Geri involved isn't the right way to go either. I have a better idea. When we're ready, I'll go to Leroy Lamb. He transferred out of the Immokalee station but he still works for the Collier County Sheriff's Office. I'll get the ball rolling by ordering the lab tests first thing in the morning. Are you available Tuesday?"

"Sure, why?"

"I don't want to wait for the plea deal to get Valentina's statement on the record. But I need a translator. I'm thinking we could go down to Venice together."

Lalo nodded. "No problem."

"Good. I'll pick you up Tuesday morning and we can drive down together."

"Aren't you forgetting something?" Lalo grinned.

Ben racked his brain, mentally checking everything off his list. He shook his head.

"It will be a while before you're ready to turn Valentina over to the cops. What's the turn-around time for the lab results?"

"I don't know, a few weeks maybe. Four at most."

"Well then, you can be the one to tell Cate her houseguest won't be leaving anytime soon."

Ben heard Lalo laughing all the way to his truck.

THIRTY-TWO

I woke to the sound of Valentina retching. Aside from patting her back as she bent over the toilet, all I could do was keep her hydrated by insisting she drink plenty of water each time she emptied her stomach. Her sheets were soaked so I changed the bedding before tucking her back in. Placing a cool, wet cloth on her forehead, I sat vigil for the rest of the night.

Come morning Valentina wandered into the kitchen, her black hair shooting out in all directions, her bare feet scuffing along the tiled floor. The clean nightgown I gave her in the middle of the night hung on her scarecrow-thin frame. A rancid odor entered the kitchen with her.

"Would you like breakfast?" I asked.

She headed straight for the refrigerator and pulled out a bottle of cranberry juice.

"If you wait ten minutes, I'll fix you eggs."

Her brown skin turned pale. "*Quiero mi medicina.*"

I took a guess at what *medicina* meant. "We'll go to the clinic after you take a shower and get dressed."

I noticed the tremor in her hand as she unscrewed the lid and drank juice straight from the bottle.

"You will find the glasses in the upper cabinet." I took the bottle from her hand and pointed. She turned and shuffled back down the hall toward her bedroom. I was about to call her back when the phone rang.

"How are you two getting along?" Ben asked.

"When is Lalo coming back for her?"

"That's why I'm calling. If it's okay with you, we'll both come to your house on Tuesday to take her statement."

That meant I only had to keep an eye on Valentina for a few more days. With a smile on my face that Ben couldn't see I said, "Good. I don't know what Lalo told you about this girl, but she's having a pretty rough time. I think she needs professional help."

Ben paused. "We're going to be taping the interview so make sure she wears something appropriate. A blouse and skirt would be good, or maybe a dress if she has one."

"All she's got are the clothes on her back. And believe me, they're hardly what I'd call appropriate."

"Can you take her shopping?"

"My first priority is to get her to the methadone clinic."

"What?"

I wasn't surprised that Lalo didn't tell Ben everything about his star witness. Nothing about Lalo could surprise me at this point.

"You heard me. What time can I expect you on Tuesday?"

"I'm guessing we'll be there in time for lunch."

"Why not plan on staying for dinner? I can make that pot roast you like and if you don't feel like driving all the way back to Gainesville, you're welcome to stay the night. After all, my guest room will be free after Lalo and Valentina leave."

"Umm . . . thanks, but I probably won't stick around for dinner. Maybe next time."

It sounded like an apology. Assuring Ben that I understood, I told him I looked forward to seeing him on Tuesday and disconnected the call.

I found Valentina back under the covers, eyes closed. She hugged Maya to her side like the dog was a stuffed teddy bear. Maya looked up at me. Valentina remained still, but from the sound of her breathing, I knew she feigned sleep.

"That was Ben on the phone. He told me Lalo will be here to pick you up on Tuesday."

Her eyes opened and closed in the same slow blink I saw the previous day.

"Valentina? Do you understand?"

She gave me a blank stare.

"Okay, we'll talk about it later. I'll be outside checking on my tomato plants while you shower."

"*Jitomates*?"

"Yes," I replied. "Toe-MAY-toes."

"Toe-MAY-toes."

I nodded, smiling. "If you were going to be here longer, I could teach you English."

She closed her eyes. "*No hablo ingles*."

"I know, but I suspect you understand more than you let on."

"*Medicina*," she whined.

I hesitated. She looked miserable, curled up in bed like that.

"I don't know much about this medicine they're giving you. But it seems to me you shouldn't go to the clinic on an empty stomach. You need to eat something."

She threw back the covers and sat up, shaking her head.

"Suit yourself. I put clean towels in the guest bathroom. You'll find a new toothbrush and toothpaste in the vanity drawer."

When I snapped my fingers, the dog jumped off the bed and followed me outside. Maya rolled in the thick grass, her black coat gleaming in the sun while she watched me pluck a large, ripe tomato from the vine. After pulling a few weeds, I returned to the house with her trailing behind. I put my ear to the bedroom door and heard the shower running. When Valentina finally appeared, I looked up to see her dressed in yesterday's clothes, her face washed clean. Obviously she left Immokalee in a hurry, leaving everything—even her make-up—behind.

She wiped her runny nose with the back of her hand and scratched the crook of her arm. "*Estoy lista*."

"What?"

She pointed to the door and pantomimed walking with her fingers. "*Medicina*." The girl had a one-track mind.

If Valentina didn't point out the Detox Center tucked into the back of a strip mall I would have missed it. There was no sign on the door, but when we entered I knew we were in the right place. Brochures on treating drug addiction were spread out on a table in the reception area and the walls were plastered with posters promoting abstinence. A uniformed nurse smiled at Valentina, greeting her in Spanish. She then looked at me and said, "You must be Mrs. Stokes. Mr. Sanchez told us Valentina is staying with you. We'll get you set up in an examination room right away."

I expected these people would give Valentina a bottle of pills and send us on our way, but the nurse grabbed a clipboard and led the way down the hall to a small closet-like space where she asked me to read and sign a sheaf of forms. As I read through them, I realized I was named as Valentina's caregiver.

"So let me understand. I have to bring Valentina here every morning so you can check to see how she is doing?"

"That's right." The nurse nodded.

"And how long will this go on?"

"Oh, she can stay on this medication indefinitely." She handed me another form to sign.

"And what about after she leaves Venice?"

A cloud crossed the nurse's eyes. "Leaves? Mr. Sanchez said she lives with you."

"He did? Well, she does . . . that is, she's staying with me until Lalo can find a more permanent place for her to stay."

The nurse placed a little pill in the palm of Valentina's trembling hand and passed her a paper cup of water. Valentina scratched the surface of the pill with her fingernail before popping it in her mouth and washing it down. The nurse shook her head and spoke rapid Spanish to Valentina.

"She thinks by scratching off the surface she'll get a quicker high," she said to me. "I told her that won't work with these. How did it go last night?"

"Not great," I admitted.

"Well, by the end of the day the worst will be over. Try to get some food into her. She's obviously undernourished." She passed me a little envelope with another pill inside. "Give this to her with dinner and we'll see you here tomorrow morning."

Back in the car, I turned to see Valentina resting her head against the window. Her eyes were closed, the corners of her mouth turned up slightly. The trembling in her hands eased. With a sigh, she reopened her eyes to reveal a thin brown band around her dilated pupils.

"Are you okay?"

She answered with a sleepy smile.

Valentina went from one rack to the next, selecting items far too provocative for a girl her age. When I found a silk blouse that I thought would look nice on her, she shook her head emphatically. Finally, she showed me a see-through blouse with an under-camisole that she thought pretty and I found acceptable. I picked out a not-too-short black skirt that went well with the blouse. Valentina came out of the dressing room and stood in front of the mirror, turning this way and that, admiring her own image. I must say, with her perfect complexion and long lashes framing her dark eyes she was strikingly beautiful. Ben would certainly approve.

After that first outfit we found several others, both of us making compromises to build a wardrobe that carried her though the next few days.

When we got home, Valentina wanted to show off her new clothes. While Maya and I sat on the lanai, she ran in and out of her room changing outfits and modeling everything for me. She saved the bathing suit—a bikini that barely covered her private parts—for last. Valentina pulled her long, black hair into a ponytail, held in place with one of the stretchy donuts that we picked up at the mall. When she spun around for me to admire how the bathing suit fit, I caught sight of the tattoo on the base of her neck. Inky black against her beautiful skin was a numbered bar code. A shudder ran through me as I remembered seeing the same mark on Luci. I reached up and brushed Valentina's tattoo with the tip of my finger.

"Who did this to you?" I heard my own voice tremble with anger.

Slapping my hand away, Valentina spun to face me. "*Mi amante*! Angel." The expression she wore earlier—a cold, blank stare—returned to her face. With a single, swift stroke she pulled her hair free from the donut and turned her back on me. As she made her way into the house, there was no trace of the bounce in her step I had seen only moments before.

Valentina slept well the second night. I, on the other hand, tossed and turned, my senses on high alert for the sound of Valentina moving around. In the morning I found her snoring, her arm draped over Maya who stretched next to her on the covers. The sight of the two of them together like that touched my heart in a way I hadn't felt in a long time.

"Rise and shine," I called softly.

Valentina groaned and rolled over. Maya wagged her stubby tail.

"Maya, get off the bed."

The dog pinned her ears against her head and came to me. Her tail wagged slowly as she licked my hand.

"Valentina," I called a bit louder. "It's time to get up."

No reaction.

"Come on now, we have a busy day ahead." I put my hand on her shoulder.

Valentina shook me off and pulled the sheet over her head. She mumbled something in Spanish, but I got the gist of it. Amazing how quickly we learned to communicate. With a little smile, I grabbed the corner of her covers and peeled them off the bed as I headed to the door.

"Breakfast first, *medicina* after," I called over my shoulder

Thirty minutes later Valentina appeared dressed in one of her new outfits, a little sundress with spaghetti straps. She greeted me with a *buenos días* and a smile before sitting down to breakfast. Maya rose to her feet and wandered out of the kitchen. Too late, I realized what she was up to. Before I could stop her, the dog emerged from the bathroom, dripping water from the toilet all the way back to the kitchen.

"Bad dog!" I shouted. "Bad Maya!"

Valentina covered her mouth, laughter spilling out between her fingers. It was almost worth mopping up after the dog just to hear that sound.

"We're going back to the mall this morning. I want to get language tapes to send with you when you leave on Tuesday."

"*Quiero quedarme aquí*. Me stay here. You learn me English."

As I looked at her, I found myself wishing we had a bit more time together. The poor thing needed a fresh start in life. But in reality, I knew Valentina needed much more than I could offer. I vowed to speak with Lalo about getting her professional help with her drug habit, even if I had to pay for it myself.

THIRTY-THREE

Stephanie listened as Ben told her Lalo had returned from Immokalee with a witness to Luci's murder and a brown paper bag with two stolen glasses and a spoon.

"What are you planning to do with that stuff?" Stephanie asked.

"I want the lab to check for fingerprints and DNA," Ben replied. "We need to put a rush on it."

"The lab's lead time is four to six weeks."

"I don't have that kind of time. I'm not sure how long Valentina will stick around."

"I didn't hear the part when you told me all this has something to do with an actual client of ours."

"Valentina saw who murdered Marcela de la Vega. I'm driving down tomorrow to get her statement."

Stephanie lifted the lid of her coffee, blowing across the surface before taking a sip. Ben fished his own cup out of the bag, leaving the two donuts for later. He looked at Stephanie, willing her to come up with an idea for how to get the results quickly.

"I have a guy, a technician in the lab. If I ask nicely, he'll get everything back to me by the end of the week. That's the best I can do."

"Who is this guy?"

"Just a guy."

Ben wondered how many 'guys' Stephanie had wrapped around her finger. He would do just about anything to be one of them. But if she had the power to fast track the process, he couldn't complain.

"I appreciate whatever you can do." Ben picked up the evidence and passed it to Stephanie. "I'll get Valentina's sworn testimony and we'll take it from there."

A few hours later, Ben was deep in thought when Stephanie reappeared in his office and handed him a bag from the corner deli.

"What's this?" Ben asked.

"Lunch. Your regular, pastrami on rye."

Ben's face broke into a broad smile. "Thanks Steph."

"No big deal. Have you finished prepping for your interview with Valentina?"

"I hope so. I've got one shot at getting this right. If Valentina skips town before we turn her over to the police, her statement is all we'll have."

"I've helped Greg prep for a witness statement or two. Do you need a fresh pair of eyes to look things over?"

"I know you're busy."

"This is a one-time offer, Shepherd. Take it or leave it."

Ben smiled. "I'll take it."

Stephanie shut the office door and settled into Ben's visitor's chair. Reaching into the deli bag she pulled out the sandwich and passed him half.

"I get the pickle. You can have the chips."

Ben passed his legal pad to Stephanie. After flipping through the pages quickly she raised her eyes to meet his. Ben could tell there was something wrong.

"Relax, it's not all bad." Stephanie pointed to the top of the first page. Ben rolled his chair closer, his arm brushing against hers as he reached for a pen.

"What's wrong?" Ben peered at the paper.

"Giving the witness an overview before you begin is a good idea. But you have to keep it simple. Don't forget you're going to be speaking through a translator. Make a note to yourself to pause after every sentence. That will give the witness a chance to ask for clarification if she doesn't understand something."

"Got it." The complication of working with a translator never occurred to him. He started marking up his work, simplifying his sentences and adding notes in the margin.

"I know it might seem obvious to you, but rule number one, don't throw any surprises at your witness. Rule number two, keep this whole thing as informal as you possibly can while getting the facts on the record."

"Right," Ben replied. He didn't look up as he continued making changes. When he finished, Stephanie gave him a few pointers on how to phrase his questions to be more direct. She reached over and flipped through the pages, pausing when she got to a point that Ben struggled with earlier.

"What's this?" She shook her head. "You can't ask your witness to admit she held the victim down while Abarco injected the heroin."

"I figured that's going to come out sooner or later so why not give her a chance to explain?"

"Definitely not a can of worms you want to open." Stephanie grabbed Ben's pen from his hand and scratched out the question. "Avoid any mention of Valentina's involvement in Luci's death if you can. I'm not telling you to censor her testimony but don't make it easy for the opposition."

"I'm hoping we won't have any opposition," Ben replied. "I intend to negotiate an immunity deal in exchange for Valentina's cooperation."

"You can't count on that. With or without that deal, if the State Attorney's office opens an investigation—and if that spoon has Abarco's prints on it they will—Valentina's sworn testimony will be part of the record. Don't think for one minute they are going to look upon her as a victim. She's a drug-abusing prostitute. In the eyes of the law, that means she's a criminal. You need to protect your client by steering clear of any questions that may come back to bite her."

Ben felt foolish. Granted, he had only practiced law for less than a year, but he should have realized certain things should be kept in the shadows.

"Anything else?"

"That's basically it." Stephanie handed him back his pen. "If things don't go according to plan, don't panic. You never know what kind of surprises a witness will throw into the mix."

Ben drew a deep breath. "I don't know how to thank you for this,"

"Just do a good job. If Valentina tells you who killed Marcela de la Vega, Greg will crown you employee of the month. If not he'll rip you a new one for going rogue. Either way, I've got your back."

THIRTY-FOUR

Maya jumped on Lalo, yelping with joy as he came through the door. I greeted him with a decidedly less exuberant handshake. After kissing Ben on the cheek I introduced him to Valentina. She took a few steps back when Ben extended his hand but he accepted the rebuff with a friendly smile. He asked where he could stage the camera equipment so I showed him to the living room and watched as he set about getting everything ready. Valentina sat on the couch, fixing him with her unblinking stare while he attached the video camera to the tripod.

In her new white blouse and black skirt Valentina's transformation was complete. Her pupils were still dilated, but there was no sign of a tremor in her hands and over the course of the past few days she had stopped scratching the crook of her arm.

Lalo settled next to Valentina and struck up a conversation with her in Spanish. Everything seemed to be under control so I excused myself and went to the kitchen to load a tray with plates of sandwiches and a bowl of guacamole. I carried the food back to the living room and set out a spread that I figured was more than enough for the four of us. Minutes later, when I returned from the kitchen with a pitcher of iced tea, I saw three sandwiches were already gone. Lalo's cheeks bulged and crumbs stuck to Maya's jowls. I popped a piece of gum in my mouth while Maya leaned against Lalo's leg, staring at him with her yellow eyes. I cleared my throat when Lalo tossed the dog half of his fourth sandwich. He looked my way, gave me a cherubic smile and stuffed the other half into his mouth.

Having finished setting up the equipment, Ben reached into his messenger bag and pulled out a legal pad. He sat facing Valentina from across the room. Only when he cracked his fingers did I realize how nervous he actually was.

"Before we start recording I want to explain to Valentina how this works," Ben said to Lalo. "I'll try to remember to pause frequently to give you time to translate but if I go too fast, remind me to slow down. Tell her that she can stop me to ask questions any time she wants."

I was proud of Ben for being so considerate. It was a good idea to help Valentina by letting her know what to expect. She leaned forward, her hands clasped in her lap, knees pressed together. Lalo sat with his legs crossed, one hand resting on Maya's head as he translated. When Valentina nodded her understanding, Ben continued.

"While I swear her in she needs to place her hand on the bible and keep it there. When she's ready, I'll ask her to state her full name and address."

Valentina's eyes darted between the two men. She asked something in Spanish.

"She wants to know if she can say she lives here," Lalo translated.

Ben shot me a glance. "Well?" he asked.

"I guess she does live here . . . temporarily."

Lalo nodded at Valentina and she flashed me a shy smile.

"After the swearing in, we'll move on to the day Luci died. It's important for her to limit her responses to the specific questions I ask. Make sure she understands that."

He paused again, giving Lalo a chance to translate.

"Finally, tell her she must always speak truthfully."

"*Yo comprendo*. I understand. I no lie."

Ben raised one eyebrow in surprise. "I thought you didn't speak English."

"I understand little."

"She understands a lot," I corrected.

Ben turned to Lalo. "Well, just so there is no misunderstanding, you should translate everything. If Valentina wants to answer in English, I guess that's okay."

Lalo nodded, repeating Ben's final instruction. With the preliminaries over, Ben turned on the camera and began.

"What is your full name?" he asked.

"Maria Valentina Muñoz de Abarco."

Ben, incredulous, stared at her. He turned to Lalo. "Is she married to Angel Abarco?"

Lalo and Valentina exchanged a few words of Spanish. When they finished speaking, Lalo turned back to Ben.

"She says in the eyes of God they are husband and wife."

"But is she legally married to Angel Abarco? If so, then we have to let her know she can't be forced to testify against her husband."

Lalo repeated the question in Spanish, his smile revealing the gap between his front teeth. "She asks what is more important, the law of man or the law of God?"

Ben sighed and asked once again if she was legally married to Abarco. Her response this time was to confirm that no, she was not.

Valentina maintained her composure as she listened to Ben's questions. She responded in a soft, clear voice, hesitating only when Ben asked how she came to be at Norma Martin's house on the day Luci died. After giving it some thought, Valentina answered.

"She says she was working in Chaparrito's when Norma called Angel," Lalo said. "Valentina could hear Norma screaming on the phone saying they had a serious problem and she wanted Angel to come over right away."

"What problem?" Ben asked.

"Luci was about to tell me who took Marcela," Lalo caught Ben's eye.

"Let Valentina answer," Ben insisted.

Lalo asked Valentina the question in Spanish and quickly translated. "She doesn't know what the problem was. Angel sent her out of the room so she couldn't hear the rest of what Norma said."

Valentina threw Lalo an annoyed look and launched into a Spanish tirade. The corners of Lalo's mouth turned up when he explained to Ben. "Valentina wants you to know that she wasn't finished answering the question and that I should give her a chance to finish before translating. She says after he hung up the phone Angel asked her to go with him."

"What did she see when she arrived at Norma's?"

Valentina explained that Norma wasn't happy when she saw her. Norma wanted Valentina to wait outside but Angel said depending on how things went he might need her help. Angel then sent Norma to her own room, grabbed Valentina by the wrist and dragged her through the house to where they found Luci curled up on her bed, alone.

"What did Angel do then?"

I heard the hitch in Valentina's voice when she answered.

"Angel told her to hold Luci's arm. But Luci struggled and Valentina couldn't get a grip. Angel started screaming, telling her to sit on Luci's stomach so she could pin both arms down. Valentina did what he said."

Valentina's face was wet with silent tears. She clasped both hands in her lap, her bottom lip trembled.

"Wait a minute." Ben looked at his notes. The crease between his eyebrows told me he wasn't happy with something. It seemed to me that he should be pleased that Valentina gave him the information he needed to nail Angel Abarco for Luci's murder.

"Let's focus on Abarco. Ask her if she saw Angel prepare the drugs that he later injected into Luci's arm."

"Yes," Lalo translated. "He crushed the pills and melted the drugs in a spoon with his cigarette lighter. Then he filled a syringe and told Valentina again to hold Luci so he could find a vein. She tried, but Luci fought hard. That's when Angel went crazy. He jabbed the needle into Luci's arm, two, three times, Valentina can't remember exactly how many. Finally Angel pushed the plunger. Luci stopped struggling and everything went quiet."

Valentina buried her face in her hands. Wrenching sobs shook her thin body.

I reached for the box of tissues on the side table and handed one to her. "Give her a minute, Ben," I said as Valentina blew her nose.

Ben glanced from his notes to Valentina and back again. Taking a deep breath he turned to Lalo. "Tell her she's doing well. Just a few more questions and we'll be done."

Valentina gave a little hiccup and wiped her tears with the back of her hand. I filled a glass with iced tea and passed it to her. She threw me a grateful look and took a sip while Ben asked his next question.

"Valentina, why did Angel do this to Luci?"

Valentina shook her head. She had stopped crying, but her eyes still brimmed with tears.

"With Angel, I cannot ask why," she said.

"Did you see Norma again before you left the house?"

"*Si*, when we leave Angel tell Norma call Moreno."

"Detective Tom Moreno?"

Valentina nodded.

"Did Detective Moreno arrive before you left?"

"*Mande*?"

"She didn't understand that," Lalo said. "Give me a minute to translate."

Valentina listened to Lalo, shook her head and responded in Spanish.

"No. They left before Moreno got there. She wants you to know Angel told Norma that if Moreno asked what happened, she was to say Luci accidentally overdosed. On the way home Angel told Valentina she could never tell anyone about what she saw or the same thing would happen to her."

Valentina bit her lower lip as the tears in her eyes spilled over.

"Can't you see how hard this is for her?" I said.

Ben ignored me. "Lalo, ask her why Abarco told Norma to call Moreno."

"She says Moreno and Abarco are friends," Lalo translated.

"Last question," Ben drew a deep breath. "Ask her who killed Marcela de la Vega."

"That wasn't the deal," Lalo said after Valentina shot back her reply. "She only agreed to talk about Luci today. If you want to know about Marcela, you have to pay her a reward."

"Tell her to answer the question."

"She says you told her she doesn't have to answer if she doesn't want to."

"Ask her again."

"Where reward?" Valentina shot back.

"I'm working on it." Ben looked down at his notes and shook his head. He turned to Lalo, "Tell her before she gets any money, I need to be sure she can help my client."

Lalo translated while Valentina glared at Ben.

"Reward first," she said. "Then I tell you about Marcela."

"What now, *amigo*?" Lalo asked as Ben drove him back to the boat.

"I have no idea. Do you think she knows who killed Marcela?"

"Well, whatever she knows, Valentina thinks it's worth *something*. Easiest way outta this is to get her that reward money."

"You know as well as I do that there isn't any reward money. I can't pay for witness testimony anyway. There has to be another way."

"You wanna play hard ball?"

"What are you talking about?"

"We could threaten to cut off her drug supply. That might get her to open up."

"You wouldn't do that, would you?"

"No." Lalo admitted.

Silence stretched between them while Ben tried to come up with something. "Maybe Cate can help."

Lalo chuckled softly. "I swear, I expected that woman to tear you apart when you told her we weren't taking Valentina with us today. Sure, she put up a fuss but deep down inside I think she's okay with keeping Valentina a while longer. Given enough time, Cate might be able to get Valentina to talk. Worth a try, right?"

"I'll have a word with her and see what she says,"

He turned off the interstate at the second Bradenton exit and headed west. As he drove through the center of town he said, "Tell me more about that place you have in mind for Valentina."

"Sarah's House is the best center for sex traffic victims in the country. I've got connections with the people there. Shouldn't take too long to get Valentina settled."

"The sooner we can move her out of Cate's house the better."

"Agreed. Besides, I think she's anxious to get back to work on the Murphy case. You know, she might be on to something with that Skinner guy."

Ben turned into the parking lot of the marina and pulled up in front of Lalo's boat. "Would you be willing to talk to Ty? Cate thinks he may be holding something back."

"I'll see what I can find out from him."

"Let me know if you learn anything."

Ben let his old BMW idle while he watched the investigator walk to the end of the pier. When Lalo turned and waved, Ben threw the car into reverse. There was still a lot of work ahead, but his gut told him Lalo was right. Valentina probably knew who killed Marcela de la Vega. And if anyone could get the girl to talk it was Cate. For the first time in quite a while, Ben felt good about the direction his case was heading.

THIRTY-FIVE

The digital clock on my nightstand glowed red as I tossed and turned thinking about Logan Murphy. I knew I let him down. After months of hitting dead ends, all I had for my efforts was a strong suspicion of Boyd Skinner. By getting dragged into watching Valentina, I put Logan on the back burner. My last thoughts before drifting off were of Tyler Fox. What was he hiding and why did he run to Boyd right after we spoke?

The phone rang, jarring me awake. Ben's voice came through the line as I cracked an eye open to see the time, nine o'clock.

"Hope I'm not waking you."

"I'll let you slide this time. Did you get what you needed from Valentina yesterday?"

"That's why I'm calling. I need another favor. Valentina is stuck on the idea of getting a reward for telling us what she knows about Marcela's murder. And at this point, my whole case revolves around her testimony."

"Do you want me to try and reason with her?"

"If you can, yeah."

"I'll see what I can do. Listen, I'm glad you called. I need to get back to Logan's case. I thought I'd give Bibi Fox a call. If I can convince her Ty knows something about Boyd Skinner, she might be able to talk her husband into coming clean. What do you think?"

Ben paused before answering. "I guess that can't hurt."

"Good. I'll let you know what she says. Do you have any idea when Lalo will get Valentina into that safe house?"

"Believe me, you'll be the first to know."

As soon as we disconnected, I dialed Bibi's home number. I counted the rings before I heard the phone click. Instead of Bibi, Tyler Fox spoke in my ear.

"Hello?"

Caught by surprise I slammed down the phone. Rather than risk calling Bibi again, I decided to ask Annie to get a message to her. By the end of the day Annie called back to say she arranged everything. We agreed to meet Friday night at the Brew Pub downtown.

As the days slid by I didn't have much time to think about Logan Murphy. Every morning I brought Valentina to the methadone clinic for her *medicina.* I was concerned about her. She slept twelve hours a day and ate like a bird. When I mentioned it to the nurse she assured me everything was normal and that it took time for Valentina's body to adjust. Aside from that, things ran smoothly around the house. The only problem was, every time I broached the subject of Marcela de la Vega, Valentina shook her head, only willing to talk if Ben produced her reward.

To keep her busy, I began teaching her English. She took to writing words on sticky notes and plastering them all over my house. DOOR. WALL. CLOCK. TABLE. SINK. CANDLE. She had a quick mind, and I was amazed at her growing vocabulary. Friday morning, while I attempted to explain the difference between "teach" and "learn" Ben called.

"She refuses to talk about Marcela," I told him.

"We're out of time. Lalo got word from Sarah's House. He's bringing her there tonight."

I felt a little hitch in my chest. Though I was frustrated with Valentina's stubborn refusal to help Ricky Castro, I had grown fond of her.

"I'll pack her things."

"Can you drop her off at his boat?"

"Sure. I'm scheduled to meet Annie and Bibi for dinner tonight, but I can have her there by three."

After hanging up I glanced at my watch. We had just enough time for one more walk on the beach before we needed to pack her things and drive up to Bradenton. When I suggested walking to the South Jetty to watch the dolphins, Valentina's eyes opened wide.

"Dolphins? Is like to me very much."

"I would like that very much." I corrected her.

"I too."

Maya trotted ahead in the soft sand, breaking off to chase a group of sandpipers before circling back to rejoin us. The weather was glorious. While people up north turned the heat on in their houses, we walked in our shorts under a cloudless sky and watched children swim in the Gulf. A Frisbee sailed away from two teenagers and Maya crashed into the water in pursuit. She emerged dripping wet and trotted back to Valentina with the plastic toy clutched in her jaws. When one of the boys came over, Valentina took the Frisbee from Maya and held it behind her back, batting her long eyelashes while swinging her shoulders from side to side. I judged the boy to be about Valentina's age. As the color crept up his neck, his eyes focused on her chest.

"Don't be a tease, Valentina. Give back his Frisbee."

She rolled her eyes but did as I told her.

Valentina flashed him a smile before we continued making our way toward the jetty. When I glanced over my shoulder I saw the boy continued to stare at Valentina as she swayed her hips seductively.

"I think he likes you."

"*Jovencito.*" She sniffed. "Only little boy."

We walked to the end of the beach where years ago the Army Corps of Engineers cut a channel connecting Roberts Bay to the open Gulf. The water flowed between two jetties made of great boulders that jutted out to sea. We scrambled over the rocks, reaching the end of the jetty as a dolphin rose above the waves to take a breath of air. Soon others appeared, a whole pod of the sleek animals swimming in a circle. They had trapped a school of small fish and the surface of the water rippled as the little ones tried to escape.

A strange look came across Valentina's face as she watched.

"What's the matter?" I asked.

"*Pobrecitos*. Poor little fishes."

I reached for her hand. Blinking away the tears she gave me an embarrassed smile.

"Valentina, I need to tell you something. Remember the place we told you about? Sarah's House?"

She pulled her hand away and shook her head. "I want stay here with you."

"They have a room ready for you. You'll be safe there. I promise I'll come to visit when I can. We have to go home and pack your things. Listen to me, this is important. You did a great thing for Luci, telling Ben what Angel did to her. We want you to do the same thing for Marcela, but you don't seem to understand. There is no Marcela reward. This is your last chance to tell me what you saw that day."

Valentina shook her head. "Luci dead, Marcela dead. Nothing change that."

We walked all the way home in silence.

THIRTY-SIX

Ben tossed his paper coffee cup into the trash bin. He stood alone in his office, staring at the timeline on his white board. Picking up a marker, he wrote down Abarco's name and a question mark and then drew an arrow pointing to the time Marcela left Norma Martin's house. A rap on the door interrupted his thoughts. He looked up to see Stephanie dressed as a Playgirl bunny holding a fat manila envelope in her hand.

"Nice costume."

"Going straight from work to a Halloween party." She waved the envelope in the air. "My guy came through. Here are the test results from the lab."

Ben's pulse quickened as he tossed the marker on his desk. "Have you read them?"

"I thought you'd want to be the first."

He snatched the envelope from her hand and paged through the report until he found what he looked for. His brow furrowed as he read the paragraph describing the findings on the glass marked with Valentina's lipstick. The technician managed to get a full set of fingerprints that he ran through the state database. No match. And though he found enough DNA on the lip of the glass to map a unique signature, by comparing that profile against other samples held in the database, he again came up empty. No match to any known criminals or unsolved crimes.

Ben skipped ahead to the spoon that Lalo removed from Luci's nightstand. Here he found encouraging, though unsurprising results. The fingerprints on the glass matched those on the handle of the spoon. *Good girl*, Ben thought. Valentina correctly marked the glass belonging to Abarco. That was exactly what he needed to prove Abarco used the spoon to cook the heroin that killed Luci.

"Well?" Stephanie asked.

"I'll call Leroy Lamb to tell him what we've got, but unfortunately there's nothing to tie Abarco to the DNA sample on Marcela's skirt." Ben passed the report to Stephanie so she could see for herself.

"That was a long shot anyway." Stephanie thumbed through the pages of the report. "The girl had sex with anyone who paid. Any defense attorney worth his salt would argue that the stain doesn't prove a thing."

"I know," Ben agreed. "Hey, listen. Thanks for getting the results pushed through. I owe you."

Stephanie didn't seem to hear him. She was concentrating on a page that Ben had skipped over.

"Hey, Shepherd, I think you missed something here."

She passed the report back and he scanned it quickly.

"Holy shit," Ben breathed.

"Good news," Ben said as soon as Lalo answered. "We've got Abarco's prints on the spoon."

"When are you going to call Lamb?"

"Right after we hang up. But get this. We got a DNA hit off the second glass that Valentina picked up at the bar. I don't know where this is going, but the same guy who drank out of that glass had sex with Marcela de la Vega."

"What? Are you sure?"

"I've got the lab results right in front of me. Did Valentina say who was drinking with Abarco that day?"

"No, just that it was a friend of his." Lalo cleared his throat. "Don't get your hopes up. That guy was probably just one of Marcela's johns. The autopsy report said it looked like maybe she was with multiple partners right before she was killed."

"Stephanie said something along those same lines, and you're probably right, but still . . . "

"Yeah, okay. I get it. You want to know who he is. I'll see what I can find out. Hey, I gotta go. I just pulled up in front of Tyler Fox's office. I'll call you later to let you know how this turns out."

"You need to be back to the boat by three o'clock. Cate is dropping Valentina off so you can bring her to Sarah's House."

"No problem. I'll be there."

After hanging up with Lalo, Ben turned to catch Stephanie staring at him.

"What?"

"Greg hasn't told you yet?"

"I don't know what you're talking about."

"He gave Kim a job. As soon as she passes the bar she's going to take your place reviewing petitions."

"What?"

"Don't worry, Shepherd. It's all good. You've been promoted."

Ben pressed the phone to his ear, listening to silence stretching half the length of Florida. He drummed his fingers on his desk, counting the seconds while he waited for Deputy Lamb to respond to his question.

"Leroy, did you hear me?"

"Right here, Counselor. Taking a minute to digest everything you just laid on me. Where are you keeping this witness of yours?"

"In a safe place."

"Well, I'm happy to hear what she has to say. Bring her in so I can take her statement."

Ben took a deep breath. "I already did that. We got a translator and recorded the whole thing."

"Playing it safe, eh Counselor? Can't say I blame you, knowing all the characters involved. But you know I have to question her myself."

"I know, but I'm asking you to work with me here."

"I'm listening."

"The witness may have assisted Abarco."

"You're telling me she was an accomplice to murder?"

"There were extenuating circumstances."

"Let me guess, you're looking for an immunity deal. Not sure about this . . . the ASA is gonna want more than 'he said she said.' What else have you got?"

"I've got Abarco's prints on the spoon he used to cook the heroin. Chemical analysis confirms China White. And there's something else that might interest you."

"Yeah? What's that?"

"Remember Marcela de la Vega?"

"Yeah, I remember. You making any progress with that case?"

"We got a DNA hit on the seminal fluid found on Marcela's skirt. And it wasn't from my client."

"Whose is it?"

Now it was Ben's turn to hesitate. He was depending on Lalo to get the name of the man who was with Abarco at the bar. The man whose DNA was on the second glass.

"Can we get that deal?"

Another long silence filled the distance between them.

"Something bothering you, Leroy?"

"You know what we're up against, right Counselor? I told you the first time we met, you're swimming with sharks."

"But we're the good guys, right? And the good guys always win."

Leroy snorted. "I'd like to think so, Counselor. I'd surely like to think so. Let me talk to the State Attorney's office."

"Fair enough. Just one thing. Remember, we need to keep this low-key."

"Understood. Give me the rest of the day to run this by my supervisor."

"Thanks Leroy. Call me on my cell phone. I'll be out of the office all afternoon."

When he hung up, Ben looked back to the white board. Picking up the marker he erased Abarco's name, leaving the question mark in place.

THIRTY-SEVEN

I fixed two glasses of iced tea and waited on the lanai while Valentina packed her things. When she reappeared clutching the suitcase I loaned her, she glared at me. As she touched the silver heart on the chain around her neck—a habit of hers—I smiled.

"Where did you get that necklace?" I asked.

"Angel," she replied. "*Un regalito*, how you say, a present." She looked at me sadly, shaking her head. "*Le extraño*, you know, I miss him."

A tear spilled from her eye. Then another, and soon both of her cheeks glistened. I wanted to remind her that this so-called boyfriend of hers was nothing more than a drug-dealing pimp. Instead I passed her a napkin and waited. She took a sip of her iced tea and with a little hiccup, blinked away the tears.

"Angel send me away." She cast her eyes downward, twisting her fingers. "That not liking to me."

"You didn't like that," I corrected.

"That what I say. Now you send me away too."

"It's time for you to start a new life."

She looked at me from the corner of her eyes. "If I get Marcela reward, I can go home. Back to Michoacán."

I started to repeat what I'd been telling her for days. That there *was* no reward. But then I realized what she just said. I could feel the hairs standing up on my arms as all my senses went on high alert.

"I didn't know you were from Michoacán."

"*Si, toda mi familia,* all my family live there. Use reward to buy Mama new house."

She prattled on about her parents, but my mind veered off in a different direction. The Spanish-speaking caller on the Jane Doe tip line said something about Michoacán. Was it possible that Valentina—a prostitute from Immokalee—knew the caller? I dared not let my hopes rise. After all, she was only six years old when Jane Doe was killed. The odds of Valentina having any connection to a murder that happened ten years ago in the woods of Snook Wallow seemed remote.

"Do you know someone called Juliana Martinez?" I fought to keep my voice even. "I think she came from Michoacán too."

Valentina met my gaze. She squinted slightly, a guarded look creeping into her eyes. "Why you ask Juliana?"

There was no doubt now. I struggled to keep my tone casual even as the blood pounded in my ears. "I have a recording of a girl named Juliana Martinez but it's in Spanish. Could you translate for me?"

Valentina followed me to my office where I pulled the cassette player down from the closet shelf. With a push of the button the now-familiar voice of the officer who answered the phone blared forth. "Tip line."

The caller replied in rapid Spanish. The only word I caught was *Michoacán*.

"Do you speak English?" The officer asked.

"*No, yo no hablo ingles.*"

"What. Is. Your. Name?"

"*Nombre? Su nombre es Juliana Martínez.*"

The officer instructed her, "Okay, Juliana, here's what we're going to do. You stay right there on the line while I find someone who can speak Spanish, and then we'll take your statement. Comprendo?"

The caller fired something back in Spanish. After a protracted pause, there was a click and the line went dead. Valentina looked up at me and shook her head. "Where picture she see?"

"Are you talking about the sketch in the paper? I've got it here somewhere . . ."

I reached into my canvas bag and pulled out a copy of the artist's drawing of Jane Doe together with the folder containing photos of her body laid out on the coroner's table. I passed the sketch to Valentina. She took one look and quickly made the sign of the cross.

"Do you know her?" I asked.

She nodded, staring at the image of Jane Doe.

"Who is she?"

"Is Juliana."

"But the caller on the phone said *she* was . . ."

Valentina shook her head and jabbed the sketch with her finger. "No, she say *her* name Juliana. Girl in paper is Juliana Martinez."

"Will you do me a favor? I want you to take a look at these photos to be sure."

Valentina accepted the folder with the ME's photos that I handed her and turned back the cover. She flipped through the pages, stopping when she saw the tattoo of folded wings on Jane Doe's shoulder. I could see Valentina mouth a prayer as she once again made the sign of the cross before handing everything back to me.

"*Es cierto*. Is Juliana," she repeated. "Is sister of Norma."

THIRTY-EIGHT

I finally knew who Jane Doe was, where she came from, who her people were. A few months ago I stood in the house of Juliana Martinez's sister, watching the paramedics remove Luci's body. A cold chill crept over me.

"How can you be sure? You were only six when Juliana was killed."

"We live same village. Angel bring Norma and Juliana to America. Norma write letter home, say life good. She say anyone want job, they can come. Many girls pay."

"They paid Angel to bring them to America?"

"Yes, five, maybe six girls. Then Norma write her mama again. She say Juliana was, how you say, *embarazada*?" Valentina made a motion with both hands in front of her belly.

"Pregnant?"

"*Si*, pregnant. Run away with boyfriend."

"It's been a long time since you saw her." I held up the photo in my hand. "Are you sure this is Juliana?"

"Angel tattoo. Very special. Only for first girls Angel bring. Norma has same."

"I have to call Lalo," I said. "He'll know what to do."

When I fished my phone out of my pocketbook, I discovered two missed messages. The first was Ben confirming Lalo would be at the boat when we got there. The second was from Lalo who had a question for Valentina, something about a glass that she picked up at a bar. I tapped "return call" and Lalo answered on the third ring. His voice was muffled as if his hand cupped the receiver.

"Hey Cate. Is everything all right?"

"Everything's fine. Valentina just listened to one of Geri's hot line tapes. It turns out that—"

"I'm in the middle of something right now."

"Sure, but I thought you'd want to know Valentina identified the victim. Her name was Juliana Martinez."

There was a long pause on the line. "Lalo? Did you hear me? The girl's name was Juliana."

"I gotta go. We can talk about this when you get to the boat."

I glanced at the clock. We were running a little late but I still had time to make it to the boat and get back in time for dinner with Annie and Bibi. I threw Valentina's suitcase in the trunk of my car with the cassette player. Minutes later we were on the way, Valentina stared straight ahead, pouting. Maya pressed her nose against the window and watched the palm trees go by.

Now that she had a name—Juliana Martinez—Jane Doe seemed real to me. I couldn't wait to see the expression on Lalo's face when I told him Juliana was Norma Martin's sister. There was a good explanation for why Norma didn't report her sister's disappearance to the police. She believed Juliana ran away with her boyfriend. Obviously that bit about Juliana being pregnant was wrong. But why did Norma tell their mother that?

We arrived at the marina ten minutes to five. Maya grew restless, poking her nose into the side of my neck. When I opened the door, she lunged out of the car and raced down the steps leading to the dock. Rounding the corner, her hind legs skidded out from under her. I thought for a moment she was going to land in the water but she recovered and scrambled to the end of the pier where the *Chilanga* lay quietly in her slip. I could see by the open cabin doors that Lalo was home. The thought of boarding that floating death trap set butterflies loose in my stomach.

When we caught up to her, Maya stood on the boat's back deck. She faced the open door, focused on something inside. The hackles on her back stood up, a low growl rumbled in her chest.

THIRTY-NINE

A face appeared from inside the boat's wheelhouse. Maya erupted into a fit of barking. My heart pounded, but Valentina climbed onto the boat and placed her hand on Maya's back.

"*Hola Ángel.*" Valentina's face broke into a smile.

"The dog, please." The man pointed to me.

I froze.

"You! Get the dog."

My heart in my throat, I grabbed the railing and stepped on board. As I took Maya by the collar, Angel Abarco came out on deck to face me.

After all the horrible things I heard about this man, it was disorienting to see his friendly, dimpled face with a smile so wide it exposed a gold tooth in the back of his mouth. He was shorter than I imagined, powerfully built with bulging biceps and a broad chest. There wasn't an ounce of fat on his body.

"What are you doing here?" I asked.

"I came to take back what is mine," he replied. Turning his radiant smile on Valentina he extended an open palm. She wrapped her arms around his waist and held on tight.

"She is not your property. Slavery was abolished in this country a long time ago."

"She is cheap whore." I turned to see a heavily made-up Latina peering up at me. She said something in Spanish to Angel that I didn't catch.

"Norma?" Valentina looked visibly shaken.

The corners of Norma's mouth turned up but the smile never reached her eyes.

I reached for my phone but froze when Norma produced a small handgun from her pocket. Maya strained against her collar. I held on tight.

"*Por favor,*" Abarco said, taking the phone from my hand. "Please, we just want to talk." He pulled Valentina into the cockpit, gesturing with his free arm for me to go in also. Knowing I had no choice, I released Maya and stepped inside. Before the dog could follow, Angel slammed the door closed.

Maya went crazy. She lunged, throwing her weight against the glass panels. With a yelp, she flew back as the glass shattered. Bracing her front feet, she launched into frenzied barking.

Abarco glanced over his shoulder, his brow furrowed. He shifted his gaze between the dog and Norma who kept the gun trained on me.

"She'll keep that up until someone calls the police to complain," I warned him. "She won't stop until you let her in."

Abarco pushed Valentina down the stairs to where Norma waited below. Pressing his body against the wall to keep his distance, he nodded. I kicked away the broken glass, clearing the way before opening the door. As Maya came bounding in I caught her by the collar. Abarco gestured for me to descend the stairs into the lower cabin. When I reached the floor below, he followed.

From the pout on Valentina's face I gathered the thrill of seeing her boyfriend was spent. While Norma remained standing with the gun held loosely in her hand, Abarco told us to sit on the u-shaped bench that wrapped around the table. Valentina slipped around the back and I settled in next to her. When Maya jumped up to sit beside me, I took the opportunity to check her paw. Removing a sliver of glass, I was relieved to see she wasn't badly injured.

"Why you here, Angel?" Valentina asked. "You miss me?"

He looked at her in surprise. "Since when do you speak English?"

"Cate learn me."She lifted her chin. "I want for you be proud."

"He doesn't care about you." I said. "You'll be working for Norma again as soon as you get back."

"Is truth?" she asked, turning to Abarco. The hurt in her eyes was heart wrenching.

When he grinned at her, Valentina pressed up against me on the bench. She looked up at Norma with a cold, hard expression. "I not work for you again."

"*Puta,*" Norma said, raising the gun.

"No." Abarco reached over and pressed Norma's arm back to her side.

I couldn't understand Abarco's rapid Spanish as he spoke to Valentina. But as he cooed and stroked her hair, I stole a glance at Norma who glared at him. Finally, out of the stream of words I caught the name Luci.

"*No digo nada.* I not say nothing about Luci." Valentina shook her head.

Abarco exhaled. A sigh so soft I thought he might start cooing at Valentina again. I never saw it coming. The force of the blow knocked Valentina over. Under my grip on the collar I could feel Maya's muscles tense. Valentina sat up, touched her hand to her mouth and glanced down at the blood on her fingers.

"Leave her alone." I wrapped my free arm around Valentina's shoulders. Looking up I saw Norma staring at Abarco, her lips pressed together in a thin smile. Outrage rose up inside me.

"Tell me, Norma, does he beat up all the girls that try to leave him?" A thought crossed my mind. "Is that what happened to your sister? Did Angel track Juliana down and kill her because she tried to run away?"

Norma gave me a sharp look. "What you say?"

"You didn't know?" The realization hit me hard. "Juliana was murdered ten years ago."

I waited to see how Norma took the news. Her hand holding the gun shook, the only sign she was coming unhinged.

Abarco looked up in surprise. All trace of the anger that flared only moments ago vanished. He spoke to Norma in the soft tones of a Spanish lover. He reached out to her but she jerked her head back and pointed the gun at him.

Valentina turned to me and said, "Angel say Juliana no dead. She stupid girl, get pregnant and leave. Say pregnant whore no good to him."

Norma threw Valentina a hateful look. Valentina smiled in a way that turned her beautiful face ugly. "Angel wrong. Cate show me Juliana photo. I know what dead girl look like. I see Luci."

Everything seemed to happen at once. Abarco raised a fist and punched Valentina in the temple. Her eyes rolled back in her head and she slid to the floor, landing in a heap under the table. Maya tore away from my grip and lunged at Abarco, catching his forearm in her razor-sharp teeth. The more Abarco fought, the tighter Maya held on. Drops of blood flew everywhere, the spatter landing on my cheek.

Abarco screamed.

Norma glanced down at the gun with a look that suggested she couldn't make up her mind. Her fingers opened and closed on the handle. Slowly raising her arm, she aimed at Maya.

My own scream rang in my ears.

I reached for the gun but Norma jerked it away. A shot rang out followed by a yelp as Maya fell.

A second shot was fired. With a high-pitched wail, Norma dropped her gun.

I looked over my shoulder to see Lalo standing at the top of the stairs, his gun pointed at Abarco, a crazed look on his face. I turned back to see Maya stretched out on the floor, her coat soaked in blood.

Lalo shouted something in Spanish. Abarco and Norma dropped to the floor. I peered under the table to find Valentina curled in a ball, her hands pressed over her ears. She kept repeating, "*Santa María, Madre de Dios*," over and over. I raised my voice, shouting over the ringing in my ears to ask if she was okay. She looked up at me, the side of her face where Abarco hit her, a bright red. I offered her my hand and she reached out to take it. Lalo kicked Norma's gun to the far side of the cabin and checked Abarco for weapons. Pulling a handgun from the man's belt, Lalo transferred it to his own. He called to me, and though my ears rang and my heart raced, I understood he wanted me to get plastic zip ties from the cabinet to bind their hands behind their backs. Abarco cried out in pain as I roughly yanked his damaged arm and pulled the tie tight. Too tight, I hoped. When I grabbed Norma's hand, she didn't make a sound. Lalo took the ties from me and finished the job, binding their feet as well.

"Are you okay?" he asked.

"What?"

"I said, are you okay?"

"I'm fine."

"Yeah, well you don't look so good." Lalo frowned at me, the ends of his new mustache turning down. He came close, peering into my eyes. I could smell his cologne rising above the sharp odor of gunpowder in the air.

"Sit down. Put your head between your knees while I take care of Maya."

"Oh my God, Maya . . ." I looked down to see the dog panting, her eyes closed. Lalo knelt next to her and placed a hand on her head. Maya's stump of a tail gave a feeble wag.

"Looks like the bullet grazed her shoulder," Lalo said at last. "What you did was stupid, reaching for Norma's gun like that."

"You would have done the same thing."

"I thought I told you to sit down."

"And I told you I'm fine."

He chuckled under his breath as he told Valentina where to find the first aid kit.

"Angel, he is bleeding." Norma struggled on the floor, nodding at the pool of blood seeping from under Abarco's arm. Lalo shrugged but after he finished bandaging Maya's shoulder he went and had a look.

The wail of sirens penetrated the cabin as blue lights flashed against the walls.

"Who called the police?" I asked.

"I did," Lalo replied. "As soon as I saw the broken glass I knew something was wrong."

I heard the thump of heavy boots as the police jumped on board. The boat rocked, causing my stomach to heave. Lalo looked up to see me holding onto the edge of the table. The ringing in my ears intensified.

"How many times do I have to tell you to sit down?" Lalo's words seemed to come from miles away.

The last thing I remember was Lalo jumping to catch me as I fell.

FORTY

Ben stood in the bright sunshine on the courthouse steps, watching as Lalo and Valentina climbed out of the truck. The diminutive Latina seemed like a small doll next to Lalo's towering hulk. A purple bruise marked the side of her face. Ben squinted against the glare of the sun reflecting off the truck's windshield. It was rare to see Lalo without his dog.

"How's Maya doing?" Ben asked as he shook Lalo's hand.

"The vet wanted to keep her overnight for observation."

"Is she going to be okay?"

"Looks that way. The bullet grazed her shoulder. Would have been much worse if Cate hadn't knocked Norma's arm right before she pulled the trigger."

Ben nodded. "Where is Cate?"

"She's supposed to be home resting but with that woman . . . who knows. Are we good to go here?"

"I arranged for a conference room so we can discuss strategy. As soon as we're done you can bring Valentina back to Sarah's House."

The room turned out to be no larger than a closet with a small round table and three folding chairs. Still, the air-conditioned space offered welcome relief from the rising heat of the day outside. And it provided Ben the privacy he needed to prep his new client, Valentina Munoz.

"I spoke with Geri a few minutes ago. I wanted to get an idea of what she has in mind. She plans to charge Abarco with breaking and entering."

"That's all?"

"No, there's more. When he broke into your boat with the intent to commit an offense—in this case kidnapping—he committed a felony. Valentina just needs to tell Geri that Abarco tried to force her back to Immokalee against her will. That will give her enough to hold him for a while at least."

He turned to Valentina. "Do you understand?"

Valentina shook her head so Lalo translated for her. When he finished, Valentina hesitated before nodding. "Yes, okay."

"Good," Ben turned back to Lalo. "Now for Norma."

"Let me guess," Lalo leaned in. "Geri will charge her with false imprisonment."

"Right. That's a slam dunk since she held both Cate and Valentina at gunpoint. And if Valentina cooperates, Geri can expand the charge to include human trafficking."

Lalo raised one eyebrow in surprise. "That's asking a lot of the girl."

Valentina was following the conversation, shifting her attention between the two men while they discussed her role in testifying against Abarco and Norma. When Ben turned to her and asked if she understood she said, "I tell police lady everything."

"Today is just the beginning. At some point you may need to testify in court before a judge."

"Norma go to jail?" Valentina asked.

"Probably, yes." Ben replied.

"Angel, too?"

Ben and Lalo exchanged glances.

"Yes, Angel too," Lalo said.

"Good."

Ben's chair bumped against the wall as he stood to leave.

"Where are you going?" Lalo asked.

"To tell Geri that Valentina is ready to talk."

"What about Valentina's testimony against Abarco for killing Luci?"

"I spoke with Leroy Lamb this morning. He's still waiting for the ASA to approve the plea bargain deal but he told me there's no way that will happen before Monday." Ben took a deep breath. "Geri can only hold Abarco and Norma for forty-eight hours. After that, if she doesn't have enough to bring them before a judge for an initial appearance, they walk."

"So the plan is to nail Abarco with what we've got right now. Leroy will bring the hammer down with the murder charge later?"

"That's exactly right."

"Let's go." Lalo pulled back Valentina's chair as far as the cramped space allowed. "*Vámonos,* Valentina. It's show time."

After they delivered Valentina into the hands of the counselors at Sarah's House, Ben climbed back into Lalo's truck, leaned against the headrest and closed his eyes. It had been a long morning but Valentina held up better than expected. As Geri Garibaldi worked her way through a long list of questions, Lalo translated for the girl. Only twice did Ben have to intervene on behalf of his client. The first was when Geri broached the subject of Valentina's immigration status. The second was when the detective asked if Valentina had ever witnessed Abarco inflicting harm on any of the girls who worked for Norma. She was fired up, anxious to charge Abarco with Luci's murder. Ben stopped Valentina from answering, telling her to invoke her Fifth Amendment rights. The murder charge would have to wait until his client was protected with an immunity agreement.

"We should see if Cate is feeling well enough to come downtown," Ben kept his head back, eyes closed. "Geri wants to get her statement about what happened on the boat."

"Geri can wait. Cate needs all the rest she can get. And you and I need to go over a few other things first. You know that second glass Valentina picked up at El Rincón? The one with the DNA that matched the stain on Marcela's skirt?"

Ben sat up straight and looked at Lalo. "I almost forgot about that. Did you ask Valentina who was with Abarco that day?"

"She said it was Tom Moreno."

The impact of what he just heard hit Ben hard. All along he discounted the DNA result, thinking it a stretch for a judge to give weight to an undated stain. Marcela was a prostitute. The dried seminal fluid on her skirt could have come from any of her customers at any time in the past. Even if they found a match, it was hardly enough to file a motion for post conviction relief. But Lalo's statement changed everything.

"Moreno had sex with Marcela?" Ben asked.

"Apparently."

"You know what this means? It doesn't matter if Moreno was with the victim on the day of the murder or before. As the homicide detective, he should have withdrawn from the investigation the moment he recognized Marcela."

"Yeah, I know. I've been thinking . . . If he paid Marcela for sex, his fingerprints would be all over the money. Moreno needed to send Leroy Lamb outside to speak with his partner so he could switch the fifty dollar bill. Valentina probably saw him kill the girl and figured you would be happy to pay for that kind of information."

"I have to bring my boss in on this," Ben's mind spun with all the legal implications. "I'll talk to him tomorrow and ask how he wants me to proceed."

Lalo nodded. "I'll wait until I hear back from you to see if there's anything else you need."

"I want you to shift gears. Have you spoken with Tyler Fox yet?"

"Yeah, yesterday. That's why I was late getting to the boat. We got hung up talking about fishing. Seems like a nice enough guy. He gave me the same line about leaving early with Skinner that night. Claims

Boyd went home, end of story. Ty said if the bartender saw someone ride off on a Harley when he closed up, it probably wasn't Boyd. We both know Charlie never saw Skinner, so there's no way to tell for sure. Still, I have to say I believed him."

"What about the hot wing sauce on the victim's hips?"

Lalo shrugged. "Everyone eats wings at a joint like that."

"So Cate is wrong about Boyd Skinner?"

"Yeah, that's how it looks to me. Listen, now that we know the victim's identity, I say we concentrate on her sister. It's Norma we should be squeezing for information."

Ben nodded agreement. He looked across the street at the courthouse. Somewhere in there, Norma Martin was behind bars, waiting for her life to take a turn for the worse.

FORTY-ONE

I sat facing Geri in the conference room after she took my statement. Ben and Lalo stood sentinel by my side. To her credit, Geri was cool and professional, nodding encouragement as I told her everything that happened on Lalo's boat. Still, recounting the horrific events of the previous day sent my blood pressure soaring. Popping two pieces of nicotine gum into my mouth I took a deep breath, anxious to go home and crawl back into bed. As I reached for my handbag, Lalo leaned across the table to face Geri straight on. "Now that you're through with Cate, the next thing you need to do is ask Norma Martin about her sister."

"Sit back and stop telling me how to do my job." Detective Garibaldi glared at Lalo. "After all these years, I am *not* going to blow a second chance at the Jane Doe homicide by cutting corners."

"Her name is Juliana," I said. "You should start calling it the Juliana Martinez homicide."

"Whatever. Norma Martin is scheduled in court to face the unlawful restraint charge tomorrow morning. If all goes well, that will keep her pretty Latina butt in jail for safekeeping. I'll have plenty of time to talk to her about Juliana later."

"Norma claimed her sister ran off with a boyfriend ten years ago," Ben said. "Couldn't you at least ask her what the boyfriend's name was?"

Geri peered at Ben over her black-rimmed glasses and tapped the table with her pencil. The gold cross she wore around her neck swung away from her chest as she leaned forward. "For your information, I did ask her. She claims there was no boyfriend. Juliana ran off with one of Abarco's other girls. Listen, don't get your hopes up. Nothing Norma Martin said gives me any reason to think Logan Murphy did not kill that girl, but like I told you already, I've got time to figure everything out."

"What was the other girl's name?" Lalo asked.

"Get out of here and let me do my friggin' job."

Lalo braced both hands on the back of his chair. "You screwed up, Geri. Ten years ago the tip line caller gave you the victim's name. You missed it."

"Get over yourself," Geri snapped. "We're way past that. You need to step back from this one."

"I don't think that's possible," Lalo said, his voice low.

Geri sighed. "Now listen up. I'm *officially* telling you I don't want your help. And I swear to God, if you interfere with my investigation I will have you slapped in cuffs and locked behind bars so fast your head will spin. You got that?"

She scribbled something on a piece of paper and passed it to him.

"I know you're taking this case personally, Lalo." Geri's ice blue eyes softened. "Just be careful."

Ben pulled me into a hug. "You did well in there. Lalo will take you home. Just try to get some rest."

I nodded agreement. A long nap was exactly what I had in mind. I climbed into Lalo's truck, more than ready to go back to bed. The cab smelled of Maya. It felt strange to not have her breathing down my neck.

"How is Maya?" I asked.

Lalo pulled out his cell phone and started tapping. He scrolled down, lost in whatever it was he saw.

"I asked you a question. What are you looking at that is so important?"

Lalo turned the phone around to show me a name and address in Fort Myers. I glanced up to see him smiling at me. "Who's Inez Calderon?" I asked. He pulled a scrap of paper from his pocket. I recognized the note Geri passed to him earlier. On it she had written two words. Inez Calderon.

FORTY-TWO

Lalo insisted on taking me home. I told him that he would have to physically drag me from the truck and tie me to my bed if he wanted to keep me from going with him to see Inez Calderon. For a brief moment I feared he would take me up on the threat, but when we passed Venice Avenue and kept heading south, I knew I had won.

"Who do you suppose she is?" I asked.

"I'm guessing she's the girl Juliana ran away with," he replied.

"Geri made it clear she wanted you to stay out of the investigation."

Lalo smiled to himself. "She *officially* told me to butt out. Unofficially she wants me to speak with Inez Calderon."

As we headed toward Fort Myers, I pondered something Geri said before we left. The more I thought about it, the more I realized there were signs all along suggesting Lalo had a personal reason for taking this case. It hit me that Lalo had a way of disappearing into his own thoughts from time to time. I first noticed it on the boat. Ben said something about Juliana being a Latina. No, wait. It was Lalo who said Juliana was a Latina. The more I tossed things around in my head the more curious I became. I stole a glance at Lalo. He gripped the wheel with both hands, his attention riveted on the road ahead.

"Why did you volunteer to help me with this case?" I asked.

Lalo gave me a surprised look. "What?"

"The moment you first you saw Juliana's photo you wanted in. What's going on, Lalo?"

Lalo went back to watching the road. His foot let up on the gas and our speed dropped back to the posted limit. "Juliana reminded me of someone."

"Who?"

He ground his back teeth. I let the silence fill the truck, giving him space to decide whether or not to tell me. We passed several mile markers before he spoke again.

"Let me show you something. It's not far from here."

He left me wondering, lost in my own thoughts. We continued south, staying on the interstate until we reached the Fort Myers exit. At the end of the ramp, Lalo turned left, leaving Fort Myers behind us. Immokalee lay thirty miles ahead.

At a fork in the road a wooden sign announced we had arrived at the Lake Trafford Cemetery. Cabbage palms stood sentry around the perimeter, patches of salt-and-pepper sand showed through the weeds. At first glance the cemetery appeared to be unoccupied but as Lalo's truck bounced over potholes, I noticed a few families gathered around the graves. Some stood, but others sat on the ground amid picnic baskets and bunches of flowers. Lalo passed without hesitation, aiming for a destination that I suspected was familiar to him.

When we reached the far side of the cemetery he pulled off the road, bringing the truck to a stop in a cloud of dust. Lalo came around and opened my door. I followed him a few steps to a spot on the ground where a brass plate was barely visible under the encroaching weeds. I watched as Lalo squatted to clear the plate with the palm of his hand. As he worked, a name emerged. Teresa Ann Sanchez Rios.

"Who was she?" I asked.

"My sister," he replied.

I stared at the dates. Teresa Sanchez died forty years earlier at the age of twenty-five.

"Teresa was ten years older than me. Old enough that everyone assumed she could take care of us after our parents died. I figure that's how I managed to stay out of foster care. I owe her for keeping us together." He lowered his voice so I could barely hear him. "I owe her for so much more."

He stood, keeping his eyes on the grave while brushing the sand off his knees. "When I turned ten, I told Teresa I intended to get a job in the tomato fields. I wanted to earn money so she could stop working the streets. Teresa went crazy and made me promise I would stay in school until I got my high school diploma." Lalo laughed, a shallow, mirthless burst of air. "I was fifteen when she died."

"Drugs?" I asked.

Lalo shook his head. "She never touched drugs." He wagged his head. "She probably picked up AIDS from a john."

In that dusty cemetery, Lalo's past took shape before my eyes. His sister worked as a prostitute to support herself and her younger brother. As I pondered the scars on his heart, Lalo spoke again.

"Do you know what today is?"

"The first of November."

"Yeah. In Mexico they celebrate it as the day of the dead. All those people we saw on the way in? They're visiting their loved ones. I suppose I should come more often but after a while I figured it out. I don't need to come here to talk to my sister."

"What do you say to her?"

Lalo turned to look at me. "When I finished high school I told her I landed a place at the police academy. And when I took the job in the Sheriff's department, I promised to help others like her. But I haven't lived up to that promise. I let Luci down."

"Next time you talk, make sure you tell her you saved Valentina."

"Let's take a walk. There's something else you should see."

We passed dozens of graves like Teresa's, not a headstone in sight. The markers were choked with weeds but again, Lalo seemed to know where he wanted to go. We stopped when we reached a spot with freshly turned dirt. I looked down to see Luci's name on the marker.

"This is the indigent section. Marcela de la Vega is a few rows over. By the way, your instincts were right about Tom Moreno."

A chill ran down my spine. "What do you mean?"

"Ben had the stain on Marcela's skirt tested for DNA. Turns out it came from Moreno. Ben is going to file a wrongful conviction motion based on police misconduct. Ricky Castro will soon be a free man."

FORTY-THREE

Inez Calderon lived in a small, trim home on the outskirts of Fort Myers. When Lalo rang the bell, she opened the door, her dark eyes turned up to meet his, an open smile on her lips. She looked to be in her ninth month of pregnancy, her swollen belly visible under a tight, stretchy top.

"Inez Calderon?" Lalo asked.

"Yes?" she replied.

"We're here to ask you about Juliana Martinez."

Her smile slowly faded as she turned to face me. "Who sent you?"

"The detective responsible for investigating Juliana's murder. We're hoping you might be able to—"

"The man who killed my cousin is in jail."

Her cousin? My breath caught in my throat.

"Detective Garibaldi thinks she may have arrested the wrong man."

Inez closed her eyes and fingered a silver ball that hung on a long chain around her neck. As she played with the thing I heard a small chiming sound. Something about the necklace seemed familiar. She opened her eyes, pressed her lips together, a hardened expression crossing her face. "I can't help you." She held tight to the doorknob. "I tried to talk to the police at the time but they didn't listen."

"You called the tip line?" I knew the answer before she nodded.

"My English wasn't good back then. But like I said, I can't help you. I have a new life now, a husband . . ." She placed her hand on her belly. "We're going to have a baby."

"This won't take long. We'll keep your name out of this if you want, but you owe it to Juliana to tell us what happened."

We sat in her living room drinking strong coffee. I soon realized how lucky we were to find her. Though she married an American, in the Mexican tradition she kept her maiden name. And as her story unfolded, I realized how lucky she was to be alive.

"Norma paid me to take Juliana away." She looked up with a start. "Does she know you're here?"

"That's how we got your name," Lalo replied. "She claims she doesn't know what happened to her sister."

"And Angel?"

"You don't have anything to fear from Abarco. He's behind bars and I reckon he'll stay there for a long time."

Inez took a deep breath and exhaled slowly. "Norma loved that creep. She would do anything—almost anything—for him. She kept six of us in that house, forcing us to sell our bodies, bringing in money for her beloved Angel. But Norma drew the line when it came to letting him touch Juliana."

Inez pulled on the neckline of her top, exposing the tattoo on the back of her shoulder. Angel wings, exactly like Juliana's.

"My husband thinks it's pretty." An ugly laugh escaped Inez' lips. "He doesn't know about my life back then. He doesn't know Angel branded us like cattle. On the day Juliana came home with a tattoo just like this, Norma knew she couldn't stop that monster. She told me to take Juliana away and to never come back. Believe me, I was glad to go. But the money she gave me didn't last long. When it ran out I did what I had to do to survive. Still, I didn't want Juliana to get dragged into the business. That's one thing I promised Norma, and I did everything possible to keep my word."

"Tell me what happened that night," I said.

"We got to Snook Wallow a few days before. At first it looked like a good place for us to stay a while. The first night I turned a few tricks while Juliana hid in the woods and listened to the music. After the bartenders closed up we snuck into one of the cabins and spent the night."

"Were other girls doing the same thing?"

Inez shook her head. "They chased girls off the property if they were caught sleeping there. But Juliana was scared. She said she didn't want to sleep in the woods so I took a chance. Anyway, the second night started out the same way. Business was good, so I gave Juliana money and told her to buy something to eat. She bought two beers instead saying it was hot and she was thirsty. Later, when I sent her back for chicken wings, two boys followed her to where I waited behind the cabins."

"There were two of them?" I asked in surprise.

Inez nodded, lowering her voice to almost a whisper. "I tried to distract them, tell them she wasn't in the business. I said if they were looking for something special I would give them what they wanted. But they weren't interested in me. One of them shoved me to the ground. I yelled at Juliana to run. She didn't get far before the other one caught her."

She looked down at her coffee, the black liquid quivering in her grasp.

"Can you describe them?" I asked.

"They were big. Both of them. The one with a knife told Juliana to take off her clothes while the other one held me down. I told her to do what they said. I thought if she didn't fight, maybe . . ."

Inez squeezed her eyes closed and a single tear rolled down her cheek. When she reopened them they were clear and dry.

"Juliana never made a sound. They took turns with her. After, one of them—the one with the knife—said he wanted her necklace as a souvenir." Inez fingered the ball hanging from the chain around her neck. "It was her bolo, the one her mother gave her. My own mother wore this one when she was pregnant with me. They say the baby can hear the chime from the womb."

"May I have a look?" I asked.

It was beautiful, moons and stars etched into two silver halves held together by a fine hinge. Something inside chimed as I handed it back.

"Juliana wouldn't give her bolo up without a fight," Inez said. "When that boy tried to grab it, she ran." She shook her head and wiped a tear from the corner of her eye. "I should have run after them but I was afraid. I never thought they would . . ."

In the silence that followed, I tried to remember where I had seen a similar necklace. "Tell me, was Juliana's necklace exactly like yours?"

"Oh no, they're all different. Hers had little angels on it."

That's when it hit me. The image of Bibi Fox nervously playing with a silver ball hanging on a chain around her neck. I looked up to catch Lalo staring at me. I gave him a little shake of my head and turned back to Inez.

"Logan Murphy did not kill Juliana. But I have a pretty good idea who did."

"Could you identify those boys in a lineup?" Lalo asked.

She stared back at him before answering. "My husband asks why I wake up screaming in the middle of the night. I tell him the nightmares are about the border patrol chasing me across the river. But my dreams are always the same. As Juliana runs, I stand there and do nothing."

"There was nothing you could do," I assured her.

"When Juliana didn't come back, I picked up her clothes and went to find her." Inez squeezed her eyes closed again. "The boys already left but Juliana was . . ."

I put my arm around her shoulders and pulled her close. "It wasn't your fault," I whispered in her ear. "Will you help us?"

She nodded as the tears began to flow.

I climbed back into Lalo's truck, raising my arm against the autumn sun streaming through the windshield. My hand, my whole body trembled.

"Are you okay?" he asked.

Though I felt faint I nodded. Lalo reached behind the seat and handed me a bottle of water. It was warm, but I accepted it gratefully.

"Looks like you were right about Boyd," Lalo said.

But it wasn't Boyd after all." I was dazed, shocked by what I just learned. "Tyler Fox killed Juliana."

"What? You can't know that for certain. Inez can pick those two boys out of a lineup but she wasn't there to see which one of them killed her."

"Ty's wife, Bibi wears a bolo. One with angels on it."

"Bolos are pretty common. Mexican women traditionally wear them when they're pregnant."

"But Bibi isn't Mexican."

Lalo pulled out his phone and tapped a message. The device made a soft swooshing sound when he hit send.

"What did you just do?" I asked.

"Sent a message to Geri. It's time she does her job."

FORTY-FOUR

Ben followed the guard down the cement-block corridor to meet Ricky Castro. When Ricky came through the open door, scowling as usual, Ben stood and reached down to take Ricky's shackled hand in his own. Ricky's expression turned to surprise. Ben had never offered to shake his hand before.

"I have good news. The court agreed to entertain our motion to introduce the DNA evidence at a post-conviction hearing."

"I'm getting out of here?" Ricky smiled, revealing a missing tooth in the back of his mouth.

"Hopefully in a few days . . . a week or two at most. My boss, Greg is going to argue the case himself. He thinks this one will be a slam-dunk."

"A few weeks," Ricky mumbled, grinning at the thought. "And how much are they going to pay me? I heard a guy got a few million for a wrongful conviction."

"We've been over this before. "You are not being exonerated, you're being released because the police—specifically Detective Moreno—did not follow the rules. In fact, the state can decide to retry you if they want, but to be honest, I doubt they will. Listen Ricky, according to Florida rule, they'll pay $50,000 for every year of wrongful incarceration. But there's a catch. Something they call the "clean hands" mandate. Remember that time you were arrested for drunk driving? That's still on your record and the state will use it to get out of paying you anything. I recommend you forget about the money and concentrate on your future. You have your whole life ahead of you."

"I don't mean to be ungrateful or anything, but don't you think they should pay me something for keeping me locked up in here? Let's sue them or something."

Ben looked at his client, wondering why he expected this meeting to go well. Ricky was never satisfied, no matter how hard Ben worked on his behalf. Anyone else in his situation would be elated, overjoyed by the news. With a sigh, Ben realized he was being selfish. After all, from his client's point of view, the justice system stole two years of his life. And despite the legal obstacles, he agreed that Ricky should be compensated for that.

"I suppose you might be able to find a law firm that would consider filing a civil suit on your behalf, but that's not the kind of law we practice at the Project. Let us get you through this hearing, and you can decide what to do after you're out."

That seemed to lift Ricky's spirits. He turned to the window and looked at the guard who stood waiting to take him back to his cell. With a big grin, Ricky flipped him the finger. The guard stood impassively, his face showing no reaction.

FORTY-FIVE

I walked toward the South Jetty, bending down to pluck an unbroken shell from the sand, brushing it off before slipping it into my pocket. As I continued to make my way down the beach, I rubbed my thumb over the inside surface, smooth to the touch. A brown pelican flew overhead, its broad wingspan casting a shadow on the sand. I looked up, shielding my eyes with my hand to watch as the bird circled and dove, beak-first into the Gulf. He hit the water with a splash, resurfacing to shake his catch down his throat. When he soared back to the sky an overwhelming feeling of loneliness descended upon me. I missed having something to do. I missed my sister back home in New Hampshire. But above all, I missed my husband.

A few weeks earlier I met Annie for lunch. She hadn't yet received confirmation that the Project would take Logan's case but Ben told her not to worry. It was only a matter of getting the paperwork in order. She grew teary-eyed as she took my hand and pressed it to her cheek, wet with tears. We promised each other to stay in touch but the days slipped by and I hadn't heard from her since.

Arriving back at the house, I left my sandals on the welcome mat and picked up the mail. As I made my way to the kitchen I rifled through the stack, separating utility bills from junk mail. Stuck between a post card offering a "free" cruise and a flier promoting a low price to clean my carpets I noticed a hand-written envelope from the local newspaper. Curious, I tore it open. Inside was a check made out to me in the amount of ten thousand dollars.

I scanned the enclosed letter, then went back and read it a second time. Stuffing everything back into the envelope, I grabbed my keys and left.

We sat together in the foyer of Sarah's House, the sun streaming through the windows. Valentina looked well, her face a bit fuller than the last time I saw her and her shoulder blades—still visible through her thin blouse—less pronounced. A young woman sat behind the reception desk casting furtive glances over her reading glasses. When Valentina caught her eye, the receptionist held up her wrist and tapped her watch. Valentina nodded and the woman turned her attention back to her computer.

"I have addicts meeting soon," Valentina said.

"Addicts meeting?" I asked. "You mean an AA meeting?"

"Yes, addicts meeting. Is okay. Better than group."

"What's group?"

"Everyone talk about why we here."

"Do you mean group therapy?"

She nodded. "Girls here have big problems."

"Have you told them about Angel?"

Valentina averted her eyes, speaking just above a whisper. "Not yet."

I reached into my purse and pulled out the envelope containing the reward for identifying Juliana Martinez. My plan was to split the money between Valentina and Inez. As far as I was concerned they deserved it far more than I.

"I received a check in the mail today," I told her. "It's a reward for—"

"Marcela reward?" Valentina's face lit up in a wide smile, Angel Abarco momentarily forgotten. "You bring me Marcela reward?"

"No, not the . . ." I caught myself, recognizing the opportunity before me. "Well, yes . . . I have the money but remember, Ben agreed to give you the reward only when you told him about Marcela's murder."

"How much reward?" Valentina scooted to the edge of her seat.

"Five thousand dollars."

Valentina's eyes opened wide. "Five *thousand*? I can go home now."

"Not so fast. You should stay here for a while, keep getting the therapy you need. And of course you need to tell Ben what you know about Marcela's murder. If there is something he can use in court, he'll expect you to testify. It will be months before everything is settled but in the end the money will be yours and you'll be free to go back to Mexico."

Valentina scooted back into her seat. She cast me a sideways glance, testing me. I bore up under her scrutiny, nodding encouragement.

"Okay," she sighed at last. "I tell Ben what I see. But first I tell you."

A blast of cold wind whipped off the Braden River. The boats in the Twin Dolphins marina strained against their lines. Without a word, Lalo removed his jacket and wrapped it around my shoulders. A few years ago, maybe even a few months ago I might have objected. It made no sense for him to suffer when I was the one who came out in this weather dressed in nothing more than a thin, cotton shirt and jeans. But his gesture was as much a part of his nature as my objection to it. I bent my head to the collar, breathing in the smell of his aftershave.

"Thanks. What's taking Ben so long?"

"He probably got caught in traffic. Let's wait inside the restaurant."

A few minutes later we sat at a table by the window. The waitress didn't blink when Maya followed us in. The black sutures stood out starkly on the dog's shaved shoulder. I was about to ask Lalo when the vet planned to remove the stitches when I saw Ben walking toward us.

"Do you know what this is all about?" Ben asked Lalo as soon as he sat down.

"No idea,"

I looked out at the angry river, wondering how to begin. Maya nudged my hand. I reached down to pat her head and the words came to me.

"I received a check in the mail this morning. The newspaper's reward for information leading to the identity of Juliana Martinez."

"How did they get your name?" Ben asked.

"Geri must have told them. But that's not important. The thing is, I decided to split the money between Valentina and Inez. If not for them, we never would have figured everything out. Anyway, I went to give Valentina the good news. She got confused and thought I meant the reward for information leading to the discovery of who killed Marcela de la Vega."

"There is no such reward," Ben reminded us.

"I know that, but she got all excited and . . . well, I kind of let her believe the money was her 'Marcela reward.' Anyway, she told me what happened in the alley that day."

"She saw Moreno kill the girl?" Lalo asked.

"No . . . let me explain. Remember Valentina said she was in the restaurant when Norma called to speak with Abarco? Well, after he hung up, Abarco left to get Marcela and returned to Chaparrito's, dragging her behind him. Valentina told me he ranted about how Marcela stole from Norma and that he would teach her a lesson. Abarco then shouted to everyone in the restaurant. 'Bargain rates,' he said. 'Fifty dollars for anyone who wants to take this thief in the alley behind the bar so she can pay her debt.'"

"One hundred and fifty dollars were in her purse. That means three different guys took him up on the offer." Lalo said.

I nodded. "Moreno was one of them."

"So if Valentina was still in the restaurant, how could she see which one killed Marcela?" Ben asked.

"That's the thing. After a while the three guys came back in. They were laughing and slapping Abarco on the back, saying Marcela was back there, waiting for him. Valentina slipped out the back door to see if Marcela was okay."

The wind howled outside and an uncontrollable shiver ran down my arms. I looked up to see the waitress approach our table with a fresh pot of coffee. She asked if we'd made up our minds about what to order. Lalo told her we needed more time but that we could all use more coffee. Silence descended over our table while she poured. I grasped my mug with both hands and took a sip. As soon as she left, I continued.

"When Valentina stepped outside, she saw Marcela—still alive—sitting with her back against the wall. The poor thing had bruises on her face, her skirt bunched up around her hips. She was sobbing, but when Valentina started toward her she waved her away, saying that she wanted to be left alone. Valentina went back inside, but as she started to pull the door closed behind her, she saw Marcela's boyfriend, Ricky Castro coming down the alley."

"Ricky?" Ben asked.

"Ricky. Valentina watched through a crack in the door. She told me Ricky yelled at Marcela, screaming that she was nothing but a junkie whore. He started hitting her, slapping her face. When Marcela put her hands up to stop him he grabbed her around the neck and . . . well, he didn't let go until she stopped struggling. Valentina didn't want to be caught so she turned and ran into the kitchen. A few minutes later Moreno went out to see what all the noise was about."

Lalo cleared his throat. "Then Moreno told the truth. He said he found Ricky bent over the body, crying like a baby."

"My client is a murderer." Ben sat staring into his untouched coffee, looking like someone had sucker punched him in the gut.

Words failing me, I placed my hand over his and squeezed.

FORTY-SIX

I accepted Geri's lunch invitation without hesitation. Sitting across from her at the Tiki Hut, I bit into my hot dog. The place was filling up. Half the cars in the parking lot bore out-of-state plates, a sure sign that the snowbirds were back for the winter. We sat by the edge of the water, a cool breeze blowing across the bay. A flock of pelicans flew overhead, heading toward an island of mangroves already crowded with the majestic birds.

"I want to thank you for giving my name to the paper. And I want to tell you that I decided to give the reward to Valentina and Inez."

"That's your call." Geri peered at me over the rim of her sun glasses. "But the way I look at it, you deserve that money. At the end of the day you're the only one who kept digging until you found out who Juliana was. Even her own sister didn't know what happened to her. You remember that newspaper sketch you gave Lalo? The one he used to write his phone number on the back? Norma claims she didn't know her sister was dead until she saw that paper in Luci's room. She made up the story about Juliana getting pregnant and running away to prevent Abarco from going after her."

"Norma kept the sketch?"

"Yeah. We found it when we searched her house."

"I'm still giving Inez and Valentina the reward money."

Geri picked up the bottle of ketchup and squeezed it over her French fries. Popping one into her mouth she shook her head. "I'll never forgive myself for missing that tip line call from Inez. And I gotta say, she's been incredibly brave throughout all of this, coming forward to testify."

She explained that Inez identified Boyd and Ty as the two boys who raped Juliana all those years ago in the woods at Snook Wallow. After they were brought in for questioning, Geri put them in separate rooms and played one against the other. Accusing them both of rape and aggravated assault, she bargained that one of them would crack and cut a deal. Her play paid off.

"You know, going into this I would have bet money Boyd Skinner murdered that girl," Geri went on, "but when you mentioned seeing that necklace on Bibi, things started to fall into place. Skinner says when the two of them caught up with Juliana, Fox ripped the necklace from her neck. Juliana started screaming, telling him that she was going to report the rape. Fox panicked."

"So they didn't leave Snook Wallow early after all."

"Right. It was Fox who convinced Skinner to lie about that. After all, Skinner raped the girl too so he would have been charged as an accomplice."

"Did you get Ty to confess?"

"He's claiming that he was so drunk he didn't know what he was doing. The thing I couldn't get my head around was that pile of dirty clothes on the floor of his bedroom. I knew I checked for blood but there was nothing there. Never considered that those were his work clothes. When I asked him what he did with the clothes he wore to Snook Wallow, he said he threw everything in a dumpster. Well, that blew his 'I didn't know what I was doing' defense because of course any idiot can see he knew exactly what he was doing."

"What's going to happen to him?"

"Tyler Fox is going away for a long time, you can bet on that."

"And Boyd?"

"That's up to ASA Hale. He was the prosecutor on this case the first time around so he'll want to settle this whole thing as quietly as possible. I'm guessing Skinner will get off with a light sentence."

I took the last bite of my hot dog and washed it down with soda. A solitary pelican broke away from the crowd in the mangroves and flew toward us. He circled, watching the water below before diving headfirst, splashing into the bay. As he rose into the sky I caught sight of the fish he held in his beak.

FORTY-SEVEN

The headline on the front section of the Herald Tribune caught my eye. *U.S. Justices call Florida's approach to capital punishment flawed.* Picking up my first cup of decaf for the day, I devoured the article. In an eight-to-one ruling, the Supreme Court decided a simple majority vote to recommend the death penalty was unconstitutional. Everyone expected the court's ruling to trigger new sentencing appeals from some if not all of the inmates on Florida's death row.

Logan Murphy would not be one of them. With Tyler Fox behind bars, Ben expected Logan to be released any day now. I clipped the article from the paper and set it aside. It made a nice, final addition to the files I accumulated while investigating Juliana's murder.

I got up from the kitchen table to pour myself a second cup. A fresh loaf of my homemade banana bread sat on the counter in preparation for my visitor. Annie didn't need to know I used common, bleached flour that didn't bear the word "organic" on the package. I figured it wouldn't kill her. At least she would approve of the two jars of stewed tomatoes that I set aside for her. The success of my crop was at least partially due to the fertilizer she recommended and there was absolutely nothing artificial in that.

Though I turned down Annie's invitation to become a regular at her drum circle, we managed to see each other often. Every Tuesday she came to my house for breakfast. We agreed early on that she should bring her own tea. She claimed the smelly concoction of leaves and twigs was an anti-toxin but there was no way she could convince me to try it. When she nagged me about the dangers of drinking coffee I smiled and told her I'd made it through all these years without worrying about toxins and I wasn't about to start now. Suffice it to say my quirky neighbor and I were becoming fast friends.

I heard the sound of a car door slamming. Since I knew it wasn't Annie—her VW Beetle was in the shop—I opened the front door to see who it could be. Maya ran up the front walk, nearly knocking me over as she barreled past me. Lalo, wearing a Baltimore Orioles baseball cap, followed.

"You might have called to say you were coming."

"Why? Do you have other plans?"

"As a matter of fact, I do." I smiled at him. "I'm expecting Annie Murphy any minute. Come in, I was about to make a fresh pot of coffee."

While the coffee brewed, I filled Maya's water bowl and set it on the kitchen floor. Water dripping from her jowls, Maya raised her head and shook, spraying slobber all over my shoes. With a sigh I grabbed a roll of paper towels and started to wipe up the mess.

Lalo sniffed the air. "Is that banana bread I smell?"

I got a knife out of the top drawer and started cutting. Placing thick slices on a plate, I set it on the table.

"Help yourself," I replied. "I'll be back in a minute."

Heading down the hallway, I closed the bathroom door before returning to the kitchen.

"This is delicious."

A quick look told me he was already on his second helping. I poured his coffee, topped up my own cup and joined him at the table.

"Have you seen the news?" I asked.

"About the Supreme Court's decision? Yeah, I did. About time, isn't it?"

"I agree. Of course it won't affect Logan. I wonder when they're going to release him."

Lalo glanced at me over the rim of his cup. "Um, I don't know. By the way, I spoke with Ben yesterday about Castro."

"How's that going?"

"It's complicated. The court can't ignore Moreno's misconduct, but on the other hand, they have Valentina as a witness to confirm Castro killed Marcela. Needless to say, the Defender Project gave up the idea of filing a motion for wrongful conviction and dropped Castro as a client."

"What will happen to him?"

"He could try to find a lawyer to take his case, but then the State's Attorney will just try him again and present all the evidence—including Valentina's testimony—to a new jury. Castro won't want to risk that, so I'm guessing they'll negotiate a deal. They'll probably end up commuting his sentence to life without parole. Who knows?"

"And what's going on with Tyler Fox?"

"It's only a matter of time before he'll be keeping company with Castro and Abarco at the Florida State Prison."

Maya nudged my hand and I reached down to scratch behind her ears. I noticed the stitches on her shoulder were gone and her fur had grown back.

"I've missed you too." I bent down and let her wash my face with her tongue.

"Yeah, well . . ." Lalo cleared his throat. "I dropped by today because I have something to tell you."

"Let me guess, you're leaving Maya with me while you disappear for a few days." I was only half-kidding. Nothing Lalo said surprised me.

"Not exactly. Maya's coming with me this time."

"Where are you going?" I asked.

"I'm taking the boat down to the Keys for a few seasons. I hear the fishing is pretty good down there."

He stared into his coffee like he didn't want to look me in the eye. I felt something in my chest, a sense of loss. Just as we came to an understanding—a promise of real friendship—he was leaving.

"What are you fishing for, Lalo?" My eyes grew moist.

He finally looked up to meet my gaze. I waited a moment but never got an answer.

"I brought you something to remember me by." He pushed back his chair. "Wait here, I'll be right back."

When he reappeared, he pressed a bundle into my arms. Looking down, I saw a ball of fluff wrapped in a towel.

"A kitten?"

"I figured he'd be good company."

"Are you kidding? I can't have a litter box smelling up my house. And cats shed like crazy. I'd have to run the vacuum three times a day." I thrust the kitten back at him. "Take it back to where you found it."

"Someone dropped him at the marina." Lalo shrugged, hands raised. "The harbor master was about to stuff the little guy in a bag and throw him into the river. I thought maybe you—"

"I don't need a cat, Lalo. I don't *want* a cat."

Lalo flashed me a smile. "Sure you do. You just don't know it yet."

Before I could object again, he whistled for Maya and started walking back to his truck. So this was goodbye. I watched as he pulled off his baseball cap and stopped, his back turned to me. After a few steps, he spun around, closing the distance between us with a few long strides.

"Remember that night I cooked you dinner?" he asked.

I nodded, too surprised to say a word.

"I wanted to kiss you that night, but you had a little too much to drink and I thought it wasn't right for me to take—"

"I'm not drunk now."

As he pulled me close, I felt the kitten pressed between our bodies. He bent down and kissed me, long and soft before letting go.

"Take care of yourself, Cate."

Then he was gone.

I watched until the taillights of his truck disappeared around the bend. As I hugged the kitten to my chest, Ben's BMW came to a stop in front of my house. Ben got out and waved before opening the passenger door for Stephanie. Holding hands, they walked up my walk as Annie appeared from around the corner. Walking next to her was a young man wearing a baseball jersey. Under the brim of his Tampa Bay Ray's cap I saw Logan Murphy smile.

Author's Note

This book is a work of fiction. Names, characters, organizations and events are the product of the author's imagination. Any resemblance to actual persons, living or dead, is entirely coincidental.

Snook Wallow is a not a real place although people may notice a similarity to a delightful place on the Myakka River in Venice called Snook Haven. To the best of my knowledge, no murder was ever committed at Snook Haven although the area does have a history of bootlegging and it is not uncommon to spot manatees munching on the vegetation near the dock. While I did my best to present Venice and Sarasota in the favorable light they so richly deserve, it is impossible for me to adequately describe the unique beauty of these two towns. And though I never noticed a Rottweiler on any boat at the Twin Dolphins Marina in Bradenton, I imagine Maya would be happy living there.

Immokalee, Florida is America's capital of winter tomatoes. While the Coalition of Immokalee Workers has been recognized for achievement in the fields of social responsibility, human trafficking and gender-based violence at work, there is still much to be done.

The Defender Project does not exist, however there are several worthy nonprofit organizations in Florida and around the country that work diligently to assist innocent people who have been wrongfully convicted. They depend largely on the heroic efforts of attorneys, law students and other volunteers who offer their services for free. Unfortunately, the need for their good work shows no sign of stopping.

I wish to extend my thanks to several people without whom this book would not exist. First and foremost, to my long-suffering friends and fellow writers, Roger Hooverman, Michele Draper, Sheila Reed, Dean Dixon and Scott Amsbaugh who selflessly provided encouragement and much needed critique along the way. To my beta readers, Nancy Merel, Jo Weiner and Willeke Heijens who waded through a flawed manuscript to offer guidance on how to improve the novel. And to Wendy Dingwall at Canterbury House Publishing, who showed faith in me.

Most of all to Pieter Heijens, my trusted advisor, my husband, and my best friend. Thank you lieve Peet, for everything.

About theAuthor

In her debut novel, *Wrongful Conviction*, Janet Heijens takes on a justice system gone wrong. Published by Five Star, an imprint of Cengage Learning, *Wrongful Conviction* drew critical acclaim by Kirkus Reviews, "Heijens premiers a rare heroine who's both gritty and reflective. Here's hoping for a series."

Following the success of *Wrongful Conviction* Heijens signed a three book deal with Canterbury House Publishing. The first in a new series, *Snook Wallow* proves once again that Heijens can keep her readers guessing until the last page is turned.

A founding member of the Sarasota Literary Guild, Heijens is also a member of the Mystery Writers of America and Florida Gulf Coast Sisters in Crime. She lives with her husband, Pieter in Sarasota, Florida.

CPSIA information can be obtained
at www.ICGtesting.com
Printed in the USA
LVOW03s0128260717
542657LV00002B/224/P